"I've been attracted to you from the first moment we met."

"I'm surprised that you would admit that. Kind of lessens your odds."

"You're assuming this is a game. I'm too old to play games. Actually, they never interested me much. How about you?"

"Oh, games can be fun sometimes."

"Tease!" Adam said with a chuckle and nipped her on the chin with his teeth.

It wasn't a kiss or a bite, but she felt it all the way down to "Red-dy and Willing," the color of her toenail polish.

Simone remembered her bad history with Cajun men and her resolution to avoid them in the future.

"Um, I think it's time to cut this flower in the bud. I am not going to do this again."

"Do what, darlin'?"

That damn "darlin'" again! "Get involved with another Cajun man."

"You're going to give me the boot just because I'm Cajun?"

She nodded.

"Well, lucky you, babe, because I'm only half Cajun."

By Sandra Hill

CAJUN CRAZY

A Cajun Novel

SANDRA HILL

AVONBOOKS

An Imprint of HarperCollinsPublishers

Excerpt from *The Cajun Doctor* copyright © 2017 by Sandra Hill.

CAJUN CRAZY. Copyright © 2017 by Sandra Hill. All rights reserved. Printed in the United States of America. No part of this book may be used or reproduced in any manner whatsoever without written permission except in the case of brief quotations embodied in critical articles and reviews. For information, address HarperCollins Publishers, 195 Broadway, New York, NY 10007.

First Avon Books mass market printing: December 2017

Print Edition ISBN: 978-0-06-256639-3
Digital Edition ISBN: 978-0-06-256638-6

Cover design by Nadine Badalaty
Cover photographs: Michael Frost Photography; © Design Pics / Getty Images (background)

Avon, Avon & logo, and Avon Books & logo are registered trademarks of HarperCollins Publishers in the United States of America and other countries.

HarperCollins is a registered trademark of HarperCollins Publishers in the United States of America and other countries.

FIRST EDITION

17 18 19 20 21   QGM   10 9 8 7 6 5 4 3 2 1

A Note from Sandra Hill

Does it feel like a black cloud is hanging over mankind? Like everything is hopeless? Like every day is a struggle through the mire of negativity?

And yet we survive?

Why? How?

It's because we are coyotes, my friends. And this book is dedicated to coyotes everywhere.

My husband was for many years a financial consultant and manager of a stock brokerage company. He believed in the principle of positivity (never start the day with a negative thought) and therefore was always coming home with new motivational quotes for me and our four sons, to the point that the boys would sometimes hide, or put their faces in their hands, when good ol' Dad started spouting his bits of inspiration. Such as, "The man on top of the mountain didn't fall there," attributed to Vince Lombardi. You could say Robert was a more elite Tante Lulu with her homespun Cajun proverbs.

The most memorable of these were the coyote ones. I remember distinctly the time Robert and I went to a business conference in Atlantic City called the Coyote Seminars. The principle behind this program was that coyotes are creatures forced to live in the wild (can anyone say Wall Street, or this political jungle of modern times?), constantly the target of hunters (CNN, Fox News, etc.) and those determined to reduce their population. The beasts have a bad reputation, for sure. Like, dare I say, some stock brokers?

But did they die off? The coyotes, not the brokers. Oh no! In fact, their numbers increased. They would be found in the forests minus a limb, dragging a metal trap, missing an eye, with several bullet wounds, fur all dirty and mangy, but limping along. In fact, a news report recently showed a male coyote trapped in an iron clamp, and its female mate coming to feed it every day.

The message here is that life is not hopeless, that no matter what life throws your way, you can survive. Yeah, get your crazy on, when necessary, like Simone LeDeux, the heroine of this book. Or get you a little St. Jude, if you are so inclined, like my outrageous Tante Lulu. But most of all, be a coyote.

Now, I must tell you that my husband is retired and has been wheelchair-bound for more than four years, following a medical catastrophe, but he still retains his wonderful sense of humor. When one or the other of us gets depressed, and we do, we've been known to give a little coyote howl. We are surviving.

Imagine what the world would be like if we were all out there howling.

Chapter One

Between the cheats . . .

Simone LeDeux replayed the voice mail from her mother, Adelaide Daigle, for the second time as she stood at the kitchen counter of her Chicago apartment. She was eating a cheese sandwich on toast and drinking a glass of cold sweet tea. She always kept homemade sweet tea in her fridge, like the good Cajun girl she no longer was. As for food, whatever!

It was midnight, and although she'd turned up the thermostat when she got home, there was a chill in the air. March in Chicago with its blustery winds was not for the faint of Southern heart.

Simone had just ended her shift as a detective with the Chicago PD. After her grueling night—images of a pre-teen girl overdosing came to mind—her mother's voice was soothing to her bruised senses. Hard to believe after the years of strife between the two of them, most of it ignited by Simone, who'd given the phrase *difficult child* new meaning.

She had to smile at the length of the message. Her mother had no concept of electronic devices. There had been a few times when her long messages—as much as five minutes—had caused her voice mailbox to shut down.

Simone also smiled at the familiarity of her mother's deep Southern accent. Simone had lost most of hers, except for an occasional lapse into a Cajunism, such as "Holy Crawfish!" Or the traditional, *"Mon Dieu!"*

However, even as she welcomed her mother's call, she felt a shiver of alarm at the synchronicity of her words. The timing was, at the least, a coincidence. Was God, or the powers that be, conspiring to draw her back to the bayou . . . her worst nightmare? Or was it just Cajun mothers who had this instinct for sensing when their daughters were in need of help, even if only a hug.

"Hi, honey. I haven't heard from you since las' week. Did ya kick that no-good Jack Landry out on his cheatin' be-hind, lak I told you to?"

"Yes, Mama, Jack is history," Simone replied out loud to her cat, Scarlett, who was enjoying the remnants of the unpalatable sandwich. Talking to her cat was nothing new, but this time it was an indication of her exhaustion and, yes, disgust, at once again being duped by a man she trusted. Honest to goodness! One year and thirteen days wasted!

"Heavens ta horseradish, girl, how you manage ta attract so many losers is beyond me, and all of them from Loo-zee-anna? Even when you move ta Chee-cah-go, you gotta latch on to a slow-drawlin' Southern man."

Simone couldn't argue with that. There was something about a man who could say *darlin'* in a husky, slow croon that could make any girl melt. Especially her, with her Southern roots. *Darlin'* was the Dixie male's equivalent to the Yankee man's *babe*, a girlfriend of hers in Chicago had said one time. Face it, she was a magnet for a Louisiana man, even if he'd lived in Chicago for almost fifteen years, as Jack Landry had. "World-class architect, low-class loser," she muttered.

Scarlett stretched with disinterest, expressing her boredom as only a cat could, pretty much saying, "Man problems again! Yada, yada, yada. You oughta be fixed, like me." The cat went off to sleep on Simone's bed, which was forbidden. The cat had heard her man complaints before. Lots of times!

"Are you Cajun crazy, or sumpin'? I remember the first time I called you Cajun crazy. It was when you were fourteen years old and you fell head-over-hiney in love with that pimple-faced hell-raiser Mark Comeaux jist 'cause he had that devilish Cajun grin . . . and a pirogue with a motor.

"I talked ta Tante Lulu yesterday an' she said some women jist got bayou mud in their eyes when it comes ta a Cajun man who's hotter 'n a billy goat's behind in a pepper patch, 'specially when they're in the middle of a stretch of hormone hot-cha-chas. I told her you were smarter'n that, bein' a po-lice detective an' all, but maybe she's right.

"Me? I got a thing fer men with a mustache, as you know. But that's another story. Ha, ha, ha!"

Yep, a billy goat's butt. She'd have to remember that one when the hot-cha-cha hormones hit her next time. Which would be NEVER AGAIN.

Her mother was right, though. You'd think Simone would have learned her lesson by now. She'd been married and divorced three times *(well, one of them was an annulment after one week—don't ask!)*, and she'd been jilted, robbed, humiliated, punked, and seduced by more men than one woman should have in her twenty-nine-and-a-half years. With a college degree and eight years in police work, she should have more sense.

"Anyways, I went ta the bone doctor t'day, and he said I gotta lose thirty pounds and I need two new knees, unless I wanna spend my las' years in a wheelchair."

What? This sounded serious.

"I'm not that old yet! I'm only fifty. I would lak ta have them new knees, though. But, nope, not an option, not 'cause I cain't lose the weight, please God, but the doctor sez I need ta have someone at home with me fer three months of out-patient rehab after I'm released from the hospital. My insurance won't cover three months in a rehab place. Oh, well. I'm gonna buy the Skinny Gals *exercise video tomorrow or sign up fer the* Prayers fer Pounds *program at Our Lady of the Bayou Church."*

Uh-oh! Was her mother pitching a guilt trip her way? Come home and help her, live with her once again in the Pearly Gates Heavenly Trailer Park on Bayou Black, best known as The Gates? *Me and Mom as roomies?* Horror of horrors!

Wait . . . wasn't it a timely coincidence that this all came up just when she'd ended another relationship?

But, no, even her mother wasn't devious enough to do that. The situation must be dire. Last time she'd been home, her mother had walked with a decided limp and could only go short distances before sitting down, due to the bad knees and her excess weight. All of which hampered her duties, even back then, as a longtime waitress at Crawfish Daddy's restaurant.

And thirty pounds was a gross underestimation, in her opinion. Her mother had been plump as long as Simone could remember, but she hid it well, being so tall and big-boned. Like all the women in her family—including Sim-one, darn it—who were always fighting diets and the genetic big butt bane. Thank the exercise gods for jogging and daily rounds of tush crunches!

Peeling off her jacket and her shoulder holster, she continued to listen to the voice mail.

"That's about all that's new here. I hear the pingin' noise. I think it means it's time fer me ta shut up. Why don't ya get a bigger mailbox? Call me, sweetie, and don't be cryin' no more tears over that Jack Landry. I'll be prayin' fer you. Kiss, kiss!"

Simone yawned widely. She would call her mother in the morning.

As for Jack Landry, Chicago architect, but born and bred in Baton Rouge . . . Simone was done crying. In fact, from the moment she'd discovered his secret life, she'd been more embarrassed than hurt. Okay, she'd been hurt, too. Badly. She'd been dumb enough to think Jack was "the one." Which was ridiculous for a twenty-nine-and-a-half-year-old woman. When would girls stop looking for "the one," and settle for the "not so bad"?

All Simone could do now was repeat an old joke that had become her motto, or should. George Strait might wail about "All My Ex's Live in Texas," but Simone would modify that to, "All My Losers Come from Loo-zee-anna."

She was thinking about having it tattooed on her butt, which was big enough.

From the mouths of babes . . .

Adam Lanier was driving his daughter Mary Sue, or Maisie, to her kindergarten class at Our Lady of the Bayou School in Houma, Louisiana. Wending his Harley through the early-morning traffic, with Maisie riding pillion behind him, he barely noticed the people who gave them double takes, not so much because of their mode of transportation, but because he was in a business suit with biker boots, and his little Mini-Me, with her arms wrapped around him, was wearing a T-shirt and skinny jeans tucked into her own tiny boots. (Yes, they made skinny jeans for five-year-olds! And teeny tiny bustiers for tykes who were a decade or so away from having any bust to speak of. But that was another story.)

There were also those busybodies who disapproved of his having a child on a motorcycle. Screw them! He'd bought a special backrest attachment for his bike seat and fitted foot pegs as well as a buddy belt harness to protect his daughter. Maisie was more likely to have an accident on her bicycle than on his motorcycle with all the precautions he took.

After dropping off the kid, he would go to his office, LeDeux & Lanier, Esq., where he'd recently formed a partnership with Lucien LeDeux, the half brother of his cousin Rusty Lanier's wife, Charmaine. A convoluted kinship by marriage that would have the average person crossing their eyes in confusion but was typical of the bayou network of families.

He and Maisie had moved from New Orleans to Bayou Black six months ago, and it was the best decision Adam had ever made. At least, he hoped so. He'd made a name for himself in the Crescent City DA's office as a sometimes outrageous, almost always winning, prosecutor. The news media had loved him, and he played up the image for his own purposes.

This was his first venture into private practice and a switch from indicting to defending. But it was a good match, working with Luc, who had an equal or more outrageous reputation for courtroom antics . . . uh, skills. Luc wasn't known as the "Swamp Solicitor" for nothing. Maybe, he thought with a laugh, Adam would become known as the Bayou Barrister.

Bottom line—the law was a game he'd learned to play, well. Didn't matter if it was in the city or in a Cajun courtroom, or whether he played on the black or white side.

Stopping for a red light, with the cycle idling, he glanced over his shoulder and inquired with seeming casualness, "So, Maisie Daisie, you settlin' in okay?"

"Oh, Daddy, stop worryin'," she advised in her too-old-for-her-five-years voice. "I'm fine. 'Specially since Paw-Paw came ta live with us. He makes better pancakes than you."

He laughed. His father made everything better than he did. Adam was one of the best lawyers in the state, hands down. And the best single parent he could be. But a cook Adam was not. Nor a housekeeper. And reliable babysitters to hold down the fort while he worked were hard to find. Thus his finally throwing in the towel and asking his widowed father, Frank Lanier, to move here from northern Louisiana.

Who would have imagined that a self-proclaimed legal (and personal, truth to tell) hell-raiser like himself, at the ripe old age of thirty-five, would be back to living with his father, who'd raised him pretty much alone after Adam's mother died in a car accident when he was seven years old and his brother, Dave, only four? But then, who would have imagined that Adam's wife, Hannah, would die of a brain tumor, diagnosed too late for treatment? She'd been only twenty-eight. That had been two years ago, and like the old cliché said, life went on.

"Thank you for taking off the ballerina tutu," he said. His dainty daughter, with her mass of black corkscrew curls, liked to pick her own attire, and if left to her own devices, the attire would have involved girly frills and ruffles, sometimes inappropriate-for-her-age choices. Like the tutu that showed her Snow White panties when she bent over.

He would be glad next year when Maisie moved into first grade where school uniforms were required. He didn't doubt for one minute that Maisie would find a way to glam up the staid plaid skirts and white blouses.

"Ya didn't give me any choice, Daddy," she pointed out, "but don't worry. I'm still wearin' my sparkle shirt."

She was, indeed, wearing a tiny red T-shirt that proclaimed in silver letters, "I'm Hot. Live With It." A gift from his brother, Dave, who was a captain in the Army, a Green Beret currently serving in some super secret, especially important black op in Afghanistan. According to Dave, that was. He was probably just banging some nurse in Tahiti, for all Adam knew. But then, Dave did have a lot of medals, so maybe he was telling the truth.

"Besides, you tol' me you would pick me up on the Harley after school if I changed. That way PawPaw kin get a haircut and a mustache trim soz he kin go ta the casino t'night with Tante Lulu and Addie Daigle."

The imp loved riding pillion on his classic motorcycle, and his father loved to gamble. The nickle slots or Poor Man Craps (a low minimum dice game). He guessed there were worse things than a bikeress-in-training and a senior citizen with a lust for the Big Payoff.

"Do ya think Tante Lulu and Addie Daigle are PawPaw's girlfriends? Kin a man have more than one girlfriend? What's *hanky panky*? That's what PawPaw said this mornin' . . . he has ta get his hanky panky on before his hanky gets rusted out. He was talkin' ta Uncle Dave. How can a hanky get rusty? Is your hanky rusty, Daddy?"

What could Adam say to that?

The light changed, thank God, and he eased the throttle to move forward.

You can go home again, but leave the motor running . . .

Simone was blow-drying her long brunette hair in the phone-booth-size bathroom of her mother's double-wide trailer in the mobile home park on Bayou Black. Although *mobile* was a misnomer since none of the tin cans here had been moved in at least twenty years.

Every time she turned a certain way, she knocked her elbow on the curtain rod. At five-foot-nine, she could easily touch the ceiling. The mirror over the sink was six inches too low; so, she had to bend her knees to see properly. The dryer heat, on top of the subtropical temperature of a unseasonably warm, late April morning in Louisiana, on top of the two-mile jogging run she'd just completed an hour ago, on top of the fifty tush crunches she did religiously every morning to hold back the posterior tide, all followed by a tepid shower, was enough to make her almost faint. Even her cat, Scarlett, which she'd brought with her to Louisiana, was panting near the door. The cubby under the sink was her favorite napping spot. Every once in a while Scarlett gave her a look that pretty much said, "And we're living here . . . why?"

"I gotta get out of this dump," she crooned softly, putting her own words to that old rock song by the Animals as she danced in place, shutting off the dryer, "and it won't be the last thing I ever do."

And she would shortly. Get out of this place.

She hoped.

No, no hoping about it. She'd be leaving, definitely, one way or another. The question was, which way to go?

There was a knock on the door. "You almos' done in there? I gotta pee," her mother said.

"Just a sec," she replied, pulling her hair off her face and twisting the mass into a long coil which she secured to the back of her head with a claw comb. Her make-up could wait till later. It would probably melt if she did it now, anyway.

She'd barely edged out of the doorway, making room for her mother, who was braced on her walker, when Scarlett scooted out. Wearing a purple floral housecoat and fuzzy duck slippers, she had big foam rollers on her head that would probably touch the ceiling (her mother was tall, too). Those big rollers were a necessity for the huge, teased hairdo her mother had sported since forever, following the Southern tradition, "the higher the hair, the closer to God." Of course that tradition of Southern women with big bouffant long hair went out about 1970, but that was her mother—stuck in the '70s. And, actually, her mother's go-to hairstyle was a back-combed French twist up-do, which had been the rage back then and was still suitable for her waitress job, which would otherwise require a hair net.

Her mother edged sideways through the door, past Simone, leaving the walker behind in the hallway.

Simone had to give her mother credit. After two months of rehab, the feisty lady had made great progress, aided no doubt by the thirty pounds she'd lost and daily exercises at the Houma medical fitness center. She really didn't need the walker anymore, and, although she had another thirty pounds to lose, she was in better shape than she'd been for ages.

Simone poured herself a mug of coffee from the blue-speckled, enamelware coffeepot on the stove. No modern K-Cup contraption for her mother. In fact, her mother made the best Creole coffee in the world. The secret being a dash of blackstrap molasses, even when serving *café noir*.

Her mother came back, walking this time without the aid of the walker. She'd removed the rollers, but hadn't combed out her hair, which was dark brown, almost black, and as clear of gray strands as Simone's, thanks to her old friend Lady Clairol. But, no, Simone seemed to recall her mother patronized Charmaine LeDeux's hair salon these days. Sometimes Simone forgot that her mother was only fifty, which was seeming younger to her by the day now that she was pushing thirty. In fact, she had a few of the gray monsters herself.

Her mother had gotten pregnant with her by that horndog Valcour LeDeux when she was only nineteen and naïve, not knowing he was already married. Ernest Daigle had married her mother soon after Simone's first birthday, not soon enough to save Simone being given the surname of the "bastard." That's the way Ernie always referred to Valcour, never using his name. It was: "The bastard won another lawsuit." Or, "Cypress Oil just hit another well, so more moola for the bastard." Or, "I heard the bastard knocked up another young lady." Or, "Rumor is the bastard has kids in Alaska. Talk about!" Ernie never made Simone feel like anything other than his little girl, though. A true father to her he'd always been.

Pouring a cup of coffee for herself, her mother eased down onto the opposite built-in mini bench of the tiny alcove kitchen table, which was just the right size for a trailer and sufficient for the two of them as Simone had been growing up. The trailer had been purchased twenty years ago when Ernie had been killed in an oil rig explosion out on the Gulf. (Not the same company that Valcour was associated with. That would be too much of a coincidence.)

Little had her mother known back then that a good lawyer could have gotten her a major settlement. A good lawyer probably could have gotten her a bundle in a paternity settlement from Valcour LeDeux, as well. Instead, Adelaide had accepted $75,000, which allowed her to buy the used trailer and the lot in the Pearly Gates trailer park, put some toward Simone's college education, and set a little aside for a "rainy day." Meanwhile, her mother had continued to work even longer hours as a waitress to support them both. She'd still waitressed until this recent knee surgery.

And that had been part of the problem between mother and daughter for many contentious years. Later—much later—Simone had realized how much her mother sacrificed for her. But back then, Simone had only known that her mother wasn't around much, and when she was she was often grouchy and undemonstrative. In fact, she'd probably been tired and grief-stricken. But to teenage Simone, she'd only seen that she was left alone at a time when she'd been missing her father and craving attention. No surprise she'd looked for love in all the wrong places. And still did, dammit.

"That Jack Landry fellow called again this mornin' while you were in the shower and left a message on your phone. I saw the caller ID," her mother said right off, motioning with her head toward Simone's iPhone sitting on the counter. "Lordy, Lordy, the boy doesn't give up, does he? He's chasin' your tail like a dog with the hornies."

The "boy," who was close to forty, did, indeed, have a bad case of the "hornies," or at least regrets for his one fall from grace. Yeah, right, like she believed that the time she'd caught him with his tongue down his assistant's throat and his hands cupping her cute little nineteen-year-old butt was the only time he'd strayed! And to think she'd actually been considering marriage! Again! When would she learn?

"Maybe you should change your number," her mother suggested.

"I'd rather not do that. He's just a nuisance, nothing threatening. I'll delete his calls without listening to them."

"You aren't thinkin' about goin' back ta Chee-cah-go, are you?"

"No. I already told you that I quit my job." She was sick of the drug detail, anyhow. "And I gave up the lease on my apartment. Everything I wanted to keep is in storage."

"You could have brought it here."

Simone looked meaningfully around the small trailer. "It's okay where it is until I decide what I want to do next . . . and where."

"Oh, Simone, cain't you stay here?"

"We'll see. I should know more today when Helene and I meet for lunch." Helene Dubois had been her best friend since childhood and was a lawyer. They were thinking about combining their respective talents—her police investigative skills, honed over eight years, and Helene's ability to file court documents—into a business.

"I'm gonna say a prayer that everything works out."

Simone smiled. Her mother was always going to "say a prayer" for one thing or another. That the roof would hold out. That the tips would be higher next week at work. That Simone wouldn't get another divorce (which was against her Catholic faith). That Cletus Bergeron would suffer an early demise while serving his latest incarceration at Angola for yet another felony.

In her mother's mind, Simone was still married to Cletus, whom she'd eloped with when she was seventeen and divorced a year later when he'd been arrested for armed robbery. How her mother justified wishing a person dead was beyond Simone's understanding of religion, but just last night she'd said, "I hear Cletus got a stud over at the prison and it's rotting off his privates. Maybe God is pullin' him ta the other side. Wouldn't that be . . . convenient? You'd finally be free."

"I'm already free. I was free when I divorced him. I was free when I divorced Jeb Cormier, that Cajun guitar player with the coke habit. And I was free when I annulled my one-week marriage to Julien Gaudet, when I got a looksee at what was on his personal computer. Talk about perversions!"

Her mother would be shocked to know what men—grown men—looked at on the Internet . . . to know that THAT was online. If anyone knew human nature, it should be a diner waitress. How her mother managed to stay so naïve after twenty-five years of "What can I get for you, sugah?" was beyond Simone's understanding. But then, Simone had been jaded by eight years of police work.

"Those other two marriages didn't count," her mother insisted.

It was an old argument and not worth pursuing. "Back to Cletus, how can a stud rot off his privates?"

"Not a stud. A std."

Simone blinked several times. "A sexually transmitted disease?"

"That's what I said. His mama told Charmaine LeDeux over at her beauty parlor that—"

"Enough!" Simone said, putting up a halting hand. "I don't want to know anything about Cletus."

"I was hopin' you might wanna go up to Angola and visit him. As long as you're stuck with him, maybe you kin kindle the fire again."

Simone's jaw dropped with amazement. "Are you kidding me? How can you go from wishing a person dead to hooking him up with your daughter again? And him with an STD, besides."

"They prob'ly cured him already with a couple shots of antibiotics." She waved a hand airily. "Let's be honest, Simone, you haven't had much luck in the love department, bless your heart. Maybe you should start from the beginning again. I'd like ta have grandbabies before the Final Judgement."

"And you expect me to manage that in a conjugal visit?"

"Well . . ."

"I'm going to pretend you never made that suggestion."

"I was just kiddin' about you and Cletus," her mother said, although Simone wasn't so sure about that, "but I was thinkin' that if you met with him, maybe you two could go to a priest and get an annulment, jist like you did from that other husband. The Church still doesn't recognize divorce, y'know."

"The Church doesn't grant annulments when a marriage has been consummated, either, Mom. Unless you go through a lot of red tape, providing grounds."

She let her mother mull that one over for a moment. But she didn't give up easily. "Anyways, back ta your meetin' this morning with the lawyer . . ."

"Not 'the lawyer.' Helene. You've known her as long as I have."

"Right. Her daddy and Ernie were on the rigs t'gether." She gave Simone a pointed look for diverting her. "When you're meetin' with Helene, you might mention that I already got some customers fer your new business."

"What? Mo-om! We haven't even decided for sure that there will be a business."

Her mother shrugged. "Anyways, as I mentioned, I

was at the Curl Up & Dye, your half sister Charmaine's shop in Houma, yesterday havin' my roots done . . ."

She didn't recall her mother mentioning being in the beauty salon. "So that's where you went after rehab. I thought you were gone a long time."

Her mother ignored her comment. "While I was there, I happened ta mention your new Cheaters agency, and everyone in the shop got excited. Two ladies wanted your business card. Do you have business cards yet? Bet I could drum up business fer you all over the place. At the restaurant. The supermarket. Church."

"No, no, no," Simone said. "There is so much wrong with what you just said."

"Like what?"

"First, I wouldn't classify the agency we're considering as a Cheaters model."

"Why not? You're gonna investigate cheatin' spouses, aren't you?"

"Yes, but more than that. We're also going to offer divorce processing, with Helene's background. And we'll work for parents who suspect their children of using drugs or engaging in illegal activities. Maybe elder abuse. A whole range of services."

"Yeah, but cheaters will be yer main business, won't it?"

"Maybe."

"I still say Bagged and Tagged would a good name fer yer business."

"No way! We're leaning toward Legal Belles, if we do decide to open this agency, *which is not certain*."

"We took a poll in Charmaine's shop. Do ya wanna know the name they all voted for?"

Not really. "I'm afraid to ask."

"Busted!"

Simone would be busted, as in burst with frustration

like a big balloon, if she stayed with her mother much longer.

"Personally, I'm leanin' toward The Honey Pot."

"No!"

"Bet I could be one of your undercover agents. Specially since I jist ordered some Spanx from the Internet. Bet I'll look like that Kim Kardashian when I'm all squeezed in the right places. Big butts are 'in' now, you know. Bet there are some older cheatin' men who'd go fer me."

Simone put her face on the table. Maybe she should go back to Chicago, after all.

Chapter Two

The things you learn in yoga class! . . .

It was Friday night, and Adam had finally gotten away from the house and was driving his Lexus up toward Thibodaux. He would have taken his bike, but it was supposed to rain later this evening. His dad would be doing babysitting duty until the wee hours. Time for some adult entertainment!

Between his busy work schedule and activities with his daughter, he didn't have much spare time, though he did play racquetball on occasion, and he'd inherited his dad's talent for poker, which he played once a month with some fellow lawyers. Adam had long outgrown clubbing; in fact, the only clubbing he'd ever indulged in had been more like bar hopping to meet chicks in college. And, although he loved his Harley, he wasn't into the biker scene.

What Adam really liked was women. Cut to the bone,

pun intended, he liked sex. And he was never one to deprive himself, not even when he'd been married. And, no, he hadn't been one of those losers who complained that his wife didn't understand him and therefore sought comfort elsewhere, blah, blah, blah. Believe it or not, Hannah had been the one responsible for that state of marital affairs, another pun intended. She'd been the horndog in their marriage. Horndog Hannah! He'd even called her that one time, and she'd just laughed. Later, she just became Hardhearted Hannah when it came to their daughter. Maisie's well-being was the only reason he'd stayed.

Soon after they had married, Hannah, a psychologist who specialized in partner counseling (That should have been a clue.), informed him that she would be having sex with multiple partners and she expected he would do likewise. Why she hadn't told him before the vows, or why he hadn't suspected, was beyond him. She claimed he was just old-fashioned.

Now, some men might have been doing the Happy Dance, but he'd always been a monogamy kind of guy. Or at least serial monogamy, as in one relationship at a time. And he'd fancied himself in love. *Foolish boy!*

"Oh, Adam!" she'd said when he'd naively voiced that sentiment. "Everyone does it. As long as no one gets hurt!"

"Bullshiiit!" he'd replied.

So he'd stayed (in a separate bedroom), and there had been lots of women; no sense building a relationship when he was already married. In fact, he'd gained a reputation as a wild and crazy guy, despite his best attempts at discretion. A player. Nowhere near as bad as Hannah, but then, he'd stopped counting after their first anniversary.

And then Hannah died. But the marriage, dysfunctional as it had been, was worth it for Maisie's sake. He'd adored the squirt from the moment she'd come squalling from Hannah's overused love channel. *That was mean! Shame, Adam, shame!* And he had to give Hannah credit; she'd been a good mother . . . most of the time.

Now he was off to a date with Sonia Easterly, a yoga instructor from Baton Rouge. He'd been hooking up with the redhead for the past five months (a record for him), ever since they'd met at a party. Sonia was teaching him things about sex and yoga that boggled the mind. Who knew there were things he didn't know about the dirty deed at his jaded age?

It was almost ten p.m. by the time he got to Sonia's townhouse, which was making this feel more like a booty call than a date, which was not his intention. He would have taken her out to dinner first, if he'd been able to leave the house earlier, and then they would have enjoyed the booty call. *Bad, Adam, bad!* Was that what they meant by "putting lipstick on a pig?" That no matter how you painted it (with dinner, flowers, a movie, whatever), it was still a booty call.

He shrugged. He didn't think Sonia was offended. He would ask her. Later. After he took care of her booty. Or was that his booty? Or both?

By midnight, he lay naked and depleted on her futon after a Frog aka Garland Pose sexcapade (Garland was a fancy name for a wide, low squat, if you asked him. Like a . . . frog.), followed by a wide-legged forward-from-the-waist bend with her hands locked on her ankles (no fancy name for this, unless you considered Downward Facing Dog as anything but down and dirty). After he regained his breath, he was going to try a Camel (these yoga folks had a thing about animals) which was pretty much a kneeling back bend. Whoa boy! He couldn't wait.

"You still need to work on drawing your energy inside,

instead of letting it all out in a rush," Sonia told him, snuggling up with her red hair spread out over his chest and one knee over his thighs.

"By *energy*, you mean ejaculation?"

"Exactly. It's more satisfying if you stop yourself from climaxing, and focus all that physical force into a spiritual buoyancy that will ripple through your body, and settle under your skin like a peaceful vibrancy."

"If you say so."

She slapped him playfully on the chest, knowing he wasn't convinced. Slipping off the bed, she said, "Let me get us a smoothie, then we'll see what else you can handle." She tossed her mane of red hair over her shoulder and wiggled her hips as she sashayed out of the room, aware of his scrutiny.

She had a great body, an athlete's body. Of medium height, but willowy thin, with muscle definition in her arms and legs. And her butt wasn't too bad, either.

He leaned back against a stack of pillows, his arms folded behind his neck. It was amazing how sex could relax the body. He'd been tired and stressed when he got here. Not anymore.

When she came back, she was carrying a glass of green slime that he declined, graciously. He was ready to engage in another bout of sex, but she wanted to talk. "I'm getting out of Dodge. Moving on, and about time," she told him. Turns out that she would be moving to California where she and her sister were going to open their own yoga studio in Malibu.

"Seems a little sudden."

"Not really. Cindy and I have been talking about it for years, and the place where she works is up for sale at a decent price."

He was already thinking, *No more yoga sex. Damn!*

"Don't look so heartbroken," she said with a laugh.

"What? I *will* miss you."

"You'll miss the sex."

True. "I like you, Sonia. You never seemed to want more."

"I don't. Be honest, Adam, you're not in love with me."

"Are you in love with me?"

"Of course not."

So, no harm, no foul. "When are you leaving?"

"In a couple of weeks. I still have time to teach you a few more yoga moves." She placed his still full glass on the bedside table, then smiled seductively at him from where she stood next to the bed. No false modesty here. With hands on hips, she openly displayed all her assets for him to scrutinize . . . her smallish breasts with their big, kiss-swollen nipples, her navel with its winking gold ring, the runway-style trim to her red bush below.

With an inborn dexterity, he rose from the bed, grabbed her by the waist, tossed her to the mattress, and moved himself atop her. "Forget your loosey-goosey hip-pie crap," he growled against her ear, adjusting his already burgeoning erection between her legs, "let me teach you a few Cajun moves. You could say we invented yoga. Have you ever heard of the Gator Slide?"

She laughed.

And then she wasn't laughing anymore.

Red light, red light, red light! . . .

"This is either the best idea I ever had, or the worst," Simone said, standing on the Houma sidewalk staring at the empty storefront. She was trying to picture the Legal Belles, Inc. sign, which would go above the double-door entrance next week, if plans proceeded.

"Stop being so negative," Helene said, nudging her with an elbow. "This is going to be so much fun, working together."

"It will be, won't it? Still, you're giving up a thriving practice, while I already gave my notice in Chicago."

"I won't be giving it up entirely. I'll still work three days a week in my office, two days here. As business picks up, I can reverse those schedules."

"Maybe you should start with one day a week here."

"Si-mone!"

"Okay, okay, but it's hard not to be a little scared. I practically emptied my savings account for this venture. Besides that, I swore I would never move back to Loo-zee-anna, and here I am, about to lock myself into a two-year lease on a business."

"Honey, the only reason you've stayed away from Loo-zee-anna is to avoid your weakness, Cajun men. And what good has that done you? They follow you wherever you go. Case in point—the architect."

"But the pool of temptation will be so much greater here."

"Pool of temptation? I like that. You're older and wiser now, Simone. You can resist. Anyhow, I'm here to warn you when . . . *if* . . . I see that certain gleam in your eye."

"Maybe we should have a safe word."

"Right. Whenever I notice you eyeballing some slow-talking Cajun devil, I'll say 'red light,' and you'll know to back off."

They both burst out laughing, and Simone gave her good friend a hug. "You're the best thing about coming home," Simone said.

Once they stepped apart and were staring at the storefront again, Helene said, "The good news is there's an apartment on the second floor, which will allow you to move out of The Gates."

Simone rolled her eyes. "There is that. Did I tell you, my mother has become a walking commercial for Spanx? And she's talking about forming a Kim Kardashian fan club called Embrace Your Inner Buttliness?"

"Noooo!"

Simone nodded. "I kid you not. And she's on this kick where she wants grandkids, and she thinks I ought to set up a conjugal visit with Cletus Bergeron. She's probably not serious, but still . . ."

"Isn't he in Angola?"

"Yep."

Helene giggled. Then, more seriously, she asked, "Well, we gonna do this thing?"

Simone hesitated, then said, "Hell, yes!"

They started to walk toward the law offices of Simone's half brother Lucien LeDeux. It was a pleasant street, she had to admit, liking the feeling of this being her new home. There was a Sweet Buns Bakery on one side of the storefront they were about to rent and a boutique dress shop called Fancy's on the other. The business space they were interested in had been occupied by an insurance agent, which suited them perfectly, with a small lobby and two separate office spaces, plus a small kitchenette and storage closets. It wouldn't require much renovation, other than a little paint. Even some of the furniture remained—desks, filing cabinets, etc.

They were both good-looking women, and knew it, and flaunted it.

It was hard not to notice the attention they got as they walked down the street, both in business attire. Helene had an appointment in family court with a client later this morning, and Simone would be meeting with a graphic artist to design and print up brochures and business cards.

Helene, a mocha-skinned beauty with some Creole blood in her veins from her maternal grandfather, wore a short-sleeved, moss green suit with a peplum jacket and knee-skimming skirt and carried a slim, leather, over-the-shoulder briefcase. Even with black high heels and her reddish-brown hair piled high atop her head in designer disarray, she was still several inches shorter than Simone's five-nine. But then, Simone was wearing heels, too. White strappy sandals that matched her white, sleeveless sheath dress, which was edged in red with a wide, red leather belt. Her dark hair was skinned back off her face into a chignon, low on her nape.

As they strolled, one or the other of them was recognized by people they knew. Invariably, the greeting would be, "Well, hello, there, Simone (or Helene). How's yer Mama?" It was a Southern thing, which made Simone smile. It also made her smile to be among people she knew. Back in Chicago, anonymity was more the norm. Not a bad thing. But she was finding this sense of community oddly welcome.

When they got to Lucien's office, a charming old Victorian-era home painted a bright yellow with green shutters, she noticed the brass plate on the door. LeDeux & Lanier, Esq. That was something new. Luc must have taken on a partner.

Luc's secretary Mildred Guidry, a gray-haired matronly type woman, who'd been with Luc for at least twenty years, greeted them, and, yes, her greeting included a "How's yer Mama?" Even before they sat down, Mildred said, "Luc will see you now." They entered the open doorway. The door to the other office was closed.

As soon as he saw them, Luc rose from his chair behind the desk and came to welcome them with a handshake and kiss on one cheek. A handsome man, still in his prime despite being close to fifty, one side or the other, she wasn't sure, he smelled as delicious as he looked thanks to a light, limey cologne. His tan suit jacket hung over a hall tree in the corner, but he wore a white, crisply starched dress shirt and a brown-and-black-striped tie, appropriate for a court appearance, which he'd told them was on his docket for later this morning, the reason they'd come into town so early.

They spent the next half hour going over and signing the paperwork that would incorporate their business and provide rental space for the next two years.

"You got a good deal on the rent," Luc pointed out. He should know, since he also represented the owner of the building where Legal Belles would be located.

"Because we were willing to commit for two years, instead of one," Helene pointed out.

"Right," Luc said. "So, Legal Belles will be your name?" Luc smiled. "I still think Ball Busters would be a better title. It's got a ring to it."

"Why does everyone have a suggestion for our name?" Simone asked, not unkindly. "Even your aunt put her two cents in."

"Tante Lulu is your aunt, too, *chère*. Sort of. So, what was her idea?"

"Beat the Cheat."

He laughed. "That would work, too."

Luc had also prepared several samples of contracts they might use with potential clients. He discussed the legal liabilities addressed in the various forms. "You need to dot all the i's and cross all the t's. Believe me, the most friendly client can turn into your worst enemy. Especially if they suddenly decide to make up with their offending partners, and you're suddenly the bad guy . . . uh, girl."

"That's happened to you?" Simone asked.

Luc nodded. "More than once. That's why I don't do divorces anymore."

"Luc is right," Helene said. "That's why I had him work up our contracts. I could have done most of it myself, but I wanted a second set of eyes. We have to be super vigilant in protecting not just our clients, but ourselves."

"Right," Luc agreed. "You know what they say about doctors not healing themselves. Same is true of lawyers. A lawyer who represents himself has a fool for a client."

Once they'd completed all the paperwork and Helene had tucked their files in her briefcase, Luc walked them to the door. "I wish you all the luck, ladies, and you can be sure I'll be referring customers to Legal Belles."

"Thanks for all you help, Luc," Simone said.

Helene was engaged in a soft conversation with Mildred, something about her niece who was attending Auburn University.

"Oh, have you met my new partner?" Luc looked toward the other office where the door was now open.

Following Luc's lead, Simone saw a man sitting behind a desk, poring over a document. He wore rimless reading glasses, and his longish, dark brown hair was pulled off his face into a short ponytail low on his neck. He was deeply tanned, like many men in the South, and wore dress clothes similar to Luc's—a navy blue suit, light blue dress shirt, and a red tie.

"Hey, Adam, you have a sec. I want you to meet my half sister Simone LeDeux and her partner, Helene Dubois, a lawyer. They're forming that new business I told you about, Legal Belles. And, ladies, this handsome devil is Adam Lanier, my new partner . . . well, six months new."

Adam stood, and Simone got an even better look at him. He had to be at least six feet tall, maybe six-one. Broad shoulders, slim waist accented by a thin leather belt, and narrow hips encased in navy slacks. A light scent of some musky cologne or aftershave wafted from his direction. Seductive.

He smiled and nodded. Helene had come in by now. But then, whoa! Adam removed his glasses. There was something about a man removing his glasses while he stared at a woman that was beyond sexy, sort of a signal that he was about to get down to serious business. Naughty business. Which was ridiculous. But, not so ridiculous, she realized when his gaze continued to hold hers, his head tilted slightly to the side, almost as if in question. His eyes were clear Cajun brown. Dancing eyes. Mischievous eyes. Dangerous eyes. And they were homing in on her.

Beside her, Simone heard Helene whisper, "Red light, red light, red light."

But it was too late.

Thunderbolt, cupid's dart, all the same thing . . .

Adam was poleaxed. No other word for it.

His heart raced. His stomach churned. And he felt a little light-headed, even though he was sitting down.

He couldn't explain what had just happened. He was afraid to find out what had just happened.

Tante Lulu—Luc's crazy-ass aunt—would say he'd been hit by some woo-woo Thunderbolt of Love nonsense. Which he didn't believe in, and which he didn't need at this point in his life, either, and which he absolutely, positively refused to accept. Not again. Yeah, he'd been in love at one time, and got himself doused in reality real quick.

But man! One look at Simone LeDeux, and his world

turned upside down. He knew it, sure as he knew that he wouldn't be seeing Sonia Easterly again, even if she decided to stay in Dodge.

One door opens, another closes.

Just so it wasn't a trap door.

Now I'm a comedian. Bullshit, bullshit, bullshit!

Maybe it was indigestion. Please, God, let it down be a stomach ailment. That crawfish omelet he'd had for breakfast at the highway diner might have been a little off, but, no, that had been hours ago. It must be the woman.

Was this what they meant by love at first sight?

No, no, no. Lust, yes. Love, no.

He'd experienced lust on first meeting an attractive woman lots of times, and it had never felt like this. Maybe he had a clock ticking away in him like some women did . . . the maternal clock winding down, an urge to nest and procreate. But what would it be for a man? Surely he wasn't looking to nest. Besides, it would be a mighty crowded nest with Maisie and his dad in there, too. Nope, he was thinking more of birddogging the woman, not birdnesting.

Ha, ha, ha! I am losing it here.

And Middle-Age Crazy didn't cut it, either. First of all, thirty-five wasn't middle-aged. *Although I did clip those extra nose hairs last week.* And second, a midlife crisis in men usually involved tomcatting, not settling down. *I am tomcat, hear me roar . . . really.*

"Oh, my God!" he muttered, putting his face in his hands. Why this particular woman? And why now?

Luc came back after escorting the two women out to the street. He leaned against the open door frame and asked, "You okay, *cher*?"

Adam shook his head. "What do you know about her?"

It was telling that Luc didn't seem surprised by his

question. Adam must look as stunned as he felt. Pitiful. "Well, Helene Dubois is an attorney. She works in a small private practice in Metairie, but now . . ."

"Not her. The other one."

Luc's eyes went wide and he came in to sit on the chair in front of Adam's desk. Just to annoy him, Luc took all the time in the world to link his hands behind his neck and stretch his legs out, crossed at the ankle, all casual-like. "Adam, Adam, Adam. So, it's my half sister Simone that has you lookin' like you been Tasered."

Adam sat down, too. Rather he sank, like a harpooned whale, or a gator down for the count on one of those *Swamp People* episodes. "You're going to go all frickin' big brother on me, aren't you?"

"Depends on yer intentions."

"I have no intentions." Yet.

"Better be careful, my friend. Simone is a cop. At least she was until recently. She's worked in Louisiana and various other states, most recently in Chicago. She could probably flip you over her shoulder and stomp on yer heart if you look at her the wrong way."

"What's the wrong way?"

"Kind of smolderin', I would think." Luc was enjoying the hell out of Adam's situation.

"Pff! I wouldn't know how to smolder if my life depended on it."

Luc shrugged, unconvinced.

"A cop? She's a cop?" Adam wasn't sure how he felt about that. Of all the women he'd had—model, waitress, realtor, teacher, rodeo rider, TV anchor, airline stewardess, yoga instructor, whatever—he didn't think he'd ever done a cop before. Not that he'd done Simone. But he was hot damn thinking about it, and if that meant he smoldered, then so be it.

"And now she and her friend are forming a Cheaters-type agency down the street. The kind that catches slime-ball men, and women, in the act of adultery or the intent to commit, then takes them to the cleaners in court," Luc continued to explain while Adam's mind had been wandering . . . or smoldering. "That's not all they'll do, of course, but I guarantee it'll be a big part of their draw."

Adam recalled Luc mentioning the new business to him a day or two ago. He hadn't paid much attention then, but he was now.

"I know a few of our clients who could very well be in their crosshairs before long," Luc said. "My dad, for one."

Luc's father, Valcour LeDeux, was a notorious womanizer, with legitimate and illegitimate children all over Louisiana, and beyond, including twins who'd arrived recently from Alaska. He'd been married for years to his second wife, Jolie, but that didn't stop his fornicating with every female in sight, some of them rather young.

"Marcus Pitot, for another. His wife has been trying to get the goods on him for years. You know him, Adam. Wasn't he a friend of your wife's or something."

Or something! If Luc only knew!

"Good thing you decided not to take him on as a client when you moved here, like he wanted you to. That could have become a conflict of interest if you do hook up with Simone."

Marcus had been one of Hannah's "friends." No wonder Adam hadn't wanted to do business with him, no matter the money he might have brought the firm. "Hook up with Simone? Whoa! That train hasn't left the station yet."

"*Mais, oui!* But I can hear the engine chuggin' from over here," Luc commented with a grin.

Adam ignored the teasing.

"Simone has been married a few times and is not too hot to walk the aisle again, or so Tante Lulu tells me."

"Neither am I. So that's a point in her favor, or my favor, depending on how you look at it. But what do you mean by a few times? What's wrong with her?"

"Actually, if you want to know more about Simone, you oughta go talk to my aunt."

"Not on your life!"

They both laughed, knowing that Adam would be opening himself up to the old lady's matchmaking she-nanigans if he showed signs of an interest in any woman, let alone one connected to her family.

Still, once Luc went off to court, and Adam was be-tween appointments, he found himself Googling Simone LeDeux on the Internet. She was almost thirty years old, a graduate of Loyola University and the North Louisiana Criminal Justice Academy. She'd worked in two police departments in Louisiana, followed by a very short stint in Florida, and most recently in Chicago where she'd only recently made the rank of detective. A lot of moving around in eight years of law enforcement. Hmmm.

And she'd been married three times. Three times! Holy crap! He didn't know what was worse. Spreading favors here and there, like his wife, Hannah, had been prone to do, while still married, or spreading favors through legitimate means, like within the bounds of mar-riage. Of course, she might have been spreading them outside, as well, his cynical mind noted.

He continued to scroll down the pages, nonetheless. Sort of a masochistic urge to inure himself to her allure. Her first husband, Cletus Bergeron, whom she must have married when she was a teenager, was currently in prison and had been in and out of the system his entire life, mostly felony robberies. Her second husband, Jeb Corm-ier, now deceased, had been a well-known Cajun musi-cian, equally well-known for being a cokehead. Adam had one of his CDs in his car, which he played on occa-sion when he was in the mood for wild zydeco tunes. And her third husband, Julien Gaudet, a computer guru, had a Facebook page, which appeared rather perverted in terms of personal proclivities.

Great taste in men, Simone! The only similarity he could see about them was they were all Cajun.

He didn't need the various photos to remind him of how she had looked, although she was especially hot in one where she was wearing a SWAT uniform. He wondered, briefly, what it would be like to make love to a woman wearing boots, a police hat, and a flak jacket, and nothing else, except maybe a black thong. No, the image of her standing in this office was the best, the one imprinted on his testosterone-teeming brain.

Tall. Not too slender like many tall women were today. Model thin, they called it. More like Skinny Minnie. He'd had sex one time with a woman whose hip bone had given him a bruise on the shoulder that lasted for a week. Simone had more meat on the bone, and muscle, from her shoulders to her ample breasts to narrow belted waist to wider hips, and she had mile long legs, and in the middle, oh, my Lord, a butt to die for. When she'd turned to leave his office, he'd noticed the way her dress cupped her buttocks. He'd never been a butt man before, but he was becoming a convert.

She was Cajun, no doubt about that, but not the sweet, petite, brown-eyed, brunette southern Louisiana belle he was accustomed to. Her eyes were alert and intelligent, daring him, or any man, to say the wrong thing. *I can think of about fifty inappropriate things right off the bat.* With her police training, she probably had a pistol in her pocket or hidden in an inner thigh holster. *God bless the male imagination.* Her lips were full, and flame-red today. Sassy, he would guess, when she let herself go. *Does she ever let herself go? She must, if she's been married three times.* And did he mention she had a world-class ass?

Later that day, Adam decided that he should buy some beignets to take home for dessert, and of course he headed to Sweet Buns down the street. That was the name of the bakery, not . . . well, never mind. It was a coincidence, of course, that the bakery was next door to the soon-to-be home of Legal Belles. Maybe he could get another look at Ms. Simone LeDeux, and see if his first reaction had been a one-off. Maybe he would notice something distasteful a second time around that would turn him off.

Even though it was a short distance, he drove his Harley, figuring he would go directly home from there. Dinnertime traffic was heavy and he would have made better time walking, but it gave him time to think. He felt a little creepy chasing after a woman, or at least uncomfortable. Would she think he was a stalker? No, he wasn't stalking. But he was behaving out of character, and that was alarming. To him.

The prospect stopped him dead. What the hell was he doing? He shook his head to clear it and turned the cycle around, heading back to the office.

He would be more careful in the future. It was not a good idea to care too much about a woman. Not a good idea at all.

And next time his sweet tooth called, he would find some other bakery. Like Haydel's in New Orleans which sold Cajunnolis, a trademarked specialty, which was Maisie's favorite. Crisp shells filled with praline cream cheese and the ends dipped in chopped pecans. Better than beignets any day. To Maisie, anyhow. He would make a special trip there soon.

That was a close call, he decided later. One he was going to avoid at all costs. And he wasn't talking . . . *thinking* . . . about pastry.

Chapter Three

It's hard work being a busybody . . .

Louise Rivard, a noted *traiteur*, or folk healer, when she wasn't busy matchmaking up and down the bayou, was standing at the butcher block table in her herb pantry mashing up crumbled alligator teeth with a mortar and pestle. Over the years, she got so many requests for her famous gator anti-itch salve, she could have bottled it and made a fortune. In fact, her nephew John, or Tee-John, said she ought to sell it in that eBay store. Hah! Like she didn't have enough work to do.

She could have used the handy-dandy mini electric food chopper that her eldest nephew, Luc, had given her last Christmas, but there was something soothing about the old methods. Grind, grind, grind. Rasp, rasp, rasp. Gave you time to think. And today she had a lot to think about.

Folks wondered about her using gator teeth in a remedy, but it made a fine abrasive. What those fancy-pancy cosmetic companies called an ex-folly-ant.

She didn't need to worry about finding the animal teeth, either. Her pet gator, Useless, who lived in the bayou out back when it suited his cranky self or when she had enough of his favorite Cheez Doodles on hand, shed them like dandruff. In fact, her nephew René, an environ-mentalist who knew everything and then some about the bayou, claimed that gators grew new teeth whenever their old ones wore down or broke off so that over a fifty-year lifetime they might replace the seventy-five teeth in their big mouths to the tune of three thousand new teeth.

Too bad humans couldn't do the same. It probably had something to do with the big sin in the Garden of Eden. God took away lots of gifts for people after that, like never growing old, because of that darn apple. She wouldn't mind looking like she had at twenty, *hubba hubba*, even if her bones were older than dirt. Whoever said wrinkles were signs of wisdom was dumber than . . . well, dirt. They were just another of God's punishments for that gol-darn apple.

When the gator tooth powder was fine enough, she dumped it in a pottery bowl and added some juniper ber-ries, peppermint oil, aloe vera, and a few other secret in-gredients before whipping the mess into a smooth cream that would thicken up after sitting for a while. Already it had a pleasing candy cane aroma.

While she spooned the salve into separate miniature tins she'd bought in a hobby shop (In the old days, she'd used little aspirin tins which they don't make anymore.), and then cleaned up her supplies, she kept thinking, thinking, thinking. Something was niggling at the back of her brain, and she knew what it was. The thunderbolt of love was about to strike again, and it needed her help.

But who was it this time?

Was it Aaron LeDeux, the pilot from Alaska? She'd heard he was up to some strange antics. Away every night. But not a woman in sight. Could it be he was gay? Now, that would be a wonder, especially since it was his twin brother, Daniel, she'd always hinted might be playing for the other team.

Or maybe it was that crazy Simone LeDeux who'd been looking for love in all the wrong places for so long it gave a body a heartache . . . or heartburn. That girl needed a GPS to find her way through the man jungle out there.

Of course, there were always more of Valcour LeDeux's children crawling out of the woodwork. Just when you thought you'd tagged them all, another one showed up. They ought to bottle up his sperm and put it in one of them fertility banks, or else cut off his wiener to end it all. She wouldn't mind doing it herself. With a rusty butter knife. She'd even offered, more than once, which was why Valcour got a restraining order against her one time. Like that would stop her if she actually got the notion!

Later, her niece Charmaine showed up, supposedly to bring her some beauty product samples from one of her salons, but really to check up on her. Her nephews and nieces did that all the time. Probably thought she was going to pass to the Great Beyond during the night. She had news for them. She had lots to do before she was ready to pass anything but a bit of wind.

Charmaine sank down into a rocking chair next to hers on the back porch facing the bayou. They both had glasses of iced sweet tea in their hands.

Louise loved this view and this simple cottage, which had been a source of peace to her for so many years after the horror and bad years following her Big Grief, which she didn't like to think about. Not anymore.

There was a stretch of lawn leading down to the water, its highlight being a beautiful fig tree that was practically as old as she was, planted by her daddy for her mother on one of their anniversaries. Then there was the St. Jude birdbath surrounded by flowers that she'd put in a few years back. And her vegetable garden, of course. She would have to pick tomatoes tomorrow, lest they go rotten on the vine. And okra, too. Lordy, that okra did flourish here. So much so, she could hardly give it away anymore.

There was something almost holy about the canopy of live oaks streaming their gray moss over a slow-moving bayou and a sun-warmed garden alongside. You could almost hear a butterfly fluttering its angel wings.

"So, Tante, what's new?" Charmaine asked, casual-like, jarring her from her reverie.

Everyone called her Tante, or aunt, even though half of them weren't actual kin. Luc, Remy, and René were sons of her deceased niece Adèle with Valcour LeDeux, while Tee-John was the son of Valcour and his wife, Jolie. All the rest—Charmaine, Simone, Daniel, Aaron and others—were Valcour's illegitimate children from various women. But Louise considered herself great-aunt to them all, blood or not.

"Is that why ya come all the way out here? Ta see what's new? I'd think ya got all the gossip ya need in yer beauty shops."

"Tsk-tsk-tsk! It's not like you ta be so sarcastic. If ya must know, I had a feelin' somethin' was up and thought I oughta come out ta see mah favorite aunt."

Bull-pucky! She cain't butter me up lak a Sunday biscuit, 'specially since I know she ain't got no other aunt. But Charmaine means well. I shouldn't take out my crankiness on her. "Ya had a feelin', too? Talk about!" In truth, it pleased her that her niece was the one who would take over as the family matriarch/matchmaker/busybody one day. It was hard work minding everyone's business, and she welcomed the help. "Someone's needin' a boost in the love department."

"Really? St. Jude tell ya that?" Charmaine teased.

Everyone knew that St. Jude was Louise's favorite saint. The patron of hopeless causes, Jude had been her go-to guy from way back when her fiancé, Phillipe, had died in the Big War . . . source of the Big Grief in her life. But she didn't want to think about that now. She was cranky enough already. "No, St. Jude dint tell me. I jist have this nigglin' sense of somethin' comin'. Sorta like the calm before the storm."

"Any idea who?"

Louise shook her head. "Ya heard anythin' more 'bout that Simone? Ya tol' me las' week 'bout that new bizness she was thinkin' of."

"It's more than thinkin' now, and she decided on a name. It's called Legal Belles. They rented Yancy Butler's old insurance office."

"Legal Belles, huh? I still say Beat the Cheat would be a better name. Tells folks right up front what they're about."

"They'll be investigatin' more than cheats."

"But that's what'll be their biggest draw."

"Are ya thinkin' about aimin' yer thunderbolt her way? She'll probably be too busy fer any kind of love life at the moment."

"Number one, I doan never aim the thunderbolt. It aims itself. And, second, when it hits, time doan matter. It's sorta lak a miracle every time it happens."

Louise looked more closely at her niece then. She was wearing a tight red T-shirt with the logo of one of her salons on it, Hair & Beyond, over black skinny jeans and red high heels. Her black hair was piled on top of her head with a red bow. Her make-up was perfect, and pretty silver crosses dangled from her ears. But that was her usual appearance. There was something different about her today. She glowed.

"Charmaine, how old are you?" Louise narrowed her eyes at her niece, who was more than forty, closer to forty-five. Well-preserved, of course, being a former beauty pageant queen, but still, no longer a young chick.

"What? Why do you want to know?"

"Because . . ." She smiled and slapped her knee with glee. "I think yer preggers."

"That's ridiculous! I'm already startin' menopause. No, it's not possible. Don't you dare pre—suggest such a thing. It would be a miracle if I was pregnant at mah age."

"Dint I jist mention miracles to ya, girl?" Louise glanced toward the St. Jude birdbath statue, and she could swear the guy winked at her.

"Old lady, did you wish this on me?"

"Oh, so now I'm 'old lady'? So much fer yer favorite auntie."

Charmaine made a low growling sound, a sign she was restraining herself from wringing her auntie's neck. Folks did that all the time around Louise.

Whatever!

"Did. Ya. Wish. It?" Charmaine asked through gritted teeth.

"Not 'zackly. I mighta wished there would be more babies what dint come from Valcour LeDeux, no offense since he's yer daddy an' all."

Charmaine growled again.

"All that growlin' probably ain't a good thing iffen ya really are breedin', girl. Too much stress killed the cat, y'know."

"That was curiosity," Charmaine corrected.

"Same thing."

Charmaine crossed her eyes with frustration.

Which also wasn't a good thing. Caused frowns, it did, which could evolve into wrinkles. But Louise refrained from pointing that out. If anyone knew about wrinkles, Charmaine did. She'd been worrying about her complexion since she was thirteen and refused to smile for a whole week because someone said smiles were just wrinkles turned upside down.

Louise had even more to think about now. And more to do. Hallelujah! Maybe she had a double mission this time. A match made in heaven and a new baby. Or lots of new babies. Now that would be a miracle!

One could only wish!

And she did!

Life was good.

It was raining miracles . . .

Later that day, after taking a home pregnancy test that turned out positive, a stunned Charmaine shared the results with her husband, Rusty, who was equally stunned, and then ecstatic with happiness. She threatened to slap him silly if he didn't stop grinning.

Soon the bayou grapevine took over. And Charmaine hadn't even called Tante Lulu. She was afraid she would say something that couldn't be unsaid later when her temper settled down.

Tee-John LeDeux, fearing a tsunami of LeDeux miracles—you couldn't be too careful with Tante Lulu—told his wife, Celine, he was buying a case of double-strength condoms. Three children were enough for him, especially with his wild Etienne. And he rubbed the

St. Jude medal he wore around his neck three times, just for luck.

Remy LeDeux, who already had six adopted and one natural child, told his wife to say a novena, or two. Rachel, a feng shui decorator, said that the energy in their home had been off kilter for some time and hoped that wasn't a sign. She started moving furniture around like a mad woman.

When René LeDeux mentioned the "threat," his wife, Val, a lawyer, said she would sue the granny panties off the old lady if she ended up with another child. They already had a boy and a girl. Two was a couple, three would be a crowd. For some reason, René recalled that he'd found a bunch of four-leaf clovers when he was out foraging with his biology class yesterday. Not that he was superstitious.

Luc, who'd had a vasectomy years ago after his third daughter was born, tried to schedule an appointment with his doctor to make sure his swimmers were still unable to swim. Unfortunately, his surgeon was on a golf vacation for the next two weeks. Luc stopped at the pharmacy on the way to his office for a super-size bottle of antacids.

Daniel LeDeux just shrugged. Married recently to Samantha Starr, they would welcome a child.

Everyone else was nervous. Love was in the air, and they all knew what love could lead to. Even worse, they knew the havoc their great-aunt could create. Had she made some kind of wish that got misdirected by the celestial powers that be?

That old black (Cajun) magic was at work again . . .

It was only two days since she'd signed the final papers in Luc's office, but it felt like two months. Simone couldn't stop thinking about that blasted hunk of Cajun temptation, Adam Lanier.

Of course, she'd Googled him on her computer and discovered he was a hotshot lawyer with a propensity for courtroom antics (in other words, a showoff . . . albeit a successful one). She wasn't too fond of lawyers to begin with, except for Helene—her courtroom experience as a cop had exposed her to more than a little sleazy legal red tape that let bad guys go free.

But, even worse, Adam Lanier was a hotshot outside the courtroom, too, if she went by the photographs taken at various New Orleans charity events and nightclubs. It was obvious that the man spread his favors, unapologetically, among many women. And this, even when his wife had still been alive! And he had a young daughter, too.

The most recent photo, taken last month at a Baton Rouge marathon, showed him with a yoga instructor who looked like a size zero in her designer tights. Simone hadn't been a size zero since she was eight years old, if then.

Nope, Adam Lanier was the worst kind of man for her. A shameless, quintessential player. Was *fidelity* an outdated word in this modern world of hookups and casual sex?

Well, her research had sealed the deal for her. A bad-boy Cajun lawyer was not for her. That was a no brainer. Good thing she'd looked him up. Informed was armed.

If only she could stop thinking about him!

Luckily, she had her new business to keep her busy. Legal Belles was taking shape faster than she'd expected. All the furniture had been removed from the first and second floors (salvageable pieces put in temporary storage), the carpet pulled up, and the golden cypress floors exposed for refinishing.

Simone was looking over paint chips with Ed Gillotte,

a contractor who worked for her half brother Daniel Le-
Deux over at Bayou Rose Plantation. He'd started work
yesterday, and already the place looked better, or at least
was showing its potential. He'd even painted the trim on
the outside of the bay window, along with the door, a
warm green and blue to match the new sign erected above
the windows.

Ed was about thirty years old but looked about forty,
every hard knock of his life showing on his haggard face.
A receding hairline led to long, reddish blond hair tied
back with a rubber band into a low ponytail. His one eye
tooth was missing. Overly thin, but with muscled arms
and shoulders, indicative of a laborer, not a gym nut. His
jeans and T-shirt and athletic shoes were well-worn but
clean.

If she hadn't known better, her police experience
would have labeled him addict, or alcoholic. He was neither. Or at least not presently. She knew from Daniel that
Ed had been on drugs at one time and was a convicted
felon (armed robbery), but he'd been clean for years,
thanks mostly to the reality check of having a little girl
with cancer. He now had a place to live, thanks to a lot of
help from Daniel, a pediatric oncologist, who'd opened
one of the plantation cottages to Ed. Living with Ed and
helping to share babysitting duties—he had three kids in
all—was Lily Fontenot, a college student who'd recently
had a baby, a little boy named Beau. The redneck carpen-
ter and the budding physicist . . . there had to be a story
there.

Most important, Ed was an expert contractor, profi-
cient with hammer as well as paintbrush. And he was
cheap.

"I think the sage green for the walls here," she told
him. "Blue for the bathroom, off-white for the kitchen,

and for upstairs I need to think about those colors a little more. I know you suggested red for the living room, but that's a little extreme for me. Too bordello-ish."

He smiled, exposing the gap in his teeth. She wondered why he didn't have it fixed, but then figured he probably couldn't afford the expense. Or maybe he didn't care. The smile was probably an indication of his disbelief that someone forming a Cheaters-type agency would be reticent about anything.

"If possible, I would like to get this reception area done first so that I can begin to do some employee interviews. All I would need is a desk and two chairs, and I wouldn't care if you were working anywhere else during that time. I can live with the noise and the paint fumes short-term."

"I'll paint the walls and refinish the floors in sections. It takes two days of no traffic for the wood to cure. You would be good to go by Friday, for this space, anyhow. Monday would be even better. Would that work for you?"

"Perfect."

An old guy, about sixty years old, walked in then, carrying a commercial-size bucket of primer, and Ed introduced him as one of his helpers. Despite his paint-spattered, white bib overalls and ratty white painters' cap, he was a spiffy-looking fellow with neatly trimmed white hair and beard and mustache. Sort of Colonel Sanders–ish. "This is Tom Dorsey. He's the one who painted your sign out front."

Simone shook hands with Tom after he set his bucket down, then said with a laugh, "I know you. Weren't you the Santa at the Our Lady of the Bayou Christmas party every year?"

Tom smiled. "Yep. For thirty-five years, this coming Christmas." He removed his cap and combed his fingers through his thick hair. "I went gray when I was in my twenties." He wagged a forefinger at her. "But you're not supposed to recognize old Santy."

She laughed. "I caught you out back having a cigarette one time, and even at ten years old, I just knew Santa Claus wouldn't smoke."

"I don't anymore, but, yeah, you caught me with that one."

Just then, the bell over the front door tinkled, and they all turned to see the most amazing spectacle enter. It was Adelaide Daigle, but unlike any mother image Simone had ever seen before.

She wore a sleeveless sheath dress with blocked colors, black in the front and back with a wide band of white from under the armpits to the hem, the kind that accentuated her hourglass figure, which was helped out by her latest obsession with Spanx. When she turned sideways, which she did to get a closer look at Simone's gapemouthed companions, the Spanx also made her bum look Kardashianesque huge.

She must have come straight from the beauty salon because her black curls were lacquered to perfection in her usual vintage French twist upsweep. Red metal hearts dangled on various length chains from her ears, matching the flame-red lipstick that outlined her lips, making them wider than their natural shape. Fake eyelashes completed the picture, except for the black high heels, which couldn't be good for someone with recent knee surgery.

"Moth-er! What in the world—"

"Hello, sweetheart. And who are these handsome fellows?"

"This is Ed Gillotte, my contractor, and his assistant—"

"Why, you don't have ta introduce Tom. We've known each other fer ages, right?" Her mother batted her false eyelashes at Tom.

"Right," Tom choked out. He was looking at her mother like she was the candy cane on his personal Christmas tree and he'd like to gobble her right up.

Eeew!

"What are you doing here, Mom?"

"I saw yer ad sittin' on the kitchen table this mornin', the one advertisin' fer employees, and I figgered I'd apply now before the mad rush."

The mad rush? She doubted that would happen, but even so . . . "What kind of job are you thinking of?"

"You know, sweetie." She rolled her eyes toward Ed and Tom, as if not wanting to say it out loud.

"Don't you think you're a little old for that?"

"Si-mone! Don't think fer one minute that I couldn't sit on a bar stool and attract some man with cheatin' on his mind. Not all men go fer females that are so skinny their bones are pokin' out, and there's somethin' ta be said fer a woman with experience."

"I'll second that," Tom interjected.

Please don't.

"Thank you, Tommy," her mother said.

Tommy? Where did that come from?

"In fact, I'd sidle right up and buy you one of those umbrella drinks. That's what I'd do."

"Oooh, I love umbrella drinks."

"Besides, a cowboy's gotta have something to grab on to when he swings into the saddle."

She exchanged a horrified look with Ed.

Taking a hint, Ed told his helper, "Well, this has been nice, but maybe we should head on to the paint store."

"Right," Tom said, his face turning red, making him look even more like the jolly old fellow. He must have figured out, belatedly, that he'd been speaking out of turn and perhaps inappropriately around his employer.

The two men left, but not before Tom promised Adelaide to come around the trailer one day to give her some of the mushrooms he cultivated in dead logs in his backyard hothouse.

Simone hoped they were *mushroom* mushrooms and not that other kind. Her mother was whacked out enough without adding psychedelic drugs to the mix.

Before Simone could say anything, though, her mother plopped down onto a folding chair and toed off her high heels. "Holy crawfish! I thought they'd never leave. Mah feet are killin' me."

"You shouldn't be wearing those shoes after knee surgery."

"It's not the knees that are botherin' me. It's the bunion the size of a golf ball on mah right foot. And if that isn't bad enough, this last Spanx I ordered came a size too small. I cain't breathe worth nothin'. You're gonna have ta cut it off me. You got any scissors here?"

"No, I don't have any scissors. C'mon, I'll walk you to your car."

"I didn't drive."

"You didn't?"

"Nope. Got a ride in with . . ." She motioned her head toward the window, outside of which could be seen a huge vintage lavender convertible which was parked catty-corner in not one, but two spaces, both of which were clearly marked "No Parking."

Getting out on the driver's side and garnering more than one gawk followed by a chuckle from passersby was none other than the Bayou Bad Girl. Tante Lulu was wearing an Elizabeth Taylor wig today and a tight, red, stretchy knit dress that showed off her cleavage. Normally, she was flat-chested, but today was about a size hot-cha-cha, which would be making her top heavy if it weren't for the balance of an impressive rear end. She must be wearing one of those butt builder panties because one cheek was higher than the other. No problem, the old lady adjusted it, right out in plain sight. Then she walked on, or rather hobbled on down the street, in a pair of orthopedic high heels.

Tante Lulu and Adelaide Daigle would look like two senior citizen hookers if they walked down the street together. Which was exactly the point, Simone realized. Tante Lulu must be looking for a job, too.

"No!" Simone exclaimed. "No, no, no!"

Seeing the direction of Simone's stare, her mother immediately recognized the conclusion she'd come to and laughed. "Tante Lulu jist gave me a lift inta town. She's on her way over to Charmaine's beauty shop. They're gonna enter a mother-daughter beauty contest at the veterans' club to raise money fer wounded soldiers."

"Charmaine isn't her daughter," Simone pointed out.

"They're gonna pretend she is. Once Charmaine puts on her Pretty Woman minidress with the black patent leather thigh boots, do you think them ex-soldiers are gonna care?"

Only in Louisiana would any of this make sense.

"C'mon. I'll drive you home," Simone said quickly to forestall Tante Lulu coming in, wanting the grand tour, and staying forever. Not that she wasn't a sweet old busybody, bless her heart.

Simone had to yank her mother up off the chair and carry her high heels while she walked barefooted toward Simone's waiting vehicle out front next to Tante Lulu's. Usually, she parked in one of the spots out back along the alley, but Ed's van had been there when she came in this morning. While they were on their way, Simone told her, "Just for the record, Mom. I am not hiring you as an undercover operative to entrap men, either."

"I didn't think you would, but it was worth a try."

"What's this all about?"

"I'm bored sittin' at home all day, and there's no way I kin stand all day at my waitressin' job. Not yet, leastways. Besides that, you'll be movin' out soon, and the lonelies will set in again."

Another guilt trip.

"I've been thinkin' about playin' some online slot machines."

"Don't you dare. They're a scam."

Simone glanced downward and her mother did, indeed, have a huge bunion on her right foot. She would need to see a foot doctor. Another thing to add to her list. With a sigh, Simone offered, "Maybe you could be a receptionist here for a while, until I can hire someone."

Her mother's face brightened.

"But it's only temporary . . . until I can hire someone."

"Sure, honey, sure." Her mother was about to ease herself into Simone's car when she exclaimed, "Holy crawfish! Would you look at that?"

Simone looked, then looked again.

It was Adam Lanier driving by. On a motorcycle. He wore a business suit with biker boots. But a motorcycle? Life was unfair. Not just a Cajun, but a Cajun on a chopper. How could she resist that?

"On second thought, don't look. I kin practic'ly hear your Cajun clock tickin'," her mother said. "I'm gonna find you a nice Yankee . . . once that Cletus pops his cork. Cain't be getting' married again while you're still bound to Cletus in the eyes of God."

Simone wasn't really listening to her mother. She was staring after the hunk on a Harley.

But wait. What . . . or who . . . was that riding pillion? A little girl with corkscrew black curls peeking out of a mini helmet—it must be his daughter—had her little arms wrapped around her daddy's waist, her face pressed lovingly—trustingly—against Adam's back. He must have just picked her up from school; she had an Our Lady of the Bayou School backpack strapped to her shoulders.

Was that even safe?

It must be. She wore a helmet, and the seat had a high backrest to prevent her falling off, and there were foot pegs installed to fit her smaller height. Plus, Adam appeared to be driving only about five miles an hour.

But, really! A Cajun playboy who was a devoted single father?

The deck was stacked against her.

That was proven true when she saw Tante Lulu observing her observations. The old bat didn't miss anything, bless her heart. "Well, well, well, I jist knew I was needed here. Give me some sugah, honey." She arched her face up for Simone's kiss, on both powdered cheeks.

"Do you want me to drive you over to Charmaine's shop?" Simone asked, eyeing the badly parked vehicle.

"Nah. It's only half a block away. Besides, I wanna stop at Luc's office." She narrowed her eyes at Simone. "Of course, you could walk along with me. Have ya met Luc's new partner yet? I saw ya eyein' him as he drove by."

"Yes, I've met Adam Lanier." She could feel her face was blooming with color.

And her mother noticed. "You didn't tell me you met a new Cajun fella," she accused her daughter.

"I didn't tell you because it didn't matter."

Tante Lulu made a clucking noise of disbelief. "I hear yer lookin' ta hire hookers," the old lady said then.

"Whaaat?" Simone glared at her mother.

"Don't look at me! I never said anything about hookers."

"Ladies what can hook men into cheatin' soz their wives kin tie their wieners in a knot when they go ta divorce court," Tante Lulu explained. "There's all kinds of hookers, ya know. Didja think I meant the other kind?"

What could Simone say to that? "Um, I won't be hiring any hookers today."

"Are ya sure? I could be yer honeypot—thass what they call wimmen lurin' men in a sting, isn't it? Yep, I would be jist lak that boxer guy. Dance lak a butterfly, sting lak a bee. I could be the best stinger ya ever used. *Sting* is a police word fer trappin' crimnals. Ya should know that, Simone."

Hookers and stingers? A Cajun busybody giving me a lecture on police vocabulary? What next?

Just then, the *coup de grace* occurred. Or rather, the two *coups de grace*. That's "what next."

A medium height, suntanned guy in a designer polo shirt and slacks—handsome as any Cajun man had a right to be—eased himself out of a low slung Jaguar. It was Jack Landry. When he saw Simone, he gave a little wave and smiled tentatively. "Hello, darlin'."

Why wasn't Jack back in Chicago? Why had he come to Louisiana? It was over. Over, over, over! Why couldn't he accept that fact? Maybe it was just a coincidence that he was here. Maybe there was a family crisis. Yeah, right. His family lived about two hours north of here in Baton Rouge.

If Jack's sudden appearance wasn't bad enough, coming up behind her, she heard another male voice say in a raspy, nicotine-like growl, "Hello, darlin'!" She turned to see a man she didn't recognize, at first. Tall, skinny, wearing faded jeans and a white T-shirt with a pack of Camels tucked into the rolled-up sleeve. How retro was that? Almost a fashion statement, of the worst kind. His skin—what could be seen of it with all that ink—was unusually pale, especially for the Deep South. Prison pallor.

Did one of those tatts on his forearm say "My Simone" inside a heart? Oh, good Lord, it did.

It was Cletus Bergeron. He must have gotten an early release.

Simone did the only thing she could. Run. Right back into her shop. Before she locked the door and pulled down the blinds, she heard Tante Lulu say to her mother, "I ain't had this much fun since I lost mah bloomers at Friday night bingo when I jumped up ta get the grand prize."

"I wonder if I gotta invite Cletus ta stay with us at The Gates since his Momma cut off all ties with him," her mother pondered.

"I dint know that," Tante Lulu said, which was a wonder since the old lady usually knew everything before it even happened on the bayou.

"Yep. Sez he ain't her son anymore." Her mother sighed. "Betcha he don't have no place ta lay his poor head. Betcha he's still in love with mah Simone. Betcha he's been pinin' away fer her all these years. Betcha he's reformed and no longer a bad guy. Betcha I could have a grandbaby by next summer."

"Did I tell ya that Charmaine is preggers? And Luc, Remy, and René might be, too. Well, their wives might be," Tante Lulu mentioned with seeming irrelevance. At least, Simone hoped it was irrelevant.

"There is hope, then," her mother said.

"It's a miracle. Good ol' celestial magic," Tante Lulu concluded.

Forget about Cajun Crazy. Simone was in Cajun Hell.

Chapter Four

There's a little hound dog in all of us, Elvis . . .

Adam sat in the courtroom, second chair to Luc, in the third, drawn-out day of a civil complaint trial against Cypress Oil. On his left was their client, Minh "Mad Mike" Pham, a second generation Vietnamese-American whose once flourishing shrimp fishing operation was no longer flourishing. He'd gotten his nickname playing football for LSU as a wide receiver. Now he was a take-no-prisoners businessman.

Mike's father, Nguyen Pham, sat beside his son. Like many Vietnamese, Nguyen had emigrated to the U.S., southern Louisiana in particular, after the 1968 Tet Offensive thanks to the work of Catholic Charities. Apparently the bayou fishing industry lent itself well to Vietnamese who had been fishermen in their homeland. And both Vietnam and Louisiana had been French colonies at one time, which had helped the immigrants blend in more easily.

Nguyen, a diminutive seventy-five-year-old, looked frail and bowed from decades of hauling shrimp nets under the grueling Louisiana skies. What a contrast the father and son were! Mike wasn't especially tall, but he still had at least eight inches on his father in height and fifty pounds in muscle.

Mike wore the blue-collar attire of a denim shirt and sun-bleached jeans with a LSU Tigers ball cap sitting on the table. He looked a mite impoverished next to the clowns from Cypress Oil, but it was a role he played well. Mike had more degrees than a thermometer and a bank account that flourished, even if his business didn't of late. It wasn't the first time Mike had been a pain in Cypress's butt, and the air reeked of hostility.

At the opposing table sat a flank of four big-city lawyers, along with Mitchell Ahearn, current CEO of Cypress, all dressed in thousand-dollar suits and designer leather loafers, some of which might even be stitched from the prized skin of alligators, the very animals that could one day become extinct because of Cypress Oil's encroaching efforts. Not to mention shrimp, crawfish, clams, oysters, and other aquatic life . . . in other words, the backbone of the southern Louisiana food chain. Mike wasn't always pleasant, but he wasn't wrong that the oil company was polluting the waters his own company fished in.

Behind the defendants' table sat lower level Cypress executives and a few big investors, including none other than Valcour LeDeux, Luc's father. Adam had never met the old guy in person, but he'd heard plenty. He had to admit that, even at seventy or so years old, Valcour was a handsome man. You'd think there would be at least one gray hair in his dark brown, razor-cut locks. He might have had some work done on his dissipated face (no hiding the alcoholic flush beneath the taut, tanned skin) because there were hardly any wrinkles, but he may have had some genetic luck. All the LeDeux men were good-looking. And hey, the women weren't too bad, either, like Simone LeDeux . . .

No, no, no! He was not going to think about Simone today. He'd done too much thinking about her every day since they'd met, and during the night, too. Hot damn, but did he think about her in his dreams! He was becoming a teenager again, wet dreams and all.

But back to Valcour LeDeux. The man had come a long way from the days when he'd been a young widower living in a rusted-out trailer with his three sons whom he'd used as punching bags regularly, all this according to Luc, who had no love for his old man. But then they'd discovered oil on his bayou property, and that made a major change in Valcour's lifestyle. Not that he'd treated his kids any better. That's when Tante Lulu—the great-aunt or something of Valcour's deceased wife, Adèle—had stepped in and taken over. To say there was no love lost between Valcour and Tante Lulu would be a gross understatement.

Adam glanced at Luc to gauge his reaction to his father being there, on the opposing side, possibly a ploy on Cypress's part to rattle Luc's nerves. No reaction at all. But then, this wasn't the first time legal action had been taken against this particular company located just outside Houma, nor was it the first time Luc had been on the complainant's side.

In a way, though, it was surprising to see all the big guns out for such small game. Nothing like the humongous class action suits filed every so many years against these destroyers of the Gulf Coast environment. No twenty-billion-dollar BP Oil–type settlement if they won. Not even one billion. In fact, the Phams would be happy with a mere million. This kind of court case was just nibbling away like ducks, that's what Luc called it. Not that nibbling wasn't important. The end result was the same. Make the culprits pay for their bad deeds and, hopefully, change their evil actions.

"Are you ready?" Luc whispered to Adam. The judge and jury had just returned to the courtroom after a midmorning break. "You do the cross on the chemist, and I'll go get our next piece of evidence."

Piece of evidence was a misnomer. More like three pieces of evidence, each of the pieces weighing about three hundred pounds. "I still don't see how you're going to get those dead gators in here."

"On a hospital gurney covered with a sheet. They're only young gators."

"I know that, but how will you get the gurney past the guards? And, man, have you checked that Gulf Coast Meats refrigerated truck out in the parking lot lately? You can smell the rot from fifty feet."

"The guard on duty will conveniently have to visit the men's room. He's a friend of a friend of Tante Lulu's." Luc grinned.

Adam should have known the old lady would have a hand in this stunt. He wouldn't be surprised if she popped up, wearing a nurse's uniform, pushing a gator in a wheelchair. "I still don't think the judge will allow us to provide the gator gang as evidence."

"Of course he won't. But by the time the defense objects and the judge rules, the jury will have gotten a whiff and a looksee at the evidence. Hard to wipe that image from the mind, or that stink from the nostrils, no matter how hard the judge rules it as inadmissible."

Adam had pulled some courtroom antics himself in the past, following "the end justifies the means" theory of law, but he was a rank amateur compared to Luc.

Mike had been talking to his father, but then turned to Luc and Adam. "What gators?"

"You don't want to know," they both replied.

Luc slipped out of the courtroom as the jury filed in and Howard Lintell, the Cypress chemist, took the stand again. The bailiff reminded Lintell that he was still under oath, and Judge Chenier looked at Adam, taking note but not unduly concerned that the lead attorney was no longer there. "Is the plaintiff ready to cross-examine?"

"Yes, sir," Adam said, standing. He went over to the table in front of the judge's bench, or raised desk, and checked on an array of test tubes that were on display, already entered in evidence. Those on behalf of Cypress Oil and those prepared by an independent company on behalf of the Phams. Then he stepped over to the witness stand where the nerdish-looking chemist in a crumpled wool suit—clearly Lintell was a northerner brought in to testify and was unaccustomed to the moist heat of the South—wiped nervously with a handkerchief at the perspiration that beaded his forehead. "Mr. Lintell, you testified this morning that the tests you ran on runoffs at the Sweet Cherry plant fell within government regulations for safety."

"Yes, I did."

"And those tests were run on April first and second?"

"Yes."

"Did you obtain those samples yourself?"

"Well, no, but—"

"Were you not alarmed that results of your samples and the ones we obtained from a private testing company differed so greatly?"

"No. Private companies are not always reliable."

"But your tests are?"

"I pride myself on the integrity of my work."

"No offense intended, Mr. Lintell. I'm aware of your impressive credentials. You testified on behalf of Great North Oil Co. last year, too, didn't you?"

"I object," the lead Cypress Oil lawyer yelled. "Irrelevant."

"Objection sustained." The judge waved a hand for Adam to continue, clearly bored. He wouldn't be for long.

"You did not gather the testing fluids yourself, is that correct?"

"That's right," Lintell conceded, again.

Adam glanced toward the jury box to make sure they drew the appropriate conclusions, implying tampering with evidence.

"But there was a chain of evidence to protect—"

"Your honor!" Adam protested. "Please advise the witness to only answer the questions."

The judge nodded and so advised Lintell.

Adam went over to the table where he opened a metal insulated thermos and poured out a glass of murky water. "This water was poured from the kitchen faucet inside Mr. Pham Sr.'s Sweet Cherry home this morning. Would you care to take a drink?"

The judge was already chiding "Mis-ter Lan-ier!" even before the defendant's counsel objected that this item had not yet been entered into evidence.

"I withdraw my offer," Adam said.

But the jury had already seen Lintell recoil at the prospect of drinking the gray water. Adam knew how to practice the law the traditional way, slow and plodding, but he also knew how to use the system and made no apologies for employing all the tricks . . . rather, talents at his disposal.

"Behave yourself, Mister Lanier," the judge warned. "You're already walking a fine line."

Just then, the courtroom door opened and Luc strolled in pushing the hospital gurney up the wide center aisle. Even before he stopped and yanked the sheet off three dead and rotting gator carcasses, the fumes were filling the air. "Your honor, I would like to introduce some new witnesses for the plaintiff. Moe, Larry, and Curly, residents until last week of Sweet Cherry Bayou. Unfortunately, they—"

The judge, with a white handkerchief pressed to his nose, finally overcame his shock and yelled, "Mister LeDeux, you are in contempt of court."

"But, yer honor, I didn't kill them gators. Cypress Oil runoff did. Why, I'm practicly a PETA person. I wouldn't hurt a—"

"Mister LeDeux! See me in my chamber immediately and get that . . . that mess out of here."

Adam glanced over to the jury box. One woman looked as if she was about to vomit, while several men barely stifled grins. Mission accomplished.

An hour later, the jury had been sent home with the trial adjourned until Monday. Luc had been fined one thousand dollars for contempt with a warning that one more transgression would land him in jail. Even Adam had been warned that the judge's patience was wearing thin.

The older Mr. Pham had already gone home, but Mike had stayed to talk over the case with them. They stopped at a nearby café often frequented by lawyers and courthouse employees.

After they discussed the lawsuit thus far and what was to come (the defense not having started their case yet), Mike hemmed and hawed before asking, "Um, assuming we're going to win this case, eventually, can you guys suggest a way to hide the funds?"

Adam and Luc exchanged "Uh-oh!" looks.

"What do you mean?" Luc asked.

"Well, there's a good possibility that I'll be getting a divorce, and, well . . ." He shrugged, his face flushing with embarrassment.

"You and Thanh? Good Lord, man, you've been married as long as I've known you," Luc said. "Longer than me and Sylvie."

Mike nodded. "Twenty-one years. The boys are in college now, and I've stuck it out longer than I ever wanted. All Thanh does is hang around the house and mope."

Luc cut right to the chase. "Is there another woman?"

"Uh . . ." Mike looked uncomfortable.

"Or more than one woman?" Adam guessed. Mike was Luc's acquaintance, not his, but Adam recognized the signs.

Mike shrugged and raised his chin defiantly.

"Thanh doesn't strike me as the type who'd be aggressive in countering a divorce action," Luc commented.

"She isn't, and I would make sure she was taken care of, for life. But I don't intend to bankrupt myself, either. She has a sister, Kim, who's as assertive as Thanh is retiring. I'm afraid Kim would get her ear, and you know how that goes. They'd have Gloria Allred flying to Loo-zee-anna faster than a kamikaze seagull."

"Allred only represents celebrities, as far as I know," Adam pointed out.

Mike just blinked at him, probably wondering if he was being sarcastic.

He was.

"There is no legal or moral way to hide assets in a divorce action," Luc said, stern faced.

If Adam hadn't admired Luc before, he would now. But then, for all his courtroom shenanigans, Luc was an honest attorney. And, no, that wasn't an oxymoron. But then, Adam had known that about Luc before he'd joined his firm. He wouldn't have aligned himself with shady legal practices.

"I have a friend who says his lawyer showed him how to hide money in some offshore account . . . Brazil or Bermuda, I think," Mike argued, a tone of belligerence in his voice.

Luc's lips thinned even more. "I don't handle divorces, but if that's the direction you want to head in, I can give you a referral. Not for illegal activity, but for divorce advice."

Mike muttered a foul word under his breath that sounded something like "Pussy!" followed by a statement that men should stick together. But then he nodded, reluctantly.

After Mike left in his own car, Luc said, "What an asshole! I never saw this side of him before."

"Are you going to recuse yourself from the Cypress case?"

"Hell, no! I've put in too much time already, and you have, too. He's got billable hours out the wazoo. Besides, there's nothing immoral about fighting against the evil oil empire. We've just got to separate the two issues. Mike the justified litigant. And Mike the jerk."

"Too bad it's a breach of ethics to make a suggestion to the other party."

"Cypress Oil?"

"No. Mike's wife," Adam said. "I'm thinking she should hot foot it over to Legal Belles."

Luc laughed. "You're right. That *would be* a breach of ethics." Luc tapped his closed lips thoughtfully. "But maybe Tante Lulu could give Thanh a business card from the new agency."

"Do they have business cards yet?"

"If they don't, they should." Luc gave him an assessing look.

"What?"

"You could go over and get a card. Or a pile of cards for our office. For referrals."

"Me? Why me?"

"Are you kiddin? Every time I mention Legal Belles or my half sister Simone, your eyes light up like a bayou moon."

"They do not," Adam countered, but not too strongly.

"Besides, Tante Lulu has you two in her crosshairs."

"For what?"

Luc shrugged. "You never know with Tante Lulu's thunderbolt. It could go in any number of directions. Love, sex, marriage, the-itch-that-can't-be-scratched, baby bumps."

Any one of those were unacceptable to Adam . . . at this time . . . with *that* woman. Besides, he could handle his own hookups, thank you very much, Tante Lulu, and he for sure could scratch if he wanted to.

But he wasn't about to let Luc get the last word in. "Rusty told me that Charmaine is pregnant and blaming Tante Lulu. Is it true that you and Sylvie might be rocking the cradle again, too?"

"Touche!" Luc said. "Touche and pray God my swimmers are still fin-less."

"Mine, too. Not that I've had a vasectomy. But I'm not looking for more kids, either. I've got my hands full with Maisie."

"None of that matters when it comes to Tante Lulu."

"Surely, she wouldn't be wishing paternity on me without the love and courtship and marriage crap."

Luc shrugged. "You never know with my aunt."

Ironically (although it was probably deliberate on

Luc's part), they were just about to pass Legal Belles, and
standing outside was none other than Tante Lulu and
some big Amazon of a woman, not just tall but hefty. But
more important, Simone stood there, hands on pretty hips
(She was wearing paint-splattered black-and-white polka
dot shorts. Not that he was paying that close of attention!),
flirting with two men who were grinning like hound dogs
at a barbecue.

Who were they?

Boyfriends? Lovers? Ex-husbands? Husband?

One of them looked like an inmate who'd just gotten
$10 in gate money and a bus ticket after being pushed out
some jailhouse doors, and the other could have stepped
out of the pages of GQ.

Shiiit!

It was just like Hannah all over again. Discovering her
men in all the wrong places. Always on edge. Always
wondering. Jealousy. Rage. Thank God he'd seen this today. You could say he'd dodged a bullet. A Tante Lulu
bullet, or a hot female bullet. Didn't matter which. Now
he could tuck Simone away as a "close call."

But Luc's car was already moving along, and when
Adam glanced his way, he saw that his partner was giving
him a knowing look. "Yep. Like a bayou moon."

Adam put a hand to his face. He *was* a little hot.

How many bullets can one gal dodge? . . .

Simone was in the middle of her third interview of the
morning, and it was not going well. Alexis Fornier, a college student looking for a part-time job and tired of wait-
ressing, thought it would be "wicked good fun" to turn a
guy on and then "whomp his ass" when she had the goods

on him. The best part, she boasted, was that she had a license to carry.

Sweetheart, I wouldn't trust you to carry my purse, let alone a pistol. "Um, that's not exactly what we do here," Simone told the girl.

"What? Oh, y'all mean what Ah said about 'whompin' ass'?" Alexis was pure Southern belle in skinny jeans, bustier, stilettos, and big hair upswept to heaven.

Yes, the girl had come to an interview dressed like a tart. Simone and Helene were continually fighting the impression that Legal Belles was no more than a cheater entrapment agency, an impression that had been spread like wildfire on the bayou grapevine. Probably by you-know-who, the Mouth of the South.

"Whompin' ass . . . that's jist an expression us young folks use, ma'am."

Ma'am? The implication was that Simone was not one of the young folks.

"Uh-huh." Simone nodded, wondering whether her next interviewee would be any better.

"Really. Ah would be amazing at entrappin' those losers. Me and mah friends often pretend ta be interested in guys at bars, just ta lead 'em on, fer the fun of it. The easiest ones ta tease are the old fogies, those guys over forty."

Definitely, I am not one of the young folks, in her world.

Next up was Sabine Gentry, a thirtysomething blonde with a slim, almost boy-like figure tucked into a sleeveless Billy Bob's Biker Club T-shirt and leather pants with boots. She had diamond climbers on her ears, a gold stud in her tongue, and myriad tropical flowers tattooed over her arms, culminating in a chain of roses around her neck.

Simone hired Sabine on the spot. She knew Sabine from the police academy and wouldn't have to instruct her in proper entrapment techniques. Sabine hadn't been working for the past seven years while she raised her three kids, the youngest of which was now in kindergarten. Sabine's husband, Brad, worked undercover for the New Orleans PD.

"You still have that thing for Cajun men, Simone?"

"Unfortunately."

Sabine laughed. "I remember how your lady parts would get all gooey when a Cajun man winked at you, or, God forbid, said, 'Come 'ere, darlin'' with that slow Southern drawl."

Yep, that's me. Fool with the gooey parts.

"Doan be gettin' all embarrassed, honey. I'm the same way. Whydja think I married a Yankee? He's the one that gets all gooey, in his man parts, when I drawl, 'Come 'ere, darlin'. I got somethin' fer you.' Southern sugah, that's what I call it."

Simone also signed on a young man from Lafayette, Gabriel Storm, which sounded like a stage name, but was not. Gabe had aspirations to become an actor and thought he could play the role of a "gigolo on the prowl." On the surface, that sounded stupid. But he was nice-looking and could be trained to follow certain scripts. His was a provisional hire, he would have to be evaluated after a trial period.

Simone intended to do "fieldwork" herself, as well. At least in the beginning. Of course, she would have to be selective in the birds she hoped to trap because she was rather well-known in some quarters. She'd be scaring off the prey before she even started if she walked into some bars or establishments where men went to meet women.

Her mother came in then, wearing another of her Spanx-requisite dresses, but with flat heeled shoes. Adelaide Daigle, name clearly spelled out on the brass plate her mother had made for her desk, had stepped into her receptionist role yesterday and had been performing satisfactorily so far. But Simone was only speaking to her when absolutely necessary, the bone of contention being Cletus Bergeron, whom her mother had sleeping on the trailer sofa these past two nights, which had prompted Simone to move, without preparation, into the Legal Belles' upstairs apartment where she was currently using a fold-out cot lent to her by Helene's parents. Scarlett was still back at the trailer until Simone could make the apartment cat-proof. "Did you see this?" her mother asked, shoving a copy of the local newspaper onto her desk.

It was an article about a Terrebonne Parish trial involving Cypress Oil and the LeDeux & Lanier law firm. The headline of the story was "The Swamp Solicitor and the Bayou Barrister Create Courtroom Stink." The photograph accompanying the article showed Luc pushing a hospital gurney with three dead gators and Adam in the background, looking all hot and professionally lawyerish but with a sinful Cajun grin on his face.

Even looking at the photograph, Simone felt the goo-eys coming on.

"Why are you showing me this?" she snapped at her mother.

"So you'd see what a mistake that Lanier fellow would be fer you, honey."

"I was never involved with that Lanier fellow. And don't think for one minute, mother, that this article or Adam being involved in some dumb lawyer tricks will make me any more willing to take Cletus back. He is my ex. He will always be my ex. And if he shows up here one more time, even to visit you, I'm going to call the police and have him arrested for harassment."

"But—"

"No buts."

"He has a job interview today," her mother told her, anyway. "He's gonna work at the Gator Packing Plant. Butcherin' dead gators fer the restaurant trade."

"I don't care if he's wrestling alligators." Simone stood and tidied the files on her desk. She had three more interviews scheduled for later this afternoon.

"You goin' somewhere?"

"Yes. I'm having lunch with Jack Landry. Then I'm off to Home Warehouse to buy some furniture, which I cannot afford and which I hadn't planned on buying until after Legal Belles was bringing in some cash."

Her mother's artfully rouged face bloomed with even more color. (She was getting lessons from Charmaine on "make-up for the professional woman.")

"What happened ta yer furniture in Chee-cah-go?"

"It's in storage. I don't have time to go back for it right now."

"I never meant fer you ta move out like that."

"I had no choice." She held up a halting hand when her mother was about to argue.

"Jist one thing," her mother said. "You're not plannin' on movin' back ta Chee-cah-go, are ya?"

Simone frowned. "Why would you think that?"

"You're havin' lunch with that architect fellow, ain'tcha?"

"That's just to say good-bye. For good."

"Did you hafta dress all sexy-like ta say good-bye?"

Simone glanced down. She *had* taken special care with her appearance. A sheer red blouse over a black bra, giving a wispy glimpse of bare abdomen, and a knee-length, black pencil skirt. Mid-heeled black slingback sandals. A redfiligreed headband held her dark hair off her face and cascading down over her shoulders, making her look younger than her almost thirty years.

There was something about looking good that was important to a girl when giving the old heave-ho to the male ho. Sort of a figurative middle finger in the air.

She'd just parked her car in the lot beside Chez Pierre's and stood outside tugging down the hem of her skirt when she noticed Adam Lanier approaching. He must have been leaving the restaurant.

"Simone," he said, coming closer.

She didn't move, little alarm bells going off, not just in her head, but all over her suddenly sensitized body. *Gooey alert! Should I pretend I don't see him? Should I jump back in the car and drive off? Should I giggle and act all girly and excited to see him? Should I wave a white flag (tissue) of surrender and just jump his pretty bones?*

It was a lost cause in the end.

Adam Lanier looked like a cool drink on a hot day, wearing a mint-green shirt with a beige tie and a light tan summer suit. Put a sprig of mint in his teeth, and he'd be a julep. This must be a work day for him, as evidenced by the suit. If he was in court, the female jurors would be salivating.

And, bless his conniving Cajun heart, the way he said her name was all soft and husky. Like he was saying "Simone," but he was thinking "S. E. X." It meant nothing, of course. It was an art form Cajun males learned at their father's knees. How to charm the opposite sex into doing whatever they wanted.

And, boy, was she thinking about all those whatevers. Darn her Cajun-loving soul!

Just as she was giving him the eye-candy once-over, he was appraising her, too. His dark chocolate eyes traveled down her body, then started up again, slooooowly, beginning with the Cover Girl "Red-dy and Willing" enamel on the nails of her toes, which were incidentally curling. Up, up, up her hose-less legs. If she hadn't shaved this morning, the hairs would surely be standing on end. Over her flat belly, as if wondering if she had a navel piercing. She didn't. But she might get one. Pausing over her sheer blouse, studying the bare abdomen, checking to see if anything important was showing at bra level. Then he licked his lips as his appreciative eyes latched on to her "Taboo-You" red lips, which had been parted, but snapped shut so fast that he grinned.

He wasn't one bit apologetic about getting caught ogling, either. In fact, he drawled out, "You're lookin' good today, *chère*."

"So are you, *cher*," she countered with an equally slow drawl. She could out-Cajun him any day, despite the revving of her hormone engine. Even so, she backed up slightly, wanting—needing—to put some space between them. Unfortunately, she miscalculated and her butt hit the driver's side door.

He moved in, shamelessly invading her personal space. With one arm braced against the roof of the car, he leaned forward and whispered against her ear, "Are you seeing anyone, darlin'?"

Low blow! The darlin' card! "Seeing?" she asked dumbly.

"Dating? In a relationship? A man in your life?"

Nope. Only a cat. And a female one at that. She shook her head. "Why?"

"Because I don't do sharing."

Do? Does he mean "do" as in "do me"? Oh, he is outrageous. She should knee him in the nuts, as she very well knew how to do. Police Academy 101. But instead, she said, "I don't share, either."

He nodded, pleased with her response. "I've been attracted to you from the first moment we met."

"I'm surprised that you would admit that. Kind of lessens your odds."

"You're assuming this is a game. I'm too old to play games. Actually, they never interested me much. How about you?"

"Oh, games can be fun sometimes."

"Tease!" he said with a chuckle and nipped her on the chin with his teeth.

It wasn't a kiss or a bite, but she felt it all the way down to "Red-dy and Willing."

She remembered her bad history with Cajun men and her resolution to avoid them in the future. "Um, I think it's time to cut this flower in the bud. I am not going to do this again."

"Do what, darlin'?"

That damn "darlin'" again! "Get involved with another Cajun man."

"You're going to give me the boot just because I'm Cajun?"

She nodded.

"Well, lucky you, babe, because I'm only half Cajun."

She might have asked him which half—she was enjoying this banter—except that Jack showed up just then. "Hey, sweetheart, sorry I'm late," Jack called out.

Simone's face flushed as she introduced them. "Adam, this is Jack Landry. An acquaintance, from Chicago."

She saw Adam's eyebrow raise at the word *acquaintance*, especially when Jack made a scoffing noise and muttered something that sounded like "Acquaintance, my ass!"

She elbowed Jack and said, "Jack, this is Adam Lanier, a local lawyer whose firm helped with the business filings for Legal Belles."

Jack tried to put an arm around her shoulder, sort of like a dog marking its territory. She made a snarling sound, which he chose to ignore.

Adam stepped back and looked from Jack to her, back to Jack, and then her again. The look of condemnation on his face told her loud and clear that he thought she'd lied, that she and Jack remained lovers. She could have corrected the impression. She *wanted* to correct that impression.

But then, she thought, *Who are you to condemn me? The man with the size-zero yoga bimbo? The man who'd allegedly laid half of New Orleans' women under thirty . . . according to Mom who heard it at the beauty parlor, so it must be true.*

Just in time, she realized the gift she'd been handed. An escape from her own bad inclinations. A preemptive call on heartbreak. He mother would say she'd almost had her crazy on again . . . her Cajun Crazy.

That was a close call.

Chapter Five

Impure thoughts aren't really impure if they're in church, right? . . .

As he sat on a stool at the kitchen island, Adam read the Sunday papers and sipped at his second cup of coffee while his dad watered his vegetable garden out back. They were waiting for Maisie to get dressed ("I kin do it myself, Daddy. I'm not a baby, y'know.") so they could go to noon Mass at Our Lady of the Bayou Church.

Adam wasn't overly religious, but he had been raised Catholic, and it pleased his father to have them attend services together. It was a good tradition to follow for his daughter until she was old enough to decide on her own. Plus, Maisie loved the music, especially the handbell choir and truth to tell, he did, too. It provided serenity in a not-so-serene world.

The sweet smell of the blueberry pancakes and syrup

that still lingered in the air made Adam set his newspaper aside and look around. There was something about Sunday mornings and reflection.

They lived in a nice four-bedroom house, about fifty years old but with a recently remodeled kitchen. Adam didn't do much cooking, but his father, who fashioned himself a "half-assed gourmet" (his words for "Cajun with a twist"), loved this room with all its stainless steel and granite and the massive island that seated four stools. His grandmother's oak kitchen table and chairs sat in a little alcove facing the side yard. And there was a separate formal dining room with Hannah's antique Hepplewhite furniture, Meissen dinnerware for twenty, and sterling flatware, which they rarely used.

Hannah had enjoyed antiquing, when she wasn't working as a psychologist or engaging in her extramarital social life, and thus had added to a family collection of hundred-year-old Newcomb Pottery from the famous New Orleans artisans. At her death, there were twenty-five pieces, some extremely rare and valuable. Only two of them—a lamp and a vase—were on view in the living room; the rest had been packed away for protection.

Maybe Maisie would appreciate some of these remembrances of her mother someday.

Adam had purchased the house just before his move here six months ago. It would have been nice to be on the bayou, but they had an in-ground pool out back, which more than made up for the lack of a running stream. And they didn't have to worry about sharing the water with gators or snakes. The flagstone patio surrounding the pool, accessed from the sliding doors of the kitchen or living room, was particularly nice for relaxing or eating outside in the evenings. Thankfully, Maisie could swim like a fish, but even so, she knew the rules. No entering the pool unless accompanied by an adult.

His father's vegetable garden was located beyond the pool and separated by a low hedge. In fact, his father came walking in now, carrying a basket containing a heaping pile of tomatoes of assorted sizes and colors, everything from yellow to almost black and various shades of red, which he knew to be heirloom varieties that his father was experimenting with this year. He'd gotten the seeds from Tante Lulu. Adam knew better than to ask his father what they were going to do with all those tomatoes. He knew that, aside from fresh slices salt-and-peppered on a plate or served on white bread sandwiches with mayo, the fruits/vegetables (whatever tomatoes were!) would end up in any number of his father's "half-assed gourmet" recipes, including the traditional gumbos, jambalayas, étouffées, and a wonderful Cajun tomato gravy and eggs dish his dad made on special occasions. Of course, they couldn't be a Southern house without fried green tomatoes. His mouth watered at the thought of the latter and he asked, "Any chance you could make fried green tomatoes for dinner?"

"Ab-so-lute-ly!" his father said. "With some shrimp remoulade. Yum!"

Maisie walked in then and exclaimed on seeing the tomatoes his father was arranging in a big bowl, "PawPaw, you dint wait fer me?"

"I figured you had enough to fill a basket from your own patch, princess. All those sugar snap peas! And I swear the radishes are big as golf balls."

Maisie made to rush out and check, but Adam grabbed her by the neck of her dress and said, "Not now. After church. You know how PawPaw hates to be late."

His father went to the sink to wash his hands while Adam checked out Maisie's attire. Her black curls were unruly but were held off her face with a diamond (rhinestone) headband, and it looked like she had some kind of pink gloss on her lips, but her dress was surprisingly appropriate, considering his daughter's usual taste. A pink-and-white-checked sundress with a bow in back, which he leaned down to tie. "You look real good, Maisie Daisie," he said, kissing the top of her head.

"I know," she said, "and I even got the day right." She bent over and flipped the hem of the dress so he could see her day-of-the-week panties, another Uncle Dave gift. Yep, it was Sunday all right. "Make sure you don't show anyone else, though."

"But, Daaaaddy, that's the fun of having good undies."

"Who told you that?"

"I heard it on TV. It was a commercial for some secret store."

It took Adam a few moments to realize that she meant Victoria's Secret. He hadn't realized they advertised on regular TV, and certainly not on a children's channel.

"Food Network," his father inserted, guessing at Adam's question.

Adam arched his eyebrows in disbelief. His father was a food junkie, loved *Chopped*, and *Iron Chef*, and *The Pioneer Woman*, but lingerie ads on that channel seemed highly unlikely.

"They were doing some kind of celebrity charity cook-off. The Rockettes against the models," his father explained, raising his chin in a "So sue me!" attitude.

Adam just laughed. Two single men raising a little girl . . . well, they were running the game without a playbook, with no woman around the house.

When they arrived at church, early enough to get his father's favorite pew—on the aisle, five rows from the back—Adam noticed immediately that Simone LeDeux was sitting in front of them, beside a woman that must be her mother. The older woman was wearing an old-fashioned, upswept hairstyle—similar to something Adam's mother had favored. Funny he should remember his mother's hairstyle from so long ago, especially since he'd been only seven when she died, and Dave had been four.

On Simone's other side was the tall, lean fellow he'd seen outside Legal Belles a couple weeks ago, the day she'd been pulling off a two-man flirt-a-thon.

So, it wasn't just the dude from Chicago she was seeing, but this man, who had a jailhouse pallor if he ever saw one. He recalled suddenly his Internet search after first meeting her and the mention of a first husband who was a convict. Cletus Something-or-other. *Great taste in men, Ms. Super Cop*, he thought. Not that he had room to talk with his one walk down the aisle with the Slut of the South. *Oh, that was mean. Speaking . . . thinking . . . of my child's mother that way. And what a subject for church!*

It didn't matter that Simone glared every time the guy tried to get her attention. Adam had seen enough to know she was not for him. He tried not to look anymore, which proved to be impossible.

Of course, he was also seeing enough of the world-class butt she displayed every time she rose or sat down in her pew, the fabric of her white linen slacks pulling taut. She had to be wearing no underwear at all, or a thong, because there was no panty line involved. Not that he was looking that closely. *Or am I?* he wondered when his father whispered in his ear, "I'm guessing flesh-colored thong."

Jeesh! He was really bad off if he was starting to share sexual fantasies with his father. Maybe it was time to hook up with Sonia again before she left for West Coast yoga land. There had been a text on his phone this morning from her, inviting him to a party. Adam hadn't called her back yet, but he wouldn't be attending. Not because he wouldn't enjoy seeing her again, and, hey, there was a lot to be said for Good-bye Sex, but it was the same day as the Dancing the Shrimp event their client Mike Pham was holding, and he'd promised to take Maisie.

He could invite Sonia to come with them instead, but, no, not gonna happen. It was probably silly of him to be so cautious, but Adam never introduced his female friends to his daughter.

After Mass, Adam would have avoided Simone, but his father stopped to talk to the older woman with her, who it turned out was indeed Simone's mother, Adelaide Daigle. From what he could overhear of their conversation, Adelaide had had knee surgery recently and was the reason for Simone coming back to Louisiana. Adelaide was also one of his father's casino pals, along with Tante Lulu and a few other senior citizens, although Adelaide Daigle was probably only in her fifties, a little young for senior status.

Despite his usual rule, Adam was forced to introduce his daughter to Simone while his father chatted away. Not that Simone was one of his women, but still . . .

"Maisie, this is Simone LeDeux. She's a policewoman, or she was until recently. Simone, this is my daughter, Mary Sue. We call her Maisie."

"I saw you riding behind your father on a motorcycle one day," Simone said, hunkering down to put herself on Maisie's eye level. "Wow! That must be fun."

And, no, he was not noticing her butt. Not now, in front of his daughter. Not really.

But then, he thought. *Already, just like all the other women, she's trying to get on my good side by soaping up my kid. Pathetic.*

As if sensing his thoughts, she gazed up at him with a look of distaste. What was that about?

"A policewoman?" Maisie said. "Like Mariska Hargitay?"

"Yes. Just like!"

Simone was no more surprised than Adam. "You know who Mariska Hargitay is?" he asked.

"Oh, Daddy. She's on *Law & Order*. PawPaw's favorite show, next to *Chopped*. He sez she's hotter than a two-dollar pistol."

Adam put his face in his free hand, the one not holding on to Maisie's little hand. *Law & Order: Special Victims Unit* wasn't children's fare. He would have to discuss Maisie's TV limits with his father. Secondly, "hotter than a two dollar pistol"?

Simone was laughing at his obvious discomfort. Especially when Maisie confided to Simone, "My father thinks I'm a child." But by then Maisie had moved on to another subject. "I like yer necklace."

A silver oval hung from a long chain nestling in the cleavage of Simone's blouse. Demure, suitable for church. The pale green blouse, not the cleavage.

Aaarrgh! My wandering mind again!

"Thank you, sweetheart," Simone said. "The medal is one I got in special recognition when I rescued a little girl from drowning. Maybe I'll tell you about it sometime."

Not if I can help it.

Maisie was looking duly impressed.

"That's a pretty dress you're wearing, honey. Is it from Zulily? I thought I saw something like that on the Internet."

"Yes! I love Zulily dresses."

"Me, too. Have you seen their mother-daughter dresses? So cute!"

Simone seemed to realize her mistake and grimaced even before Maisie revealed with a little pout, "I don't have a mother anymore."

"I'm so sorry." She reached over and adjusted Maisie's headband, tucking a few of her curls behind her tiny shell ears. An unconscious, maternal action that Adam couldn't condemn, especially when Maisie leaned into her hand.

"Maybe you could come over to our pool today, and you could tell me about the drowning girl," Maisie said, brightening suddenly.

Whoa, whoa, whoa! "Not today, Maisie," Adam interjected. "I have to go into the office, and PawPaw has some friends coming over."

The knowing look on Simone's face annoyed the hell out of him, and he almost invited her to come, anyway. Luckily, he caught himself because just then a car tooted its horn, and he saw the skinny guy from church behind the wheel. The car had Illinois plates, and he assumed it was Simone's.

"That's Simone's husband, Cletus," he heard Adelaide telling his father.

"Ex-husband, Mom. Ex-husband," Simone said as she stood and grabbed her mother by the arm, yanking her toward the waiting vehicle. At the last moment, she turned and waved at Maisie, "Bye-bye, honey bun."

"She called me honey bun," Maisie whispered to Adam in awe.

"What's yer hurry?" Simone's mother asked her daughter as Simone continued to frog march her toward the waiting car.

"Why is Cletus driving my car? He doesn't even have a key."

"Well, maybe he learned how ta jimmy a starter or somethin' in prison. How do I know?"

"Next time you invite me to church, let me know that Cletus will be there, too."

Adam just shook his head. Another dodged bullet.

"I like her, Daddy."

Get over it, sweetheart. I certainly will!

But then his father, the traitor, said, "We ought to have a pool party sometime. We never did have a house-warming."

Adam wasn't sure if his father was looking at Adelaide Daigle or Simone LeDeux as he made the remark, or whether he was picturing the older woman or the younger in a bikini. Either was equally alarming to Adam.

"Yippee!" Maisie said. "Can we, Daddy? Can we? Me and PawPaw been talkin' about havin' a housewarming fer a long time."

He doubted if his daughter even knew what a house-warming was. But it looked like he was going to be forced to host a party.

That's what happened when a sinner went to church.

If that wasn't bad enough, Tante Lulu came stepping down the church steps on the arm of Father Bernard. She called out, "Yoo-hoo! Just the person I wanted to see."

To Adam's dismay, he realized that she was looking at him. The few people remaining in the parking lot, including his father, Maisie, and some lagging parishioners, all turned to stare at him.

"Ya gotta come over ta mah cottage real soon," she told him. "I have a hope chest fer you."

Adam groaned, knowing what that meant. The old lady, who was a self-proclaimed matchmaker extraordinaire, made hope chests for all the men in her family and a few close male friends.

"Uh, I'm real busy these days, Ms. Rivard," he said, deliberately not using her Tante prefix to put some distance between them. A wasted effort.

"Doan ya be Mzz-in' me. I'm Tante, and ya know it. An' fergit about busy. Ya cain't be too busy fer love." She glanced at the departing car that held Mrs. Daigle, Simone, and the husband or ex-husband or whatever he was. Then she looked at Adam. "I hear thunder. Do ya hear thunder, too, boy? Ya better 'cause me and St. Jude're smellin' ozone in the air, a sure sign of the thunderbolts ta come."

"The only thing I smell is trouble," he muttered under his breath.

On the way home, thunder struck, and rain pounded on the roof of his Lexus, rat-a-tat-a-tat, like bullets from an AK-47 (or a celestial weapon). It was just a coincidence.

Ooey, gooey, for sure . . .

The open house for Legal Belles was an invitation-only event for friends and businesses they might deal with and persons or agencies in a position to make referrals. Like surveillance equipment companies, social workers, police, doctors, and, yes, lawyers. And the news media.

Tomorrow, they would be officially opened for business, and already they had six clients who'd insisted on signing up for services, including a mother who was certain her thirteen-year-old daughter was having sex . . . *with a teacher*! She didn't want to make accusations until she had proof. (Um? Nighttime tutoring in math?) There were also two Vietnamese women who came in personally to schedule an appointment for next week, but wouldn't say why.

The open house was being held in the late afternoon so that people could come before heading home for the day and not be fearful of having a glass of wine, or two, before going back to work.

Hosting the party were Simone and Helene, helped by their secretary, divorcée Barbara Rae Ozelet (aka The Barracuda, taken from her name, BArbara RAe, as well as her take-no-prisoners attitude, despite her petite appearance), and Simone's mother, Adelaide, who was still the temporary receptionist and digging in her heels over any replacement. BaRa, her dark hair cut into a short bob, wore a white sheath dress and four-inch white high heels, but she still only came to Simone's shoulder.

Legal Belles now had seven part-time "undercover" agents or contract employees, as well, none of whom were present today, for obvious reasons. Their association with a Cheaters-type agency needed to be private, or they would be ineffective in catching people engaged in bad deeds. And, actually, that secrecy was necessary for all their investigative work, not just cheaters.

Adelaide had shimmied herself into another Spanx outfit, a jade-green, sleeveless jumpsuit, with bands of white down both sides, giving her a surprisingly shapely figure. Simone might have to try some Spanx herself. Or not. That might give the impression she was trying to attract male attention, which she was not. Especially after Adam Lanier's obvious horror at the possibility of being paired with her when they'd met after church last Sunday. She didn't have to be a super sleuth to recognize that if he'd had his choice, he would have avoided talking to her at all. *Why?* She wasn't sure. Whatever the reason, it hadn't been flattering. Not that she'd wanted to talk with him, either.

Even so, Simone dressed in her favorite outfit today. A short-sleeved, scoop-necked white dress with a knee-length, A-line skirt, cinched in at the waist with a wide, black belt. Completing the picture were strappy black stilettos. Her dark brown hair was twisted into a neat

French braid, and large pearl stud earrings were her only jewelry. The heels put her head above most of the women and half the men in attendance. A power play.

Helene waved, beckoning her from across the room where she was talking to a reporter from a New Orleans TV station. Simone declined with a quick shake of her head. Let Helene handle the media. She did it so well. And she looked good today, too, in her usual business suit with a flair . . . this time, a lavender one with a skirt that ended mid-thigh.

While Simone and Helene networked, Adelaide and BaRa manned the refreshment/drinks table where small finger foods and wines were being served. They'd considered offering more hard liquor or even beer, but decided against it. People had to be extra careful today. The person supplying booze, even at a private party (not just a bar) could be held liable in DUI accidents, along with the drunken driver.

In any case, they'd started more than an hour ago, and should be done in another hour or so. At any one time, there were thirty people circulating through the offices, some leaving, some arriving, so that in the end Helene had predicted they would have about fifty people. A good number! And most had taken brochures or business cards with them.

Just then, Simone sensed someone standing behind her. Close. She recognized the light musky cologne before she felt the whisper of breath against her ear, "Are you going to show me around?"

It was Adam Lanier, of course. A late arrival.

She turned.

Adam had clearly come directly from his office, or the courthouse. His brown-and-beige tie had been loosened over a crisp white dress shirt with rolled-up sleeves, tucked into dark brown, belted suit pants. A not-unattractive (darn it!), late-day stubble shadowed his jaw. He was probably a two-times-a-day shaver when he had nighttime activities on his agenda, none of which she was envisioning. Nope. None. (In any case, wide shoulders, narrow waist and hips. Long legs. Duly noted!)

"Adam. Welcome to Legal Belles," she squeaked out.

"Sorry I'm late. I know Luc was here earlier, but I couldn't get away until now."

"You didn't have to come."

"Well, yes, actually I did," he said enigmatically. (*Enigmatic* being another word for Cajun male magnetism in her personal dictionary, when accompanied by smoldering brown eyes.)

Glancing around, he remarked, "Wow! What a transformation! I saw this office when it was still an insurance agency. Pretty much drab gray all over the place."

Legal Belles' premises *were* actually quite lovely now, not just utilitarian as Simone had originally envisioned. "We have Rachel LeDeux, Remy's wife, to thank for all this. She's a feng shui decorator. Look at those original paintings on the walls. We could never have afforded the extra expense, but Rachel talked some local artists into lending them to us." Simone was babbling but didn't seem to be able to control her nervous tongue.

"They do add a touch of class," Adam agreed. "I especially like that one that looks like a bunch of wet vaginas."

"Adam! Those are calla lilies with dew on them."

"Oh." He winked at her, having known what they were all along, apparently. "Well, you can't tell me this Tabriz carpet is a loaner, or cheap, either." He glanced down at the rug they both stood on in the lobby. "My wife inherited one from her family worth twenty thou."

He mentioned his wife casually, not with any particular affection, or grief. But maybe she was putting too much importance on that.

The oriental carpet did add a pop of muted color (gold and burgundy and ivory) as a contrast to the pale green paint Simone had chosen for the walls in that weeks-ago meeting with Ed.

"More like two hundred dollars. If you look a little closer, you'll see the worn spots and a honking big hole under the magnolia tree in that humongous jardinière, which, incidentally, has a crack in the bottom. Rachel found them both in an antiques shop."

"Maybe I should invite Rachel over to look at the house I bought six months ago. My dad and I just moved everything in from his place and mine with no particular plan, other than couch–living room, bed frame–bedroom, pots and pans–kitchen. We're still looking for stuff in boxes out in the garage."

"I'm sure she'd be happy to help."

"I don't want any fancy designer place. Done that, not interested in a repeat."

Another reference to his deceased wife . . . in a less than loving way? Hmm. "Rachel would give you whatever kind of design you wanted, or make suggestions that you could take . . . or not."

He nodded, then pointed to the hallway. "The tour?" he prodded.

She led him into her office, of which she was especially proud, even though most of it had been Rachel's doing again. A low, red velvet sofa before a wooden coffee table, which sat on another carpet that was only about six-by-eight, but stunning. This time it was a much-worn, hand-woven, Cajun carpet from a hundred years ago, depicting what appeared to be the scales of silvery fish on a sea of blue waves. Very unusual and not the kind of thing Simone would have ever picked for herself in a store.

"This is what I call an office!" Adam said, surprise in his eyes. "Rachel again?"

"Mostly," she conceded.

He continued to look around and touch various pieces, like the leather recliner, also in red, that sat before the double window overlooking the small patio out back, which could be accessed only from the kitchen. The separate stair access to the second-floor apartment led from the patio, but now Simone would have to park out front and walk around the side of the building, or enter from inside the office. No hardship, considering the results. There was also a comfy easy chair upholstered in a red-and-black check pattern with a matching footstool.

The metal desk that had been in the office was gone, replaced with a modern, egg-shaped, Lucite desk with a surprisingly comfortable Lucite office chair. Adam sat down in it and leaned back until it almost tipped over. Then he crossed his legs and rested his ankles on the desk. "Cool!" he concluded.

In front of the desk were two vintage chairs with wooden arms and backs, but buttery yellow leather cushions.

"All of these colors should have been garish, but instead they make for a cozy, inviting office space, one that should be comforting to a client, inviting confidences, don't you think?" Again, she was babbling. She bit her bottom lip to stifle her nervousness.

"Absolutely."

There was even an old, refinished sailor's chest in one corner, with an assortment of books and toys for the client who may have been forced to bring a child along for the consultation. Adam stood and walked over to pick up an

American Girl doll and said, "My daughter has one just like this."

Unlike his tone when he mentioned his wife, his voice and his eyes lit up at mention of his daughter. In all her years with police work, Simone had developed a talent for the reveals a perp (or any person, for that matter) made with a mere break in the voice. Voice language was as important as body language.

Adam was now studying some photographs on the wall of Simone in police uniform, and some framed diplomas (college and law enforcement), there was also a landscape painting of Bayou Black, a gift from Tante Lulu done by one of her great nieces. It even included the old lady's pet gator, Useless.

He pointed at the one picture where Simone stood in a flak jacket and rifle following some terrorist training exercise. "I saw that photo on the Internet."

"You just happened to see a picture of me on the Internet?"

"I Googled you the minute you left our law offices two weeks ago."

"You did?" She didn't have to put a hand to her face to know it was flaming hot.

"Of course. And don't tell me that you didn't do the same for me."

She wasn't about to deny a fact which was obvious. "So, what did you learn about me? Other than my police background?"

"That you get around a lot."

She sat down in one of the visitors' chairs in front of the desk. Now her face was heated with consternation, not embarrassment.

Sensing her consternation, he said, "You've been married at least three times."

"And you think that connotes 'getting around a lot'? Like a slut?"

"I didn't use that word."

"You implied it."

"Like I told you the other day, I don't do sharing."

"And you think I do?"

"The guy at church . . ."

"My ex-husband . . . for more than ten years."

"I heard he's living in that trailer with you and your mother."

"With my mother. I moved out, into the apartment upstairs, the day he moved in." At the puzzled expression on his face, she explained, "My mother is old-school Catholic. She doesn't believe in divorce. So she thinks I'm still married to Cletus."

Adam was back to sitting behind the desk, his fingers tented before his lips, thoughtfully. "How about the dude in the Chez parking lot? Another ex?" he asked in a snide manner that was starting to annoy her.

"Yes, another ex. An ex-fiancé who didn't have the same morals as you about sharing. But you know what, Adam, you don't have much room to talk." Her tone of voice put him in the Raging Asshole category, she hoped.

"What does that mean?" His feet dropped to the floor and he leaned forward across the desk.

"According to *my* Internet search, you were the Horndog of the South for years, even while your wife was alive. Rumor is that you screwed so many women that Black & Decker wanted to put your name on a drill."

His face was the one flaming now. "Don't believe everything you read."

She arched her brows. "I could say the same thing."

He glared at her for a long moment, then sank back. "What are we going to do about this thing between us?"

She didn't bother denying the "thing" he referred to. "Not a damn thing!"

"Why?"

"Because you have no respect for me, and I have even less for you."

"Maybe we had an information malfunction," he conceded. "Besides, the way I hear it, you have no more interest in another marriage than I do."

"Marriage? Who said anything about marriage?"

He ignored her question and went on, "So, what does respect have to do with wild, no-holds-barred, screaming sex?"

Screaming? Me or you, buddy? She wasn't about to ask him which. He would probably answer her in ways she might not like . . . or like too much. "Think a lot of your talents, do you?"

He shrugged. "And don't you dare mention Black & Decker screwing again."

She laughed.

"I could wipe that smirk off your face in a nanosecond," he said. "C'mere." He crooked his finger at her and motioned toward his lap. "Plant your sweet ass right here, sweetheart. And, yes, I've noticed how sweet it is."

"Not a chance!"

"Are you as turned on as I am?"

"No."

"Prove it. Come over her and let me kiss you a little. Betcha I could make you as wet as those cally flowers out there."

"Oh, that was crude. And they're calla lilies, not cally flowers."

"The best sex is always a little crude."

"This is not sex."

"Are you sure about that?"

Actually, she wasn't. And, to her inner dismay, she *was* a little wet . . . or was that "gooey," as Sabine had accused Simone of getting every time a Cajun man winked her way. Yep, the bane of her life. Cajun goo.

She stood suddenly. Time for her to go out and mix with the remaining guests, some of whom had passed the open door of her office, peeked in, and then passed with a wave when they saw it was occupied.

"Well, it's been nice chatting with you, Adam. Do come again." She realized her mistake immediately.

Even before he grinned and said, "Oh, I intend to. *Come* again."

"Crude again? Tsk-tsk!"

As he passed her on the way out of the office, he gave her a little smack on the butt. "You don't know crude yet, darlin'."

"That amounts to sexual harassment," she called after him, not really upset.

"So sue me. I can recommend a good lawyer." He turned to waggle his eyebrows at her.

She gave him the finger.

They were both laughing when they reentered the lobby area, which was almost deserted, except for her mother, Helene, BaRa, and Tante Lulu. They must have been in her office longer than she'd realized.

Her mother took one look at her and Adam and sighed to BaRa. "She's got her crazy on again. I see the signs. Cajun Crazy! I'm gonna pray fer her."

"I'm gonna pray fer her, too," Tante Lulu said. "Ta St. Jude. But I 'spect mah special intentions are different from yer special intentions."

"You're not still hoping for a reconciliation with Cletus, are you?" Helene asked Simone's mother.

"Goodness' sakes, no! Cletus's grandmother from

Houston came ta mah trailer and dragged him with her by the ear. If I'd known he had a grandmother, I never woulda taken him in. I only let him move in 'cause I felt sorry for him when his mama shut her heart ta him. Anyways, Cletus's grandma said all his troubles started when he got involved with *mah* family. The nerve! That boy was stealin' pennies when he was in grade school, dollars by junior high, and cars by high school. To tell the truth," her mother confided, "I think he called his grandmother ta come rescue him. Scarlett took a dislike ta the boy right off. Scarlett is Simone's cat, which she seems ta have forsaken in her rush ta leave. Almost scratched Cletus's tattoos off one day. Cletus got ta be afraid the cat would slip a hairball in his mouth while he was sleepin', which was most of the time."

Simone didn't know about anyone else, but her brain went fuzzy just listening to that long discourse in answer to a simple question.

"Then what's the problem, Addie?" BaRa asked, after blinking several times.

"He's a Cajun!" Simone's mother said, as if that was answer enough.

The "he" in question, Adam, just stood poleaxed before her, stunned that all these women could be discussing him as if he wasn't even there.

"What we need ta do is find a Yankee fer mah daughter . . . one what's a little dull and homely-like," Addie said.

"Well, I can't claim to be boring, and I try my best not to be dog-ugly most days," Adam said.

Several of the ladies blushed, not having realized he was listening.

What did they think . . . he was a potted plant just standing there with no ears? Jeesh!

"But as for being Cajun, I can't help that," Adam continued. "I am a little bit Yankee, though, from one of my grandmothers. I suspect that part is lodged in my big toe that looks slightly Yankee-ish and has a tendency to twitch sometimes."

Helene snickered and gave him a thumbs-up.

Tante Lulu was slapping her knee and cackling, "A Yankee toe! Doan that beat all?"

Her mother was not amused.

BaRa just looked confused.

Adam turned to Simone then and whispered, "Does a guy have to go through this gauntlet every time he wants to get close to you?"

She tilted her head at him. "Depends on how close."

He grinned. "Real close."

Beware of too much happiness . . .

Adam was smiling when he got home. And he was smiling after taking a shower that evening and taking care of some necessary business . . . in the shower. He was still smiling when he came down for coffee the next morning.

Maisie was eating a toasted bagel with cream cheese. Already dressed for school, she had a big-ass pink bow in her hair, holding back a mass of black curls that had only been half brushed. A good wind and she'd be carried away like a hot air balloon. She was wearing blue jeans with a T-shirt that read "My Uncle's an Army Stud" and black ballet slippers. Kindergarten fashionista!

He couldn't object today.

"What bug is ticklin' yer funny bone?" his father grumbled from where he sat at the table, sipping at a giant mug of black coffee. Adam assumed he'd lost at poker last night.

"Daddy is jist happy, PawPaw," Maisie chastised his father.

"Yeah, well I wish he'd pass the happy pills," his father responded.

Adam poured himself a cup of coffee and waved aside his father's offer of a bagel. He'd grab something on the way to the office. He sat down at the table opposite the pipsqueak. "Nice bow!" he remarked.

"I did it myself." Maisie beamed.

"Don't think I don't know what's got you all grinnin' like a dog with a sweet bone." His father was still on that subject. "Tante Lulu told everyone about your meetin' up with that Simone LeDeux at the open house. Whoo-boy! She said the air was a-sizzlin' and a-smokin'. I take it yoga is no longer in fashion."

His father was becoming as much of a busybody as Tante Lulu. That's what comes of a grown man living with his father. It's against nature. "Tante Lulu talks too much. And since when is that old lady in your poker group?"

"She isn't. She told her niece Charmaine who told one of her customers, Maudine Earhart, whose husband Leroy's cousin plays poker with us guys."

The bayou grapevine!

"See-mone? Is she the lady from church?" Maisie wanted to know.

He nodded and reached across the table to dab at her milk mustache with a paper napkin. "She's the one."

"Kin we invite her ta our pool party?"

The pool party again! He glared at his father, who put up his hands in surrender. "I didn't say anything."

He wasn't sure if his father referred to Simone, which had been Adam's thought, or the party idea. He decided to home in on the latter, but he would talk to his father later about discussing matchmaking for Adam with his daughter. "You're the one who mentioned a homecoming party at church."

"Well . . . um . . . Maisie and I got the idea together."

"I have a list, Daddy, of everyone we kin invite ta our pool party."

"A list, huh? And when is this party going to be held?"

"Not till school is out fer the summer, in two weeks. You are comin' ta my graduation, aren't you, Daddy?"

"I wouldn't miss it for the world . . . not even for a hundred million Tootsie Pops." Those were her favorites, cherry preferred.

"Oh, Daddy!" she said.

"Will this be a kiddies-only party?"

She shook her head, almost dislodging the giant bow. "All kinds of people."

By that, she meant all ages, he assumed. He was getting mighty suspicious, though. His daughter had a devious mind. "And what will we be celebrating? Kindergarten graduation? Losing your loose front tooth? Summer?"

"Dad-dy! A party doesn't hafta be a celebration. It kin jist be a happy time."

"Oookay!"

"But maybe it could be a Fourth of July party."

"That sounds good." And it was almost two months away. She'd probably forget about it by then.

"And make sure See-mone gets an invitation."

Yep, devious! And that's what happened when you introduced your child to one of your ladies. Not that Simone was one of his ladies. Yet.

His father was amused, clearly understanding his discomfort. "You could invite your yoga friend, too," he suggested with more mischief than helpfulness, "if you're worried about See-mone getting the wrong idea."

"The yoga friend is moving to California."

"Aaah!" his father said, as if that explained everything.

By the time Adam got to the office, he was no longer smiling so much. Clearly, he had to think this whole Simone attraction over more carefully. Not jump right in where lust beckoned.

The first thing Luc said to him, though, was, "Hey, buddy. I heard you and my half sister are a thing."

"We're not a thing."

"Yet?"

"Yet."

"Oh, boy!"

"What does that 'Oh, boy!' mean?"

"It means Tante Lulu has her work cut out for her this time."

They went off to court then, for yet another day of proceedings in the never-ending Pham versus Cypress Oil lawsuit. After three long weeks, they might finally have closing arguments today. The wheels of justice moved slowly, and there had been many a spoke in the wheels during this trial. Such as the judge having a scheduling conflict. And the defendants calling for a sidebar on every other issue, causing innumerable delays. Cypress Oil failing to provide discovery, which called for more sidebars and arguments without the jury. In essence, the tactic was to slow the process down so much that the litigants would be so irritated they would drop their suit. Which hadn't worked.

Luc and Adam had several times been threatened with wrongful conduct fines. But that was another story, and par for the course.

By noon, both sides had closed. The jury would begin deliberations at one p.m., right after lunch.

Now he and Luc were leaving the courthouse with

Mike. His father hadn't been feeling well lately and had chosen to stay home. Actually, there hadn't been many spectators today at all, boredom having set in, Adam supposed. Valcour LeDeux himself hadn't been around for more than a week. Supposedly, he and his young (compared to him) wife were off to Bermuda.

Was he that confident of Cypress winning the case? Or did he just not care? Probably the latter. He personally wouldn't suffer so much as the company itself and the value of its stock, if they lost.

Thankfully, Adam hadn't thought about Simone LeDeux all morning . . . until Mike mentioned that he'd found a business card for Legal Belles in his wife's purse.

Uh-oh!

Could Adam be saved from a relationship misstep by something as simple as "conflict of interest"? For some reason, he wasn't smiling.

Chapter Six

The wheels of justice made odd turns . . .

Simone was staked out in front of Luther Ferguson's home. He was the teacher who was supposedly providing nighttime math tutoring to a thirteen-year-old girl, Darlene Rossi.

Her Mazda sedan, parked several houses down the street, was a dark blue that blended in with the surroundings on this starless night, a portent of bad weather to come. She hoped the rain didn't come until she was done here. It wouldn't be the first time she'd worked in inclement weather (Winter blizzards in Chicago came to mind.), but she'd prefer not to.

It was a waiting game at this point, although Simone was prepared for every eventuality once Darlene arrived . . . if she did. Cell phone, zoom lens camera, recording device, Mace, a pistol, even doggie treats. Luckily, the neighbor's pet Lab had been taken inside. What she didn't want or need was a barking dog alerting the perp of her presence.

Angela Rossi, a single parent, never married, had informed Simone fifteen minutes ago that her daughter Darlene just left their home after yet another argument. She lived only four blocks away.

Simone was prepared for all situations, not just investigating a crime, and she'd already informed Angie, "I'm a mandatory reporter of child abuse. If I gain this evidence for you, it has to be turned over to the police. Otherwise, I'm liable for huge fines and even jail time myself. More than that, I can't in good conscience let this kind of predator loose to repeat his crimes."

"But what about Darlene?" her mother had argued. "I don't want her name in the papers. She'll be ruined before she ever enters high school. Can't we just tell the school principal and get him fired? As long as he's out of the picture, Darlene would be safe."

Simone had shaken her head. "Not a possibility. First of all, it's a crime. Second, if not Darlene, it will be, and probably has been, some other girl."

"I just don't know." Angie had wrung her hands in dismay, and Simone's heart had gone out to her. The woman worked hard as a waitress at an upscale Houma restaurant and had even given up her more lucrative night shift when she'd suspected her daughter's involvement with the teacher.

Counseling had accomplished nothing in the past, according to Angela. Still, Simone could try to suggest counseling, because Darlene's problems wouldn't end with the incarceration of Luther Ferguson. The very fact that the girl could be seduced by the man as well as her refusal to stop the "tutoring" sessions, was indicative of other problems that needed to be addressed.

"Okay, here's the deal," Simone had offered. "I have twenty-four hours to report from the time I witness a crime. Let's say I get the evidence. How about if I make arrangements, ahead of time, with a lawyer I know, who will go with you to law enforcement to file a complaint. Darlene's a minor, so her name shouldn't be made public. I know in small towns news can travel fast, but we'll do our best to keep things quiet. I guarantee if this case goes to trial, there will be other girls coming forward."

Angie had nodded.

"And in return," Simone had demanded, "I'll have a counselor in place to immediately work with you and Darlene . . ." Simone had held up a halting hand when Angie had been about to protest, once again, that counseling hadn't worked before, and continued, "because there is every possibility that Darlene will want to protect the creep and will hate you for taking him away."

So Simone had talked with Luc, who'd agreed to take on the case, if needed, pro bono, and she'd contacted an old school friend who was a psychologist, as well. Now, all she needed was the evidence.

While she waited for Darlene to arrive . . . and, hey, maybe she wouldn't come, and maybe her mother had been wrong about the teacher. *Wishful thinking!*

By this time . . . Simone checked her illuminated watch . . . yep, eight-thirty . . . Sabine would be propped on a bar stool at the Swamp Tavern, casing out Sam Ellison who stopped every night for a beer . . . and maybe something else. His wife was hoping it was only beer. It was probably more. Almost always, by the time a spouse suspected infidelity, it was a done deal.

Gabe Storm, the actor who'd envisioned himself as the "gigolo on the prowl," was posing as a wealthy Internet tech tycoon with a proclivity for giving expensive jewelry to appreciative ladies. Thus far, the woman, who attended the same health club as new member, Gabe, hadn't bitten his bait, which was points in her favor.

Most disturbing, in a personal way, was Simone's meeting this morning with the two Vietnamese women. Thanh Pham, married to Michael Pham, the plaintiff in a lawsuit being handled by LeDeux & Lanier, was accompanied by her sister, Kimly Bien, a professor of women's studies at Tulane. Thanh, a quiet, more traditional Vietnamese woman in both demeanor and attire, had clearly come at the prodding of her more aggressive, and protective, sister.

Helene had sat in on the session, too, and they both agreed that this one could get nasty. The verdict was expected any day in the Pham versus Cypress Oil Case, and it could be a (well-deserved) windfall for Michael Pham and his father's shrimp fishing company. But would it be a windfall for Thanh and her two sons, as well? Kimly didn't think so. Why? Thanh had suggested shyly that her husband of twenty-one years had other women. Her sister, Kimly, had snorted at that and amended, "Lots of women! And he's acting like a man who's about to make a big move."

Money could turn even the most generous family man greedy. Mike Pham wouldn't be the first man to hide his funds when he was contemplating extracurricular activities, or even divorce.

Would her half brother Luc or his partner, Adam Lanier, help their client bury his assets from view? She hoped not.

"Proceed with caution" had been their advice, for both sides. The women and themselves. It was a "wait and see" game at this point.

Just then, she saw Darlene walking up the street with

her backpack over her shoulders. It was dark by now, and Simone could hardly see. Darlene was tall for her age, a little chubby, and, Simone knew from pictures her mother had provided, beginning to develop curves . . . breasts and butt. Tonight, the girl was wearing a pair of yoga pants and a tank top. She didn't hesitate to go directly up the sidewalk to the front door, and without knocking, she entered the bachelor's ranch-style home. A definite red flag.

This was Simone's cue. Quietly, she exited her car and crept across the side yard toward the back of the house where there was a lighted window. She wore dark clothing and black sneakers, and her hair was pulled off her face into a ponytail, but none of that mattered. Speed and stealth were the most important things.

When she got to the back window, she was disappointed to see that a shade had been pulled. But then she moved to another window, which had been raised to allow some air to enter through an old-fashioned window screen. Using one of the handy tools in her pocket kit, she eased the screen aside and inserted the long lens on her camera below the shade, just enough to give her a view. And she turned on her cell phone's voice recorder.

Bingo!

Good ol' Luther already had Darlene down to her bra, the backpack and tank top lying on the floor. He was kissing the girl voraciously, and Darlene was kissing him back. This was not a new scenario, obviously. It was a game that had been played out before, probably many times.

Hard to see the attraction. Luther was more than thirty with a receding hairline, although he had a bodybuilder's physique, emphasized by the tight jeans and T-shirt he wore. Darlene had the slightly chubby body of an adolescent girl and was probably insecure, as girls her age often were. Attention from a male of any age would be a big boost to her morale.

"Oh, baby, you are so hot!"

"Take off your clothes for me, real slow. Show me your pussy."

"That's the way. Now, bend over. Yeees!"

And Simone thought, *Gag me!* She'd seen enough. Evidence enough to convict the guy and end his career as a teacher. She didn't need to see actual penetration.

In the meantime, Simone needed to end this particular sexual event. As she raced toward her car and turned on the motor, she called Luther's number, which she'd programmed into her phone. The phone rang a half dozen times before voice mail picked up. Disguising her voice, she said, "This is Neighborhood Watch calling to warn you of a fire in your vicinity. Go outside immediately, and do not go back inside until the fire trucks arrive."

She waited for less than a minute before more of Luther's lights flicked on, and he and Darlene, both disheveled, rushed outside to look around, confused to see they were the only ones in their yards. Hopefully, that ended the fun and games for tonight, at least. She waited. Yep! Soon Darlene came running out, dragging her backpack over one shoulder. She was clearly spooked.

Good!

Only then did Simone ride off. She wanted to stop at her apartment first. Hopefully, she could meet Luc at his office down the street to bring him up-to-date and they could go to the Rossi house together. But no, best to act now. She pulled over into a drugstore parking lot that had enough outside lighting for her to see.

Picking up her phone, she noticed that she had an email with an attachment from someone with the address, curlylocks@cajuncajun.com. The subject line read: "You're

Invited." Was it a porn link? No, she didn't think so, not from the cajuncajun.com email server, which was known to be reputable. She clicked it open and saw a pink background with a grinning frog reclining on a pool float with the words, "Ya'll Jump In. Ribet, Ribet." Scrolling down she found an invitation to a Lanier family pool party on the Fourth of July. Or, rather, a "Save That Date" card since the party wouldn't be held for a while yet. "Splish, splash. A Fourth of July Bash. Fun and Food. Get in the party mood." It was from Frank, Adam, and Mary Sue Lanier, but, clearly, the cute invitation had been Maisie Lanier's choice. The question was: Who had decided to invite her?

So much for conflicts of interest!

She was interested.

But she had more important things to do now.

She called Angela and apprised her of the situation involving Luther Ferguson and her daughter. "When Darlene returns, don't say anything. Wait until I get there with the lawyer. We'll be there in ten minutes. Try to act normal. Honestly, I promise, Angela, this will be over soon, and you'll be glad you handled it the right way."

"Oh Lord, oh Lord, oh Lord!" Angela kept saying. So much for acting normally. Well, maybe that's how she acted around her daughter, anyway.

Then, she called Luc's office on the off chance he might be working late. No answer, except for an answering machine inviting her to leave a message. Next, she called Luc's cell phone. Same thing. Finally, she tried his home number. His wife, Sylvie, answered the phone.

"Hey, Sylv."

"Simone? How are you? I heard your open house was a success. Sorry I couldn't make it, but I do have a referral that will be coming in to see you any day now. A chemist friend of mine with an unusual problem . . . but I'm rambling. You called . . . ?"

"Is Luc around?"

"No. He went to Baton Rouge on emergency business. Won't be back until tomorrow afternoon."

"Oh, damn!"

"Is this business or personal?"

"Business."

"An emergency?"

"Oh, yeah!"

"I'll give you Adam's cell number. He's taking Luc's calls."

She groaned. "Okay, give it to me."

When she called Adam a few seconds later, she could hear music in the background. "Lanier here."

"Adam?"

"Simone?" He was clearly shocked to hear from her.

"Listen. I have a situation here, and Luc is unavailable. Can you help?"

"Can you repeat that? I can hardly hear. Let me go out in the hallway."

"Where are you?"

The background noise level was more subdued now. "The Swamp Tavern. I came here with a few buddies for a beer after a racquetball game at the athletic club."

She wondered briefly if Sabine was still there trolling for a hit from their client's husband. No matter. "Are you drunk?" she asked Adam.

"Hell, no! Why would you ask that?"

"Because I need you sober to go with me to meet a client."

She tried to explain, but again the loud zydeco music interfered.

"Meet me here," he shouted, trying to be heard, "and I'll do whatever I can to help."

Lord help me, she thought as she put the car in gear and went out again to make the fifteen-minute drive to the

Swamp Tavern. No sense going home to change clothes or doing anything else. Best to get this over with asap.

But she couldn't help but think that every time she decided that she would not, could not, should not get involved with Adam Lanier, the Fates tossed him in her path again.

And, no, no, no, it was not the thunderbolt crap.

Just then lightning lit the skies and thunder clapped in the distance. She was going to be caught in the storm tonight, one way or another. The question was: Which storm?

Meanwhile, down in the swamp . . .

Adam waited for Simone's arrival at the Swamp Tavern with mixed feelings.

He hot damn wanted to see her, no matter the reason. And his daughter had insisted on including Simone on her pool party guest list; so, he would be seeing her one way or another at some point, if she accepted the invitation.

On the other hand, every instinct in his body warned him that she was a mistake about to happen. Clue number one: married three friggin' times. (Exactly how many men had she been with, curious minds wanted to know, in and out of marriage? Not that he had any room to be critical. Still . . .) Clue number two: not the type of woman he wanted in a forever kind of way; no woman was. Clue number three: a member of the LeDeux family, any one of whom would break his bones if he hurt her. Not that he had any plans to hurt her. Not in a bad way, anyhow. Clue number four: a "relative" of the notorious Tante Lulu who could be the biggest pain in the ass if she sniffed love . . . or sex . . . in the air. Clue number five: possibly involved in a case that conflicted with one of his.

Despite all the warning signs, Adam's body was on high alert. Testosterone amped up. Blood practically humming in his veins.

A number of the men in the tavern turned when she arrived, and he felt oddly irritated, as if she was his alone. She wore a black hoodie, which she shrugged out of as she entered the steam heat of the bar, exposing a black tank top and black spandex calf-length tights, with black sneakers. Her hair was pulled off her face into a ponytail, and she didn't appear to be wearing make-up.

She was tall for a woman, and big boned. Not fat, but not thin, either. Curves, she had lots of curves, delineated by the tank top and the spandex pants. Bust, waist, hips, and a sweetly rounded, tight butt.

She was not smiling as she approached him at the bar.

"Do you want a drink?" he asked.

She shook her head. "No time." But then she noticed the guy behind the bar. A big, bald-headed black man with a thick mustache and unibrow, and a gold hoop earring in one ear only. He looked like a friggin' pirate. "Hey, Gator, how you doing?"

"Still hangin', sweet cheeks. How about a drink, on the house?"

She shook her head. "Not tonight. I'm working."

"As a cop?" Gator asked with a little alarm, perhaps wondering if something was about to go on in the bar.

"No. I gave that up. New job now. Have you seen Sabine tonight?"

The bartender nodded. "She left about a half hour ago with some guy."

She and Gator exchanged some meaningful glance, meaningful to them, anyhow.

"Who's Sabine?" Adam asked.

"An employee," she said, rather reluctantly.

A customer at the end of the bar called for a refill and the bartender went off.

Adam arched his brows at the bartender and then her.

"I've known Gator since grade school. He's worked here ever since he left the military back in the nineties . . . some kind of special forces . . . and is a co-owner now, I think."

Her long explanation was probably due to his obvious, mistaken conclusion that he was another of her men. Hell, he still might be, for all he knew.

"Should we sit down so you can explain the situation?" he suggested.

"Can I explain on the way?"

"Sure," he said. "Where are we going?"

"A neighborhood on this end of Houma. Otherwise, I would have had you come in to my office."

"Should I drive?"

"It'll be faster if I drive since I know the area."

He got in the passenger seat of her Mazda and adjusted the seat way back to accommodate his long legs.

As she put the car in gear, she glanced his way. "Just come from the gym?"

"Yeah. Racquetball. I told you that on the phone. Why do you ask? Do I stink?" He raised an arm and sniffed his pit. Just smelled like deodorant to him.

"Nah, you always smell kinda musky. Good musky, not bad musky. I was referring to your clothes. I forgot that you mentioned the racquetball."

Musky? So, she notices my aftershave, which I put on this morning. Talk about a long life! But she was right. T-shirt, shorts, athletic socks, and shoes would be a clue to where he'd been. And he had showered before leaving the gym. Of course, he could have been practicing yoga. But she didn't know that.

She explained the situation then, regarding the young

girl and the teacher. He asked several questions, and he looked at the digital images on her camera, which were certainly incriminating.

"So, exactly what do you want me to do?"

"Talk to them about the legal ramifications of the whole situation."

He glanced down at himself. "I'm not really dressed for a client consultation."

"I don't think they'll care. Besides, I'm no better. Anyhow, in addition to giving them the legal view on what will happen, could you then set up a meeting for a complaint to be filed with the police, either at the station or in the Rossi home. Do you have any contacts in the department? If not, I could ask John LeDeux to give us some names. He's a cop."

"I know who to call." In fact, Max Salter had been his racquetball opponent a few hours ago. "Do you want to get the police involved tonight, or in the morning?"

"Tonight. I'm afraid Darlene will somehow manage to contact Luther Ferguson and tell him what's happening. And, frankly, the mother is skittish. Give her enough time, and enough persuasion from Darlene, and she might refuse to file a complaint."

"Okay. Got it." He pulled out his cell phone, scrolled down to the number he wanted, and set the device on speaker so Simone could hear both sides of the conversation. "Hey, Max, I have a situation here. Can you put on your detective hat and help me out?" He explained the situation.

"This isn't Ferguson's first adolescent girl rodeo. We've had complaints before, but nothing substantial enough to prosecute."

Simone made a snorting sound of disgust.

Adam put a fingertip to his lips to indicate silence. Cops had an aversion to recording devices, or speakerphones, which sounded like recording devices.

"I'll bring my partner with me," Max said. "Give me the address."

Simone jotted it quickly on a scrap of paper and he repeated it over the phone. "Wait for an hour so we have time to get our ducks in a row. And, Max, it's really important that we keep this girl's name out of the public eye."

"She's underage, so that won't be a problem, anyway."

"Yeah, but you know how these things slip out."

"I'll take extra care that she be protected. Is that what you're asking?" Max's voice sounded a little testy, as if he resented Adam questioning police protocol.

"I appreciate it, buddy."

"Yeah, well, next time don't beat my ass so bad on the courts. My wife says I look like I've been through the wringer. I could barely walk up the steps without groaning." The testiness was gone, replaced with teasing.

"Well, you *are* getting older."

"I'm no older than you, Lanier. Thirty-five and in my prime!"

Adam smiled and clicked off.

"Will the arrest take place tonight then?" Simone asked.

"It should."

"I appreciate your help with this, Adam. I owe you one."

"One what?"

"Favor."

He grinned. There were favors, and then there were favors.

Some teenage activities never get old . . .

The meeting with Angie and Darlene Rossi went surprisingly well. Oh, Darlene was upset . . . more embarrassed than angry over her "relationship" with Luther Ferguson being discovered. Turns out, she'd wanted to break it off for some time now, but Luther had threatened to spread the word around school that she was a slut.

That was Darlene's story, anyhow, which Simone wasn't buying. She had the camera evidence of the girl responding enthusiastically to the perv's kisses.

But then, the mind of a thirteen-year-old girl worked in mysterious ways. And, besides, it didn't matter whether she had been willing or not. Sex between an adult male and underage female was against the law. Even though Darlene had "consented", as a minor, she didn't have the maturity to know that what she was doing was wrong.

Adam had been wonderful dealing with the girl. Firm in his directions, but gentle when she became emotional. Probably due to experience with his own little girl. They didn't teach sensitivity training like that in most law schools as far as she knew.

He was also impressive in dealing with the police once they arrived. One of them, a friend, kept looking at her, then Adam, and rolling his eyes when he thought no one but Adam was looking. Adam ignored the eye rolling and was professional in the way he represented Darlene as his client to the police, getting assurances for her privacy that might not have otherwise been provided. In fact, he talked them into taking the complaint here in the home, rather than having Darlene and her mother be required to go to the police station.

Darlene would not be going to school the next day. Instead, a counselor would work with her, giving particular attention to how Darlene should handle herself post-Luther and the school scandal, which was sure to follow. Even if her name was not mentioned, there would be peer speculation over who the girl could be.

More than two hours later, Simone was driving Adam back to the Swamp Tavern parking lot where he would pick up his car. The storm that had been rumbling all evening broke loose just as she turned off the highway. The deluge hit the car with pounding pellets. She could barely see through the windshield as she eased into the slot next to Adam's Lexus.

They sat still for a moment, waiting out the downpour. Showers usually lasted only a few minutes here in the South, then dried up quickly in the hot weather.

"Good thing you didn't drive your motorcycle tonight," she commented.

"It wouldn't be the first time I got caught. It came in handy during Hurricane Katrina when I was a new lawyer in town and the streets were a mess. But then there was the time last year when I got hit with hail the size of marbles. I was black-and-blue for a week."

"The perks and perils of open-air driving. Here on the bayou, the dangers can be different. I was out on a pirogue with some friends when I was thirteen or so, and we rode right into an alligator's nest. Talk about fast rowing to get out of there."

"Thirteen, huh? At least you weren't humping a teacher. Or were you?"

She straightened indignantly. "That was insulting."

"Yeah, it was. I'm sorry. It's just that I'm nervous."

She turned to look at him, barely visible in the cocoon created by the foggy windows and loud rain. Under normal circumstances, they could have heard the band playing in the tavern. Not now. "Why are you nervous? Oh, you mean the aftershocks from everything that happened tonight."

"No, Simone, I do not mean what happened tonight. I mean everything that has been leading up to this night."

Huh?

With a long sigh of what sounded like surrender, he undid his seat belt, then leaned over to undo her seat belt, as well. With a skill that had to have been perfected in cars throughout his teenage years and beyond, Adam yanked her up and out of the driver's seat and over onto his lap. Before she could say, "What the hell . . . ?" or, "Stop!" or, "What a great idea!" he was kissing her. Wide-mouthed, wet, hungry kisses that went on forever. There might have been tongues involved, too, but she wasn't sure if was his or hers. And hands! Oh, my! His hands were everywhere. Cradling her face, cupping her but-tocks, shaping her breasts, tugging her closer, adjusting her position, making wide sweeps from her shoulders to her thighs and back up again. No interruptions in the kisses or the caresses.

And she was no better, or worse. She tugged at the rubber band holding his hair off his face in a little pony-tail and combed her fingers through the strands. She nipped at his earlobe, and he moaned, arching up into her so that his erection pressed against her hip. She was touching him all over, too, except that one place, which she was saving for later.

She started to tell him she was too big for this space, and that he was, too, but somehow they fit. In more ways than one.

The whole time they kissed and touched, they mur-mured sexy words at each other. Or they seemed sexy, in context.

"Oh, darlin'."

"Yes!"

"Please."

"More!"

"Does that hurt?"

"Hurts so good!"

Laughter.

Giggles.

"I feel like a teenager again."

"Yes, you do, stud."

"Are you teasing me?"

"Do you feel teased?"

"Oh, yeah!"

Who knew where this might have led if there hadn't been a sharp rapping noise. Adam eased her off his lap with a painful groan, and since the car had still been running, he was able to open the electric window on his side. For a moment, they couldn't see clearly the person standing behind the flashlight shining into the car, but they were able to tell that it had stopped raining because the man standing there appeared to be dry.

"Uh-uh-uh!" a male voice chided. It was Adam's police friend, Max Salter, who was grinning at them. "Well, well, well, Mis-tah Lan-ier, I thought I might find you here where you'd left your car, but I didn't expect . . . this."

"Bullshit!" Adam said, opening the door and shoving it hard against his friend's belly so that he had to step back with a laugh. "What are doing here, Salter? Demoted to patrolling bar parking lots now, are you? Looking for DUIs?"

"Nah. I just thought you'd like an update on what happened at Ferguson's house." Peering around Adam's shoulder, Max waved at Simone who was leaning across the passenger seat to hear what was being said. "Hey, Ms. LeDeux, whatcha doin'?"

She made a sound of disgust, and Adam put himself between Max and the car so that the detective couldn't see her anymore. Chivalry and all that!

"It all went down short and sweet. We didn't even need to call for backup. He's in lockup, as we speak. Of course, he's already lawyered up. That creep Jessie John Daltry from Nawleans."

"I know Daltry. He doesn't come cheap. Wonder where Ferguson would get the cash for such a high-priced attorney? Teachers don't make that much."

"Family money," Max told him.

"Does that mean this case might be dropped?"

"Not a chance!" Max said. "We got the bastard this time."

"Well, let us know what's happening and if you need any more help," Adam told him.

"Will do." But then the detective added, "Behave yourself," as he walked away, chuckling. Over his shoulder, he added, "By the way, you have a hickey the size of a French Quarter praline on your neck."

Adam said a foul word and put a hand to his neck as he walked around the front of the car. The motor was still running, and the lights were still on. He then checked his watch.

Simone checked the dashboard clock, as well. Almost midnight. Good Lord, they must have been making out for a long time. Like teenagers. And a hickey? Surely she hadn't done that. Had she? Well, he sure didn't do it to himself. *Can he see how red my face is? And, oh, my God! What if I have a hickey, too?*

She put her window down when Adam bent his knees to put his face into her view. "Are you going to be all right going home alone?"

I don't see any hickey. But his lips look all puffy and raw. Kiss-swollen. Get your act together, Simone. He asked you a question. Something about needing an escort home or something. What? She was a cop . . . or had been.

What does he think I am, some fragile Southern belle? Who gives world-class hickeys. Aaarrgh! "Of course," she said, as calmly as she could manage, wanting to get out of there as soon as possible so she could go home and cover her head with a blanket for a week or two.

Neither of them mentioned the big elephant in the parking lot . . . the still simmering attraction between them, the chemistry that had led them to behave so irresponsibly. The hickey.

Enough! She'd behaved badly. She'd been saved by the bell . . . uh, knock. No harm done! Time to move on.

She could tell that he was having second thoughts, too.

"Thanks for your help tonight, Adam. See ya!"

He inserted a hand, just before she closed the window. "Not so fast, Simone. Aren't you forgetting something?"

"What?"

If he asks for a good-night kiss, I'm going to scream.

If I don't get a good-night kiss, I might scream.

"The party's not over yet, sweetheart."

That sweetheart *was kind of ominous. Or maybe it was just the immature kind of thing a teen boy says when he hasn't gotten his rocks off yet.* "What party? Oh, you mean the pool party at your house," she said, playing it dumb.

"No, Simone, that's not the party I mean. The *other* party."

Yep, definitely Boys 'R Us.

But then she was feeling a little bit girlish.

Chapter Seven

What they needed was a party to celebrate . . .

The verdict in Pham versus Cypress Oil came down the next afternoon. Guilty on fifteen of twenty counts. There would be a two-week continuance before the trial was reconvened for the penalty phase when a decision would be handed down on fines and compensation for damages. In the meantime, post-trial motions would be filed, including any appeals Cypress wanted to make.

Everyone on Pham's team was ecstatic, especially Mike Pham. Adam and Luc high-fived each other once they were out of view of the judge and jury, not wanting to appear too unprofessional, or be cited for contempt of court . . . a line they'd crossed a number of times, according to the judge.

"Why didn't we get them on the other five charges?" Mike wanted to know the minute they were alone.

Adam was tempted to stuff his fist down the ungrateful jerk's big mouth, but Luc spoke first, "Hey, Mike, be satisfied with what ya got. Those five charges involved premeditation, and that's hard to prove in this kind of case."

"Yeah, I guess," Mike conceded. "Let's go celebrate. Oyster shooters at the Swamp Tavern?"

"Not in the middle of the day for me. Sylvie would kill me. I have to attend my youngest daughter's swim meet at five."

Mike gave Luc a look that pretty much labeled him as pussy-whipped. He turned to Adam and said, "You got a wife hanging on your tails, too?"

"No wife, but I have work back at the office, including some paperwork involving this case." He just had to add then, wanting to needle the bastard, "I wouldn't celebrate too soon, though, Mike. You never know what courts will award. Might be just one dollar."

"Whaaat? They wouldn't dare!"

Luc, catching Adam's cue, said, "Yep, sometimes the juries, they jist wanna give a message, not money. One time I had a client sue fer sexual harassment, and the court ruled in her favor, but gave her a measly one hundred dollars fer pain and sufferin'. My commission, it was about fifty cents. Talk about!"

It was amazing how Luc slid in and out of Cajun dialect so easily, and it appeared to be unintentional. Except when he deliberately exaggerated his language, wanting to come off as redneck dumb. Like the time he appeared before the State Supreme Court against some Manhattan bigshots trying to swindle a farmer out of his land for a shopping mall. They thought they were dealing with Barney Fife with a law degree, but instead got Matlock, but that was another story.

Mike gaped at the two of them, horrified. "Yer shittin' me!"

Adam shook his head slowly, as if in sympathy.

Luc said, "We kin only hope you'll get a fortune, *cher*."

When Mike stalked off, Adam said to Luc, "*Cher* my ass! He's not your friend."

"I know. And the sad thing, ironically, is that he'll probably walk away with at least a million bucks. Losers are losers even when they win. By the way, did you know you have a hickey on your neck?"

"I got hit by a ball when I was playing racquetball last night," Adam lied. He hoped Max would keep his big mouth shut, but that was probably an impossible wish. Cops loved to find something to annoy lawyers. "It about knocked me out."

"Yeah, right. And I suppose a racquetball caused yer lips ta be all red and puffy, too. When we get back to the office, maybe ya should suck on an ice cube."

Adam told Luc what he could suck on.

Which didn't bother Luc. "Guess it's best that I do the TV interview, unless ya want the reporter askin' if ya been bee stung."

Once again, Adam noticed how sometimes Luc's language got more Cajun and Southernish than others. Not just when he wanted to fool the unwary, but when he wanted to tease, as well. By the twinkle in Luc's eyes, though, Adam could tell that Max had already been blabbing. Luc must have run into the cop in the courthouse.

"Bite me!" That was the best retort Adam could come up with, which turned out to be an unfortunate choice of words.

"Looks lak ya had enough bitin' already, pal," Luc drawled.

Yep, unfortunate.

When they got back to the office, Adam found his father in the lobby chatting with their secretary, Mildred Guidry, who was an avid home gardener, too. After congratulating them on winning the case, Frank went back to discussing pesticides with Mildred while Luc began making preparations for the interview with the local television station about the verdict and Adam went into his office, where Maisie was sitting behind his desk tapping away on his laptop.

"Maisie! Honey! You shouldn't be using Daddy's laptop. You might accidentally wipe out some important files."

"Oh, Daddy, I brought mah own flash drive."

He should have known. Kids knew more than adults about computers today. Not that he was a computer idiot, but Maisie could probably teach him a few things.

"I'm workin' on the VeePees fer our party," she told him.

"Huh?"

"The RSVPs."

"RSVPs? Where did you hear of that?"

"PawPaw tol' me it was a way to see how many people would come. And mah friend Phoebe's sister Christine showed me how to do it on my computer."

Oh, great, a conspiracy! "So, you got a lot of those RSVPs already?"

"Ten." She smiled happily, as if she'd just won an Oscar.

"Really? You just sent them out."

"Mostly they're from my kindergarten friends so far," she admitted.

"And you're using a computer to plan this whole shindig, huh?"

"Of course." She motioned for him to come behind the desk and peer over her shoulder. "I have files fer everything. Guest list . . . forty-three so far. Food . . . Tante

Lulu sez she kin make a Peachy Praline Cobbler Cake fer us. Drinks . . . we're havin' pink lemonade with little umbrellas. And beer . . . yuck! Decorations . . . red, white, and blue fer the Fourth of July. Extra pool floats . . . we gotta have some flag ones, this bein' a theme party. Games . . . me and mah friends are gonna plan those."

"And this Christine helped you set this all up? How old is she?"

"She's really old. Fourteen. But PawPaw helped, too."

My father? What is he thinking? And did I hear Tante Lulu mentioned in that spiel? Oh, Lord! I don't want to know how Maisie knows that old lady so well. Must be Dad who involved her. I am definitely going to have a word with him. And a "theme party"? We're having a "theme party"? But for now, he just said, "Wow! You've put a lot of thought into this, haven't you?"

"A good hostess is first of all a good party planner."

He smiled at her adult language. "Where'd you hear that, my little hostess? From Christine? Or PawPaw?" *Or, God forbid, Tante Lulu?*

"Food Network. 'Parties for the Younger Set.' I'm the Younger Set. But you're not old, either, Daddy. Well, not tooooo old!"

He had to laugh. After last night, making out in a car like a horny teenager, he was definitely not feeling old.

"I have a folder fer you, too, Daddy. Wanna see?"

He was about to say yes, but Luc stepped in and waved a folded newspaper at him. Luc signaled with his eyes that Adam had to see the headline.

"I'll be right back," he said to his daughter and walked out, following Luc into his office. "What's up?" he asked Luc. "Too soon for news on our trial, isn't it?"

"Look," Luc ordered, spreading the newspaper out on his desk.

Adam swallowed a gasp of surprise. The headline read, "Houma Teacher Charged with Statutory Rape." There was a picture of Luther Ferguson, flanked by Max Salter and two uniformed officers, doing the perp walk from the parking lot to the courthouse for arraignment early this morning.

"They sure work fast," Luc said. He already knew about the situation that had come up last night, even though he'd just been returning from Baton Rouge early this morning when they'd gotten the verdict call. While they'd waited for the jury to come in, Adam had brought him up-to-date on the prior night's happenings . . . minus the make-out session with Simone.

"According to Simone, they had to act fast because . . ."

"*Mais oui!* I shoulda guessed," Luc interrupted. "Simone is the one who gave you the love bite. Wait till Tante Lulu sees that. Whoo-ee! Weddin' bells will be a-ringin'."

Adam ignored Luc's jibe and skimmed the article. It wasn't just statutory rape Ferguson was being charged with but a whole slew of other crimes, like sodomy, child pornography, and solicitation of a minor. "Oh, no! They granted him bail."

"Yep. A hundred thou. Cash. Apparently his family has money. Somethin' ta do with designer popcorn in Nebraska. Ya ever heard of FergiePop? Zebra stripes, peppermint cane colors, polka dots, that kind of thing. And outrageous flavors, like Cajun Spice, Arctic Ice, Thai Ginger. They've been grownin' the stuff fer a century or more, but always adaptin' ta the times. No more simple salt and butter."

"Yeah, Maisie wants to get some of the pink cotton-candy flavor for her party. But, man! If ever there was a flight risk, he's it. He could skip town in a flash with that kind of money behind him."

"Not so fast. He's under house arrest with an ankle monitor. And the arraignment was fast-forwarded, so I expect the trial to be expedited, too."

"Max hinted last night that there might be other victims."

"There always are with these kinds of perverts."

"Max also said something about Ferguson already being lawyered up with Jessie John Daltry."

"Hah! Daltry's a slimey s.o.b., but I'm not sure he can do much for a pedophile."

The reporter for the TV station arrived and Adam was forced to participate in the interview about Cypress Oil along with Luc, merely because he hadn't managed to escape the office fast enough. Maisie didn't understand what the oil company case was about, but she was practically jumping with pride, watching her father being interviewed. Adam's father was beaming, too.

Later that evening, when everyone was asleep, he called Simone. "Hi," he said, not bothering to identify himself.

"Hi," she said back, knowing who it was.

Was that a sign of something, that they recognized each other's voices? Or just Caller I.D.?

"Were you sleeping?"

"Just getting ready for bed."

"Alone?"

"Adam!"

"Sorry."

"How about you?"

"Alone or in bed?"

"Both."

"Same as you. I'm wearing black cotton sleep pants with red tongues imprinted all over them, a warped Christmas gift from my brother, Dave, that I wear as a concession to having a daughter in the house. How about you? What are you wearing? Or not wearing?"

"Adam! That is such a cliché! Next you'll be asking me to come over and see your etchings."

"No etchings here, but I do have a baseball card collection packed away in the closet from when I was a kid."

"I'm wearing silk. Boxers and tank top." She paused. "And nothing else."

"Tease!" he accused with a laugh. Then, "Want me to come over?" Not that he could. Not without giving his dad notice that he was going out. And all that would ensue . . . questions, raised eyebrows, the works.

"Be serious."

"I am." *Sort of. I might even risk my father's scorn if you say the word, honey.*

"Congratulations on your win today."

"Thanks." He waited for her to mention something about Mike Pham, assuming his wife had come in to see her at Legal Belles, but she said nothing more. "Any further word from the Rossi girl?"

"Yes. She stayed home from school today, and a counselor worked with her. Hopefully, she'll be back in classes tomorrow, that way her absence would be less obviously connected to Ferguson."

"Where's the kid's father?"

"Absent. Never been around."

"I think I'd kill the man who did that to my girl."

"Yeah, well, that wouldn't help much since you'd be in prison."

"So logical!" There was a poignant silence before he said, "So, we gonna do this thing?"

She hesitated before asking, "What thing?"

"Don't be coy."

"No, really. Do you mean the attraction between us? A

quick hookup or two to relieve the itch? Dating? Something more than that, like a, God forbid, relationship?"

He said a foul word under his breath. "Why do women always have to overanalyze everything?"

"Maybe because we're the ones who usually get hurt. Look, Adam, I don't deny there's this spark between us, but I've felt the spark before . . . and been burned. My mother would say I've got my Cajun Crazy on again. I do have a thing for Cajun men."

"So, I'm just one Cajun man, any of whom would do?"

"That's not what I meant."

"What *do* you mean?"

"I mean that I am older and wiser now. I hope. I'm going to be more cautious this time around."

"You weren't that cautious in the car last night."

"Ouch!"

"That's not an insult."

"Felt like it. But you're right. I wasn't cautious. You caught me off guard. A blip on the radar of my new resolution."

"I'm afraid to ask . . . what resolution?"

"No more Cajun men."

"That's not fair. Besides, I keep telling you, I'm not totally Cajun."

"Cajun enough. And stop smiling."

"How do you know I'm smiling?"

"Women's intuition."

"What does your women's intuition tell you that I'm doing right now?"

"Adam!"

"Not that. I have a notepad next to my bed and I just wrote a note to myself. 'New Resolution: Seduce Simone.'"

"I thought you already did that."

"Oh, darlin', I haven't even begun."

"Say that again," she said on a groan.

"Say what?"

"*Darlin'.* Kinda slow and smoldering."

Smoldering? How do I smolder? But he gave it a shot. "Dar-lin'," he repeated, all hokey slow and Clint Eastwood raspy.

There was an odd sound then, and he asked, "What was that noise?"

"The sound of dumb female bones melting."

Gossip Central, for sure . . .

Louise had a late-day appointment to have her hair done at Charmaine's Houma salon, Curl Up & Dye. She wasn't sure whether to go with Red Velvet or Pink Panic today. So many choices!

The first thing she noticed when she entered the shop was the missing life-size St. Jude statue in the lobby. "Charmaine!" she called out. "Better phone the po-lice. Someone stole yer St. Jude."

"Uh, it's not really stolen," Charmaine said, coming out from behind the counter. "I put it in the storage room."

"Why?" Louise put her hands on her hips and narrowed her eyes with suspicion.

"A customer complained that it was politically incorrect to have a Catholic statue in a public place."

"Whaaat?" More lak idjit-incorrect ta be insulted by St. Jude. Didja tell the lady that St. Jude is the patron saint of all hopeless people, not jist Catholics. Holy Sac-au-lait! What'd she want? A Buddha?"

Charmaine put up her hands in surrender. "I'll bring it back out."

"Ya better. Otherwise I may hafta stage a protest with

mah friends from the Our Lady of the Bayou rosary society."

"Please, auntie, no protests. The last time ya staged a protest, it was over at Bayou Bob's Strip Club, and I had ta bail the bunch of you outta jail."

"We was framed."

"Yeah, right. Come on back to my station."

Louise followed her niece, who was all decked out today in a red jumpsuit with high heels, about three pounds of teased-up black hair, and enough jewelry to sink a boat. Charmaine owned at least five of these beauty shops around southern Louisiana, along with a spa up at her husband Rusty's ranch, The Triple L. A bimbo business-woman, that's what Charmaine was, and proud of it.

Louise, on the other hand, was just wearing her pink "Proud to Be a Cajun" sparkly T-shirt over white capri pants and orthopedic shoes with ruffled socks. Simple attire, for her. You could say, her going-to-be-beautified outfit, she chuckled to herself.

And, whoo-boy, did she need to be beautified today! Those beauty shop mirrors showed every little flaw. For example, right now Louise's face, with its layer of foundation and powder, looked like a white prune. *Oh well,* she thought, and decided to just squint while she was here so that her view would be filtered, sorta like cataracts . . . the good kind.

Even so, Charmaine oughta invest in some of those magic mirrors that made a person look younger and slimmer. Maybe she would buy her some for her next birthday, though Charmaine claimed not to want any notice taken of her birthdays anymore. Louise knew how she felt. She didn't like to talk about her age, either. Of course, Charmaine wasn't old. Always conscious of her appearance, Charmaine had been hiding her age since she was twenty-one and entered her first national beauty contest.

Louise didn't want to think about what she'd been like when she'd been twenty-one. Happy, for sure. Her fiancé Phillipe Prudhomme had been alive then, and life had been—

"What's the big occasion?" Charmaine asked as she propped her up on two pillows on a swivel chair, then arranged one of those silky cover-ups over her shoulders. "You usually come in on Saturdays."

"I gotta be all spiffied up fer mah big date t'morrow night."

"Lawdy, Lawdy!" Charmaine said under her breath. Then, "Who's the lucky guy?"

"Well, it's not a date, exactly. There are a bunch of folks goin' out on the town t'gether."

"Y'mean dancing?"

Charmaine held up two hair-color chips, and without speaking, Louise picked the red. Somedays she felt like pink, but at the moment, red was calling to her.

"No, not dancing. Though I could dance if I wanted to, even with these bunions. Nope, it's 'Eats and Slots' night at the Lazy Dazy Steamboat Casino on Lake Charles. Eat 'til yer beat, and slot 'til ya rot. Tee-hee-hee."

Charmaine groaned at her joke, which *was* kinda lame, she had to admit. After slathering the hair dye on her head and setting the timer, Charmaine sat down to chat for a moment. Her next client wouldn't be in for another fifteen minutes.

"And it's not t'morrow night, exactly, either," Louise went on. "Older folks like ta get a head start on an evening so they kin be home in time ta watch reruns of *The Golden Girls* by nine. Of course the men—the old farts—prefer reruns of *Charlie's Angels*, the old series, with Farrah Fawcett. Practically porn in its day. Anyways, we'll prob'ly be headin' out by three or four. And speakin' of my gal Farrah, kin ya spruce up mah Farrah wig. It's beginnin' ta look scarecrowish."

Charmaine rolled her eyes, as she often did when Louise rambled on.

Does she think I don't notice?

Does she think my brain's so old it don't know when it meanders from one subject to another?

Do I care?

Louise thought a moment. *Nope.*

Young folks just didn't understand that the reason older folks rambled on was that they had to get all their thoughts out at once, just in case they dropped dead unexpectedly. Also, they tended to forget things if they waited for as much as five minutes. Last week, Minnie Holbein went to confession and halfway through forgot where she was and began telling her son Rufus, who lived in Florida, what she thought of his new wife.

"By the way, how's mah favorite great-great-great niece?" Louise asked, referring to Charmaine's daughter, Mary Lou. It always saddened her that Charmaine and Rusty had been able to have only one child. They'd certainly tried hard enough. Of course, that might all change if the baby bug spreading around had bit Charmaine, too, like she suspected. But she would wait for Charmaine to bring up the subject. Best not to rile Charmaine while Louise had a pound of dye on her head, or she might walk out of here bald.

"Now, auntie, you say that to all your nieces and nephews. That they're your faves."

"Well, in the moment, they are. So, it ain't lyin'."

"Mary Lou is her daddy's girl, as ya know. She refused ta let me enter her in a beauty contest when she was a cute little princess, and I've have had less luck during her teen years. All she wants to do is ride horses and work the ranch with her father." She sighed.

Louise patted Charmaine's arm. "Pageants ain't fer everyone."

"I know, but it feels lak she's maybe ashamed of mah title." Charmaine had been Miss Louisiana more than twenty years ago and had enough beauty pageant crowns and titles to furnish a museum. Louise really thought she should make a display of them in her shop window.

"Mary Lou is not ashamed of you. She's jist followin' a different path." It was funny how insecure women always were. Here was Charmaine, a noted beauty who had used her assets to start her own business, then expand it so she was practic'ly an entrepreneur, married to the hottest Cajun cowboy who ever rode a horse, with a daughter who never got in trouble, and she worried that she was lacking in some way. It was Hollywood and all that nonsense on TV, in Louise's opinion, but that was another pet peeve of hers to be aired another day. "Yer a good mother and allus have been."

"I s'pose. Anyways, she's takin' a gap year before goin' ta college. She's thinkin' about becomin' a veterinarian."

"See! Be proud of her, honey, and be proud of the good job you've done in raisin' her."

Charmaine swiped at her eyes and gave Louise a hug. "I always feel better after talkin' ta you."

"Truth to tell, honey, I come ta yer beauty shop on a reg'lar basis ta get mah gossip fix," Louise said, wanting to lighten Charmaine's mood. "Where else could I hear everything about everyone? Under the hair dryer."

"Ain't that the truth? It's lak a therapist's office."

"So?" Louise prodded.

"Well, ya already knew that Cletus moved out of Addie Daigle's trailer at The Gates, but didja know . . ."

For ten minutes, after Charmaine filled her in on the latest gossip . . . uh, news, and after rinsing her hair and blowing it dry, Louise remarked, "Speaking of Addie . . . I doan know what I'm gonna do 'bout that daughter of hers."

"Why? What has Simone done?"

"Nothin'. Thass the point. By now, she should be hop, skip, and jumpin' t'ward the altar."

"And she's not, I take it."

"I give her a man what's hotter than asphalt, and what does she do?"

"What?"

"Resists."

"How do ya know she's resistin'?"

"Ya get any weddin' invitation yet?"

"No, but—"

"I'm thinkin' we need ta plan an intervention."

"Oh, boy! Fer Simone or Adam?"

"Both of 'em."

"A double intervention. Is there such a thing?"

"I doan know. Guess we could start with Simone. I got some herbs that we kin slip into her mornin' coffee."

"What's with this 'we' business? I'm not druggin' anyone. Ask her mother ta do it. She's closest to the office coffeepot, anyway."

"Hah! Addie thinks her daughter is still married to that Cletus bum."

"I know, but she's startin' ta bend on that issue after havin' him live with her for a few days. When she was here yesterday, she said he drank so much beer, her recycle bin was overflowin'. And she said it will take her a month ta get rid of the smell of beer farts in her furniture." Charmaine paused in spritzing hairspray on Louise's soft red curls and said, "So, herbs in the coffee fer Simone. Is that all?"

"Well, ya know them Laniers are havin' a pool party on the Fourth of July. I was thinkin' Adam and Tee-John and Luc and Remy and René could put on some special entertainment."

"Ya doan mean The Cajun Village People! I thought we retired that act a long time ago."

"Ya never retire a good thing." Over the years when someone needed a shove in the love department, the LeDeux family put on their own Cajun version of the old Village People act.

"Ya think ya could talk Simone into doing this?"

"Not Simone. Adam."

Charmaine perked up with interest. "Do tell, auntie."

"Well, we could have a special music revue around the pool, and at the end Adam could come out all lawyer-like in a business suit, but then strip down in a little bump and grind 'til he's down to his . . ."

"His what?"

"What do ya call those skimpy men's bathing trunks?"

"A Speedo?"

"Thass it."

"Son of a bayou gun! I'd lak ta see that. But somehow I doan see Adam as the Speedo type."

Louise shrugged. "I'll think of somethin'."

"That's what I'm afraid of," Charmaine said.

Chapter Eight

All in a day's work . . .

Simone did a lot of smiling the next day. Who was she kidding? She'd done some smiling in bed, too, after ending Adam's late night phone call.

Yeah, he was sexy as hell on wheels. And good-looking. But more than that, or equal to that, he was fun. She enjoyed bantering with him. And, no, she was not imagining what else she would enjoy doing with him.

BaRa was already there when Simone went down to the office at eight-thirty a.m. Her secretary liked to come in early to open up, after dropping off her twin boys at Our Lady of the Bayou School where they were third-graders. She also left at three-thirty to pick them up, but the flexible workday was an inconvenience they could work around. "Looks like someone got some last night," BaRa observed.

"Hardly," Simone replied, trying her best to hide the blush that was heating her face. "What's on the agenda for today?"

BaRa, whose short, dark hair was still damp from a morning shower, wore her usual four-inch heels (to give her some height) with a green, cap-sleeved, office-friendly pantsuit. She went to her desk, which sat in an anteroom just outside Simone's office and, beyond that, Helene's. Picking up a folder, she read, "Office meeting at ten with Sabine and Gabe, past reports and future assignments. Those last two job applicants will come in at the tail end of your meeting, as you requested. Noon lunch with Angela Rossi at the restaurant where she works. Two new potential clients scheduled for two and three. And an appointment with Kimly Bien and Thanh Pham at four.

"Oh, and the community college wants to know if you or Helene would like to teach a course in its women's studies department next semester, something about women and marriage law. I told them you'd get back to them on that."

"Good publicity for the firm. Ask Helene if she has time."

"Okay. The Internet tabloid newspaper *Aha!* keeps calling, as well. Not sure what they want. Probably just fishing for news."

"Bad publicity. Not the kind we want, or need."

"And here's a tentative schedule for the next three days." She handed Simone a printout.

BaRa was very efficient and Legal Belles was lucky to have her. She'd been working many years for the insurance agency that had been in this spot previously and hadn't wanted to relocate to another satellite office in Morgan City. Despite the acrimony between her and her ex-husband, Alan Ozelet, or Ozzie, an oil rigger, she wanted to keep her kids where they could see their father often.

"How did your meeting with Ozzie go last night?"

"Pfff! The bum wants a reconciliation. Claims his cheatin' days are over. More like, he's sick of livin' in an apartment with no one to clean up after him."

"Maybe he really has changed."

"Do alligators suddenly wanna cuddle with porcupines?"

"He is good-looking."

"Looks only go so far. That man's wiener has been in more buns than Oscar Mayer. And I haven't had a taste for meat since I kicked his sorry ass out the door."

BaRa did have a way with words. Must be hanging around Tante Lulu too much . . . or Simone's own mother, truth be told.

"And he claims I need a man around to protect me. Hah! I got a bat in my car, and a pistol in my bedside table. That's all the protection I need."

"And the boys?"

"Ah, well, that's another story. They do love their daddy." With a sigh, BaRa informed her, "There's fresh coffee in the kitchen, and an extra breakfast baguette from Sweet Buns."

"Thanks," she said and headed in that direction. The coffee she would welcome, the baguette she would bypass, despite her rumbling stomach.

Adelaide Daigle came ambling in at nine. They didn't really need a receptionist *and* a secretary at this point, but Simone didn't have the heart to fire her mother. And, besides, she was working for practically nothing.

Her mother was wearing another of her Spanx outfits, purple and lavender today. Simone also noticed the black heels she was wearing. Not stilettos, but heels nonetheless, mid-height and strappy. Surely not recommended for a lady with two new knees who was still going to rehab twice a week.

"Hello, hello, everyone," her mother said, even though Simone and BaRa were the only ones around. "Beautiful day outside."

"Mom! Do you really think you should be wearing heels?"

"It's okay. I take them off when I get here. I have slippers in mah purse . . ."

Oh, great! A receptionist in fuzzy duck slippers.

". . . but I wanna wear 'em when I go out later t'day."

"Out where?"

"The casino. With Frank Lanier and Tom Dorsey."

Oh, Lord! Adam's father and the Santa/painter? "You're going on a date with two men?"

That was a little weird, even for her mother.

"Not a date, exactly. Tante Lulu is comin', too. And Sabine's mother, and Aunt Mel from over at Bayou Rose Plantation. She's visitin' her nephews Daniel and Aaron LeDeux. She's a less-be-an, y'know. I'm not sure how I feel about that. She better not hit on me. Oh, and Sam Starr from Nawleans, a friend of Tante Lulu's. He's the guy from the Starr supermarket chain, Samantha Starr LeDeux's grandfather. He's so cute, looks jist like Colonel Sanders, *with a mustache*."

Her mother and men with mustaches! And a lesbian! Would wonders never cease? "And you're all going to a casino?"

"Yep. Dinner first. Early bird special fer seniors at the Rumpus Room on the Lazy Dazy Steamboat in Lake Charles. They have an all-ya-kin-eat buffet with two hundred dishes fer only ten dollars. After that we'll do a little gamblin'. Of course, I'm not quite a senior citizen, but I think I kin sneak in. Would be the first time I tried ta look older."

"Why would Sam Starr need to get bargain dinners? I hear he has money out the wazoo."

"How you think he got all that money? Bargains! We're all goin' t'gether in one of the Starr Foods vans. He offered a limo—we would have all shared the cost—but that's too fancy-pancy fer us. And what's a wazoo, anyhow?"

"I have no idea," she said, and walked off to prepare for her day. Why had she ever imagined that her mother was lonely living alone while she'd been in Chicago? It appeared she had more of a social life than Simone did.

Thoughts of last night's phone conversation came suddenly to mind. That was the extent of her social life.

But she was smiling again.

Her meeting with Sabine and Gabe went well.

Sabine looked ultra-feminine this morning in a blue-and-white polka dot sundress and nude sandals, unlike her usual biker girl, leather attire, even though the floral tattoos up her arms and around her neck were even more prominent. No piercings showed, except for tiny pearl post earrings. Her blond hair, which had been all spiked and edgy last time they'd met, was now loose with subtle waves about her face. A surprising beauty!

Sabine reported that her target had engaged in a conversation with her at Swampy's and had bought her not one, but two drinks. However, all he did was talk about his wife who was ruining their marriage with her jealousy. Sabine ended up giving the guy advice on how to make his wife feel more secure. So, that was a good news/bad news case. The wife would, or should, be pleased with the results. But short and sweet, meaning not much cash for Legal Belles. But that was okay. They'd done their job. Case closed. That one, anyhow.

Gabe amused them by arriving in his IT tycoon persona. In fact, with his hair neatly parted, he looked like Bill Gates with black framed glasses and geeky clothes . . . a vee-neck sweater over a button-down dress shirt and tie. He even threw a bunch of Internet-savvy words into their conversation, like *encryption*, *gnutella*, *kibibyte*, *qwerty*, and *optical media*, which had Simone and Sabine staring at him in wonder and thinking they needed to buy a modern dictionary for the office.

"It's all part of acting," he told them. "Just like writers toss in a word or two to give their books authenticity, such as in police procedurals, actors do the same with technical words or accents or attire or body language."

Once again, Simone and Sabine just stared at him. Gabe was either smarter than she'd realized or a really good actor.

Gabe's target, Tammy Allerby, whose fiancé wanted a prenup, was taking the bait, finally, he told them. In fact, he'd taken Tammy to a nearby jazz club for drinks after their health club routines last night. "I should be paid time and a half for all this exercise. Keep it up and I might even get a six-pack. Ha, ha, ha!" he told them, half jokingly.

Maybe I should join the gym. For a week.

"Tammy is very interested in my 'assets.'" He grinned and adjusted the frames of his glasses up his nose. "My first inclination is to tell her fiancé to not only get a prenup, but to back off completely."

"Well, keep up the good work," she advised him, "but be careful you don't overstep the line into entrapment. And it's not our job to tell clients what they should do with the info we give them."

"Got it," he said. "Appeal, but don't be aggressive. Gather the news, don't be part of the news."

"Right."

Two other applicants came in looking for jobs then. Legal Belles really didn't need any more employees in its "stable," but these two were part of the initial call for applications and hadn't fit into the first round of interviews. One of them interested Simone very much, a Creole woman of color with a private detective background. She had previously worked for a big New Orleans law firm.

The other applicant, not so much. Not because she wasn't talented in terms of office procedures, but at this time, in the early stages of Legal Belles, BaRa and Simone's mother could handle everything that came in.

"I need you to come with me for lunch at Tres Bien Restaurant," she told her mother at a quarter to twelve.

"I cain't do that. I'll be too full fer the all-ya-kin-eat at four," her mother said. "Besides, I'm about ready ta pop outta mah Spanx as it is. The bloat, dontcha know?"

Yeah, Simone knew about "the bloat." Women had been blaming it for everything but hemorrhoids since the beginning of time. Eve probably told Adam she was bloated when he commented on the size of her little belly—from apples, in her case.

"You don't need to eat anything. Just have a glass of tea, or a cup of coffee. It will be less conspicuous for me to be meeting with Angela Rossi before her shift starts if you're with me."

"You mean, we'd be sorta like partners. Like Cagney and Lacey."

"Who?"

"Never mind. Maybe I kin have a little order of Tres Bien's raspberry soufflé with salted caramel sauce. We could share a plate," she mused, standing to remove her fuzzy duck slippers and put on her high heels.

Eyeing the shoes, Simone said, "Maybe we better drive over," even though it was only two blocks away.

They sat in a back booth of the plush restaurant with Angela before her shift started. She wore a black uniform with a tiny white apron and black pumps. Her blond hair was pulled off her face into a neat chignon, and her make-up was minimal but flawless. At only thirty-five or so, Angela was an attractive woman, and Simone wondered about her history, the missing father of Darlene and all that.

"You look so much more relaxed," she told Angela.

"I am, thanks to you," she said, reaching across the table to squeeze Simone's hand. "I don't think I would have had the nerve to go to the police on my own."

Simone was touched. "And Darlene?"

"She went to school today, and we'll just wing it to see how that plays out, but that counselor you referred us to has been so helpful. She's young enough, about twenty-five, to understand how an adolescent girl could get involved in such a situation. She's already talked Darlene into joining an after-school fitness program as well as band. Darlene used to play the flute really well, but gave it up when some kid said it was dorky. Her counselor convinced her that flutes were cool, and a good flute player could even get a college scholarship. Please, God!"

"No misgivings about Luther Ferguson's arrest?"

"None that she mentions. That lawyer friend of yours has been an angel."

"Luc . . . I mean, Lucien LeDeux?"

"No, the one you brought over to our house. Adam Lanier."

Adam, an angel? "How has he been helpful?"

"He's offered to represent us if we have to go to court. But even if we don't, he says he'll be our representative with the police. He told us not to talk to anyone, including the cops, unless he's present. Isn't that nice of him?"

"It sure is." And Simone's suspicious mind wondered if Adam's offer had anything to do with the attractive Mrs. Rossi. Which was grossly unfair of her, she knew. But then, he was always quick to jump to conclusions about her, as well, just because she'd been married a few times.

After that meeting, during which her mother had in fact eaten the entire soufflé while Simone had been talking, they went back to the office where Max Salter, the detective friend of Adam's, was waiting to speak to her. In the meantime, he'd been speaking with BaRa. He and her ex-husband, Ozzie had worked together on a shrimp boat when they were teenagers.

"Maybe I could do a little work for you guys, on the side," Max said, once they were in her office. He grinned as he added, "I have a pair of tight black jeans that my wife says make my ass look hot."

"And you think hot asses are a criteria for employment at Legal Belles?"

"I'm jist sayin'."

Simone couldn't be offended. The guy was just teasing. "So what's up?"

"I need your signature on some documents, giving us permission to use those photographs and the audio you recorded of Luther Ferguson." He took some folded sheets out of his pocket and slid them across the desk to her.

"Do I need my lawyer to look this over before I sign?"

"You mean Adam?" he asked with a smirk.

She couldn't help but blush, knowing what he'd witnessed in the Swamp Tavern parking lot. "No, not Adam. Helene Dubois, my partner, is a lawyer, and my half brother Lucien LeDeux is, too."

Max shrugged. "It's a fairly simple release, but you can have it looked over first if you want."

"How's the case against Ferguson going?"

"I can't really say, but your work and the evidence from the Rossi girl will go a long way to putting this guy behind bars. Where he should have been a long time ago." Those last words were a hint to her that they had other girls lined up to testify, as well.

"Good working with you, Simone," Max said before he left. "I expect it won't be the last time. Other cases, and all that."

That was probably true.

Simone signed on two other clients after that. One of them involved a woman who wanted a divorce and just wanted a female attorney to represent her. Helene could handle that one easily. The other was the usual Cheaters-type case. Saffron Pitot of New Orleans whose husband Marcus Pitot was the wealthy owner of Cypress Lumber, a generations' old company, as well as numerous other businesses. Saffron wanted the goods on her husband who had been engaged in some kind of perverted sex club for years.

"Why come all the way from Nawleans to hire an investigator?" Simone asked. "You have plenty to choose from in the Big Easy."

Saffron, a former soap opera actress of no particular fame, was in her forties, but with enough work done on her face and body to make her look ten years younger. "I read about your agency in the feature section of the *Times-Picayune*, and it struck a chord with me. I checked my horoscope and then double-checked with my astral advisor, and Madame Bouche said Legal Belles was the place I should go for help."

Ooookaaay. "What exactly do you want us to do, and what is your ultimate goal? Do you want a divorce?"

"I don't think so. The old fart leaves me pretty much alone, but I've gotta get evidence of his activities, just in case."

"In case . . . what?"

"In case some sweet young thang in his orgies gets her claws into him, and he tries to push me out the door. You know how men are once a woman hits forty. They start looking for sweeter, younger meat."

Whoa! Lots to chew on there. First of all, Simone took umbrage at being lumped with the over-forty crowd. Second, what was it with the meat references today? And third, orgies?

"Tell me about the club. What's its name?"

"I don't think it has a name. Just a group of men and women who get together and have orgies at their different houses. Lots of times they use Marcus's lodge up on Lake Pontchartrain."

"What makes you think it's a club? Which people? Can you give me names? Has it been going on for a long time?"

"At least ten years. And mostly the same group of about ten people. They only add new people when someone drops out, or dies, like Adam Lanier's wife, Hannah, did two years ago."

Sirens went off in Simone's head. "What? Who did you say? Adam Lanier?"

"Not Adam. His wife, Hannah. What a piece of work that one was! All respectable married woman, a psychologist or something, with a child and a husband most women would die for, but a slut underneath. She was the organizer of lots of these 'events.' I think Marcus wanted to hire Adam to handle some of his legal business when he moved from the prosecution to the defense side of the bench, but I don't know if that ever panned out. Adam was never involved in the clubbing, as far as I know. I mighta wanted to join if he did." Saffron waggled her obviously tattoo-enhanced eyebrows at Simone at that jest.

Simone was not laughing. In fact, if she hadn't been

sitting down, she would have had to, so deep was her
shock. Not about the sex club. They were nothing new,
and, in fact, were more acceptable today in society as a
whole. Live and let live. If no one gets hurt . . . That kind
of thing. But this put a whole new picture on Adam
Lanier, and the kind of life he'd led before moving here.
She'd been under the impression *he* was the player. But
now . . . Hmmm.

She wasn't sure who she would send to investigate that
one. She might have to do it herself.

After that, she and Helene met with Kimly Bien and
her sister, Thanh Pham, and Simone was zapped by yet
another "connection" with Adam Lanier. She supposed
that was the way of the bayou. Forget about "six degrees
of separation," in Cajun land, it was more like three. Not
that Adam had anything in particular to do with the complaint of these two ladies. Still . . .

The two women couldn't be more different. Thanh wore
the traditional black silk pants with a frogged tunic, also
black but beautifully embroidered, possibly by herself,
with multicolored birds. Kimly wore a white oxford col-
lared, fitted shirt over skinny jeans and sandals. Thanh's
black hair hung in a single braid down her back. Kimly's
black hair was piled atop her head with a claw comb.

"Do you want a divorce?" Helene asked Thanh bluntly.

"No! No divorce!" Thanh said vehemently. "We were
married in church. No divorce."

"Well," Kimly interjected. "Let me argue with that. I
believe that Thanh's husband, Mike, is going to file for
divorce once he gets a settlement in this Cypress Oil case.
And I believe that Mike is going to screw my sister, financially, once he does. My sister is not so convinced."

Simone looked at Thanh.

"Minh would not be so cruel." Minh was Mike's Vietnamese name.

"Hah! You don't think twenty years of infidelity is cruel, Thanh? You don't think twenty years of having you on a pittance of a household budget is cruel, while he drives around in a rigged-out fifty-thousand-dollar truck?"

"I asked him about that, and he said he needed it for the business," Thanh said to her sister.

"Bullshit!" Kimly exclaimed.

Thanh flinched at her sister's vulgarity.

"What exactly do you want from us?" Simone asked. "Evidence of infidelity?"

"That will be easy enough to get, and it's probably a good idea to have it on file," Kimly said, "but we need advice on what Thanh is entitled to under Louisiana law in the event this ends in divorce."

"First of all, Ms. Bien, as you are probably already aware, getting a divorce in Loo-zee-anna can be difficult," Helene said. "There is nothing as easy as 'no fault' and there has to be a two-year separation first when children are involved."

"But if he does file, he has two years to hide his assets, doesn't he?" Kimly noted. "I have friends with horror stories of how their spouses claimed poverty, then suddenly lived the high life shortly after the divorce decrees."

"That does happen. Of course, he could go to some other state like Nevada for a 'quickie divorce,' where there's only a six-week waiting period."

"And that's why I want my sister to be aware of this Cypress Oil court settlement. She has no idea what assets they have now, but—"

"Minh says we have lots of debt. Lots," Thanh said in her husband's defense.

Once again, Kimly looked skeptical, and continued with a prediction, "His claiming poverty is just him setting the stage."

"Why do you say that, Kimly?" Helene asked.

Kimly looked at Helene. "Mike doesn't even let her have a credit card or checking account. The big man taking care of his little woman. But forget about what they already have, or don't have. If we learn through public records that he gets, let's say, a million dollars in the Cypress Oil case, he will have to account for every penny of that, won't he?" Kimly squeezed her sister's hand while talking, not unaware of how difficult this situation was for the more timid woman.

"You're right," Helene said, "and, Thanh, even if divorce never comes about, you are wiser to know where you stand financially."

"There's one more thing you should be aware of," Kimly told Helene and Simone. "Our parents owned a small fishing fleet on the Gulf. When they died, I took a cash payment from the Pham family, which allowed me to go to college and grad school, and Thanh's half share was in the form of all the boats and equipment which were just folded into the Pham company. I don't think there was anything shady about it. The elder Mister Pham was in charge at that time. But who knows how it looks on record now? Is Thanh considered a part owner of their company?"

"Good points," Helene said.

"Let us get started on this. Discreetly," Simone suggested. "I'll do some preliminary investigative work on Mike Pham, and Helene can research court and business records. We'll get back to you as soon as we have anything. Hopefully, in a week or so."

After the women left, Helene and Simone were alone in the office. BaRa had already left to pick up her children and Adelaide had gone off to the casino.

"So, how are you feeling about the business so far?" Helene asked.

"We're busy, which is good. And I'm enjoying the work, so far. How about you? Your opinion?"

"We're getting good press, though that will die out, thankfully. We're better off operating under the radar. To answer your question, I'm glad we did this." She smiled.

"I am, too," Simone said, and smiled back.

As she was picking up her purse and some folders, Helene asked, "Heavy date tonight?"

"Yeah, right. With a cat. I'm going over to The Gates to pick up Scarlett. I left her there when I moved out suddenly when . . ."

". . . when Cletus moved in," Helene finished for her.

"Right. He's gone now, but my mother says if she wanted a cat, she would have gotten herself one a long time ago. Besides, she thinks it detracts from her image as a hot middle-aged bachelor woman."

"Middle-aged?" Helene scoffed.

"If you live to be a hundred. Now that Mom has discovered Spanx and her inner Kim Kardashian, she sees herself as a swinger of sorts. Oh, not the wild swinger type. That would be contrary to her Catholic upbringing. More like an available lady of a certain age."

Simone walked Helene to the door, which she intended to lock before putting up the "Closed" sign.

They were still laughing over the idea of her mother as a swinger, but only until Simone noticed a motorcycle going by, slowly, with a suited guy driving and a little girl wearing a ballerina outfit and a tiara riding pillion, both of whom waved at her.

"Mercy!" Helene said.

"Yep!" Simone agreed.

"Remember your safe word, Simone. Is it too late to say 'red light, red light'?"

"Way too late."

Chapter Nine

*D*ear Abby, they were not . . .

Adam had a decision to make.

Sonia's plan to move to California had fallen through, and at least for the short-term, she was staying here in Louisiana. Can anyone say, more yoga sex?

On the other hand, in his warped code of moral standards, reconnecting with Sonia would end any possibility of a connection with Simone. Connection in the sexual sense, that was. One man, one woman, at one time.

But he hadn't had sex for weeks, and Sonia was temptation in and out of her tight yoga pants.

And he'd yet to get in Simone's pants of any kind. In other words, no harm done. Easy enough to end a relationship that had never begun. Well, except for the make-out session in her car and the almost phone sex.

Mixed in with these confusing mind games was the

other female in his life, the most important one. Maisie. He was still committed to a single parent role in raising his daughter. No more marriage or relationships that intruded on that bond with his daughter. He insisted on a strict line separating his family life from his love life. Thus far, Sonia had been okay with that. Would Simone? He doubted it, but you never knew. Simone had been burned by a bad marriage, or marriages, just like he had.

Back and forth these thoughts went in his brain, like ping-pong balls. He left his office and went out to ask Mildred if she had any headache pills.

"Ask Luc. I gave him my bottle this morning after he had breakfast with his aunt."

After taking a couple pills, he sank down in the chair in front of Luc's desk. "You have a minute? I have a dilemma." The more he explained, the more Luc grinned, which should have clued him in that seeking advice from a LeDeux was a big mistake.

"Let me get this straight. You're askin' me fer sex advice? Wow! I'm flattered."

Adam started to rise. "Forget about it."

But Luc held up a hand. "No, no, give me a chance. I was just surprised. Most men wouldn't complain about having two women on the line. Hell, most men would have day-of-the-week women if they were given a choice."

"I'm thirty-five years old, Luc, not fifteen."

"First of all, ya gotta know I would pick Simone because that would mean yer part of the LeDeux fam'ly."

"Not if no wedding bells were involved."

"Adam, Adam, Adam! Do you honestly think Tante Lulu would let you escape if you got that close to Simone? I had breakfast with her this morning, and my head still hurts. She's wantin' to provide some entertainment fer that pool party of yers."

"Huh? Do you mean the Swamp Rats?"

"Among other things." Luc waved a hand. "Don't worry. I've almost talked her out of it."

"I wouldn't mind the band, and Maisie would be putting together a playlist if she found out."

"Forget the band fer now. I gotta tell ya, she's buildin' a hope chest fer you, and that's all I'm gonna say on the subject."

"I've heard of those bullshit hope chests."

"Oh, Lord, doan ever let her hear ya say that. They work, my friend. I can attest to that, as will my brothers Remy, René, Tee-John, and Daniel, as well as some male friends of the family. All married now!"

"Stay away from Simone, then. That's your advice," Adam said and felt a heavy weight press down on him.

"No, no, no! I dint say that, *cher*. Jist be careful, and know the consequences."

"That's what I've been doing, and it hasn't got me squat. I'm practically a monk these days."

"Well, ya could always screw till yer blue with the yoga lady . . . and by the way, doan think I'm not imaginin' all that flexibility. Then, when you've had enough of that, you could move on to Simone."

"And you think Simone would wait?"

"Hell, no! I'm still picturin' all those flexible positions."

So much for getting advice from a law partner who has an inborn Cajun gene for teasing. Adam would never hear the end of this.

"I will tell ya one thing," Luc said, more seriously. "When she's The One, you'll know it."

"Yeah, but that's the point. I'm not looking for 'The One.' I'm just looking 'For Now.'"

"Tante Lulu is gonna make bayou mush of you. Hey,

did it ever occur ta you that Simone might have some yoga moves of her own?"

Now, there was an image implanted in his brain like an erotic chip.

If that wasn't stupid enough, he broached the subject with his father that night after dinner. Well, not after dinner, exactly, his father and some friends—male and female—had gone to a casino for dinner and a little gambling. He returned by nine p.m., whistling.

When was the last time I whistled after a date?

When was the last time I had a date?

Really! My sixty-six-year-old dad has more of a social life than I do. Notice I said . . . no, thought . . . social life, not sex life. That would be too bizarre to contemplate.

After he outlined his dilemma to his father, minus the sexual aspects, the old man took his questions seriously, unlike Luc who considered him a moron for not just taking on both of the women, not just at the same time, but probably in the same bed.

"Son, you need to get over this idea you have that all women are alike. Just because Hannah turned out to be a rotten peach doesn't mean that other fruit can't be sweet. That sour taste in your mouth about marriage is just one bad bite. Get over it."

"I know that all women aren't like Hannah, but it's not just me that I'm concerned about. It's Maisie. I don't want her becoming attached to a woman, thinking she'll be some forever kind of mother, then have her go away."

"You'd be surprised at how well kids can adapt. And did you ever weigh the benefits of Maisie having a mother against that risk?"

Adam stiffened. "I do well raising Maisie on my own . . . with your help."

"No one says you don't. For heaven's sake, boy, get the

pike outta your ass. Oh, I forgot. Tante Lulu gave me something tonight to pass on to to you."

"It better not be a friggin' hope chest."

"Huh?" His dad paused as he was tugging something out of his jacket pocket. He handed Adam a small statue. Even before he explained what it was, Adam knew.

"A St. Jude statue? She sent me a St. Jude statue?"

"Yep. St. Jude is the patron saint of hopeless cases," his father explained.

"I know that," he sniped. Hadn't he gone through twelve years of parochial school?

He was feeling a little hopeless, though, he admitted, but only to himself.

"By the way, Tante Lulu was wonderin' if you'd mind some live entertainment at our pool party."

"Entertainment?" He was suspicious. The old lady was devious.

"The Swamp Rats, that band her nephew is in."

He shrugged. Luc had already mentioned the possibility. That sounded harmless enough.

"Another thing . . . that yoga lady friend of yours called this afternoon, and I think Maisie might have invited her to the pool party."

Adam groaned and put his face in his hands. Simone and Sonia, together? Looking down at the statue in the palm of his hand, he muttered, "This is either going to be the party from heaven, or the party from hell."

He could swear the statue smiled.

Keeping score in the game of love . . .

Simone was in the Starr Foods Houma supermarket after work, buying cat food and other pet supplies along with

some take-out food from the deli for her evening's meal . . .
an oyster po' boy (So much for her diet!) and a salad with
raspberry vinaigrette dressing (low-cal, of course). She ran
into Adam and his daughter as she turned away from the
counter and saw them behind her, waiting to be served.

Adam was wearing a Tulane T-shirt and denim shorts
with rubber thongs, and his daughter was all cute little
girl in pigtails and a matching outfit right down to the
rubber thongs, both pairs of which were pink.

"Simone!" Adam said, clearly surprised to see her. In
fact, he was uncomfortable.

And she recognized why, as his eyes darted from her
to his child. It was just like after church. He didn't like his
women mixing with his daughter. Not that she was his
woman, but he put her in that category.

"Adam," she acknowledged with as much grace as she
could when she wanted to smack him with the cat toy that
protruded from her cart, a long stick with a bunch of
feather teasers on the end. Then she turned to his daughter and shook her tiny hand, "Maisie, isn't it? We met after church last week."

"Yes, I remember. Yer Daddy's friend."

That was debatable, especially at the moment.

Adam turned from them and asked the clerk, "Do you
have an order for Lanier?"

Simone bent her knees to put herself more at eye level
with the girl, "Is that your dinner that Daddy's picking up?"

She nodded. "Hot wings fer Daddy and PawPaw, and
mac and cheese fer me, and we're gonna get a fruit tart
from the bakery. Do you like mac and cheese?"

"I love mac and cheese."

"You could come over ta our house and eat with us."

Adam was back and looking alarmed, again.

She should have accepted, just to annoy the ass. But

she wouldn't hurt the kid to hurt him. She rose and said, "Oh, no, honey, I have to get home and feed my cat."

Maisie glanced at Simone's cart, saw the cat toy, and her little eyes lit up. "You have a kitty?"

"I have a cat. Her name is Scarlett."

"We doan have a kitten. Or a puppy." Her lips turned down. "Daddy said we could get one when we moved ta the bayou, but we doan have one yet." She batted her eyelashes at her father as only little girls could.

"Now, Maisie, you know we're waiting until after your birthday in August to go to the animal rescue farm."

"I know, Daddy. But I could go see Miss See-mone's cat, couldn't I?"

"Uh," Adam said.

"Sure," Simone said, giving Adam a dark look. "In fact, why don't you come over right now, after you drop off your PawPaw's portion of the hot wings?"

She was as surprised by her invitation as Adam was, and with the little girl jumping up and down with glee, there was nothing Adam could say, except "Sure!"

As they were both paying for their purchases and leaving the supermarket, Adam leaned over and said, "I don't know what game you're playing, but . . ."

". . . but what?"

"Game on!"

There's a little bit of crazy in all of us . . .

The hell with it!

Adam was sick up to his gullet with the "Should I?"/"Shouldn't I?", "Will I?"/"Won't I?" crap. Life was a gamble, and he was tossing the dice. Let them fall where they may!

Like my big, honkin' fool of a body. Crash, bam, fall-ing!

Maisie was so excited at the prospect of seeing a damn cat that he found himself feeling guilty. But, no, he couldn't give her everything she wanted when she wanted it. Otherwise, they'd have a dog *and* a cat. Forget that, she'd have a pony, too. And a herd of rats running on wheels in a cage. He didn't care if they called them gerbils, they were rats to him.

No, there had to be rules.

Like the rules for relationships you're about to break, his conscience prodded.

When they were climbing the steep stairs to Simone's apartment, which were located on the outside of the building facing the alley, Maisie changed her excitement gears. "She lives in a place *above* her office? Oh, Daddy, that is so cool! Maybe you and me and PawPaw could live in a house . . . an a-part-ment . . . over yer law office. I could see you anytime I wanted."

"Then you wouldn't have a pool," he pointed out. "Or a pool party."

"Oh. Doesn't Miss See-mone swim?"

"I imagine she does. Maybe she has friends with pools, or she could swim in a lake." *And I am not picturing her in a wet bathing suit. Or naked in my pool, after the party's over.*

"What's that yummy smell?" she asked, changing gears again.

"There's a bakery next door."

Her eyes went wide. "Really? I would love to have a bakery next door."

"Then I'd get as fat as a blimp, and your grandfather would sink to the bottom of the bayou when he went fishing, and you'd get a million zits from all that sugar."

"I'm too little fer zits, Daddy. What's a blimp?"

"Never mind. Anyhow, my slim, flawless-skinned angel, we can only stay for a little while. We don't want to make a nuisance of ourselves."

"Oh, Daddy! She likes us."

"How do you know, princess?"

"Everyone likes me," she said, with a lack of humility that was endearing, rather than obnoxious, "and she looks at you kinda funny when yer not lookin'."

"Funny . . . how?"

"Lak I do on Christmas morning when I see my presents fer the first time. Before I unwrap them."

He had to smile. What man wouldn't like the idea of being a woman's special, unwrapped gift? What man wouldn't be imagining the unwrapping?

The door swung open before they even knocked. Simone, smiling warmly—at Maisie, anyhow—motioned them in. "Welcome, welcome! You're my first visitors." She held a big white cat in her arms that she only set down once the door was closed. The cat immediately took off down the hallway with Maisie racing after her.

He handed Simone their take-out bag, and she turned, which caused her ponytail to practically whip him in the face, he was that close. Stepping back slightly, he had only a blip of a moment to take in her luscious body in a black Legal Belles T-shirt and white jogging shorts that barely covered her nicely curved butt and left a long, long stretch of legs bare down to white sneakers. Luckily, she didn't notice his perusal or his grin as he followed her into a small kitchen.

"I'm sorry to inconvenience you this way," he said right off. "I know Maisie pushed you into an invitation."

"No, Adam, your daughter didn't push me. You did."

He arched his brows in question.

"You were being an ass."

He was about to argue, but then said, "You're right. I have issues, obviously."

"Well, don't involve me in your issues."

"You are my issue."

They stared at each other, and he wanted to kiss her so bad he barely restrained himself from reaching out and yanking her into his arms and never letting go. He was fifty percent sure . . . maybe even sixty . . . that she wouldn't resist.

"Let's start over. Hi, I'm Adam Lanier."

"I've heard about you."

"Uh-uh! We're starting over. Clean slate."

"Okay. I'm Simone LeDeux. Welcome to my humble abode."

Fortunately, Maisie yelled then, "Daddy, Daddy, come see what I can do!"

"Go," Simone said. "I'll get the food ready. Will Maisie take sweet tea or milk?"

"Milk," he said. "Me, too, if you have enough."

"Milk and hot wings?" She laughed.

"I left the wings for my father. I figured you'd share your po' boy with me."

"I thought you had a thing about sharing."

"Tsk-tsk!" he said, tapping a forefinger against her lips. "Starting over, remember."

She pretended to nip at his finger, which he wouldn't have minded. In fact, he'd like her to suck on the tip and—

"Uh-uh," she warned, reading the licentious thoughts on his face, apparently.

Note to self: Don't show licentious thoughts. "Sorry. It's hard to stand so close to the fire and not get hot."

"Puh-leeze!"

She wasn't going to let him get away with anything.

Switching gears again, he told her, "I also brought half of the fruit tart for dessert."

"Are you trying to sweeten me up?"

"Oh, yeah!"

She shook her head at him. "What am I going to do with you?"

"I have some ideas."

"I bet you do."

They both went into the living room to watch Maisie play with the cat. In fact, Simone got down on the floor to show his daughter some of the cat's tricks. Meanwhile he checked out her apartment.

It was sparsely furnished with newly refinished cypress wood floors. Probably a work in progress since she'd only moved here a few weeks ago.

A woven, gold area rug sat in the middle of the room, which was painted a warm rust color with a low sofa and two matching chairs upholstered in shades of tan, green, and orange, arranged about a circular coffee table. There didn't appear to be a TV set, a must for any bachelor pad, but maybe there was one in the bedroom, which he could only see partially through a half-open door. A bay window, facing the street, held a window seat with soft red cushions . . . a perfect spot for reading that was probably the cat's favorite spot. Maisie would have all her dolls spread out there like a private, little girl alcove.

After they ate their dinner on the coffee table, he sat on the sofa next to Simone, watching Maisie cuddle with the cat and make little cooing noises that she probably thought the cat would understand. Maybe it did. Adam wasn't a big fan of cats, but he would put up with one, if that was the pet Maisie decided on. His father was trying to influence her toward a black Lab, which had been the breed of Adam's youth. Personally, he didn't care, except he didn't want a really big dog, or a really small one, either. His dad would be the one in charge of training the mutt, or cat, while Adam was at work. In other words, it would be whatever Maisie wanted, or whatever caught her eye, or heartstrings, the day they finally went to a shelter. Except for a pony . . . or rats.

He could see that Maisie was practically asleep. They would have to leave soon. He reached over and ran a fingertip along the edge of Simone's jaw so she would look at him. "Thanks for having us here. I know you would have rather we didn't come."

"And I know you didn't want to come . . . and no double entendres."

"I have reasons for wanting to separate my family life from my personal life," he tried to explain.

"Because you think I'm unsuitable company for your daughter."

"No!"

"Yes! Be honest. I'm a woman who's been married three times. Somehow that makes me kind of immoral. Certainly not the mother figure you want your daughter to look up to."

"Whoa, whoa, whoa! No one said anything about mother figures. I have no intention of getting married again, and I was under the impression you felt the same way."

"I do, but that doesn't mean I can't be insulted when I'm considered a slut."

"I don't know you well enough to consider you a slut. If I thought you were a tramp, that would definitely be reason to keep you away from my daughter. But there are other reasons for my rule."

"A rule now?"

He ignored her sarcasm. "Maisie tends to attach herself to people easily. It's not so much that she's needy, as overly friendly. She doesn't understand when people don't reciprocate, or suddenly disappear."

"Like your women do?"

"Like they would if I introduced them to her. I'm not much of a long-term relationship guy."

"I'm not stupid, Adam. If I had a child and was raising it as a single parent, I would be real careful about introducing a third person into the relationship."

"So we're good then," he leaned over to kiss her.

She ducked away and stood. "Hell, no, we're not good. Let me ask you a question. These short-term relationships of yours . . . do they involves dates . . . you know, dinner, movies, concerts, that kind of thing? Or just wham-bam booty calls?"

His red face gave him away, and she started to laugh.

"Not always," he protested.

She continued to laugh.

"Okay, Ms. Smart Ass, would you like to go out on a date sometime?"

"I don't know. Try me again after you've had a chance to stop hyperventilating."

"I am not . . ." He stood and tried to grab for her—he was laughing now, too—but the coffee table was between them. And Maisie began to whine as children did when they were overtired.

"Say good night, sweetie," he told his daughter as he picked her up.

Maisie lifted her sleepy head from his shoulder and said, "Good night, Miss See-mone. Good night, Scarlett."

"Good night, Mary Sue. Sweet dreams." With one hand she held the door open for Adam to pass through; in the other arm she held the cat who would probably dart out into a neighborhood she was still unfamiliar with.

"Good night, Simone. Sweet dreams," he whispered as he leaned down and kissed her lightly on the lips. Even that light brush of lips on lips was erotic madness waiting to happen. *If this is Cajun Crazy, then welcome to the funny farm*, he decided with sigh of surrender. "We have a date . . . sometime. . . . right?"

She hesitated, looking from him to his daughter and back to him. She could have cut him off at the knees then with one of her sarcastic remarks. Instead, she sighed, too. "Right."

If she was the honey, who would the bee be? . . .

Simone was falling in love, which both exhilarated and scared her. Last night's visit from Adam and his daughter only cemented the feelings that were already there.

Love was nothing new to Simone, of course, being almost thirty years old and "dating" since she was fourteen. Married three times. Four long-term relationships (of more than six months). Innumerable dates. Just a few . . . okay, three . . . one-night stands.

That was a lot of baggage for any man to take on.

It was sad, really, this endless quest for a forever kind of love. Did she even believe anymore in the possibility of "true love"?

The answer was yes. But she just wasn't sure it was in the cards for her.

As a result, she was going to tread carefully this time, not just because Adam was Cajun (her bane), or because any relationship they had would be short-lived (or not, which might be even worse), but she also worried about getting involved with a man who had a child. She didn't want to hurt Maisie any more than her father did.

That being said, she was keeping her emotions to herself. Not even her best friend could know. No more jumping impulsively into a new man's arms . . . or bed.

Simone and Helene were discussing the two most important cases on their schedule . . . Marcus Pitot and Mike Pham. They were sitting on the back patio of Legal Belles eating a take-out lunch from Sweet Buns Bakery next door . . . chicken salad on homemade croissants, replete with crunchy green grapes and walnuts, topped with leaves of crisp local arugula. The pitcher of sweet tea was from her own fridge.

"I wish you could be the one working Pham, but I'm afraid he might recognize you," Helene said.

"My picture hasn't been in the papers or on TV whenever Legal Belles was discussed," she argued. "And he's at least five years older than I am, so we didn't go to school together or at the same time."

"Yeah, but you know what the bayou is like. A small community, in many ways, encompassing many towns. And the grapevine is a Ripley's wonder."

"Guess you're right," Simone conceded. "And there's that concern over a conflict of interest with LeDeux & Lanier."

Helene nodded, probably thinking of the ties with Simone's half brother Luc, not knowing precisely how close Simone was to "ties" with Adam.

"Anyhow, I'm thinking about hiring that new woman, Cecile Bastian, to do some legwork, following the creep, checking out his personal contacts. CiCi has a remarkable talent for digging out the least detail that others might overlook. Years of detective type experience."

"Sounds good. I worked with CiCi a few years back on an embezzlement case."

"And the actual sting operation . . . well, Sabine would

be good for that. In fact, she's already started since she finished up that Sam Ellison case."

"The one where the wife suspected the husband of cheating, but he wasn't?"

"Yeah."

"Wonders never cease."

"Tell me about it." They both laughed. Then Simone asked, "Have you had a chance to check the public records on Mad Mike's dealings?"

"Oh, yeah. Kimly Bien has reason to be concerned on her sister's behalf. The Pham business is solely owned by the Pham family, father and son only. Nowhere does Thanh have a share, either in ownership, stocks, or fixed assets. In fact, the home she lives in is listed only in her husband's name. He, by the way, also owns a condo on Grand Isle."

"Surprise, surprise! What can she do?"

"Lots. I'm going to prepare a lawsuit for her, seeking an appropriate share in the business, full ownership of her home, and other financial remuneration. But I won't file until the Cypress Oil settlement is announced or until Mike Pham has filed for divorce, or both."

"It should come soon, according to this morning's paper."

"Right. Also, I understand that he went to Las Vegas last weekend. That might just be a coincidence, but on the other hand, remember what I said about the six-week divorce available there. He could have been renting a short-term residence. I suspect he's already started the divorce application process. I have a detective working on that now."

"He's a piece of work," Simone said, shaking her head with disgust.

"Yes, but unfortunately not so unusual. Now, can you

set up another meeting for us with Kimly and Thanh?" She checked her iPhone calendar. "How about Tuesday afternoon?"

"I'll put BaRa on that right away and confirm with you."

"Now, onto the Pitot case. Are you willing to do the groundwork yourself? To be the honey trap?"

"I am."

"You'll have to spend some time down in Nawleans where he lives and this club operates."

"No problem."

"Be careful. These are powerful men, and women, who don't like being thwarted."

She shrugged. That was nothing new. Power corrupts, whether in politics or private life.

"Maybe you and Gabe should work it as a couple."

"That's a good idea. Let me talk to him and work out a plan."

"I would feel better in this particular op if you had a partner."

"You mean I would be safer with a man protecting little ol' me?"

Helene laughed and put up her hands in surrender. "Sorry. I keep forgetting you've been a cop and know better than most men how to protect yourself."

"I shouldn't be so sensitive," she said in response, not wanting Helene to feel bad.

Helene checked her watch, then stood suddenly. "Damn! I didn't realize it was so late. I have to be in court in a half hour . . . a contested will case. Call me." Grabbing her shoulder bag, she rushed away.

Her next appointment wasn't for another hour, so Simone took a moment to just sit and relax, sipping at the last of her tea.

She wondered what Adam was doing now. He might be in court, as well. What would he think of her posing as a swinger, looking to join a sex club with her husband, Gabe? He would probably want to halt her activity, a protective action much like Helene's. Or he might just walk away in disdain, considering it another in her lifetime of wanton activities. Or he might offer to take Gabe's place and take part in the sting with her. Now, that was a scenario that would never happen but posed lots of interesting possibilities.

She had to smile at her mind wandering. Cajun Crazy again, that's what her mother would say. Or was it just plain Cajun Love.

Simone was cleaning up the lunch debris, still smiling, when she heard a voice call out from inside the office, "Yoo-hoo!"

It was Tante Lulu.

Simone did the only thing any sane woman would. She ducked through the back gate and down the alley. Suddenly, she felt the need for a noontime jog to the park. And it didn't matter that she heard thunder in the distance.

Chapter Ten

*T*here *was something fishy going on . . .*

It was crazy. Adam knew it was crazy, and still he was driving down the empty streets of Houma in the pre-dawn hours of Saturday morning with Maisie still half asleep beside him.

They were going fishing.

And the crazy part? He was heading toward Simone's apartment to invite her to go with them.

Sometime during the middle of the night when he'd been unable to sleep, it occurred to him that all his past relationships, once he'd been reality-checked by his wife with her liberal marital views, had been geared strictly toward sex with a permanent relationship, meaning involvement with his daughter, being an impossibility. And it wasn't as satisfying as it should be . . . at least not after ten years of short-term, somewhat meaningless hookups.

Part of it was probably due to his approaching thirty-sixth birthday.

What if, his sleep-deprived brain had asked him, he went about this in the opposite direction? Invite a woman he liked into his family circle, then see where it led in terms of sex and a more permanent relationship.

I know—crazy.

And it would make a lot more sense if the woman he invited into his family cocoon was more librarian-ish or younger and therefore not so "experienced" or anyone but Simone LeDeux.

It was what it was, he said to himself, and told Maisie, "Wait here, honey, while I go up and get Simone." He parked his father's pickup truck, which he'd borrowed, in the alley behind the office building, as the sun was just beginning to rise in a warm haze. It was going to be a scorcher by afternoon.

Maisie awakened totally then, blinking her eyes with surprise at her surroundings. "Can I come, too? Maybe we kin bring Scarlett with us?"

"No cats. And you stay here where I can see you so we can get out to the bayou before the fish go to sleep." He'd told her the same old fish tale his dad used to tell him, that fish slept under rocks and deep underwater when the sun was hottest overhead. He didn't know if it was true or not. Besides, they were going for crawfish as well as the usual bayou fish—bream, bass, catfish, or sac-au-lait (white crappies).

He was wearing his usual fishing gear—a purple-and-gold LSU baseball cap that read "Geaux Tigers" in faded letters; his lucky denim shirt with the sleeves torn off and a fishing license clipped to his breast pocket; khaki cargo shorts with lots of pockets for hooks and line and even bait, which might not have been washed since the last time he'd hit the bayou; and sockless, tattered, once-white sneakers. He hadn't bothered to shower or shave and he probably smelled kind of fishy. In other words, cool fisherman. He hoped.

He leaned on the doorbell of her back door until finally it opened a crack, and then wider as Simone realized who it was. He'd obviously awakened her from a deep sleep. Her long, dark hair was a mess of waves and tangles and bed-mussed erotica (erotica being in the eye of the beholder). She wore no make-up and there was a sleep crease on her one cheek where she must have lain on a wrinkled sheet. She wore a pink sleep shirt that hit only mid-thigh and was saved from being Victoria's Secret hot and sexy by the grouchy Garfield cat on the front with the caption "Seriously?" Her toes, painted a bright red, were curled against the cool floorboards.

"Adam! What are you doing here? What's happened?" Then she seemed to take in his attire and added, "Are you nuts?"

"A little bit. What's on your agenda for today?"

"Huh?" She blinked sleepily and waved to Maisie who had opened the electric window of the car door and called out to her.

"Hey, Miss See-mone? Where's Scarlett? Kin she come out and play?"

"Uh, not right now. She's asleep."

"Do you have to work today?" He clarified his first question to Simone and reached over to tug on one of the long strands of hair that was caught on the drool by her lips.

She slapped his hand away and said, "No. Not really. I was going to do laundry and wash my hair and . . ." Midway, she yawned widely and he got a good look at her even, white teeth.

"We're going fishing," he declared. Then he thought of something. "Do you like fishing? I mean, have you ever even been fishing?" That wasn't such an outrageous question. He knew—had dated—women who wouldn't touch a fish, unless it came from a can.

She straightened with affront. "Ah do declare, Mistah Lanier," she said in an exaggerated Cajun drawl. "Ah was born 'n bred on the bayou. We learn ta fish before we kin walk. Talk about!"

He grinned.

"What are you up to, Adam? Why are you here?" she asked, the expression on her face turning serious.

"I have no idea." He shrugged. "It seemed like a good idea."

She hesitated, staring at him.

"Wanna go?" He prodded her big toe with the tip of his sneaker.

She nodded, reluctantly.

"Then get your ass in gear, darlin'." He took her by the shoulders and turned her around, giving her a little push and a pinch on the butt. "Hurry up and get dressed."

She yelped at the pinch, but walked away from him, giving her hips a little extra sway, just to get the last "word" in. Smiling, he went down to the car and told Maisie, "I see the lights turning on in the Sweet Buns Bakery. What say we go over and see if we can talk them into some food for our outing?" He'd brought a cooler with bottled water and lemonade and several pieces of fruit that had been sitting in a bowl on the kitchen table—bananas, apples, and grapes. He'd figured to buy something more substantial along the way. Or else, Maisie would become bored before noon and they'd eat when they got home.

"Yippee!" she said.

They came away with several bags of leftover dinner sandwiches from last night—still fresh, the proprietor assured them—and warm sugar-crusted beignets right from the oven. Simone was already at the car waiting for them. She was wearing a baseball cap, too—Chicago PD—with her ponytail pulled through the hole in back, a black tank top tucked into a pair of red, belted Bermuda shorts, and flip-flops. She carried a huge canvas shoulder carryall that probably served as a gym bag.

Maisie ran up and hugged Simone around the waist, saying, "I'm glad yer comin' with us, Miss See-mone."

This was just the kind of thing he'd always been fearful of regarding his daughter and his "women." His daughter was so needy, and she latched on to people too easily.

So, it was surprising, even to him, when he looked at Simone and said, "Me, too."

Gone fishin' . . . and other stuff . . .

Adam hadn't had so much fun in years.

Maisie had insisted she sit in the backseat of the truck with Simone, so Adam drove them like a redneck chauffeur in a pickup truck. They all laughed at the image they presented.

They stopped at Boudreaux's General Store for bait, where they covered all their bases with a selection of catalpa worms, night crawlers, minnows, chicken livers, and canned corn. Not surprising to him at this point was the fact that Simone didn't shrink back or go all "Oooh, oooh!" at sight of the slimy critters. Either it was the cop in her who'd seen slimier things, or it was the Cajun who had, indeed, done her share of fishing, or it was just

Simone, who was different than the average girl . . .
thank God!

The old-timey store also sold tackle, crushed shells for
driveways, and Avon beauty products. Simone bought a
fishing license, just to be legal. And Adam bought some
chips and a jar of Mrs. Boudreaux's homemade spicy
pickles to go with their sandwiches. He also got paper
plates and napkins as well as several bags of ice and a
Styrofoam cooler for any fish or crabs they might catch.

It was a good thing Adam had borrowed his father's
truck because his Lexus never would have made it over
the rough roads that led to the remote fishing hole he'd
chosen, far enough away from town or oil company con-
tamination that might spoil the fish for eating. It was a
lovely spot showcasing the best of what the bayou had to
offer. Bald cypress trees in the water with their knobby
knees protruding upward here and there. Age-old live
oaks dripping gray moss. Myriad floral bushes exuding
beautiful scents, in contrast to the swampy smells of mud
and decaying vegetation. And, of course, the slow-
moving, coffee-colored stream that was hopefully teem-
ing with fish.

While he cased the area for danger—snakes, gators,
red ants, and the like—Simone spread out a large, tightly
woven mat from her carryall, which was probably intended to be a beach blanket, but served well as their picnic tablecloth. On it, she arranged the carryout bags and
other items, making several trips back and forth to the
bed of the truck. He was pleased to see that she involved
Maisie in her "work." Meanwhile, he arranged the rods
and reels and long-handled nets and bait at what he
deemed a good spot by the stream.

It was the kind of spot where a man, or woman, liked
to just sit and enjoy the peaceful sounds of the bayou—

the rush of the current, the various bird calls, the rustle of leaves in the slight breeze—which was impossible with Maisie. In her excitement, she just couldn't stop talking and laughing. Which, of course, was a good sound to him.

"Betcha I catch a gazillion fish t'day," she told Simone as they smoothed out the edges of the blanket.

"At least," Simone agreed. "When I was your age, my father took me noodling for catfish up the bayou, and I got one so big we ate catfish for a month. Noodling is when you stand in the muddy water and tickle the fish with your fingers until you latch on and pull the critter to the surface."

Adam wondered idly if she meant her birth father, Valcour LeDeux, or her stepfather, Ernest Daigle. It had to be the latter, of course, since Valcour had never had much to do with any of his kids as far as Adam knew.

"I know, I know," Maisie said, jumping up and down. "Me and PawPaw saw it on Animal Planet." She turned toward Adam, assuming he'd overheard, "Kin we noodle t'day, Daddy? Kin we, kin we?"

"Not today, sweetie. The waters here aren't conducive to noodling."

At her downcast expression, he added, "We'll catch the old-fashioned way. Probably two gazillion."

By then, Maisie was off on another subject. "I lak yer nail polish, Miss See-mone." She was looking at Simone's bright red toenails. Her fingernails were short and unadorned, though nicely trimmed. Another remnant of her police days, he assumed. Hard to gather blood evidence with two-inch nails.

"I like your polish, too," Simone was saying. "That color of pink is my fav. Did you do your nails yourself?"

Both her tiny fingernails and toenails were neon pink,

even though Adam had encouraged her to go for clear, or at least pale pink. Try being a grown man in the cosmetics aisle at the drugstore picking out nail enamel, arguing with a five-year-old girl with a taste for pizz-azz.

"Nope. Mah daddy did them fer me. I'm too little ta get inside the cute-culls." She gave her face a little moue of disappointment.

Simone glanced up and met his gaze, with raised eyebrows.

He just shrugged.

And Maisie was off on another subject. "Do ya have any children?"

She shook her head.

"Doan ya lak children?"

"I love children."

"Are ya gonna have children some day?"

"Maybe. Why do you ask, honey?"

"'Cause I'd lak ta have a brother or sister ta play with. I was gonna ask Santa fer one las' Christmas, but I wanted another American Girl doll more."

Whoa, whoa, whoa! This was the first he'd heard about her wanting a sibling. And why was she looking to Simone for a brother or sister?

Simone was laughing, not at Maisie's words, but at the dismay that must have been apparent on his face.

"You could always ask next Christmas," she encouraged Maisie, just to tease him, he could tell.

Maisie bit her bottom lip, a habit she'd developed when deep in thought. "Maybe. I'm almost six years old, y'know. Pretty soon I'll be too old fer dolls. I think I would be a good babysitter, though, don't you, Miss See-mone."

"I'm sure of it. All that doll baby practice!"

"Enough dawdling, you two," he said then.

"First we need to put on plenty of sunscreen and insect repellant," she cautioned.

"Right," he agreed. He wouldn't have forgotten if he wasn't so distracted by talk about babies, or by Simone herself. He was further distracted over and over again as she expertly wielded her rod and line over the bayou waters or helped him net a fish, or when she showed him an old Cajun method for catching crawfish by skimming a leafy limb over the water near the muddy banks till the mudbugs climbed on and they were able to scoop them up.

By noon, they'd caught two large catfish and a one-pound catfish, which was small by bayou standards but a keeper because a wildly ecstatic Maisie had been the winner of that bout and she wanted to show it off to her grandfather. They also had an impressive bushel of crawfish. They'd released a lot of smaller fish they'd caught—trout, bass, and crappies.

It would have been enough fishing for Adam for the day, especially since they'd depleted all the food and most of the drinks, but Maisie had been a die-hard angler, claiming there were lots more fish to be caught. Right now, the die-hard was fast asleep on the blanket, her face resting on her folded arms, her little butt in the air.

"Should we wake her?" Simone asked as she packed up some of the empty food containers and put them in a bag for trash to be carried back home.

"Not yet," he said, sitting against a tree, his long legs stretched out before him. Thank God Simone had remembered the bug repellant. Insects could be seen buzzing over the water in hordes. He patted a spot beside him, indicating she should come sit beside him.

She hesitated but then plopped down next to him.

He put an arm around her shoulders, tucking her closer. She didn't resist, which he took as a good sign.

"This is fun," she said then. "Thanks for inviting me. Will you be cooking all this fish when you get home?"

"I won't. *We* will."

"I don't have a pot big enough for a crab boil," she told him.

"I do. We can stop at my house and cook them. Maybe stop for some fresh corn on the way. If I call my dad, he'll have some sides prepared before we get there."

"That sounds an awful lot like a relationship."

He didn't say anything.

But then she asked, "Scared?"

"More like resigned."

"Thanks a bunch."

"I didn't mean that as an insult." He kissed the top of her head to demonstrate his sincerity. There were a few bits of duckweed in the dark strands. Her baseball cap had fallen off when she and Maisie had been in the stream trying to noodle. To no avail, of course, as he'd warned them. In any case, the cap was probably out in the Gulf by now.

"Well, I'm scared, too. A little. I'm way too scarred by past heartaches to open myself up again."

"Scared, scarred, whatever! Wanna make out a little while the kiddo is asleep?"

She laughed. "You do have a way with words."

"I have a better way with other things," he said and lowered his mouth to hers.

She resisted at first, leaning away from him, which caused his lips to just skim hers. But he cupped her face in his hands and held her firmly in place so he could kiss her properly, which he did.

Not to brag, but he was a good kisser.

The problem with many men was that they considered sex a mad rush of a trip from start to finish, with finish being the "good stuff." He, on the other hand, considered every spot along the road to be "good stuff." The kissing, definitely. Caresses, all kinds, all places. Looking—just looking—at the scenery . . . the breasts, the belly, the butt, the knees, the toes, the small of a woman's back, and the mysterious valley between the highways. Intercourse. The final climax. And then the afterglow.

Some men boasted about the number of times they'd taken a woman in one night. He much preferred one time, all night long. Or two.

He wet her lips with his tongue. He moved his mouth back and forth across hers until he got the perfect fit (yes, a perfect fit of lips, not that other perfect fit), and then he kissed her deep and openmouthed. Tongues. Teeth. Hungry, hungry kisses. Then slower and gentler, seeking. Back to wet and demanding.

She moaned against his open mouth, and he no longer had to cradle her head because she had her arms around him, kissing him back, with as much hunger, and, yes, expertise, as he wielded. There was something to be said for a woman who knew what she wanted and went for it, especially when she was with a man who knew what he wanted (everything) and went for it.

"You taste like Mrs. Boudreaux's pickles," he said.

"That is just great."

"I like pickles."

"Well, good, then."

Somehow, she was half-lying across his lap with his one arm under her shoulders holding her up. How had that happened? Had he tugged her across, or had she shimmied over herself? No matter.

Ooh, this was dangerous . . . a temptation not to be fulfilled with his daughter sleeping several feet away and likely to awaken at any inopportune moment. He wanted to tug both her tank top and bra straps down enough to expose her breasts so that he could look and touch and taste. He wanted to use the heel of his hand against the vee of her legs and bring her to a small, pre-orgasm, an appetizer, so to speak. He wanted to be inside her and feel her welcome.

And his daughter was awake.

He sensed her presence, hovering over them, before she spoke. "Whatcha doin', Daddy?"

Little Maisie was becoming his safety valve against unwise decisions. Because apparently he was incapable of being wise anymore when it came to Simone.

Simone jumped up and off his lap.

He put a paper plate over his crotch. "Um, just talking, sweetheart. Are you ready to go home?"

She nodded. "I hafta pee first."

"Okay, but you'll have to go in the bushes. I'll take you."

"No. I will," Simone said. "Us girls have to stick together." She grabbed a couple napkins and an empty plastic grocery bag for trash, along with her carryall, then led his daughter away.

"Be careful of snakes," he warned.

"Not to worry," Simone yelled over her shoulder. "I have a pistol in my carryall."

What?

Did she really?

Probably.

Shaking his head in wonder, he reaffirmed in his mind what he'd already thought before. Simone was different from all the women he'd known before.

And he was pretty sure that was a good thing.

Planning a party . . . a sex party, that was . . .

Simone met with Gabe on Monday morning to discuss strategy for the Marcus Pitot case.

"First of all, we have to set up a temporary home in the Nawleans area," she told him. "Even if we're claiming to be newcomers to the area, we should at least have an apartment."

"I know the perfect place," Gabe said. "My parents go north for the summer months. We can use their place. It's not big, but it's in an exclusive, gated community outside the city."

"Will they mind?"

"Nah. In fact, they'd get a kick out of being associated in any way with a sex ring. My mother used to be a preacher."

She arched her brows at that. "Must have been a pretty progressive church."

"Not really. She just has a great sense of humor."

"Okay, so we have a base of operation. Who are we?"

"I'm thinking that I'll be a doctor."

"Isn't that a little risky? You could be caught in a mistake if someone asks a question about your work."

"Again, I rely on my parents. My dad was a proctologist before he retired. You do not want to know everything I know about hemorrhoids."

She had to laugh. "Some family!"

"Yeah, and my sister Faye is a forensics scientist in Los Angeles, and my little brother Eli is studying sports medicine at UCLA."

"Why aren't you on the West Coast if you want a career in acting?"

"I was, but my girlfriend, Livia, is finishing her PhD at Tulane. I'll stay while she's here, one more year. Then, we'll probably go back."

Wow! Gabe was proving to be lots more interesting than she'd realized. Maybe that was true of all people, delve a little deeper and you'd be surprised at what you discovered.

Like Adam.

She had to smile, just thinking about him and the day she'd spent with him Saturday. They ended up at his house, cooking the crawfish and catfish they'd caught, along with the corn on the cob they'd picked up on the way home. Adam's father, Frank Lanier, sliced an assortment of some wonderful tomatoes fresh from his garden and drizzled olive oil over them with salt and pepper. Yum! In addition, his dad had whipped up a super broccoli and cauliflower pasta salad, the vegetables also from his garden.

They'd eaten out by the pool on a screened-in patio. The bugs got vicious by evening, or in the daytime when attracted by food or water.

Maisie had talked nonstop and shown Simone her American Girl collection up in her pretty lavender bedroom. "It's not pink and it's not purple. Lavender is mah favorite color," she told Simone. The cutie! She also talked about the dog, or cat, she was going to get for her birthday. Unless she changed her mind and wanted another doll.

Simone had also talked a lot with Adam's father who was a retired New Orleans policeman, comparing notes of the jobs they'd covered. She had seen Adam raise his brows a time or two when she mentioned some of her edgier cases, like the time she'd rappelled out of a three-story building when being chased by a drug dealer, or when she'd infiltrated a female biker gang in Chicago for two months. Maisie had her repeat the story of how she'd gotten a medal for saving a drowning girl.

Frank was an old-fashioned guy, priding himself on having been a beat cop his entire career, never aspiring to be a detective or in a supervisory position. "We got to know the people in those days. You can bet there wasn't so much crime then, that's for damn sure. Forget I used a bad word, Maisie. If I saw any drug dealing in my neighborhood, I just whomped the boy on the side of the head and sent him home to his mother, who would whomp him twice as hard."

They had all laughed at his tactics, which would be deemed police brutality in today's politically correct society.

"You never whomped me," Maisie had pointed out.

Her grandfather had touseled her curly head. "That's because you're an angel who never deserves whomping."

At the end of the evening, Adam had driven her back to her apartment, his father having offered to put Maisie to bed. It was a sign of how tired they all were that neither Maisie or Simone complained . . . Maisie about having to go to bed so early, Simone about being alone with Mr. Temptation.

Adam had surprised her by not asking to come inside when he dropped her off. Oh, he kissed her. A lot. Till her knees turned to jelly and she was moaning into his open mouth. He'd explained, "The first time we get together, and I mean that in the Biblical sense, I want to take my time. I want us both to be wide awake and know what we're doing. I figure I will need at least three hours to do the job properly."

Three hours? "You are so full of it."

"No. Delayed gratification, darlin'. It makes the meal all the more satisfying."

She wouldn't let him get the last word, though. As she'd given him one last peck on the lips, she'd told him, with an exaggerated moue of disappointment, "I guess I went without panties today for nothing. Oh, well!" And she'd shut her door on his gawping face. She'd heard his laughter on the other side of the door, though.

She was beginning to think that humor had been missing in lots of her other relationships. Love *and* laughter, that was the combination she should look for this time.

If she was looking.

Hah! How could she help but be looking?

"Why do you have the loopy grin on your face again?" Gabe asked her.

They were sitting in her office, she behind her Lucite desk, and he in the chair on the other side. She shoved a sheet of paper toward him. "These are notes from Mrs. Pitot on places her husband and his club members often hang out. I suggest we just try going to each of these until we make a connection. We don't want to be overt in making contact. It has to appear accidental, at first."

"I agree," Gabe said.

"Let's start with The Hangout, that bar up near the Pitot lodge."

Gabe nodded. "Y'know, Mrs. Pitot is going to an awful lot of trouble and expense to get the goods on her husband, just in case he threatens to leave her."

"She can afford it. And, frankly, she's probably wise to get her ducks in a row for the time when he takes off with Suzy Snowflake, or the next sweet young thang. That's what rich old guys do."

"Cynical, cynical!" Gabe chided.

"A fact."

"And she doesn't want us to go to the police or anything, right?"

"Right. Although I have warned her that if I witness illegal activities of a certain type, I have no choice."

"Such as?"

"Forced participants. Pedophilia. Danger."

Gabe nodded. "How far are we going to carry this thing? I mean, you and me. Naked? Shaking the sheets? Ménages?" He waggled his eyebrows at her. "Whips and chains?"

She laughed. "Not that far. Don't get any ideas. We can

pretend to be into whatever they do, but I personally don't intend to do any of it. What you do is your choice."

"Livia would kill me," he said. "So when do you want to do this thing?"

"How about . . ." She checked her calendar. "How about next week?" She made that suggestion because she had a date—an actual date—with Adam for next Saturday. She figured that once they started the Pitot investigation, she might be spending several days away from Houma. She didn't want to have to cancel at the last minute if something came up in New Orleans.

"Oh, one more thing. If you're going to be a doctor, what am I going to be?"

"Hmmm," Gabe said, then grinned as he surveyed her body. "How about a former stripper?"

Chapter Eleven

*G*ive me that old-time . . . seduction . . .

Adam was getting ready for his big date with Simone. And, man, did that make him seem old!

Most single people he knew either hooked up for sex or traveled in groups to parties or bars where they then hooked up for sex. Hardly anyone under the age of thirty dated anymore, or so he was told by TV and the news media, and some of his bachelor friends. Of course, he was thirty-five. Not that his age should make any difference. Or should it?

He didn't mind giving dating a shot, though. He kind of liked the idea of an old-fashioned courtship. *That has got to be a Tante Lulu word. Even Dad isn't that behind the times. More like* Little House on the Prairie–*ish. Yeah, that's me. A big ol' Michael Landon.* Not that this courtship with Simone was leading to anything serious, like marriage, God forbid. Yet. Never. Maybe never.

Oh, hell, he was overanalyzing everything.

He'd even had his hair cut . . . oh, not short short. But the little pony tail was gone. He was making some kind of half-baked declaration of new beginnings.

"Dad-dy!" Maisie had said when he came in from the barbershop. "Ya look jist lak Justin Bieber."

What? That was not the look he was going for.

His father had said, "Nah. He looks more like Ryan Gosling in *La La Land*. Ya goin' ta trip the light fantastic t'night, son?"

Also not the look he'd been going for. If there was any tripping to be done, it would probably be actual tripping, not some frou-frou dancing in the streets. *Frou-frou? Oh, my God! Another Tante Lulu word!* If anything, he'd prefer to be Christian Grey in *Fifty Shades of Grey*, but, no, his hair was too short for Adam's taste. Whatever!

The house was a mess of game equipment being put together for the Fourth of July pool party to be held in a few weeks, like pool ping-pong paddles and a net. Thus far, thirty people had indicated they would come. He feared it would be lots more than that.

He was wearing a dark blue suit, pale blue shirt, and a blue striped tie when he picked up Simone at seven-thirty. He was taking her to a restaurant that featured fine dining and dancing. The last time he'd been on a date, it had been with Hannah, at Brennan's in New Orleans, after which he went home to relieve the babysitter and she'd gone off to one of her other "dates." *Is it still a date if it involves more than one man?*

He might have been a little embarrassed over the extra care he'd taken with his appearance, but he soon saw after knocking on Simone's door that she had done the same. Wearing a red dress with thin straps (*She must not be wearing a bra.*) that molded her body right down to her upper knees and black strappy high heels, she was dressed for a night on the town. Her dark hair was tucked off either side of her face with combs. Her make-up appeared to be nothing but pure Southern suntan (probably expertly applied cosmetics) but highlighted by crimson lipstick to match her dress. He noticed a light musky scent rising from her skin when he leaned forward (with her high heels she was almost his height) to kiss her cheek in greeting.

"Don't you look handsome tonight?" she said as he helped her with a hand under her elbow down the steps and over to his Lexus.

He gave a little bow and a whistle. "Likewise, darlin'."

"Oh, that's not fair. I never should have told you how I'm affected by that word."

Huh? Oh. She means the "darlin'" drawl. "All's fair in . . . whatever," he said.

Simone had to laugh, staring at Adam as he slid into the driver's seat. The fool couldn't even say the word *love* aloud without breaking out in a sweat. "Where are we going?"

"The Chateau. They have a band and a dance floor for after dinner. Is that okay?"

"Perfect."

On the way to restaurant, he told her funny stories about the upcoming pool party that was getting out of hand. "My daughter has become a miniature Bill Gates and Martha Stewart combined. She uses her laptop—yes, my daughter has a laptop, a cheap one without bells and whistles—where she has all these files related to the party: guests, food, entertainment, fireworks, and so on. Then she's been hitting Martha Stewart's website for recipes."

"She knows how to maneuver around the Internet like that?"

"Oh, yeah, with some help from my dad and a friend's older sister. But that's the good part. The bad part is that my father's the cook in the family, and the two of them have been going at it like cats and dogs over the menu. Dad wants hamburgers and hot dogs on the grill, with some salads and a flag cake. Maisie wants crab-cake sliders, s'mores made on his grill with Godiva chocolate and homemade graham crackers, blueberry coleslaw, and tomatoes stuffed with shrimp-infused quinoa."

"Quinoa? I can hardly pronounce that myself."

"Yeah, quinoa. Which is just chewy rice, if you ask me. Anyhow, my dad's fussy about his grill and marshmallows dripping onto those polished grates is enough to make his eyes roll back in his head, but when she mentioned his tomatoes . . . well, you have to know my father is possessive about his heirloom tomatoes."

"I saw how proud he was of his garden when I was at your house," she interjected. "And especially those delicious tomatoes. He's a Master Gardener, isn't he?"

Adam nodded. "Bottom line, I don't need to buy any fireworks, there are enough sizzling in my house."

Simone was laughing so hard by then that she had to dab at the tears in her eyes with a tissue. "Whose idea was it to have a party?"

"Maisie's, of course. Egged on by my father. They supposedly got the idea from one of the numerous Food Channel shows that my father watches. Apparently, they heard one of the hosts say that when you move into a new home you're obligated to have a housewarming party. Then Maisie decided it had to have a theme. Thus, the Fourth of July."

"She's adorable."

Adam looked at her and smiled. "Yeah, she is."

"And you're blessed to have your father to help you," she added.

"Don't I know it!"

When they got to the upscale restaurant, the maître d' escorted them to a table on the far side of the room, away from the band, which would give them a chance to talk below the din. Adam guided her in front of him with a hand at the small of her back. It seemed as if the silk fabric of her dress moved slightly against her skin, under his palm. Sort of a caress. But she might be mistaken.

She hoped he wasn't looking at her butt, which more than filled out her tight dress. She should have borrowed her mother's Spanx. Oh, well! Too late now.

After sitting down, they placed their ordears . . . a shared Roast Oysters with Tarragon Butter appetizer and a Praline Bread Pudding dessert, a Gulf fish sampler entrée for her with a side of cheese truffled grits, and Steak Oscar for him, medium rare filet mignon topped with asparagus, lump crab meat, and hollandaise and a side of Cajun Quinoa, instead of the usual baked potato. They both laughed at the mention of quinoa.

The meal, heightened by a bottle of red wine, was sublime, as would be expected at a five-star restaurant. And the conversation was equally excellent. There was never a lull.

"Tell me about your marriages," he urged, probably wanting to get the subject out of the way from the start.

He watched her closely as she dipped a large crab claw in lemon butter and sucked out the succulent meat. She licked her lips just to tease him, and he smiled, giving her a little salute.

It was a game they were both playing.

"I married Cletus when I was seventeen, soon after I graduated from high school. My mother and I weren't getting along, and I probably looked at him as an escape. I realized my mistake almost immediately and left after a couple of weeks. My divorce didn't take place until a year later, but by then I was in college. I blame it all on humming hormones."

He propped his elbow on the table with his hand under his chin, studying her. His position caused the sleeve of his jacket to ride up, exposing more of his neatly starched dress shirt, highlighted by gold knot cuff links. She did like cuff links on a man. Like eye glasses . . . when a hot man took off his glasses or cuff links, while gazing at a woman with erotic intent, well, it just about melted her bones.

"I'd like to see you with humming hormones," he commented.

It took her a second to realize that he was referring to her remark about blaming her early indiscretions on humming hormones. "Darlin'," she replied, drawing out the word, "I've been humming around you from the get-go."

More of the game.

His dark Cajun eyes danced with humor. But then he straightened and took another bite of his steak.

She liked watching him eat, as much as he liked watching her. He chewed his food slowly, closemouthed, with an expression of pleasure on his face. Noticing her study, he stabbed a portion of steak with a sliver of asparagus and a lump of crabmeat and held it out across the table.

She had no choice but to open her mouth for him, a blatantly sexual act of seeming surrender, which he clearly enjoyed as much as she did. In fact, several times during the meal he stabbed one of the items on her plate and ate with relish. Whether it be redfish or shrimp or scallop, the sharing was almost like an erotic ritual. At least she hadn't offered food from her fork to his mouth.

Yet.

Oh, I am in deep trouble!

All of her senses were heightened. The smell. The taste. The sounds. Even the feel of the velvet seat under her rump.

So caught up in the intimate aura was she that at first she didn't hear him ask, "So, what was wrong with Cletus?"

She blinked several times to clear her head. It must be the wine. It had to be the wine. Otherwise . . .

"What wasn't wrong with him? I found out right after the wedding, which took place at a seedy justice of the peace in Alabama, by the way, that he already had a rap sheet for breaking and entering, and burglary. Small-time stuff then. He hasn't stopped since, moving onto bigger crimes, like armed robbery and auto theft. In fact, he was only released from Angola a few weeks ago."

"I heard," he said. "Your mother's roommate for a week or so, wasn't he?"

"Yes, and the reason I moved out of her trailer so quickly."

"Which brings us to husband number two," he prodded. "The musician, Jeb Cormier, I think."

"You've done your homework."

"A little."

"I married Jeb when I was a senior in college. Not as dumb as when I married Cletus, but totally naïve when it came to drugs. Sadly, Jeb was an addict. Especially sad because he was a gifted musician. When I play his CD *Louisiana Lost*, with that deep baritone and that wailing Cajun sound, it brings tears to my eyes."

"Sounds like you really loved him."

She shrugged. "Maybe. Probably. But it died out before I left him, long before he died of an overdose. It's probably why I ended up going into law enforcement, though, seeing the damage drugs can do."

"Sorry to have injected a sad note into our evening."

"It's okay," she said. "A long time ago. Don't you want to know about the perversions of my third husband, Julien Gaudet, the computer entrepreneur?" She waggled her eyebrows at him.

He laughed. "Sure."

"Well, I'm not going to tell you. Suffice it to say, when I found out where he was getting his big inflow of cash, I was out of there. If you count up the actual time, I spent with my three husbands, it amounts to about six months. Pathetic, I know."

They'd finished their meal and sipped at their glasses of wine while the waiter removed their dishes and brought out the dessert, a huge bread pudding with two spoons. Simone was stuffed but she had to try at least a bite, and then she sighed aloud and couldn't stop herself from taking more.

"Your turn," she said then.

He nodded. "My life hasn't been quite so interesting as yours. One marriage, but it was a whopper."

She arched her brows.

"I was a beginning assistant DA in Nawleans when I married Hannah. She was a psychologist specializing in couple counseling. That should have been a clue, I realize, in hindsight."

"Who was it that said hindsight is twenty-twenty?"

"Billy Wilder," he informed her. "The Hollywood director. And, yeah, the things we wish we could undo! Not that I would undo my marriage, because it gave me Maisie."

"Of course."

"You talk about being naïve when you married at seventeen. Hah! How do you excuse a grown man of twenty-six, falling brain-dead, head-over-ass in love with a woman, five years older, by the way, and marrying her, without knowing she was into extramarital affairs, ménages, sex clubs, and all kinds of perversions? Yeah, I know, you probably thought there wasn't a perversion I didn't welcome. Betcha I could match you perversion for perversion with Hannah and your Gaudet creep."

Simone's jaw dropped open with shock. Yeah, she'd known about Adam's wife being involved in a sex club, but to hear him tell it so bluntly was shocking.

"I didn't even know they had sex clubs like the one Hannah was into, that's how clueless I was at the time. Now, I understand, there are tons of them around. You would probably know, having been a police officer."

"Um, did you participate in them?"

"No!" He hesitated, then wiped his mouth with a napkin and placed it on the table over his plate. "I have to admit, I went to one of their parties . . . okay, two . . . just to see what they were about. Not my thing!"

"Because of their activities or on principle?"

"Both. Don't get me wrong. I'm not an angel. Far from it. After many futile attempts to get Hannah to give up her wild personal life, I began having affairs myself. One-on-one affairs, not orgies. Yeah, I know, I'm splitting hairs with my moral preaching." He shrugged. "Guess I'm kind of an old-fashioned guy living in a modern world. I still believe in the sanctity of marriage, but not for me," he was quick to add. "Once burned, twice shy."

There were so many things Simone wanted to ask, especially about the sex club, but she couldn't begin her Marcus Pitot investigation based on info she'd gleaned from Adam. First of all, it was unethical. Second, he would believe she'd used him; he would never forgive her. So she tried to veer the conversation in another direction. "How did Maisie fit into this picture?"

"Funny you should ask! She didn't. Hannah never wanted a child. She alternately blamed me and some anonymous donor for the accident."

Simone gasped. "Are you saying that Maisie isn't your child?"

"Oh, she's mine all right. But that's how Hannah kept me from filing for a divorce and taking Maisie with me. She needed the cover of a respectable marriage to carry out both her legitimate couple counseling business and her personal orgies. So, she always implied that Maisie wasn't actually my child and if I left, she'd get custody."

"Oh, Adam!" She reached across the table and covered one of his hands with hers.

He turned his hand over and linked his fingers with hers.

"It was only after her death that I had a DNA test done, which proved Maisie is mine, but it wouldn't have mattered. Blood or not, Maisie was mine by then."

She squeezed his hand, speechless.

"So, that's my story."

Their gazes held for several long moments. Finally, she said, "Sounds like we've both been through the grinder."

He nodded. "I'm falling a little bit in love with you, y'know."

The frown on his face prompted her to say, "And that's a bad thing?"

"Could be. As I just said, I've been burned."

"Wanna compare scars?"

He grinned and raised their clasped hands so that he could kiss the inside of her wrist. "Wanna dance?" Without waiting for an answer, he tugged her to her feet.

The band, which had been playing soft background music, now transitioned into louder and more rhythmic dance sounds. As they walked through the dining tables toward the dance floor, following some other couples, she asked, "*Can* you dance?" Lots of men couldn't.

"I dance," he said.

And he did. Oh, boy, he did! Nothing fast and flailing. More slow and swaying, holding her close, letting the rhythm of the music control their body rhythms. It wasn't a klutzy substitute for cool dance moves. It was an expert type of non-movement. Sway dancing, if you will, at its erotic best.

"Are you seducing me?" she asked against his ear.

"I hope so," he said and licked her neck, a quick flick of his tongue that made her jerk and him laugh. He leaned his head back to look at her face. "This dating thing is turning out better than I expected."

"No kidding!"

He pulled her flush against him. With her high heels, they were the same height. His arms were wrapped about her waist, down low, hers were around his neck. Cheek to cheek. Breast to chest. Belly to belly. His thighs bracketing hers. More swaying.

The band had a female lead who had been singing old blues songs by favorites like Bessie Smith and Lena Horne, but now she belted out the modern Adele song "Crazy for You."

Yep!

The things clueless men will do! Or not do! . . .

They danced and drank and talked until midnight when they left the restaurant to go home. By then, Adam had come to a whole new enlightenment: Dating was sexier by far than just hooking up, and he hadn't even kissed her yet or copped a feel or whispered something dirty in her ear, all of which he would surely do. Just not yet. Not tonight. It was all about the build-up, the heightened senses, the anticipation.

Not that they were going to have sex tonight. Not *sex* sex, anyway. It would ruin the process, in a way. Anyways, this was his new theory. Yet to be tested.

And, no, he wasn't giving up the real deal. But, just for a change, this was fun.

I wonder if Simone is aware of these facts.

Probably not. Hasn't she a history of jumping into relationships, rather, marriages, without prolonged courtships?

I'll surprise her, he decided, *not with a "Wham-bam, thank you, ma'am" but with a "No thank you, ma'am." Not that I'm thinking prolonged here. Just not Wham-bam. Crazy, huh?*

Especially when I've been carrying around a half hard-on all evening. Mr. Happy isn't going to be too happy with tonight's outcome.

On the other hand . . . hand being the keyword here. Ha, ha, ha!

Holy crap! I'm talking to myself. I could probably write a book about this, his crazy-assed brain went on. *Sex without Fucking. Or Dated but Sated. Or What Grandpa Didn't Tell You about Courtship. Or Restrained Lust: The New Sex.*

Or, the voice in his head countered, *Man's Brain Shorts Out over Lust Overload.*

"Why are you smiling?" Simone asked when he walked her up the back stairs to her apartment. He had an arm around her waist, to hold her up (Really.) since she was a little "tipsy," her word, while he was only half buzzed. Half hard and half buzzed . . . what a combination! *If I get tired of being a lawyer, maybe I could be a stand-up comedian.*

"I'm thinking about becoming an author," he told her.

"Huh?"

"It's a personal joke," he said, squeezing her even closer to him.

"Okaaay." She started to take her door key from the tiny purse that dangled from a long chain about her shoulder but he stopped her. "No. Not yet."

Instead he backed her up against the door and for the first time all evening he let himself press his body fully against her so that she could feel his erection. No more brushing of body parts, like when they danced. At the same time, he put his mouth on hers and almost swooned at the sheer pleasure of the tactile sensations. *Really, Adam? Swooned? Like a freakin' Southern belle? Okay, light-headed then, a better word. More manly? Aaarrgh!* In any case, his light-headedness caused him to lean into her more. It was a long, long kiss, and when he took a break, he murmured, "I've been wanting to do that all night."

"Me, too," she said and took his face in her hands, kissing him back, openmouthed and hungry.

Meanwhile his hands were caressing her body, the silk of her dress moving under his palms. Her back. Her narrow waist. Her butt. *Is that a thong I feel underneath? Hallelujah!* Mr. Happy lurched. Her breasts. Another hallelujah discovery . . . no bra, as he'd guessed earlier. More lurching.

She moaned and arched into him.

He was doing a little inner moaning himself, still caught back there with the no bra, no panties discovery. He couldn't help himself then as the line he'd drawn for himself tonight moved a little further into No-no! land.

With a sigh of resignation, combined with sublime appreciation, he tugged the straps of her dress down to her elbows, trapping her elbows at her sides. "Oh. My!" he said along with a more graphic four-letter word.

"Touch me," she urged in an embarrassed whisper.

"With pleasure," he said and used just the tips of his fingers to examine the ample mounds. Lightly, lightly, lightly, avoiding the center of her heightened sensation. She squirmed from side to side and arched her breasts outward.

But he was taking his time. Studying her breasts, with his eyes and then his fingers. Barely touching the skin. The areolae were pink, like a virgin's, or a woman who hadn't yet carried a child, and the rose-hued nipples were turgid with arousal.

"More," she demanded. She probably would have yanked his head down if her hands were free.

He chuckled and flicked the tips with his thumbs. Just once. "Tell me."

"What?" she gasped out.

"What you want." Another flick.

She squirmed against the restraint of her own dress, then admitted, "Your mouth . . . I want your mouth on me."

"Your wish is my command, darlin'." And, yes, he used that *darlin'* deliberately since she'd told him it was her bone melter, or other melter. Slowly, he lifted one breast from underneath and lowered his head, taking the tight bud into his mouth, wetting it with his tongue, then drawing on it with a slow rhythm. At the same time, his free hand worked the other breast.

Almost immediately, she shuddered and her legs gave way as she melted into a sweet, instantaneous climax. He grabbed her by the waist to hold her up and pressed his knee against her pubic bone. He never stopped sucking on her breast, harder and faster.

Note to self: Simone's breasts, number one erogenous zone.

But wait. Maybe it wasn't her number one spot. He almost smiled, thinking of all the explorations to come, discovering each and every one of her secrets.

But not tonight, he cautioned himself. *Remember. Dating. Prolonged Anticipation. A new way of doing things.*

He began to draw up the straps on her dress, covering her once again.

She blinked at him with surprise. "Well, that was embarrassing."

He tilted his head at her. "Why?"

"Because I went off like a rocket while you're all cool and calm down on the launch pad.

"Not so cool or calm," he said, placing her hand over his cock which was no longer half hard, more like hard as steel. He pulled her hand away almost immediately before she had a chance to grab on or caress him in any way that would shoot his good intentions to hell. "This was a great date, Simone. Wanna try it again?"

"Huh? You're not coming in?"

Coming being another keyword, which he decided not to mention to her at the moment. Instead, he shook his head. "Not tonight." He kissed her lightly, very lightly, to assuage any ruffled feelings. She might have bitten his lip if he lingered. "Let's try another date, or two, and see where things lead."

She started to turn away from him in affront. "This is just a game to you."

"No, it isn't." He turned her back to face him. "I've discovered stuff about myself tonight, and you, too. I like it."

"And?"

"I think we should pursue this dating thing some more."

She appeared unconvinced.

"If I come in now, we'll screw each other's brains out for a few hours. And maybe we'd repeat that another time or two. Wild monkey sex, probably, but same old, same old. Don't you want something different?"

"I don't know. Wild monkey sex sounds kind of interesting."

He chucked her under the chin for teasing. He assumed she was teasing. She better be teasing. He needed backup from her, not a tease-to-please come-on. "I have a prior commitment for tomorrow. A golf game with potential clients up in Morgan City, and I might be tied up in court this week, it depends on the judge in the Cypress case. He should have reconvened by now."

"Are you worried?"

"Not really. It just means that Luc and I have to be ready on a moment's notice. I can't really make plans."

"I can't, either. I have an out-of-town case."

"Really?" When she didn't elaborate, he asked, "How about next Friday night . . . no, I can't get out then. My dad's poker night. Saturday night again?"

"I just don't know. I might still be out of town."

"How about after work? Maybe an early movie or something? What do people do on dates now, anyhow? Do you play racquetball? No. Golf? I didn't think so. How about a ride on my Harley?"

That last drew some interest, but then she put up both hands. "Just call me, Adam. I'm a little confused right now. And I really do need to play it by ear this week in terms of my schedule. No, I'm not mad." She laughed then. "After all, getting laid isn't the be all and end all, right?"

It's not? I mean, of course, it's not. Down, Lurch, down!

"Lord, I can't believe I said that." She turned the key in the lock. Then she turned to him with a wicked Jezebel smile.

Uh-oh!

With mock regret, she said, "Too bad you can't come in tonight. I had this thing I was going to show you with handcuffs."

Son of a friggin' crawfish! He stood staring at the closed door for several moments before chuckling aloud, "Touche, babe!"

Unable to wait until he got home, he called her number from his car, a few miles down the road. It rang several times before she picked up.

"Adam?" She must have read the caller ID. "When you said you'd call, I thought you meant tomorrow."

"I couldn't wait," he said. "One question. Handcuffs?"

She laughed and said, "Good night, Adam."

Chapter Twelve

preparing for a road trip . . .

Simone spent all day Sunday doing the things single women do when alone on a weekend. Laundry. Cleaning Scarlett's litter box. Grocery and toiletry shopping. Manicure and pedicure. Shaving legs. Hair conditioning. Scrubbing the toilet.

Adam called in the middle of the afternoon while she was at the laundromat but left a text message when he got no answer: Just finished 9 holes. Thinking about u. Wish I cld see u tonight. About those handcuffs . . . ?

She texted back, although he was probably still playing golf. Just got home. How's ur game?

Shitty. Picturing pretty red dress mishap, he texted back immediately.

U wouldn't want 2 see me in my condition today. Not pretty.

What condition?

Olive oil on hair.

I can shampoo. I do dgter's hair.

Not same thing.

Def not. You have 2 B naked.

Why?

So I don't splash suds around.

Suds?

Frothy stuff shampoo makes.

Would U B naked 2?

If U insist.

Where R U now?

Club house. Dinner next. ZZZ.

Have fun.

Spking of fun, U ever used those handcuffs?

```
LOL.  I M a cop.

In bed?

I ref 2 answer on grnds that . . .

Have I mentioned fantaC I have of
nailing U on UR glass desk?

LOL.
```

After that, Simone spent a lot of time planning her work week. And it was a good thing she did because it proved to be a madhouse, starting as soon as the office opened the next morning.

First off, she had to deal with BaRa, who came in sporting a black eye.

"What happened?" she asked with shock.

"Would you believe I ran into a door?"

"Ozzie?"

BaRa blushed, which was unusual for her. The petite woman had been through the mill with her cheating, oil rigger ex-husband and gave the impression of taking no prisoners anymore. Nothing seemed to embarrass her. Except, apparently, her own weakness. "Uh, I might have decided to rake the fool's coals last night . . . and ended up getting hit in the face with the rake, the rake being my own failure to hold the line."

"Huh?"

"The sex got a little energetic, and I fell off the bed and hit my fool head on the bedside table. Ozzie had been playing ball with the boys all afternoon and looking good in gym shorts and no shirt, and I was feeling horny. Good thing I swerved at the last minute or I might have lost an eye. Talk about!"

Simone gaped at the woman who'd said on innumerable occasions that she couldn't stand her philandering ex-husband. "Are you getting back with him?"

"Hell, no! One booty call does not a marriage make." BaRa was at her desk, turning on her computer while they talked.

That was a proverb to live by. "Are you sure you don't want to stay home for the day?"

The question surprised the secretary who stood and tilted her head to one side. "Why? Do I look that bad?"

Actually, she looked good, except for the black eye. At only five-foot-five, at most, even with four-inch heels, she was a trim little package in a smart lavender dress with a dark purple belt. Her bobbed dark hair was parted on one side and swept forward today in an attempt to hide the damage, but it wasn't long enough to do the job.

"You look fine. I have a really good concealer upstairs in my cosmetics bag if you're interested, but only if you want to avoid questions. I personally don't care."

"I'll take you up on that, on the off chance that Tante Lulu drops by. No way would she buy the door excuse."

"She'd probably put together a posse to go after Ozzie. Even out on the rigs."

BaRa grinned at the mental picture. "By the way, you should see Ozzie. When I hit the table, I bit his lip, which caused him to flip over and off the bed, pulling a hammy. So he not only has a fat lip today, but he's limping, too."

"Just deserts," Simone commented.

"For sure."

Her mother came in at nine and started to tell her about a meeting she'd had with Father Bernard after church yesterday. For once, she was wearing a pantsuit, not one of the form-fitting dresses. She'd mentioned yesterday that holding in her stomach for so long was giving her gas. Her hair was still in the same neat French twist, though. Some things never changed, including her fixation on Simone's marriage status. "I happened ta mention how it would be nice if the Church annulled your marriage ta Cletus, and he tol' me . . ."

Simone walked away in the middle of her mother's discourse. She was tired of telling her mother to forget about Cletus. The marriage was over. End of story.

"Anyways, good news!" her mother called after her. "Father Bernard sez it don't matter none since you were never really married. Justice of the Peace vows don't count."

"Aaarrgh!" was Simone's only comment.

Next she met with Sabine and CiCi related to their work on the Mike Pham case. The two women were working together as a team, Sabine being the actual "honey trap" while CiCi provided all the investigative work, including places that Mike hung out, friends, girlfriends, and lots of other juicy details.

CiCi was a mocha-skinned Creole of unusual height for a woman . . . about six feet tall, at least. She wore her reddish-brown hair in a long braid, which, along with her high cheekbones, made Simone wonder if she might have some American Indian blood in her, as well. There were many Native American tribes indigenous to Louisiana, including the Houma Indians, an offshoot of the Choctaw Nation. Today CiCi wore black leggings with a loose, tunic-style blouse embroidered with an intricate design that might very well be indicative of that very culture.

Sabine was in full biker gear today, her slim figure encased in black leather pants (Good thing it was early morning; she would be sweltering by this afternoon.) with a red tank top. All her piercings and tats were clearly visible. Her blond hair had been moussed off her face into a sleek, almost mannish style. The girl had style! And it changed from day to day.

"He likes submissives," CiCi announced, right off the bat, without warning.

"As in BDSM?" Simone asked. She was sitting behind her desk, and the two ladies were in the chairs in front. And, no, she was not thinking about Adam's fantasy involving her desk. Not in the last fifteen minutes, anyhow.

"Yeah," CiCi said. "He's a closet sadist."

"Good to know." Simone was tapping her chin thoughtfully. "Definitely a change in dress for me. No heavy leather, dominatrix-type stuff. Maybe a dog collar. Doms love dog collars on their women. And contrast that with a sweet nice-girl persona."

"On the other hand, you could hint that you have a piercing with a ring to hold a chain down below," CiCi advised. "Actually, combine the two. Miss Innocent with wanton ways."

Simone's eyes went wide. Not that she hadn't heard all this and more in her police work. But hard to associate it with an average guy . . . which Mike Pham apparently wasn't.

"He's got a special room at his condo on Grand Isle," CiCi told them, checking her notes.

"Special room?" Simone asked.

"Yeah. Have you read *Fifty Shades of Grey*?"

"Oh, boy!" Simone said. "How do you know?"

"I talked to the guy who installed the 'dungeon,'" CiCi told them. "Wrist hooks and straps on the walls, fold-down spanking bench, X-frame cross, pulley system on the ceiling, that kind of thing."

Holy Moly!

Sabine just arched her brows. "My husband bought me a flogger for Christmas, but that's as far as we go."

And people think I've led a wild life! "Can we can get pictures?"

"I guarantee it," Sabine said. "I haven't made a connection with him yet, but CiCi gave me the name of a bar he frequents on Monday nights. I'm going tonight. We'll see if I can get him to invite me back to his place."

"Be careful," Simone cautioned.

"Always," Sabine said.

"In the meantime, I do have lots of data and a few photographs of him with other women. One or two of the disgruntled ones might be willing to testify, if needed." CiCi looked at Sabine. "Your info will be the shit icing on this boy's downfall cake."

Later that afternoon Simone was preparing to go to New Orleans with Gabe to look over his parents' place and perhaps hit a few bars where Marcus Pitot was reputed to hang out. CiCi was working on background research on this case, too, and had already given them some places and people to check out.

The question was how to dress, what personality she wanted to portray as a potential swinger wife. Not blatantly sexual, in her opinion. That would be too obvious. She settled on a capped-sleeve, short, black lace dress with a sweetheart neckline, exposing only a bit of cleavage. Red stilettos with ankle straps, that she hoped made a statement; they were Jimmy Choo knock-offs, the illegality of which the cop in her conveniently ignored since they'd been a gift. Crystal chandelier earrings matching the crystal barrettes that held her hair off her face . . . hair which was a shiny mass of waves today thanks to her olive oil treatment. Very subtle make-up that gave her a natural look. Except for the red shoes, she looked demurely sexy.

She packed a small case, just in case they needed to stay overnight. Then she went downstairs to wait. She'd already sent her mother home with a protesting Scarlett in her crate. It was either that or invite her mother to stay in her apartment, which she didn't want to do. Best to avoid precedents in that regard.

While she was waiting—everyone had already left—she was surprised to see Tante Lulu wobble in. And *wobble* was the correct word because the old lady was wearing high-heeled pumps . . . in a putrid pink color to match her putrid pink sundress. That was mean. The color was actually just bright pink, kind of neon-y. And actually her hair was slightly pink, too, and her lips were definitely pink. Pretty in pink, it was not. But typical for Tante Lulu, whose outrageous appearance often aimed to stun.

"I gotta pee," Tante Lulu said right off, rushing into the office and down the hallway. When she came back a short time later, she apologized. "Sorry about that but mah bladder ain't what it used ta be. I was outside in the car when the urge come on me."

"You didn't drive in yourself, did you?" Simone glanced out the window. The last time Tante Lulu had driven into town, she'd parked catty-corner in two spaces out front.

"No, I came in with Tee-John. He's next door at the bakery buyin' some doughnuts. I tol' him I could make beignets better than any store-bought pastries, but he wouldn't listen ta me. Sez his wife has a cravin' fer cream-filled doughnuts. Tee-hee-hee!"

"Uh-oh!"

"It ain't fer certain yet. Leastways Celine sez it ain't certain, but I know. Thass why I'm wearin' pink, jist ta give Celine's ovaries a nudge. We ain't got enough girls in our family."

That made as much sense as eating bananas to produce a boy, which one of her Chicago friends had done after already having three girls. What she ended up with was potassium headaches and another girl. "And what's the big event that has you all dressed up?"

"Oh, we're gonna celebrate Etienne's thirteenth birthday. He wanted ta eat wings at a strip bar. Talk about! We're gonna have cake and ice cream at home, instead." She grinned at Simone. "I wouldn't have minded a strip club mahself, but no wings. They give me gas."

TMI. Just then, Tante Lulu seemed to notice Simone's appearance. "Wow! Ya goin' out on a job t'night. Ya pretendin' ta be a hooker?"

"What? Do I look like a hooker?"

"Not a hooker 'zackly. More like one of them high-priced hall gals."

It took Simone a second to realize that the old lady meant *call girl.*

"No, this is the way I dress when I go out—"

"—on a date? Ya have a date? Oh, boy! I knew the thunderbolt was workin', but this is really fast. Is it Adam?"

Just then, who should walk in with perfect timing but . . . yep, Adam.

"Hey, darlin', I got done early and thought I'd drop in to see if you were free for . . ." His words trailed off as he noticed Tante Lulu, and then a close second later, he noticed Simone's appearance. "Whoa! That's some outfit!"

"Don't you like it?" She turned to give him a full view.

"I love it, but how did you know I was coming?"

"I didn't. I'm on my way out of town. A job."

His eyes surveyed her attire from head to foot and noted the overnight bag near the door. "Some job!"

She shrugged. This was what she did. He either needed to accept that . . . or not.

"I said she looked lak a hall gal, but she sez she's goin' on a date," Tante Lulu told him.

"I did not say that," Simone protested.

"Huh?" Adam said.

Just then, a car horn blew outside and they could see

through the glass doors Tee-John LeDeux, handsome as always in cut-off denims and a Ragin' Cajun T-shirt. He yelled from where he stood by the open car door, "Tante Lulu, get yer pretty little ass out here, or I'm leavin' without you."

"Oh, that boy!" the old lady said about her great-nephew who was not Tee, or small, at six-foot-plus, nor young at thirtysomething. On those words, she began to wobble out again, calling out over her shoulder to Adam, "Yer hope chest is finished."

"That is just super," he muttered.

"Whadja say?" Tante Lulu asked, just before she shut the door after herself.

"Thank you," he muttered to the closed door. Then he just stood and shook his head for several seconds. The old lady had that effect on people. Turning back to Simone, he asked, "A date?"

"No."

"You're working?"

She nodded.

"Where you going?"

"I'd rather not say."

"A cheating spouse case?"

"I'd rather not say."

"Are you going alone?"

"No."

"Let me guess . . . you'd rather not say with whom."

She nodded again, then added, "I wish I were free tonight, Adam." And she meant it. He looked so good in his rumpled suit and afternoon stubble that she was tempted to cancel her trip to New Orleans and show him all the things a Cajun girl could show a mostly Cajun boy. But she was more responsible than that and just put a hand on his arm to show her sincerity.

"So do I," he said huskily, and took that hand in his, squeezing.

Just that squeeze did something to her girl parts. "You're not mad, are you?" she rasped out.

"No, not really." But there was a hesitancy in his voice. "I don't have any right to be mad. Do I? Not yet?"

"I'm not sure you'd ever have that right, Adam. This is my work. Doesn't matter if it's Legal Belles or as a cop. Sometimes I've just got to do what I've got to do."

That sounded ominous, even to him as evidenced by his arched brows. Then he nodded his acceptance of her words, but again there was a hesitancy. "Can I call you later?"

"How about I call you, in case I'm tied up?" Oh, Lord, that sounded bad.

"Sure. He gave her a quick kiss, then glanced at her overnight bag. "You're not taking your handcuffs with you, are you?"

"No, Adam, I'm saving those for you."

A watched phone never rings . . .

Adam found himself waiting eagerly for Simone to call him that evening, and he didn't like it, not one bit. Not that he objected to her doing the calling. No, it was the fact that he was waiting for the call like a nervous teenager. He even took his cell phone into the bathroom while he poured bubble bath into the tub for Maisie and sat on the closed toilet lid listening to her chatter about her day.

Afterward, he watched a *Charlotte's Web* video with his little Mini-Me for about the fiftieth time. It was her favorite, next to *The Little Mermaid*. Then they made some jewelry with colored rubber bands. After that, he tucked Maisie into bed and promised to take her to Jungle Gardens on Avery Island sometime this summer. She'd heard about the place from a girl down the street. He'd been there on a field trip as a kid, but then it was to see the huge salt dome and tour the Tabasco factory.

His dad, who was watching *Iron Chef* in the den, gave him an update on the party that was turning into a massive bayou bash and giving him a rash. Really! His father's arms and legs, visible in white undershirt and Bermuda shorts, were covered with calamine lotion. But it was probably from working in his garden near some poisonous weed.

Distractedly, because he was fixated on the stupid show, his father related that René LeDeux had been there this afternoon, at Tante Lulu's urging. "He checked out our exterior electrical outlets to see if they're capable of handling his band's equipment and lighting."

"Lighting? Why do we need lighting? I thought this was a daytime pool party."

His father shrugged. "It might run into the evening."

Adam groaned. He was starting to feel a little itchy, too.

"Another thing. René asked if we want him to bring one of those wooden platform things, and I told him to ask you."

"What? This is getting totally out of hand. Why can't we just have some kind of stereo music? Why the hell does this house have a sound system if we're not going to use it, anyway? And since when does a five-year-old's party need live music?"

His father shrugged. "It's your party, too."

"Since when?"

"You're arguin' with the choir, boy. Tell it to Tante Lulu."

No way was he risking any excuse for the old biddy to

bring some lamebrain hope chest over here. "Why can't you? I'm not the one making all these plans."

"Me complain to that sweet woman? Not a chance. We're pals since she joined our casino gang. I wouldn't want to hurt her feelings."

"And I would?"

"If the shoe fits."

"I'm beginning to think that impromptu parties are much better. We never should have told Maisie she could plan a party two months in advance. All that time is not good for party planning. Didn't they tell you two yahoos about that on the show that gave you this crapola idea to begin with? Who the hell needs a theme party?"

"Yahoos? Now you're callin' your daughter a yahoo."

"I'm callin' you a yahoo, and Maisie a yahoo side-kick."

"Ha, ha, ha! Mr. Comedian! How come you're so antsy tonight? Maybe you need to visit one of your girlfriends."

"*Dad!* Are you suggesting sex to calm my nerves?"

"Always worked for me."

"*Dad!*" he repeated.

"With your mother."

TMI! Time to change the subject, or come back to the subject. "I'm afraid to ask, but just how big is this party by now?"

"Fifty."

"Aaarrgh!" Adam got up and decided to take a shower. His father didn't even notice his leaving, so engrossed was he once again in the show where some guy was making trout ice cream.

By eleven o'clock Adam was ready for bed and decided to give Simone another half hour before hitting the sack. He picked up a Grisham thriller he'd been reading off and on for a month and then half reclined on the bed against a couple of propped pillows. After an hour of not flipping even one page, he gave up, slamming the book down and turning off the light. "To hell with it!" he muttered, arranging the pillows flat on the mattress under his head. "Where are you, Simone?"

As he dozed off, second thoughts crept in. Maybe this dating crap wasn't all it was cracked up to be. Or maybe he was just becoming cracked.

The perks of working overtime . . .

After stopping off at the house on the outskirts of New Orleans where they would be staying, Simone and Gabe ate a quick dinner at a French Quarter bistro, then headed for the wine bar frequented by Marcus Pitot. By slipping a twenty dollar bill to the hostess at the Grapes of Wrath, Gabe managed to get them seated within viewing distance of the table where their target had made reservations. She and Gabe were calling themselves Dr. Lawrence and Diane Storm, using Gabe's actual surname in case Pitot should check the ownership of the house where they were staying, which was in his parents' name.

Gabe was looking very business professional—i.e., physician newly arrived in town—in a gray suit by Hugo Boss with a crisp white shirt and black tie. His hair had been dyed blond, or maybe that was his natural color, and although longish, it was combed off his face neatly. His face was tanned, giving the appearance of a man with money enough to get out on the links or his sailboat on the weekends.

The Grapes of Wrath was a cozy basement establishment where a jazz trio played in a back corner, but the music was soft, allowing people to talk. Around the room

singles and couples sat on bar stools at high tables, and
on low couches and comfy chairs arranged in conversation pits.

Simone and Gabe sank down into one of the sofas and,
after checking the menu, ordered the "house special of
the day," which was a cabernet sauvignon costing twenty
dollars a glass. The bill for Mrs. Pitot was getting bigger
and bigger.

They leaned back on the soft leather and chatted between sips of the wine, which was delicious.

"What does your girlfriend think about this work
you're doing?"

"Livia knows I work for Legal Belles, but she doesn't
know about this case precisely. I know how important secrecy is to you."

"Would she mind?"

"Nah. Liv's so happy that I was willing to move here
that she wouldn't care if I was hooking. Just kidding."

"Is it a serious relationship?"

"Oh, yeah. When she graduates, we'll move back to
L.A. and once we're both on our feet financially, we'll
make it legal. Hey, maybe when this is all over, Saffron
can give me some leads on TV work. I'm not too proud to
do soaps."

"*The Old and the Dutiful.*" She laughed. "You never
know."

"And you? Anyone special in your life?"

She wasn't sure what she would have answered because just then Marcus Pitot walked in. With a woman.
Who was not his wife.

Gabe held his cell phone in front of his face pretending
to read a text. Instead, he took a photo of Pitot with the
woman. Not that a photo with a woman was important to
this case; Saffron had plenty of those. What was needed

was evidence linking Pitot to a sex club and "unusual" sexual activities . . . the types of things he wouldn't want made public. In other words, infidelity, okay; whips and chains, not so okay.

"That's Caroline Bannon, Pitot's latest mistress," Simone told Gabe. "Used to be a call girl. Now she's Pitot's exclusively."

"She is hot."

"Yeah, and about half his age. It's amazing what money can buy."

"Meow," Gabe said.

"Fact of life. Sex sells. Men buy."

"And women don't?"

By the grin on his face, Simone could see that Gabe was teasing, and she laughed.

Which caught Pitot's attention for a moment, and he glanced their way. He was sixty-one years old but looked fifty, with a receding salt-and-pepper hairline but taut skin that might be due to a facelift. If she hadn't been aware of his proclivities, she would have said he was an attractive man. Except for his eyes which were icy steel. Mean eyes.

Gabe moved closer to her, and the two of them played their roles then. Feeding each other bits of the finger foods provided with the wine—cheese straws, glazed pecans, and mini tapas. Touching each other often, his fingers trailing down her bare arm, her hand resting on his sleeve, and then his thigh. Exchanging knowing gazes, even the occasional small kiss.

At one point, Gabe frowned at her and pinched her arm, hard, murmuring a bunch of gibberish intermixed with words like *pretend*, *argument*, *you'll like it*, and *friggin' yes!* One of the words he spoke, sotto voce but loud enough to carry was *ménage*. When she flinched away from him, he drew her back forcibly and murmured more angry whispers at her. Finally, she nodded, and he leaned down to kiss the bruised arm.

She wasn't sure if Pitot was watching or overheard anything they'd said, but they sensed his scrutiny as he passed by. The man was clearly a regular customer. He and his "date" circulated, talking to various people, but then they made for the nearby conversation pit that had been reserved for them and where two other couples clearly waited for them. Were these other members of the sex club?

When Pitot went to the men's room, Simone headed toward the ladies' room just as he was exiting. She bumped into him, putting her hands on his chest, then apologized profusely. "Sorry, I'm such a klutz. It's these shoes." She stuck out one of her stilettos, along with a long length of bare leg, for Pitot's perusal.

He steadied her with hands on both her arms and studied her.

She let him, then patted her chest in a fluttery fashion—just making sure he noticed that she had a bosom, ha, ha, ha—and said, "Forgive me. I've had a little too much to drink."

"No problem, sweetheart."

She smiled and wobbled away from him.

When she got back, Gabe remarked, "He watched your ass when you walked away."

"Pfff! Everyone looks at my ass." Her butt might be the bane of her life, but Simone wasn't above using it when necessary.

Now, it was time to put their plan into action. She and Gabe had already discussed this possible scenario. What would make Pitot think that she and Gabe would go for their group antics? Well, one thing would be an interest shown by either of the married partners in other men or women. That's where they would start. Gabe got up and went to the bar, leaving her alone. Soon he was chatting up a woman, clearly establishing that he was a man with interests beyond his wife.

To her surprise, Pitot's mistress came over and sat down beside her. "Hello. I'm Caroline Bannon."

"Hi. I'm Diane Storm."

Caroline put a hand on Simone's arm. "I saw you sitting alone and thought I'd keep you company till your husband returns." She let her hand remain when Simone made no protest at the familiarity.

"How nice of you! We're new in town and don't know anybody." Simone gave a little moue of girlish disappointment.

"Well, that's easily fixed," Caroline said and motioned for the waiter, ordering two glasses of wine, whatever Simone had been drinking.

They both took several sips.

Simone glanced over to Pitot's group and saw that the man was watching them. Clearly, he had sent his mistress over.

"That *is* your husband, isn't it?" Caroline glanced at the diamond wedding band on Simone's finger and then over to the bar where Gabe had his hand on some woman's ass while he whispered in her ear.

"Yes. That's my husband, Larry. He has a wandering eye . . . um, hand." She giggled and put a hand to her mouth. "I'm a little tipsy."

"And you don't mind . . . the wandering?"

"No. It doesn't mean he doesn't love me." Simone leaned over as if to tell Caroline a secret. "Sometimes he brings women home, to our bed."

"Wow! Does he ever bring men home?"

"Oh, Larry's not gay."

"I meant for you."

Simone pretended to blush. "Not yet."

Caroline tilted her head. "But he wants to," she guessed.

"Oh, yeah."

"You say you're new in town . . . Where you from?"

"Chicago. Larry's a cardiologist, and he's joining a practice down here. We got tired of all the cold."

"And you don't know anyone here?"

"Oh, Larry has some relatives here, but they're out of town for several months. We're staying in their house till we can find a place of our own. We're looking for a condo. Do you know any good Realtors?"

"I do. The man I'm with owns a building just outside the Quarter, but I don't know if there are any empty units," she said. "Any kids?"

"No!" she said emphatically. "Not for at least five years."

"Listen, I gotta go, but let's do lunch. You free tomorrow?"

"Yes, that would be wonderful." Simone wrote the number for her disposable phone on a napkin and Caroline did likewise with her number. They agreed to meet the next day at Galatoire's at noon.

Caroline went back to her group and Simone noticed that she was imparting some information to Pitot. As the three couples left, Pitot paused by Gabe at the bar, said something, shook hands, and then the two of them exchanged several words.

A short time later, Gabe came back. "Pitot introduced himself. Said he understood I was a doctor new to the city and wanted to give me a warm Nawleans welcome. How about you? What did the babe say?"

"Casing me out," she said, taking a long swallow of her wine. "We're having lunch tomorrow."

"That's settles it. We're staying tonight, right?"

"Right."

Gabe said he would do some legwork in the morning, tracking down women who'd been known to participate in Pitot's perverted activities, not just in the sex club. And he would visit Pitot's apartment building as a prospective tenant. Simone was going to use her police connections to see what they had on Pitot. Cops knew stuff!

Even though she hadn't done anything bad or even witnessed anything bad, yet, she felt smarmy just having been around such people. So she took a really long shower. Once she climbed into bed, Simone checked the bedside clock. Twelve thirty-three a.m. Surely too late to call Adam, as she'd promised.

But then her phone rang.

And it was Adam. And he hollered, so loud she had to hold the phone away from her ear. "Where the hell *are* you?"

Call me maybe . . . when you're in a better mood . . .

At first, Simone was angry. What right did Adam have, taking that tone with her? But then she was suddenly concerned. "Is someone hurt? Oh, Lord, did someone die?"

"What? No."

"Why are you yelling at me, then?"

"Because it's after midnight!"

"And . . . ?" *Does he think I'm some kind of Cinderella?*

"I don't have a frickin' clue where you are."

Not at the ball, Prince Charming. "And . . . ?"

She heard a sigh before he said in a calmer, but still irritated, voice, "I've been worried about you for the past three hours."

Aah, how nice! And no glass slipper to give you a clue.

"Please tell me you haven't been out trolling for creeps in a bar all this time."

Trolling? That's how you categorize my work? Not so nice! "Yes, I've been working, Adam. Yes, I was in a bar for part of the evening . . . a wine bar, if that makes any difference. And no need to worry. As I've told you before, I can take care of myself."

"No, you can't, Simone. Not all the time. No one gets a safe card for all situations all the time."

"I'm a cop, Adam. Or I was."

"Sorry if I overreacted. You said you'd call, and when you didn't, I began to imagine . . . well, I was worried."

"I was just about to call but decided it was too late. Can we start over?"

He hesitated. "Sure."

"Hi, Adam. Just got home and was thinking about you. What kind of day did you have?"

"Busy." He explained that his work day had been spent mostly in the office, meeting with clients and doing legal research. He'd eaten at home where his father did most of the cooking. Tonight it had been fried green tomatoes with remoulade sauce, one of his favorites, and home-made mac and cheese, one of Maisie's favorites. Video watching and jewelry making.

She liked picturing him watching *The Little Mermaid* and his big hands making tiny bracelets.

And he went on to complain about the never-ending pool party preparations. "You will be coming, won't you?"

"I hope to," she said. It was about two weeks away. Surely this case would be finished by then and she could be more clear about her schedule.

"How about you?" he asked. "What did you have for dinner?"

She had to laugh at his obvious ploy. "I started with a Jackson salad. Yummy quail eggs and bacon and—"

"Arnaud's? You're in New Orleans?" he guessed.

"Nice try, Adam. I was just kidding."

"You can't blame me for trying." He paused. "I kept thinking about you today."

"While you were so busy?"

"In between. Thoughts of you kept nagging at me."

"Like a bad toothache?"

"Or some other ache."

"Uh-oh! Are we about to have phone sex?"

"I didn't know that was an option."

"It's not. I'm too tired to think of anything creative."

"Oh, well, same old same old is just as good sometimes."

"You an expert on phone sex then?"

"Hardly. But I'm willing to give almost everything a try."

"You're not going to start with that old cliché, are you?" She made her voice all male and husky. "What are you wearing, baby?"

He laughed. "No clichés? But have a little mercy, sweetheart. That wiped out ninety percent of my repertoire."

"You have a repertoire?"

"I'm thirty-five years old, Simone. Just for the record, though, I'm naked and lying here like a regular sex god waiting for action."

"Really? You're naked?"

"Don't I wish! No. Not with a five-year-old daughter in the house. But I can pretend."

"Okay, I'll pretend, too, then. I'm wearing the same red high heels I had on this afternoon with black stockings, a black thong, a garter belt, and a black lace demi-bra."

"To sleep in?"

"If sex gods can be naked, then sex goddesses can wear whatever they want to bed."

He laughed. "What do sex goddesses do when they can't sleep?"

"Read a book."

"What kind of book? Something boring, like *War and Peace*?"

"No, something sexy."

"Do sex goddesses masturbate while they're reading sexy books?"

"Hmmm."

"What are you doing, Simone?"

"Hmmm."

He laughed and said, "Hmmm." A short time later, he said, "Well, that was good for me. How about you?"

"I think I can sleep now."

Chapter Thirteen

How does one dress for an orgy? . . .

At eleven a.m. the next day, Simone was ready for her noon luncheon with Caroline Bannon. She wouldn't leave for another half hour or so since it was only a fifteen-minute trip into the city. Gabe would be dropping her off in their rented BMW.

Gabe had been a busy beaver already, having gone out at nine this morning. She'd spent the morning turning herself into an upper-class trophy wife. A white, nubbed silk, mid-thigh designer suit (with the label cut out) and black Manolo Blahnik slingback pumps, the first being an upscale thrift-shop find from two years ago, and the latter a guilty-pleasure indulgence she'd been unable to resist when passing a Chicago boutique window last winter and which she'd conveniently labeled "My Christmas Present to Me." Her brown hair, still glistening from her hot-oil conditioning several days ago, was upswept into deliberate disarray. Simple pearl stud earrings and her diamond wedding band. No blouse under the suit jacket which gave a clear view of her no-bra cleavage, just enough to tease but not enough to be slutty.

All this had taken more than two hours. How—or why—did women waste so much time doing this? And some of them did it every day!

She was standing at the kitchen counter talking with Gabe, who was drinking a bottled water he'd taken from the fridge. She was drinking nothing, afraid to spoil the effect of her make-up.

Gabe was going for the casually affluent look today, too. Dark brown pleated slacks, a golf shirt with a Palm Springs Polo Club logo on it, and loafers that probably cost as much as her Blahniks. When she'd raised her eyebrows on first seeing him this morning and remarked, "Expensive tastes!" he laughed and told her, "I raided my dad's closet upstairs."

"Tell me more about your morning," she prodded him. He'd already mentioned some "research" he'd done just by chatting up some folks who had businesses in the vicinity of Pitot's offices, on the supposition that he frequented some of them. He did. Including a jewelry store that loved him for his generosity to his wife. Yeah, right. It wasn't his wife he was buttering up with expensive trinkets.

Then there was the outdoors store where Pitot bought a lot of rope, Gabe had told her.

Rope? She didn't want to know.

Gabe had told her, anyway. "Thin, flexible rope, that easily works itself into slip knots. And harnesses. He also favors harnesses, the kind mountain climbers use and men who like to see women in . . . gear."

Eew!

"I also cased the apartment building that Pitot owns about a half block from his offices. He wasn't there, but his property manager will undoubtedly mention my having dropped by. I get the feeling that Pitot keeps a close hand on all his projects."

"That's why he's so rich."

"Probably. There aren't a lot of people who can afford $5,000 a month rent, and that's only for a one-bedroom."

"Just how wealthy is Pitot?"

Gabe shrugged. "Billionaire, I figure."

"No wonder Saffron is willing to pay us so much for the deets on Pitot if it ensures that she gets a share if—when—he dumps her."

"What does she look like? I mean, why so insecure? Is she a dog?"

"Hardly. Saffron isn't bad, for her age. But no woman, no matter how beautiful, can compete with youth. Caroline, or females like her, will always be younger versions of themselves."

"I guess."

"If Pitot is such a hard-nosed businessman, I wonder how closely he checks up on people before inviting them into his close circle. What if he finds out you're not a doctor?"

"Simone, my family is brimming with doctors, all over the country, and abroad. There has to be a Storm cardiologist somewhere. As long as there's no photograph when they Google my fake name."

Just then, they heard the sound of a car pulling into the driveway.

"Uh-oh! Your parents?" she inquired of Gabe.

"Nah. I talked to my mom last night. They won't be coming back until October."

They went through the hallway to the front entryway and opened the door to find Caroline Bannon exiting a shiny silver Jaguar, which made their rented BMW look like a rustbucket. Oh, well. Money talks.

"Caroline!" Simone said, walking out the door to the front steps.

"Diane!"

For a moment, Simone forgot that she was supposed to be Diane Storm. But then she extended her hands and Caroline responded with air kisses on both sides of her face. The scent of some expensive perfume wafted from her. Joy, Simone guessed.

Simone's favorite since she was a teenager was Diorissimo, a much cheaper scent than Joy. But she'd forgotten to bring any perfume with her. As a result, the only thing wafting from her was olive oil and the Caress soap that had been in her guest shower. "I thought I was meeting you at the restaurant." Simone frowned with confusion. Maybe last night's wine had been more potent than she'd realized.

"You were, but I was in the neighborhood and thought I would save you the effort."

Yeah, right. More like Pitot had sent her to see if they really did live at this upscale address.

"How nice of you!" Simone said. "Especially since we have only the one rental car here, until our vehicles arrive next week. Right, sweetheart?" she said to Gabe.

"Right," Gabe agreed. "Now, I won't have to drive you into town, honey. I can check out a few golf courses since I already had my meeting at the hospital this morning." Then taking Simone's cue, he turned to Caroline and stepped forward, extending a hand. "I don't think we've met. I'm Lawrence Storm. You can call me Larry." He gave the woman a manly scrutiny, designed to show that he appreciated her beauty.

And beautiful she was in a jade-green, sleeveless sheath with pale green alligator pumps, both of which were undoubtedly designer quality. Her diamond earrings, if they were real, could provide a down payment on most people's houses.

Caroline gave Gabe an appreciative once-over right back. "And I'm Caroline Bannon, but you can call me Caro." Gabe had released her hand, but she let her fingertips trail over his wrist.

Signals . . . it was all about signals. *I like what I see. I'm willing. Are you?*

"Did your meeting go all right at the hospital?" Caroline asked with seeming casualness.

"Yes. If I decide to open a practice here, I'll need hospital privileges. Just a technicality." He made a fake grimace of distaste at the need for such an inconvenience.

Simone was more and more impressed with Gabe's ability to come up with impromptu details.

On the way to the French Quarter, Caroline talked about all the places she thought Simone might be interested in as a newcomer to the Crescent City. Beauty salons. *Can anyone say olive oil?* Catering companies. *Mothers . . . the Cajun version of catering companies.* Home cleaning agencies. *I wield a mean toilet brush.* Only once did she shock Simone, or rather catch her off guard, when she asked, "Do you wax?"

Simone thought about joking with, "What, furniture?" But she knew exactly what Caroline meant. "No. Larry likes me better with a neat trim down there. Reminds him of a golf course. The man does love golf. Of course, he would go for getting my pubes de-haired if he could watch me screaming my ass off."

"You're probably right to go that route. Frankly, so many women go bald today that I'm thinking the trend will go back. And bedazzling! Who wants jewelry pasted on your landing strip? I'll take my diamonds around my neck or on my fingers, thank you very much."

Simone was beginning to like Caroline. She wasn't at all the bimbo that she'd imagined she would be. "How did you get to . . . um, be with your friend?'

"Be his mistress, you mean. No need to beat around the bush, ha, ha, ha. I've been with Marcus for more than a year. Before that I was a call girl."

Whoa! Shades of Tante Lulu and her hall gal reference! "Why . . . I mean . . . oh, never mind."

"Ask me anything. I graduated from college with a teaching certificate and I worked two years trying to pound English literature into brain-dead high school juniors for a pittance. One day I decided to reevaluate my life. I asked myself, what do I like to do? And the answer was sex. I like sex. All kinds. And I'm good at it. So why not get paid for my services?"

"Well paid if this car is any indication," Simone said.

"Right. And I have enough money stashed away that if I get too old to attract a desirable partner—I'm very selective—or if decide I want to do something else, I can."

"So, you're not looking for marriage?"

"Hell, no!"

"I can't really blame you, Caro," Simone said, being deliberately familiar with her nickname. "I was a nurse who married the doctor. What kind of cliché is that? Every mother wants her daughter to marry a doctor because they make so much money. Not that I don't love Larry madly."

"Of course you do. Love is fine, but what about sex? Do you like sex, Diane?"

Talk about blunt! "Definitely."

"What kind?"

She pretended to be flustered. "All kinds, I guess."

"Anything kinky?"

Wow! This was some conversation for new acquaintances. "A little. Some spanking. Sex toys. And other stuff."

"Don't you ever get bored with just one man?"

"Larry is really good in bed."

"Nice to know, but that doesn't answer my question."

"I suppose," she revealed, pretending embarrassment. "Larry wants to try it . . . you know, a ménage . . . but I just don't know. How can I love Larry and do it with another man?"

"Maybe it's the ultimate act of love. Surrendering your wishes to the man you love. If Larry wants to engage in a ménage, it doesn't mean he doesn't love you. Just the opposite."

What a crock! Gag me with a silver-plated teaspoon. "I never thought of it that way."

"I remember the first time I did it with two guys, it about blew my mind. Take the best orgasm you've ever had and multiply by ten."

By then they'd reached the Quarter, and Caroline swung expertly into a parking space that conveniently opened up on the side street just off Bourbon where the historic Galatoire's Restaurant, noted for its French Creole cuisine, was located.

Simone had shrimp étouffée, which was good, but she wished she'd ordered what Caroline had when she saw her Crabmeat Sardou, a yummy dish that included artichokes with creamed spinach and lump crabmeat under a blanket of hollandaise. Not for the diet conscious. They both sipped at white wine. Their conversation was normal, like that of two new friends getting acquainted. Movies they liked. Sports they didn't like. Fashion. Men.

Then it was not. Normal, that was.

When they were both done and sipping at strong Creole coffee, Caroline said, "Listen, Diane, I'd like you to meet Marcus and some of our friends. Can you come to dinner on Friday night?"

"I appreciate the offer, but—"

"Marcus has a lodge up on Lake Pontchartrain that is lovely this time of the year. It's only ten miles away."

"That sounds great, but—"

"There will be two other couples. We'll all be staying overnight. You can stay, too, if you like. Not good to drink and drive, y'know! Ha, ha! Or you can go home to your own bed, if you like. It's all a matter of choice."

There was clearly a message in those words, *matter of choice*.

Simone thought quickly. Today was Tuesday. If they made plans for Friday night, she could go back to Houma and work for a few days before returning. Then, hopefully, she and Gabe would get all the info they would need in that one night, and be done with the case.

"I'd love to come, but let me check with Larry first and get back to you. I was going to decline because we need to fly back to Chicago tonight to take care of some last-minute details involving the sale of our condo. We should be back by Friday."

"Wonderful," Caroline said, whipping out a platinum Amex card before Simone could offer to pay, which she had no intention of doing.

As they were exiting the restaurant, Simone asked, "How should I dress?"

Caroline gave her an amused look and said, "You are so sweet."

Simone couldn't recall the last time anyone had called her sweet. Maybe Adam when he'd been sucking on . . . No, no, no! No thinking about Adam right now. She put a deliberately confused expression on her face. "I meant, cocktail party dressy or lakeside casual?"

"Sweetie, you can wear anything you like." And Simone thought she heard Caroline add, under her breath, "Or nothing at all."

The question was: Who was the real winner? . . .

Adam was in court with Luc and Mike Pham at one-thirty when he got Simone's text message, I'll be back this afternoon!

He smiled but was unable to text back anything but, Good. Date tonight? and see her immediate response, Yes! So pathetic was his desperation for her becoming that he interpreted her exclamation mark for wild enthusiasm. And it didn't even matter that he was still a little mad at her for making him worry last night.

The jury entered the courtroom once again and the judge read them instructions for deciding on damages in the Cypress Oil case. A half hour ago, Luc and Adam had declined Cypress's last-minute settlement offer of five hundred thousand dollars on behalf of their client, even though his actual damages had been less than that.

To both Luc's and Adam's consternation, Mike had that sleaze lawyer Jessie John Daltry with him. Not sitting at the bench, of course, since it wasn't his case, but just behind them, offering unwanted opinions. Adam assumed, but refused to ask for both personal and ethical reasons, whether Daltry's appearance meant the divorce was proceeding or some effort was being made to hide funds. He almost hoped the rumor was true that his wife was seeking help from Legal Belles, but he couldn't ask Simone.

Once the jury went off to deliberate, lawyers for both sides met with the judge in his chambers to discuss various legal issues, including Cypress's plans to appeal. "You can do whatever you want, gentlemen, but I don't think you have any grounds," the judge said. "My suggestion is, tighten your belt and prepare to pay. Then get your shit in order before some other shrimpers, or the whole blessed bayou, decide to sue."

The Cypress lawyers were not happy campers and were heard muttering something about "judicial bias" as they stormed out. Luc and Adam were only back in their office for an hour when there was a call announcing a jury verdict. They contacted Mike who was out for a liquid lunch with Daltry, and they met the two of them, reeking of bourbon, back at the courthouse. Adam handed Pham a sleeve of breath mints.

Valcour LeDeux had showed up by then, flanked by some Cypress execs, all looking grim faced. Mike's father was there, also, but not his wife. There was a Vietnamese woman, dressed in smart business attire, sitting in the back of the courtroom, but Adam knew it wasn't Thanh Pham. It was probably her sister—a university professor, he believed.

The verdict was for one million in actual damages, and three million in punitive damages. Their law firm had taken the case on a contingency basis (no win, no cash), and after expenses, like investigators and expert witnesses, Adam and Luc would rake in a cool thirty-three percent. More than one million dollars.

Of course, Daltry was probably telling Mike that he would have done the job better and for less. Which was bullshit. Daltry was known for screwing his clients with exorbitant commissions and expense accounts.

No matter! It was cause for celebration. The elder

Pham appeared dazed, and the Vietnamese woman had already left the courtroom. Valcour muttered to Luc as he passed, "Ya did this ta spite me, son."

Luc bristled at the word *son* and replied, "No, Daddy Dearest, the size of your wallet means nothing to me."

Luc and Adam shook hands with Mike and clapped each other on the shoulders.

"How soon do I get my money?" Mike wanted to know as they walked down the courthouse steps and put Mike's father in a taxi.

"Not right away," Luc told him. "First, we have to see if there's an appeal, in which case you would get nothing for a while. Often defendants use that as a delaying tactic and then offer a much lower amount to settle."

"I'm not settling."

"I wouldn't suggest that you do," Luc said.

"If you ask me . . ." Daltry started to say.

"No one asked you," both Adam and Luc said at the same time.

"If there's no appeal, you could cash out within a few months," Adam told Mike, trying to soften the tension. "Hey, lighten up, everyone. It was a good day. We should all be happy."

"I am, I am," Mike assured them.

"When can Mike get court papers spelling out the verdict?" Daltry asked.

"Possibly tomorrow. Why do you ask?" Luc had some history with this guy and was having trouble maintaining a civil tone.

"Because I might need to show them to the bank if I want to get a loan against future cash inflow," Mike revealed before he noticed Daltry motioning him to keep quiet.

"That is not a good idea," Adam said. "You never

know what might happen in these cases. I've seen companies declare bankruptcy and then show up months later under a different name to avoid payouts."

"Cypress Oil isn't about to go bankrupt," Daltry interjected.

Luc ignored Daltry and said to Mike, "As my Tante Lulu is wont to say, 'Don't trust the gator who brings wine to the table.'"

"What the hell does that mean?" Mike wanted to know.

Luc just arched his brows as if Mike should know without being told, which of course irritated Mike, which was Luc's intent.

"How about a drink to celebrate?" Mike suggested in a more conciliatory tone.

"Maybe later," Adam said before Luc could say something more antagonizing.

"I'll be out of town later," Mike said. "At least the next few days."

"Oh?" Adam asked.

"Going to Vegas. I'll be back on Thursday."

"Really? I didn't know you were a gambler," Luc remarked.

"I'm not. It's business."

"Don't say anything," Daltry advised.

Which caused both Adam and Luc to exchange glances. What business could a shrimper possibly have in Vegas? And what did Daltry have to do with said business?

Whatever. Their relationship with Pham would soon be over.

They all shook hands and parted ways, with a promise to connect again once they heard more from the court.

When they got back to the office, after being congratulated by Mildred and raising toasts with cups of water from the cold dispenser, they went into Luc's office where they discussed upcoming cases, strategy, and who would handle what for the next two weeks.

"So, how are you going to celebrate?" Adam asked Luc.

"Hah! Sylvie won't talk to me since it turns out my swimmers, which I thought were de-finned, are still swimming."

"She's really pregnant then?"

"It appears so."

Adam grinned. "So, there's an epidemic of LeDeux pregnancies. You and Sylvie, Charmaine and my cousin Rusty, Tee-John and Celine, and how about Remy and Val?"

"Still waiting to find out."

"And you all blame Tante Lulu?"

"Oh, yeah! She has an in with the celestial powers." He glanced meaningfully at the St. Jude statue on his desk.

"I think it's kind of nice."

"You would. You're safe . . . for now."

"For good," Adam proclaimed. "I have no plans for more children."

"Oh, so naïve! Have you heard the story about how God laughed for the first time? It was when he heard a man say, 'I have a plan.' It was probably that other dumbass Adam." He grinned and shook his head. "So, how are *you* going to celebrate our win?"

"I have a date."

"Really? Another one. This is getting serious, my friend."

"It's just a date." When would he learn to keep his mouth shut?

"Hah! When a Cajun girl has more than one date with a fellow, her Mama starts crocheting pillowcases."

"I have plenty of pillowcases and mine are a gazillion threads to the inch from my marriage, thanks to Hannah's insistence on only the best." He regretted immediately having mentioned his dearly departed wife. What a way to put a damper on a good day! "What does one do on a date, anyway?" *More blabbing! I must have a late-onset clueless gene. Or maybe I was always clueless . . . can anyone say nympho wife? Well, in for a penny, in for a pound, as Dad always says. If Luc can quote his relative, so can I.* "I've already taken her fishing and out to dinner."

"Adam, Adam, Adam." Luc looked at him as if he was . . . yep, clueless. "Are you really asking me what to do on a date?"

"Other than *that!*"

"Whoa, whoa, whoa! Are you on some kind of crazy-ass abstinence kick?"

"Not exactly. Not permanently, anyhow. And just for a little while." He sighed on seeing Luc's incredulous expression. "You probably think I'm crazy."

"You ought to talk to Charmaine. She decided to become a born again virgin at one time."

"I am not becoming a born again virgin. Jeesh!"

"Well, of course you're not. You have no little thingee down there to sew back up. Although you could probably get uncircumcised, but . . . ouch!" Luc put a hand over his crotch.

"This is a ridiculous conversation. Forget I said anything."

Which didn't deter Luc at all. "At your age, I would think you've had lots of experience dating."

"Not really. It's been more than ten years since I married Hannah, and then in the past two years, since she died, the whole man-woman scene has changed drastically. They don't date anymore, Luc. They just hook up. Not that I haven't done plenty of that. But still . . ."

"I was born too early," Luc complained. "When I was single, a guy had to work hard to get in a girl's pants. Now, it seems, the ladies are just as likely to dip into a man's tighty whities when he bends over to pick up her hanky."

"Hanky? What are you . . . ninety years old?"

"What's yer point?"

"Bottom line. I'm trying dating, for a change. And I'm at a loss as to what to do."

"Well, I like the fishing. Good choice there. Did you catch any fish?"

"What does that have to do with anything?"

"Holy crawfish! Someone's irritable."

"I am not irritable. I'm in a good mood."

"How about a movie? Seen *Fifty Shades of Grey* yet?"

"Can the jokes, Mister Comedian."

"I am not being a comedian. I'm serious. Sylvie and I watched a video of that movie, and, whoo-boy, that's probably when she got pregnant. For an old guy, I still have moves. Wanna know—"

"Forget I asked for your advice."

Luc ignored him and went on, "A concert would be good."

"What concert?"

"I don't know. The only live music I listen to is Remy's band, and wild zydeco isn't very romantic. Did I ever tell you about the time Sylvie and I had to hide out in a swamp fishing cabin for days and the only music available was Barry White, and I'd been threatening her with nude dancing since we were in kindergarten, practically. Hey, how about nude dancing for a date?" At Adam's glower, he shut down that line of advice and made a great show of wiping a hand over his face to remove the smirk. Then, with only a smidge more gravity, he said, "Of course, you could always try a simple walk in the park."

"What park?"

"How do I know what park? Any park."

"A movie seems the safest route, but not some porno flick," Adam mused.

"I'm not sure *Fifty Shades* qualifies as porno," Luc said.

Are we really going to have a discussion over the definition of pornography? Now? I don't think so! Adam waved a hand dismissively and rose to leave Luc's office.

"Congrats, buddy, on winning the good fight today in court."

"Back at you," Adam said.

Just then, Mildred came over. "I forget to tell you that Tante Lulu was here earlier, and she left a gift for you, Adam."

"For me?"

"This oughta be good," Luc said, following Adam as he opened the door of his office and almost tripped over something that sat on the floor. It was a large pine box decorated with flowers and intertwining vines. Pretty, in a primitive sort of way.

"It's yer hope chest, *cher*," Luc announced gleefully.

"That is just great." With trepidation, Adam opened the lid. On top was . . . what else?

Crocheted pillowcases.

Chapter Fourteen

To the victor belong the spoils, for sure. . . .

Simone made good time getting back to Houma by three p.m., after her lunch with Caroline. She knew when she saw Helene's face that something important must have happened.

"What's up?" she asked as her friend dropped a brief-case down to the floor and sank into the chair in front of Simone's desk.

"It's over. Pham was awarded four million dollars."

Simone let out a little shriek of happiness and the two partners hugged. "Now our work begins. I'll be so sorry to spoil Pham's windfall! Not!?"

"Same here. His wife and her sister should be here any minute. Are you free?"

Simone nodded, still smiling. "Now the you-know-what is going to fly, right?"

"Like a typhoon. Wish I could see the creep's face when he gets served the papers."

Simone's office phone rang, and BaRa announced, "Thanh Pham and Kimly Bien are here to see you."

"Send them in." She and Helene stood and greeted the two women, one of whom was looking jubilant, the other confused. "Let's sit over here," she said, indicating the sofa and two chairs, "so we can be comfortable."

The sisters sat next to each other on the couch.

Simone perched on the edge of the red-and-black upholstered chair, and Helene pulled the matching footstool over to the coffee table and spread out her folders.

"As I told you on the phone, Ms. Bien, Mike Pham and his father were awarded four million by the court today. I assume you have relayed this info to your sister."

"Yes, and you can call me Kimly or Kim."

Helene nodded. "Now we have to decide exactly what we want to do. I can tell you what I think, and how to proceed, but first, let's hear what Simone has to tell you from her investigation. It may influence your decisions."

Simone leaned forward and laid her folder on the coffee table next to Helene's. "Number one, no question in our minds that Mike Pham will be seeking a divorce. It looks like he's already started the process of establishing residence in Las Vegas for that purpose. In fact, he has reservations for a flight there this evening, returning on Thursday. He rented an apartment there weeks ago."

"But he never asked me for a divorce," Thanh said.

"He doesn't have to," Helene interjected. "Until he actually files for divorce and you are sent the papers, he has no legal obligation to tell you. Besides, he wants time, now that there's a money verdict, to hide the funds."

Kim said several words in Vietnamese that were probably the equivalent of "The bastard!" To Helene and Simone, she commented, "The fool thinks we won't know the amount. And, actually, if I hadn't intervened, my sister probably wouldn't have. She doesn't much pay attention to what's around her."

"What if I do not want a divorce?" Thanh asked, raising her chin defiantly at her sister's assessment of her cluelessness.

Why would a woman want to stay with a man who no longer wanted her? Well, that was nothing new, Simone supposed. Lots of women were more comfortable in marriage, even a bad marriage.

"It doesn't matter," Helene told her. "He will get a divorce if that's what he wants."

Kim put an arm around her sister's shoulders and squeezed. "How do we protect Thanh? Like you said, now that the lawsuit is over, Mike will probably attempt to hide the cash. Even if we confront him about the amount, he will say there were all these expenses, lawyers and such."

"Not if we act quickly. Preemptive strikes are the key," Helene said and looked directly at Thanh. "First of all, I have already prepared legal documents requesting a change in ownership of several properties. Specifically, that the house title should be changed to your name, along with one of the vehicles, a Toyota RAV4, which is being used by your sons in college, and half ownership of the shrimp business."

Thanh's eyes widened. She apparently hadn't been expecting so much. Little did she know what a pittance it was compared to Mike's share.

"You think he will agree to those changes?" Kim asked.

"No, he won't," Helene told her. "But it's a starting point. The house and car are deal breakers, but here's what we want. Thanh agrees to give up her request for half ownership of the shrimp business in favor of her two sons, and in return, she gets one million in cash from the Cypress lawsuit, college tuition and support for her sons until they reach age twenty-five, and all her legal expenses paid."

Kim frowned. "Why would Mike agree to all this?"

"Because Thanh will give up rights to his condo on Grand Isle, his other vehicles, and other assets."

Thanh frowned, "What condo?"

"That's what Simone will tell you about. And this is where we have our most leverage with Mike Pham. He will not want any of this information to go public."

Thanh's brow creased with puzzlement, but Kim was beginning to understand, and she grinned.

"Are you sure that you want to know all this?" Simone asked Thanh.

"Know what?" she asked.

"Things about your husband's personal life."

"I know there have been women."

"It's more than that," Simone said as she slid a series of photographs over to Kim with a raised eyebrow, silently questioning whether she thought her sister could handle such graphic details.

Even Kim was shocked by what she saw as she flipped through the photographs of Mike's condo and some of the half-naked pictures of himself and females in very distasteful postures. The one of a young female chained to the fake stone wall even drew a gasp from the sophisticated woman.

Kim closed her eyes, thought several moments, then said something to her sister in Vietnamese before gently handing her the photographs.

"What did you tell her?" Simone wanted to know.

"I told my sister to be strong, that it was better to know than be ignorant like a sheep before the slaughter."

Thanh viewed the pictures slowly, one after the other, as if imprinting the graphic details on her brain. To everyone's surprise, Thanh did not weep or question the validity of what she saw, though she looked as if she could throw up. Instead, she skimmed through them a second time, then said, "It is done. I do not know this man. Where do I sign?"

By the time he came back from Vegas two days from now, Mike would know that his wife was going to fight him, and that she had a posse of women behind her. In fact, Helene took great relish in paying a server overtime to deliver the subpoenas to Mike at the airport.

Simone and Helene talked softly after that. No high fives or whooping congratulations. Maybe those would come later because, for sure, there were going to be some hard times ahead in this case. But it was a start. A good start.

After Helene left for the courthouse, Simone met with BaRa to discuss appointments she'd scheduled for the next few days with potential clients, four spouse Cheater cases, a business embezzlement, two nanny surveillances, an Internet stalking, and a youth drug possibility. After that, she got updates from Sabine and CiCi, who'd not only been working on the Pham case, but several others. And there was a lot of paperwork to get caught up on. As a result, when her cell phone rang, she was surprised to see it was five p.m.

"Hey, darlin'," Adam said.

"Hey."

"Busy day?"

"Very. Congratulations on the court verdict today."

"You already heard about that?"

"Yes." She wasn't about to tell him about Mike's wife and her sister being in her office earlier. "You know how news travels on the bayou."

"Are you still free this evening?"

"What did you have in mind?"

He laughed, a low, husky sound that needed no words. "How about a movie?"

"You mean a video. Here at my place?"

"No. I don't trust myself alone with you."

Her self-confidence rose about ten notches. "So we're still doing the dating-without-sex thing?"

"For now. What? You don't think I can last?"

"We'll see." She was going to do her best to test his strength. "So, a movie, huh?"

"Yep. Popcorn, soda, holding hands, the works."

"I like the holding hands part, but I prefer Milk Duds over popcorn."

"See you at seven?"

"I'll be waiting with bells on," she said.

"As long as there are no handcuffs."

Who knew surrender could be so sweet? . . .

So, Tuesday night he took Simone to a movie. Something with Matt Damon. He couldn't remember the details. What he did remember was her hand in his, the occasional nudge of her thigh, and the tantalizing feel of her breath in his ear when she leaned over to whisper something about the show.

Adam had been sexually active for almost twenty years, but he discovered that night that his ears were highly erogenous zones, almost hypersensitive, connected like electrical circuits to every fine hair on his body, the tips of his fingers and toes, and especially the biggest sexual conductor of them all, which was getting bigger and more frustrated by the moment. That night, later, in the shower when he used his fingertip to ream out the soapy whorls, he about blew his wad just picturing Simone's tongue doing the same.

Pathetic, huh?

He could see the headline now, "Grown Man Electrocutes Himself in Shower with Hot Finger."

Taking care of business, himself, just wasn't doing it anymore.

The next day, Wednesday, he decided to take the afternoon off, and Simone did likewise, so that the two of them could go sailboating, along with their chaperone, little Miss Maisie.

On the way to the lake, he stopped at a convenience store for some ice where he ran into John LeDeux, who was on his way to work as a cop up Lafayette way. John, who'd stopped for gas, smirked at him and said, "Really, *cher*? Chastity in a Cajun? It just ain't natural." He waved at Simone and Maisie in his dad's pickup truck. Then he added to Adam, "Good luck with that."

Apparently Luc's big mouth had already been at work.

He got the last word in with John, though, when he remarked, "I hear congratulations are in order. A new baby, huh? And your youngest is . . . what? Eight? Good luck with that."

"Be careful. If Tante Lulu gets you in her crosshairs, ya might be in the same tight spot."

Adam didn't tell John that he was already in the old lady's sights, but not for babies. He hoped. *Note to self: Stock up on condoms. Extrastrength. Just in case I get lucky. Someday.*

It was a good thing Maisie was with them on the sailing expedition because the sight of Simone in cut-off shorts and a bikini top were enough to make Adam's skin boil if the Louisiana sun didn't. Adam wasn't sure how much longer he could hold off.

Being out on the water was fun, though, and Simone had more patience than he did with Maisie, he had to admit, especially when the kid had a couple of near falls. Yeah, she wore a life vest and knew how to swim, but still, it was good having a second set of eyes and hands to restrain the energetic five-year-old. Besides that, it gave Maisie another set of ears to listen to her babble on about her upcoming party.

And, no, I am not thinking about ears.

That evening they went to a small jazz club where they spent several hours just listening and talking softly. He'd thought about taking Simone for a ride on his Harley, but he feared all that vibration would shake up too many teetering parts.

While at the club, they ran into René LeDeux, who apparently appreciated all kinds of music, not just the wild Cajun stuff his band played. René told him he would be over early next Tuesday, the Fourth of July, to set up for the entertainment.

"You're going to have live entertainment?" Simone asked with surprise.

"Tante Lulu's doing," Adam explained.

Enough said.

"I heard you're on the wagon," René remarked. "Not for long, I wager," he added as they both watched Simone wend her way through the tables toward the ladies' room. The backside view in a belted tunic over tights was, well, a sight to behold.

"Luc again?"

"Nah, Remy told me, and he heard it from Charmaine, who heard it in her beauty salon."

Adam groaned. "That is just great. I'm the laughing stock of the bayou."

"Not at all, my friend. Well, not to everyone. The women all think you're Mr. Perfect. The men, not so much. We don't want you giving our wives ideas."

It ended up an early evening since they were both tired from being out in the sun all day. Besides, Adam couldn't take much more of just kissing and petting on Simone's doorstep. And by the sound of her moans, she was weakening, too.

Just how long did this dating crap go on in the old days? he wondered.

On Thursday afternoon, he found out via a phone call that Simone had to work that night. "One of those cheating spouses traps?" he asked.

She didn't answer, which he took for an affirmative.

"At a bar?"

"No. Somewhere else."

"Can I come, too?"

"That defeats the whole purpose, doesn't it?"

"I don't know. I never tried to trap a cheating spouse before," he grumbled.

"Are you going to be difficult, Adam?"

"No. Just disappointed."

"I meant to tell you, I have to go out of town again tomorrow."

"Overnight again?"

"Yes."

"How many days this time?"

"I don't know for sure. Maybe just one, depends on what happens."

"I can't pretend to like this, Simone."

"It's just a job. Would you feel the same if I were still a cop and out on arrest warrant?"

"Probably."

"Do you still want to date?"

"Hell, yes!"

"I guess I'll see you when I get back then."

"Will you call again tomorrow night?"

"I don't know if I'll be able to."

That sounded ominous, but he held his tongue, knowing any concern he voiced would only be taken as a negative. They said their good-byes, and he went back to work on some trial prep he needed for a new case. Or tried to.

He kept thinking about Simone.

Abstinence sucked. But it was more than that. He was ready to move to the next level with Simone. Not some nameless body. Simone. She was smart, and she was sexy, with a sharp tongue. And she made him laugh. And swear. She was turning him inside out with confusion and wanting, even resentment. Lust with a twist.

Once he got home, he was so grumpy that his dad took Maisie out for ice cream, deliberately not inviting him to come along. Adam decided to go for a one-mile run, which became a five-mile run. And the only difference? He was now not only grumpy but sweaty and exhausted.

He took a shower, first hot, then cold. No better.

By ten o'clock he'd had enough. Calling out to his dad in the den, he said, "I'm going out for a while."

"Hallelujah!" his father said.

By the time he got to Simone's place, it was ten-thirty. Thankfully, her lights were on, indicating she was home. He hoped.

He took the steps two at a time and pounded on her door.

When Simone answered, she was wearing some kind of pajama outfit. Short-sleeved, scoop-necked top over long pants. Cream color. Clingy material. No bra. Bare feet. Her hair was damp, as if from a recent shower. Her skin exuded the scent of flowers . . . and sex. *Okay, wishful thinking on that one. But then, anything would smell like sex to me at the moment.*

"Adam?" She tilted her head to the side. The door was only open halfway. Probably to keep the cat from darting outside. But, no, he could see the feline beyond the hallway, preening its fur with nonchalance, as if Adam weren't worth the effort of getting off the couch.

"Darlin', I give up," he said with a sigh of surrender. "Are we gonna do this thing?"

At first, she just stared at him. But then a slow grin emerged on her lips. Delilah couldn't have done it better just before she snipped off Samson's hair. "You had me with *darlin'.*"

It's true what they say about Cajun men . . .

Adam picked her up in his arms and kicked the door shut behind him with the heel of his athletic shoe. Shades of Rhett! Except there was no sweeping staircase, just a long hallway. And he was wearing sweats and a T-shirt. Still, swoon-worthy.

Simone was not a small woman, and she couldn't remember the last time a man had carried her—if ever. But Adam was managing very well, even when he tripped over Scarlett who'd come to investigate why a male was being granted entry into their abode. She screeched when Adam's toe hit her fur and ran off to hide under the coffee table and send cat scowls his way.

Heading directly for her bedroom, he edged the open door wider with his hip and tossed her on the brass bed. It was only a double size to fit the small room . . . no queen- or king-size, which most people seemed to prefer today, and which would probably have better suited her large frame, especially when shared, or about to be shared, with a gift-from-the-gods large man.

The bed had been left behind by the previous owner. Simone had purchased a new, extrafirm mattress but just polished up the old frame to its former glory. And, glory be, but the little old lady who'd lived here before had surely never entertained a man like the one who was prowling about the room now, like a hungry tiger. With deliberate care he removed his wallet, cell phone, and a strip of condoms from his pocket, placing them on the bedside table. Too bad he wasn't wearing glasses and taking them off—that would have been her last straw. Still, she was having a good time watching him tear off his shirt, toe off his shoes, shrug down his sweatpants and kick them aside, the whole time staring at her with smoldering eyes.

You've got to love a guy who can smolder his eyes. He had a nice body, too. Tall, broad-shouldered, narrow waisted and hipped. Muscular like an athlete but not steroid ripped. Light brown hair fuzzed his long legs and arms and chest.

Wearing just boxer briefs, which left nothing to the imagination, including his erection, he leaned down to turn on the bedside lamp. The room flooded with a warm glow, since the high watt bulb she used for reading in bed was softened by an amber shade.

"Ooh, I don't know, Adam. I do better in the dark. Too many imperfections."

"I like to see what I'm doing," he told her in a gravelly voice as he tugged both her pants and low-rise underpants down and off, flinging them back over his shoulder. Next came her top. "And I intend to explore every one of your imperfections . . . and perfections."

She raised her arms to hold on to the headboard bars. Otherwise, she might have bolted, for fear she would be incapable of meeting the intense need she saw in his eyes, which appeared golden brown, burning. She just wasn't that hot, in her opinion, despite all her marriages and relationships.

But Adam misinterpreted her posture as a tease and murmured, "Witch!" That was all right. Let him think she was more confident than she was.

He spread her legs, and then moved over her, kneeling between her thighs. Thank God, she'd shaved her legs tonight.

"Look at you," he murmured appreciatively. His eyes twinkled at her, and he smiled.

And she melted, knowing perfectly well that her hair, when it wasn't blow-dried, became a wavy mess, knowing her body was less than perfect, knowing that Adam was probably seeing her through lust-hazy eyes. But that didn't matter. He made her feel, not perfect, but highly desirable, and that was a huge boost to her self-confidence. "I think maybe I'm ready . . . already," she confided with a heated face.

"Duly noted," he said, glancing pointedly at the joining of her thighs where she was no doubt wet . . . and not from her shower.

"Spoken like a lawyer."

"Whereas you are a cop, or former cop, and will soon be reading me my rights. Wherefore I, as the second party—"

"Have only the right to get on with this party," she sniped and released her grip on the brass bars, reaching for him.

"Uh-uh." He forced her arms upward again. "I've waited too long to gulp down this meal. Slow savoring."

"At least take off your undies so we have an equal playing field."

"Uh-uh," he repeated. "This is my chastity belt."

"Hey, stud, I've got news for you and Calvin Klein. Your chastity belt is about to burst its seams."

He laughed and pinched her nipples into even tighter, rosier sentinels of arousal. Like a male erection, their condition was hard to hide. In case anyone didn't notice, nipples yelled, silently, "Hey, look at me. I'm blinkin' hot and aching for you."

She gasped and arched upward at the painful pleasure. "More," she demanded.

"Definitely," he promised. "Later."

"At least kiss me."

"Definitely." His fingertip was outlining her lips and brushing over the full surfaces. "Later."

She nipped at his fingertip, and he withdrew it, chuckling.

So, this was how he was going to play it. Well, two could play that game. She would just lie here like a loaf of bread and pretend indifference until he gave in and did it her way. Not that she had a "way."

With maddening slowness, he explored her then. Her shoulders and arms, her sides from pits to thighs, down the center of her body, between her breasts, over her navel, down to but not touching her pubic hair. Then he flipped her over, and did the same to her back, paying special attention to the back of her knees and her buttocks.

The whole time he made murmured sounds of appreciation.

"Your breasts are like sweet mounds of hardened ice cream topped with candied cherries. Have I mentioned I have a sweet tooth?"

Down, cherries! Down!

"Have you ever worn nipple rings?"

No, but I liked when you pinched them.

"How about a navel piercing? I know a fellow . . ."

Not gonna happen. And I'm not gonna get waxed, either.

"I like that you don't go bare down here."

Oh. Well, I'm okay with your chest hair, then.

"Some women's pubes look like plucked chickens."

Seen a lot of female landscaping, have you?

"Did you know the small of a woman's back is considered an erogenous zone?"

No, but I can think of a few others. One of which wants you to get on with it.

"Oh, man, oh, man! Your ass! Do you exercise a lot to get those cheeks so round and tight?"

No, they came that way. Darn it! How am I going to resist a guy who admires my big butt?

He flipped her again and now he arranged himself atop her, carefully, and began to kiss her. Holding her face in both hands, he savored her mouth with deep, wet kisses that got her squirming under him.

She put her arms around him and caressed the cords of his neck and muscles of his back and even his cloth-covered buttocks, which were also nicely curved and hard. But she wasn't about to ask how he got his that way. She was still trying to maintain an impression of low arousal when in fact her hormones were not just humming, they were screaming for completion.

Simone liked kissing, and Adam was good at it, but right now she wanted more. She arched her hips upward, lifting him only slightly, then grinding back and forth against his erection, which she could swear grew even more.

He groaned and pressed his forehead against hers, bracing himself on straightened arms. Then he raised his head, showing her glazed whiskey-colored eyes. "Slow down, sugar."

"How do I slow a runaway train?"

"We have miles to go before . . ." He waggled his eyebrows at her.

You might have miles, I have inches.

Singing the blues of a different sort . . .

Adam looked down at Simone and smiled. He'd imagined that they would be good together. He hadn't imagined big enough.

"What are you smiling about?" she grumbled, still discontented that he wasn't conducting this night's activities in the fast-forward fashion she wanted. Or thought she wanted. He intended to convince her otherwise.

I am the chief engineer on this train, baby. For the moment. Not that he would tell her that.

"You are one handful of a woman," he murmured as his hands swept over her breasts and belly. "That's why I'm smiling. No skin-and-bones model type, but flesh and curves, and places for a man to sink into."

"Fat! You're saying I'm fat."

"Definitely not!" he protested as she tried to swat at him.

He linked his fingers with hers and raised their arms above her head. "Feisty female!" he grumbled against her neck. Oops, he hadn't meant to say that aloud.

She shoved his face from her neck by tossing her head and grumbled right back at him. "You mean, I have a mind of my own, that I'm not easily controlled."

"Sure," he conceded, with a smile. "And you're smart,

probably smarter than me with my supposedly high
I.Q. Did I tell you I have a high I.Q.?" That sounded stupid, even to his own ears. And totally irrelevant to their
situation. *And speaking of ears . . . I wonder what she
would say if I asked her to stick her tongue in my ear and
jiggle? Or just blow in my ear?*

"Street smarts," she commented. "And who cares how
high your I.Q. is? It's not your brain I'm concerned with
now, it's that other organ." She bucked her hips up against
said organ, just in case he didn't understand.

He did. "Maybe I chose the wrong words to express
myself," he conceded with a laugh. "You're funny, sweetheart. I didn't realize what a great sense of humor you
have."

She gave him a cross-eyed glower. "All these left-
handed compliments just to slow the action down!" she
accused him.

"Left-handed?"

"Like a woman wants to be a comedian in bed!"

"It is funny when you pretend not to be highly aroused
while you're weeping hot oil from sex city."

Her face flushed, and she tried to knee him off her.

No way! He was firmly planted, chest to breast, hip
to hip.

Having lost that battle, she tried another. Ridicule.
"Wow, Prince Charming, you do have a way with words.
Hot oil?"

Little did she know that the only way ridicule worked
with a man when both of them were naked was if a
woman ridiculed his most precious part! At this moment,
said part wouldn't come down if the cast of Comedy Cen-
tral was surrounding the bed. "I could have said warm
honey from your private ewer of paradise, but that sounds
too romancey."

"Ewer, huh? *You're* so full of it! And God forbid you should be romancey!"

He leaned down and kissed her, real quick, before she bit his lip. "Really, darlin', is there anything better than a woman who can make a man smile in bed?"

"How about a man who can make a woman smile in bed? Or better yet . . . a man who can get . . . on . . . with . . . it."

She humped him, upward, a couple times for emphasis. Like he needed emphasis at a time like this!

He got the message, and in fact he was more than ready to "get on with it." Sliding off the bed, he stood and shrugged out of his briefs, carefully. Glancing downward, he saw the blue veins standing out on his cock. One of those rare, but much to be desired Blue Steelers. He couldn't help but smile.

"When you're done admiring yourself, my ewer is starting to yawn."

He was outright laughing as he pulled on a condom and arranged himself on her once again. And she was laughing, too.

But not for long.

For either of them.

He pressed himself inside of her and gritted his teeth against the intense pleasure of her inner folds spasming around him in welcome. She raised her knees, which gave him even more access. Have access, will travel, said his happy part.

"You feel so hot inside," he told her.

"You are so hard," she told him. "Are you wearing a ribbed condom, or is it those big blue veins I'm feeling?"

The first was a no. No ribbing. The second was just plain impossible, but his ego about went through the roof, anyhow. And, of course, he answered, "It's my big blue veins." Which was ridiculous, but who cared!

As he withdrew, her vaginal muscles tugged on him. Nature's way of keeping the male inside where he could procreate. Or Simone's body's way of saying he felt so good, please stay. Probably both.

She wrapped her legs around his butt, and he began the serious business of thrust and retreat, shove forward, drag back, in and out. Slow, then fast, then slow again, until he was no longer capable of thinking, just doing. His vision was blurry, his heart was racing, and Simone was moaning in an endless stream of, "Oh, oh, oh, oh, oh!"

When she came with an almost painful grab on his cock, then convulsed around him, he immediately followed by arching his back and shooting out his own orgasm. There was a roaring in his ears, and blood drained from his head, leaving him weak and sublimely sated.

For a long moment, he just lay atop her, trying to slow his breath down to a pant. The roar diminished gradually, and he felt like he might actually survive.

Until . . .

Damn, but didn't she take that moment to breathe in his ear! In fact, she was blowing. Little spurts of air. In a rhythmic pattern. It was probably just her attempt to get her own breathing under control, but sonofabitch, he didn't know whether to say, "Hallelujah!" or, "Have mercy, Lord."

Not that God had anything to do with sex outside of marriage, although St. Jude might have, if Tante Lulu had sicced him on them with her thunder of love crap. But, no, even the saints didn't get involved in the sex act, did they?

"Simone," he said, raising his head to look at her.

Her eyes were half lidded and she was breathing evenly through parted lips that were rosy and swollen from his kisses. But, no, no, no, she was not going to fall asleep on him. "Wake up, Simone. You can't sack out after blowing me back to life."

Her eyes shot open. "I gave you a blow job? In my sleep?"

"No, darlin'. Not that kind of blow job." He rolled over on his back, and held on to her waist, forcing her to sit upright. On his standing half-soon-to-be-full-again erection!

Her eyes went even wider as she noticed said half-stand, and she jiggled her hips a little just to make sure. "Are you serious?"

He might have seen stars for a moment, or maybe it was just the flash of amber light from her lamp as he blinked rapidly. "Serious as any man can be who's about to have his first ever multiple orgasm."

She smiled slowly, pleased, and tried to move her hips some more, which he couldn't allow. Not yet. "Be still," he ordered. "I want to look at you."

"Seems to me, you already did enough looking when you commented about my being fat."

"I never said you were fat. Now, shhh."

Her knees were folded on either side of his hips, and her buttocks rested on his upper thighs. Her hands were on his chest so that she was leaning forward slightly.

He used that opportunity to examine her ample breasts, recalling how sensitive they'd been on those occasions he'd petted them to orgasm on her outdoor landing. Lifting them from underneath. Palming them. Flicking the pale pink nipples which he'd already roughed to a rosy hue. You could tell she'd never borne a child; otherwise, the nipples and areolas would be much darker. The best part was watching the expression on her face as he played with these most erogenous parts of her lush body.

"Come closer," he urged as he leaned upward.

She arched her neck back as she did so, giving his mouth access to her breasts. As he took one into his mouth, drawing deeply and squeezing the other, she came apart inside and around him, just like she had before in their petting sessions, but this time—praise God and pass the gumbo, as Tante Lulu often said—his cock was there to feel every seizure of her inner muscles. It was a sign of his out-of-control excitement that he could think of the old lady at a time like this and not go limp.

This was not a violent orgasm, but a sweet wash of sexual pleasure that was wonderful to Adam because of its gentleness. Not that he didn't appreciate screaming, explosive, mutual climaxes when they came (pun intended), but wasn't the human body amazing for its variety?

It must also be a sign of his out-of-control excitement that he could have such philosophical thoughts at a time like this. Especially when his half arousal was now full and ready for some friction.

Simone was sitting upright again and was staring at him through glazed eyes, as if she couldn't believe what had happened, but then she smiled. And, oh, man, he knew he was in trouble by that smile. It was the kind Boudica the Celtic warrior queen gave the Romans before she led her army forward.

She merely rocked at first, forward, then back. Several times.

But he wanted more than that, and he took her hips in his hands, showing her the movement he liked best. A quick learner, she rode him then. Hard.

He held on to her buttocks at first. Then he rose to a sitting position, knees raised, and they rocked each other while he tongue kissed her. Then she Frenched him back. And they were so good together. He wanted it to last forever, but of course it ended much too soon. Or just in time.

This time, when she lay depleted under him, he rose and went into the bathroom to discard the condom and wash himself off. When he returned to the bed, she was stone-cold asleep, the kind of sleep only a perfect orgasm could bring.

He knew that Simone had insecurities about her body, but, oh, man, if she could see herself the way he saw her! Her hair was a mess of shiny brown waves spread out on a white pillow imprinted with multicolored butterflies. She had pulled a matching butterfly sheet up over herself, but her shoulders and arms and upper breasts were still exposed. A sex flush still infused her cheeks and neck and chest. Her lips looked bruised and that might be whisker burn on her chin. He liked that he'd put his mark on her.

In fact, he was beginning to think he was falling in love. It had been a long time since he'd felt like this, and then only for one woman . . . in the early days with Hannah. And look how that ended up.

Why Simone? He had no idea. He'd certainly fought the attraction.

And why now? Could it be as simple as some scientific principle where the human psyche yearned for some kind of destined bonding every so often? Or maybe it was connected to middle-age madness.

Whatever the cause, he just knew that he thought about her all the time, and when he looked at her, he felt happy inside. His heart swelled, literally. Corny, he knew. But maybe not so absurd. Medical researchers had announced recently that people could actually die from a broken heart. Was it so impossible then that the heart could actually inflate with love?

On the other hand, could Tante Lulu and her St. Jude nonsense have anything to do with this awful/wonderful assault on his emotions? Probably not. But still, everyone had warned him about steering clear of the old lady.

On this confusing note, he decided that this would be a good time for him to leave. He liked to be there when Maisie awakened in the morning. But it was only one a.m. Plenty of time. So, he slid into bed beside Simone, pulled her into his arms, and covered them both with the sheet.

Just before he fell asleep, he noticed the cat in the doorway glaring at him. He suspected that he'd usurped the feline's nighttime spot. "Tough luck, Scarlett," he said on a yawn. "Tomorrow is another day."

Little did he know what tomorrow was going to bring.

No regrets . . . yet . . .

Simone was late getting up the next morning, and her first look in the mirror over the bathroom sink almost scared her into ducking back under the covers again. It was going to take twice as long as usual to fix herself so she didn't look like a woman who had been thoroughly fucked. *Excuse the crude expression. It fits!* But did she mind? Heck, no! Not the fucking or the extra effort required to repair the damage.

Too bad she wasn't going to Marcus Pitot's lakeshore house until tonight. One look at her in this condition, and everyone would assume she was ready to party. Sex party.

Her hair resembled a wild mass of waves due to its drying naturally and her writhing in bed. She wet-combed it tightly off her face into a ponytail, which looked more like a bush than a tail. She'd have to rewash and style later.

Ice cubes on her lips did little to reduce the swelling

from so many deep, deep kisses. Women paid big money for this botoxed look, but they didn't get it at home, overnight. Everyone would guess the cause, and she wanted to hug the secret of her and Adam to herself for a while longer.

Make-up hid the whisker burns on her face and neck. The other places he'd abraded were her not-so-guilty pleasure.

Simone had awakened once around two a.m. to find herself snuggled up against a sleeping Adam. She'd thought about shaking him and sending him home, but she was too sleepy, and he was so warm, and her body was so relaxed, that she'd drifted contentedly back to sleep.

But then she'd awakened again about three a.m. from a deep, erotic dream to find herself already aroused. They were both on their sides, spoon fashion, and Adam had been lightly caressing her body's intimate parts while she slept, bringing her up to not-quite-orgasmic levels.

"What . . . no . . . that's not fair," she protested.

"Shhh," he said. "Let me . . ."

Before she'd known what was happening, she'd been on her knees, face in the pillow, and he'd been taking her from behind. She'd still been only half awake; so, it had been a dreamy sort of sex, until his one hand played with her hanging breasts and the thumb of the other hand strummed her clitoris, which was still engorged from previous bed play. In a nanosecond, she'd jump-started from This-Is-Nice to Holy-Freakin'-Magic-Fingers!

Good thing she had no neighbors—nighttime ones, anyway—because, for the first time in her life, she'd screamed out her ecstasy. Talk about explosive orgasms. And Adam had been no better. The male roar of triumph! What a thing to hear! Under normal circumstances she would have laughed. Neither of them had been laughing.

Until four a.m. when she'd awakened him to say it was time to take a shower and go home. She'd gotten back at him then by giving him an ear orgasm while he'd leaned against the shower tiles. He'd already told her how sensitive his ears were and how he'd had fantasies about her tongue, and, *well, you get the idea.*

She'd been back in bed and almost asleep again— *What girl wouldn't be after all those climaxes?*—when Adam, fully dressed and about to leave, had leaned down to kiss her and said, "Call me."

In fact, she could have sworn he'd said, "Call me, love."

Chapter Fifteen

All in a day's work . . .

When she got downstairs to the office, the first one she saw was BaRa who remarked, "Someone's been ridden hard and put down wet."

So much for all of Simone's efforts to appear normal.

Her mother, who was wearing a one-piece, black spandex body suit patterned with red chevrons, which made her back end look like a Chevrolet *(Where is she shopping these days?)*, took one look at Simone, then did a double-take. "I knew it. Cajun Crazy again!"

Tante Lulu, who had just "stopped by" on her way to the bank, must shop at the same place as her mother because she was all dolled up in a black-and-red herringbone shorts set. The old lady cackled and said, "God bless thunderbolts!" But then she wagged her finger at Simone, cautioning, "But God doan like no hanky panky outside marriage. Best ya be callin' the banns real soon."

Ed, the painter, who was finishing up some last-minute detailing, muttered when he saw her enter the kitchenette, "Some guy's walkin' bow-legged today."

And Helene, when she came in for a ten a.m. meeting, just grinned.

"Kimly Bien called me late last night. Mike Pham went berserk when he was served and made all kinds of threats against his wife."

"Oh, no! Was she hurt?"

"No. If she had been, we could have hauled his ass to jail today. But she was afraid, and called her sister. The question is how to protect her now."

"She wouldn't be safe with her sister?"

Helene shook her head. "That would be Pham's first place to look for her. And Kimly's biggest concern is Thanh herself. Her husband, once his rage is tamped down, will try to cajole his wife into dropping all the 'nonsense.' He told her, 'You know that what is mine is yours, too. We don't need any papers to prove that.' And already Thanh is weakening."

"And the solution?"

"I was thinking she could stay with your mother."

"At The Gates? I hate involving my mother in this kind of thing."

"She'd love it. And it would get her out of your hair here for a few days. Besides, you'll want her to babysit your cat again while you go out of town, just in case you need to stay an extra day."

"Oh, please let this be a one-night deal. I feel dirty just thinking about what those people do."

"I would think you'd been in a bit of dirt already," Helene remarked, looking pointedly at Simone's puffy lips.

"Good dirt," Simone told her.

"Anyhow, be safe tonight. All we need from you and Gabe is some audio with Pitot making perverted suggestions, and some photographs of the stuff these people do at these parties, or the accessories. His wife already has the goods on his affairs. She needs stuff he would never want made public."

"Accessories?"

"Hey, if Pham has his condo equipped with a special room, you can be sure Pitot has accommodations to suit his guests' specialized requests."

"I'm gonna have to bathe with lye soap after this."

"Call me," Helene said before she left.

Which reminded Simone of Adam's last words to her.

"I meant to tell you, that Ferguson creep got a plea bargain."

"What? Don't tell me they released him."

"No, he's going to serve ten years minimum, lose his teaching license, have to pay fifty thousand dollars in various fines, and be a registered pedophile. Which was a gift to him, actually. Girls were creeping out of the woodwork, willing to testify against him. At trial, he could have gotten lots worse."

"At least Darlene won't have to testify in open court, and she and her mother can, hopefully, start getting their lives back on track."

"Right," Helene agreed.

After that, they spoke to Simone's mother about having Thanh as a guest for a few days.

Adelaide surprised both Simone and Helene by being not only willing but enthusiastic about the idea. "My feet have been killin' me, and the doctor says I need to rest my knees more," she revealed.

Simone could have said, "I told you so," but didn't.

"Maybe she kin teach me how to make Vietnamese food," Adelaide mused as they walked toward her car. She was going to follow Helene to the Pham house where Kimly's sister was helping Thanh to pack.

"Or maybe you can teach her how to make gumbo," Simone said.

Things settled down after that until Gabe came to pick her up midafternoon. She'd gone next door to buy a few items from the boutique, items suitable for a lakeshore dinner. White slacks, a blue-and-white-striped blouse, white sandals, and a pretty red, soft-as-kitten-fur pashmina in case it got chilly.

It was only later when they arrived at the lodge that Simone realized things were not going to go according to their plans.

First of all, their car was blocked in the driveway so they couldn't make a fast getaway if it was required.

Second, the evening's agenda included a quick swim before dinner. And she hadn't brought a bathing suit. But neither had anyone else.

Third, one of the guests—a short, bald guy, Sam Salter, who owned a chain of gyms in Biloxi and had the steroid muscles to show for it—had taken an instant liking to her, and he had the hands of an octopus. Besides, he liked to brag, explicitly, about what he could do with that bald head.

Fourth, she and Gabe had gotten separated right from the start, with Caroline latching on to him like he was the new best thing. Gabe—bless his actor's heart—was playing right into Caroline's flirtation by pretending to be horndog happy at her attention. At one point, Simone heard him say to Pitot's mistress, "I drank two bottles of pineapple juice today. Makes my happy juice taste like piña coladas."

Eew! Where does Gabe come up with this stuff? Maybe it's just a man thing . . . the male genetic inclination to crudeness.

And, finally, sharknado alert! Marcus Pitot had the mean, steely-gray eyes of an ocean predator, and he was watching her every move. Whatever he was into, it was going to be painful. The music from *Jaws* played in her head.

For the first time, Simone began to question her new profession.

It was raining rage . . .

Mike Pham came storming into LeDeux & Lanier that afternoon in a rage. "My wife has lost her friggin' mind. I oughta have her committed. Can I have her committed? Otherwise, I just might have to kill the bitch."

Mildred backed up, frightened by the red-faced man, even though he was yelling toward Adam and Luc who'd come out of their offices, and not at her. Any minute now she'd be reaching for her Mace.

"Whoa, whoa, whoa! Enough of that kind of talk!" Luc warned, motioning Mike, as well as Adam, into his office, shutting the door behind them. "Now what's going on?"

"I got back from Vegas last night, and some kid slapped these papers in my hands in the middle of the airport."

"A process server?" Adam asked.

"Yeah, some pimple-faced asshole of a college kid. Shoved the papers in my hands and ran."

Wish I'd been there!

Adam and Luc looked over the documents, which appeared to be various subpoenas and court filings related to the Pham shrimp business, a home, and other property. In addition, meek little Thanh Pham was preempting her husband by filing for divorce first. *Would an air fist pump be out of order?* Adam wondered. The divorce petition mentioned grounds of adultery and "living separately and apart."

"You haven't been living at home?" Adam inquired.

"Sometimes I do. I have a place on Grand Isle that I prefer." He shrugged with defiance, as if he had every right to do so.

"It says that your business is in your name and your father's. Any reason why your wives' names aren't on it?" Luc asked.

"My mother is dead, but her name was never listed as an owner, either. It's a Vietnamese thing. The man is the head of the family and the business."

That didn't seem so bad. Sexist, and old-fashioned, but not anything to raise legal alarm bells.

"And the house?" Luc asked.

"Same thing." Mike's flushed face said there was more to the story.

"Have you talked to your wife about these?" Luc pointed to the documents.

Mike nodded. "Thanh wants a million dollars, the house, a car, and a bunch of other stuff. Which she is going to get over my dead body. Kimly put my wife up to this, I know she did."

Something more was going on here. "Excuse me a moment," Adam said and went into his own office where he called Kimly Bien. And, boy, did he get an earful!

Fifteen minutes later, when he returned to Luc's office, he said, "There are pictures."

"Of what? Me screwing some woman? Big deal!"

"More than that." Adam looked at Luc. "It would seem there's a room in Mike's condo on Grand Isle called 'The Dungeon.' And photographs to prove some unusual activities."

Mike's face went beet red. "It's not illegal."

"Probably not, but what *could be* illegal is your business setup," Adam said. "When you married Thanh, did she bring a number of shrimping boats into the business in exchange for which it was intended that she become part owner of the company?"

"Like I said, it's a Vietnamese thing."

Luc exchanged a quick glance with Adam. "Look, Mike, you were our client for the Pham versus Cypress case. And that's all. This other crap, including a divorce, will have to be handled by Jessie John Daltry. I want nothing to do with it."

"That's bullshit. You lawyers are all alike. In for the easy kill, out when it requires some work."

"Um, I think enough's been said here today," Adam said, going over to open the door. "It's been nice working with you." *Not!*

Mike said a few foul words before gathering up his paperwork and storming out. "I'll see you two shysters in court. And not on my behalf. I'm gonna sue your asses off for malpractice."

"Go for it!" Adam said, following him out, just in case he punched in a wall or scared Mildred even more than she already was.

Afterward, he and Luc agreed that it was good riddance. They did not need clients like Mike, despite any money they might bring in.

Adam was driving home later that day, and was stuck in the downtown rush-hour traffic when he noticed Adelaide Daigle, Simone's mother, standing outside the Legal Belles office waving him down. He frowned with confusion. It was five-thirty, Simone was out of town, and the office should have been closed for the day.

He pulled over into an illegal parking spot and opened his window, "Hey, Addie, what's up?"

"I jist stopped by the office ta get some pain pills I left here earlier today."

"And . . . ?"

"I need ta take a bag of kitty litter back ta the trailer park with me, but it's upstairs and my knees are killin' me t'day."

"You want me to help?"

"I'd be much obliged."

He followed her inside the office, and asked, "Where's the bag?"

"In the pantry closet of Simone's kitchen upstairs."

He used the interior stairway to access Simone's apartment and had no trouble locating the fifty-pound bag. How Addie was going to get it from her car to the inside of her trailer, he had no idea. Maybe a neighbor would help.

About to heft the bag onto his shoulder, he noticed the open laptop on Simone's kitchen table. He shouldn't look, but his attention was caught by the picture on the screen. It was a cedar-log lodge-type dwelling on a lake. Very attractive. Was Simone looking for vacation possibilities? Maybe a dirty weekend for the two of them?

But wait!

The fine hairs stood out on the back of Adam's neck. He recognized that place. It was Marcus Pitot's place on Lake Pontchartrain. The site of many of the sex club orgies that Hannah had frequented.

What did it mean?

Was Simone, the woman he was almost certainly in love with, into those types of perversions? He didn't think so. Yeah, she'd blown his brains out with the sex last night, but it had been normal stuff. On the other hand, in the early days, when he'd first fallen for Hannah, he never would have suspected her of such perversions.

A rage began to build in him.

Duped again? Was that possible?

He knew it was unethical, but Adam sat down and began to play with Simone's laptop. He soon realized that this was a job, not some personal perversion of Simone's. She, and her agency, were investigating Marcus Pitot on behalf of his wife, Saffron Pitot, who was as flaky as a Southern biscuit but who seemed to have some good reasons to suspect her husband was up to no good. And there was a MapQuest page with driving directions.

His rage should have abated, but it didn't.

Had she any idea what she was fooling with? Nabbing cheaters was one thing. Messing with a sadistic bastard like Marcus Pitot was another. To say he was dangerous was a vast understatement. Adam recalled rumors that Pitot had ordered one of his partners "eliminated" when he crossed him one time. And Adam knew for a fact that a woman who dropped out of the sex club, and talked about it, somehow ended up with a mugging that cut her face so badly she needed numerous plastic surgeries.

I thought you were smarter than that, Simone, he fumed, as he stood and picked up the cat litter and carried it down the steps and outside. After he tossed the bag into Addie's trunk, she thanked him profusely. It was only as the car began to move away that he noticed the woman slumped down in the front seat with a head scarf pulled forward to cover her face.

No, it couldn't be. He blinked and looked again. *Oh, my God! It was Pham's wife, Thanh.*

Adam's rage amped another few notches. Now, it wasn't just Simone who was in danger, but her mother, too.

Was this the kind of woman he wanted around his daughter? One who had no care for her own safety, let alone those around her?

He practically saw red as he drove off, and not just because there was a parking ticket on his windshield.

What should he do?

How about nothing?

How could he go home, eat dinner, and play with Maisie when he knew where Simone was? Impossible!

But then, no one would expect him to be some Prince Charming coming to her rescue. In fact, Simone would reject that idea, vehemently. He knew how she valued her independence and police skills.

Pff! Marcus Pitot didn't play by any rules the police academy taught.

She'd get what she deserved for being so stupid.

What if he scarred Simone? Hell, what if he killed her? A drowning at the lake . . . nothing unusual in that.

Who was he kidding? He was going after her, and he'd cart her home over his shoulder if he had to, like that bag of cat litter. But how did he barge into a private party, without an invitation, without giving up Simone's game?

He thought of something suddenly, an excuse he could give Pitot for showing up unannounced. Driving home, he waved to his dad and Maisie, who were in the pool, and went upstairs to the file cabinet he kept in his office closet. It was a sealed manila envelope marked "Hannah," which he placed in a slim leather briefcase.

"I'm going out for a while," he yelled to his father from the open sliding door in the kitchen.

"How about that rage?" his father remarked before Adam had a chance to turn and leave. The old man was sitting on the edge of the pool in swimming trunks, his legs in the water.

"Rage? What rage? I'm not in a rage," he lied.

"Huh? I didn't say *rage*, I said *stage*. How about the stage that René LeDeux delivered today for the party?"

Adam noted then that beyond the pool, a miniature stage had been erected. And a wooden dance floor on the grass! So much for the expensive lawn care service he'd contracted! And holy crap! Their neighbors would have a bird over the noise, unless they invited them all, which they would probably have to. What was another twelve or so people?

"Dad-dy," Maisie complained as she climbed out of the pool, dripping water from her sagging suit, and came toward him, "you promised we would go shopping."

"I'll go shopping with you tomorrow. Cross my heart, sweetie," he said, marking an X on his chest before letting her give him a wet hug.

The big pool party would be held soon, and he'd been promising that he would help with a trip to Party Circus. Tomorrow he would pay up with a chore he hated . . . shopping.

For now, he had another chore to complete. And he couldn't help but wonder if Simone would be around to come to their party.

Home, home on the range . . .

After skinny dipping in the lake, all the women wore long silk scarves, working them into sarongs, some more transparent than others, while the men wrapped shorter lengths of fabric around their hips. Claiming modesty, Simone had worn her underwear into the water, which proved amusing and somewhat of a challenge to all the others. Gabe had no problem going full monty, whether in his personal life or for a job, apparently.

She sensed that everyone was cautiously studying her and Gabe, gauging their reactions to the setting and any innuendo of sexual activity. Nothing overt was revealed yet, except for Sam the Hands, who'd toned down his groping after a while, probably after a few words of warning from Marcus. She had noticed when they'd entered the lake that Sam was unusually well-endowed (Like porno-star huge!), which could only be an asset for a club like this. Otherwise, he was a little crude compared to the others.

Though Simone was sticking to white wine, lots of alcohol was being consumed, mostly hard liquor, and Caroline had a preference for dirty martinis. Twice, Simone had surreptitiously dumped her drink in a potted magnolia tree. She'd seen Gabe do the same with some fifty-year-old Scotch. Yeah, not very original, but effective so far. But poor tree! She vowed to herself that she would give a donation to the Save The Trees Foundation as a penance.

So far, she and Gabe had gotten lots of pictures and audio thanks to the high tech devices they used, but so far nothing extreme enough to satisfy Saffron Pitot's wishes had happened.

They sat down to dinner in their scant attire out on the wide porch overlooking the lake. A first clue that things were starting to get steamier was that the servers, two young women, wore only skimpy aprons and high heels. No bras and the flimsiest of thongs. The busboy—or busman, since he was in his early twenties—wore nothing at all, not even shoes. No one paid any attention to their nudity, so she didn't comment, either. She could tell that the others were watching her and Gabe for their reactions, but other than a blush from her, and a wink from Gabe, they pretended nonchalance.

The meal was, of course, excellent. Native red snapper with baby potatoes and snap peas, followed by a decadent chocolate soufflé. And potent lemon liquors to cleanse the palate . . . or freeze their brains. Despite her rationing of alcohol, Simone was feeling a little woozy. She hoped they hadn't drugged the drinks, as well. That could be a disaster.

Besides Marcus and Caroline and Sam Salter, there was Sam's wife, Heidi, a young, muscle-defined example of his female fitness program, who was several inches shorter than his bald head, but buff. Really buff! In fact, she'd won a number of weightlifting competitions, her claim to fame being that she could bench press two hundred pounds.

And there was James Allard, a New Orleans real estate developer, and his wife, Chantung (Really!), a former model whose blond hair and pale skin were a sharp contrast to James's coal-black skin. They were an attractive couple, both tall and very thin, and surprisingly intelligent, as evidenced by the dinner conversation that evolved around several topics—the economy, crime in the Big Easy, and recent movies. They supported the New Orleans Opera Association in a big way.

Gabe could hold his own on the subject of movies and the theater, and Simone knew plenty about crime, big city and otherwise, although she managed to appear not too knowledgeable. Thus far, there had been no big gaffes.

It was no surprise that, as the meal progressed, the talk became sexual.

"I was invited to be in a porn movie," Sam informed them. "A guy who came into the gym checked me out in the showers and made an offer right on the spot."

"Are you going to do it?" Marcus asked.

"Nah! I'm saving Big Betsy," he said, palming himself, "for my wife and a few of my friends." He waggled his eyebrows at said friends.

Simone sipped more lemon madness to hide her revulsion.

"I was in a porn flick one time," Gabe said.

Whaaat?

"Seriously, dude?" inquired Sam, not at all pleased to have his thunder stolen.

"When I was in college," Gabe explained. "Needed to earn some extra cash for tuition."

"That's amazing, Larry," Caroline said, placing a well-manicured hand on Gabe's arm and squeezing.

"Was it fun?" Simone asked, not sure if Gabe was serious or not.

Gabe shrugged. "Actually, it got kind of boring, as I've told you before." At the hoots of laughter from the other males at the table, he elaborated, "Most of the folks were drugged out, especially the women, and, frankly, I don't take it in the ass for any amount of money."

Whoa! Simone had to bite her lip to keep from gasping out her shock, but the others at the table loved his candor.

"I do," Heidi revealed, "for the right person." She glanced pointedly at James.

Everyone laughed at what must have been a private joke.

I am so out of my comfort zone here.

Which got even more uncomfortable when Chantung announced, "I got my nipples pierced. Wanna see?"

Everyone, including herself, truth to tell, said yes.

And so the former model, whose perfect breasts were surely silicone enhanced, tugged the top of her sarong down—*Right in the middle of the dinner table!*—exposing two engorged nipples through which two small gold rings flashed in the candle light. She left the silk fabric lying in her lap while she arched her back and preened.

Compliments abounded. Chantung even let Sam tug

on one of the rings to see the effect, which was a gasp from her lips. Pleasure or pain, it was hard to tell. "If she was mine, I'd put a chain through those suckers and lead her around like a pet dog," Sam said.

To which James should have reacted negatively, but he just smiled.

"Maybe her husband will let you do that, later," Marcus suggested as he stood and asked, "Refills, everyone, before we move to the Play Room?"

"Play Room?" she mouthed at Gabe, who got her message, and said, "Listen, Marcus. I'm game for just about anything, but Diane here is a little timid. No offense intended, but you're gonna have to give us a chance to make up our minds if this kind of activity is for us." He paused and added, "If you want us to leave now, no hard feelings."

Marcus was not a happy camper, but he exchanged looks with the other members of his club, then told Gabe. "You can stay and watch tonight, if you want, or join in at any time, if the mood hits you. But if you don't participate, I better not hear about this around town. Anywhere, for that matter. Am I making myself clear?" The steely warning in his eyes was more than clear.

She and Gabe both nodded.

Marcus smiled then and said, "We're gonna do some role playing tonight, but first we have a little live entertainment that I'm sure you'll enjoy. Caro, why don't you show Diane the costume gallery?"

"Sure. Come on, girls." Caroline stood and motioned for not just Diane, but Heidi and Chantung, to accompany her. "Bring your drinks with you."

The costume gallery? Oh, boy!

Whatever she'd been expecting it wasn't this! Practically a department store of nothing but costumes. It was like Dragon Con, Comic-Con, and Porno Con combined in a large room with numerous open closets and clothes racks and shelving units. At a quick glance, she could see Star Wars costumes, as in Stormtrooper does Alien Women, she supposed; pirates, both male and female; superheroes; Roman soldiers and raggedy female attire (Rape of the Sabine Women, Caroline explained.); cops and hookers; dom and dominatrix; doctors and nurses. Amazing what money could buy! And the foolishness it could be spent on.

"We're doing the Old West tonight," Caroline told Simone. "The men already took their costumes to the downstairs dressing room."

"Oh, goody! My favorite," Chantung said. "I take dibs on being the horse tonight."

Whaaat?

"You always get to be the horse," Heidi grumbled. "Okay, I'll be the Indian captive."

"Diane and I will be plain old cowgirls, then," Caroline said.

We will?

When Caroline handed her a buckskin skirt and a shirt, Simone said, "These will never fit."

"Sure they will. The fabric is stretchy. One size fits all."

"My underwear is probably still wet. It's still in the downstairs bathroom."

"No underwear." The message in Caroline's tone was that this was one concession that would not be made. "You might want to take your jewelry off."

Simone shook her head. "I'd rather not." She was recording everything she could with her earrings scanning the room, although Caroline was probably referring to the three-carat, synthetic diamond ring on her finger.

A short time later, Simone stood before a full-length mirror wearing a cowgirl hat and boots, a pair of toy pistols holstered in a belt around her waist, a leatherette skirt that hung low on her hips and was so short the lower curve of her buttocks would be exposed if she leaned over even a little, and a snap-button blouse that only started buttoning about mid-abdomen and which was fitted so that it was skintight from waist up to the ruching that acted as an uplifting device under the breasts. The result was that her bare breasts were practically bursting out. And, frankly, the calico material was way too thin.

She felt silly.

But it was nothing compared to her companions. Caroline's cowgirl outfit consisted of thigh-high, leather fringed hooker boots, a tiny leather thong, also with fringes, and a leather vest that exposed rather than covered her breasts and was held together by a thin leather cord. Her cowgirl hat hung down her back from a loop around her neck. She carried a whip in one hand and a lasso in the other.

"Yippee ki yay yay," Simone joked.

And Caroline retorted, "Ride 'em, cowgirl."

Then there was Heidi, the Indian maid, whose only resemblance to any Native American Simone had ever seen was a feather in her braided hair. Suffice it to say, there were lots of beads and a pair of moccasins.

The biggest shock came with Chantung's costume. She wore a leather harness fitted between her bare pierced breasts and around her back where reins dangled down. On her head and hanging down her back was a horse's mane and strapped to her backside was a lush horse's tail. She wore high heels with taps on them that sounded like horseshoes clippety-clopping when she pranced around the room. When she bent over she wiggled her butt and neighed.

Welcome to bizarro land!

But that was nothing compared to what she saw when

she entered the Play Room. First of all, the room was a vast homage to male fantasy. Dim lighting. Low armless chaises and circular couches. Several ottomans similar to ones she'd seen advertised in the back of *Cosmo* magazine, ones designed to align the body in the so-called perfect sexual position. A very large flat-screen TV. There were probably all kinds of toys and whips and chains in the closed shelving units around the room. In fact, there were a number of brackets in the walls that might be used for restraints, and there was a weird metal contraption hanging high up on the ceiling, but overall it was upscale sexy compared to Pham's Dungeon Room, which was more lower-class sleaze.

Not that this room didn't give her the creeps. It did. Big time.

And then the men walked in.

She didn't know whether to laugh or run for her life.

Gabe was playing the naked cowboy, or almost naked cowboy, wearing a white cowboy hat, a white Speedo or thong, hard to tell from this angle, and cowboy boots. But Gabe was the most conventional of the bunch.

James was the Mexican bandito, all in black with ammunition belts criss-crossed over his chest. He carried a rifle (fake, she hoped) in one hand and a whip in the other. Oh, and did she mention he wore assless black denims and red-embossed leather boots?

Sam had taken on the role of Indian chief, to complement his wife, Simone supposed. He wore a full feather headdress, a bow in hand, and a quiver of arrows slung over his shoulder. War paint formed designs on his face and shaved chest. Beaded wrist and ankle bracelets rattled as he walked. His "Big Betsy" was bare and . . . well, big.

And then there was Marcus. If they got a picture of

him, she and Gabe could leave for the night. His costume was so ludicrous and insanely perverted. He was a bull with a headpiece that was furry and sporting horns. There was also a cloak of fur pelts hanging from his shoulders. Devices resembling hoofs circled his ankles and wrists. And between his legs was strapped a dildo so big it would do any bull in stud proud; it swung from side to side as he walked into the room.

She had to blink several times to keep from going bug-eyed. Gabe came over to her and gave her a kiss on the lips and a pat on her butt. "You okay, sweetheart?"

"I'm fine, sweetheart," she said back at him, in case anyone heard them. They would certainly be watching for their reactions. She tried to smile. But under her breath, she whispered to Gabe, "How soon can we get out of here?"

"As soon as I can slip out and get our car free," he whispered back, pretending to be nuzzling her neck.

"Sit down, everyone," Marcus ordered. "We'll have a little entertainment before our own games begin."

There was a tittering of laughter around the room, and James remarked, "Yee-haw!"

She and Gabe sat down on a low couch thingee that was curved upward slightly at both ends. They immediately found out that the darn thing rocked, like a see-saw.

The others laughed when they noticed the two of them almost falling off the ends. But they then sat close together in the middle, for balance, and the fun began.

In walked their two servers and the busboy/man, all naked, pushing one of those mechanical bulls on rollers. When they got to the middle of the room, they put locks on the legs. And Simone could see that this mechanical bull was different in that there was a wide hole in the center of the saddle.

To the tune of Aerosmith singing "Back in the Saddle

Again," the three of them did the most incredible things with that bull. On it, under it, to themselves, to each other. Dancing, gyrating, masturbating, copulating as the music got louder and louder, then ended with a crash of silence, as they bowed to the clapping crowd and Marcus walked them to the door, dildo swinging, presumably to pay for their services. Meanwhile Sam and James were moving the bull off to the side. Not out of the room, though, she noticed.

What would she do if they asked her to ride that thing? Bare-assed, as she was?

"Well, that was disgusting," she said to Gabe.

"Um," he replied.

She gave him a look, and saw that he was turned on. *Men!*

"Hopefully, their car is the one blocking us in," Gabe said. "I'll check as soon as I can."

Marcus was back, and he walked over to them, "Are you having fun so far?"

"Terrific!" Gabe said.

"How about you, Diane? Still feeling timid?"

It was hard for her to answer at first because with them sitting and Marcus standing, it put the dildo at eye level. "I'm still not sure," she said and had no trouble pretending to blush.

They were saved by the bell then, literally, as the doorbell rang.

Everyone in the room went still, glancing worriedly at Marcus.

Marcus put a fingertip to his lips, cautioning silence. "It's probably those three who just left. Probably forgot something and locked themselves out." Even so, he removed his bull head piece and put a toweling robe over the rest of his costume, leaving the room.

The door was shut, but still they could hear voices.

"What the hell are you doing here?"

"I found one of Hannah's folders—the one you keep pestering me about. I was in the neighborhood and thought I'd drop it off."

"This is not a good time. Hey, you can't just barge in here and—"

"Not barging. This will only take a second. Oh, I see that you just finished dinner. Oops. Is this one of your club nights?"

"Just leave the damn folder on the table."

"Uh-uh. You are signing off on these things. I don't want you to be bothering me about any missing photos anytime in the future."

"Why now?"

"I have a daughter who's nosey. I don't want her finding these."

"Okay, let me see them. Whoa, where you going?"

"Just checking to see what you have going on tonight."

"Why? You were never interested before."

"I'm lots older now . . . and wiser."

Everyone was standing now, looking toward the door. She and Gabe were closest, but she'd recognized the voice before the door even opened. It was, of course, Adam Lanier in a rumpled business suit with a five o'clock shadow, looking sexier than anyone in the club, and angry as a bear if that tic in his jaw was any indication.

She groaned. "He's going to ruin everything."

Gabe looked at her. "Who is he?"

"My boyfriend, sort of. Former, as of this minute."

"Folks, you remember Adam Lanier, Hannah's husband," Marcus said, trying to take charge of the situation, knowing how uncomfortable everyone was feeling, especially in their costumes. "Don't worry. Everything's fine."

Adam glanced around the room, nodding at each of the couples before he got to her and Gabe. He arched his brows and said, "And these new folks are . . . ?"

"Dr. Larry Storm and his wife, Diane. They just moved here from Chicago. Why don't I get you a drink, Adam? Scotch and water as I recall?" Marcus was clearly trying to save the night and soothe his club members' rattled nerves.

"Sure," Adam said, even as he shook Gabe's hand, then just gave Simone a head-to-shoulders lookover. "What's this, Simone?" he asked. "Annie Oakley Does Dallas?"

"No. It's about to be called Ex-Cop Kills Dumb-Ass Lawyer."

"Will you be wearing a cop suit that shows half your ass, like you are now?"

She bared her teeth at him, and at the same time tugged down the hem of her cowgirl skirt.

"I think Diane is losing her timidity," Gabe joked loud enough for others to hear, then walked over a few feet to chat with Caroline, who'd already indicated an interest in Simone's doctor husband. She heard Gabe remark to Caroline, "Who's this new guy? I sense a spark between him and Diane." Clearly, Caroline, as well as the others, must be wondering why Adam was suddenly interested in sticking around. An interest in Diane/Simone would be one explanation.

"And you don't mind?"

"Not as long as she shares the honey and goes home with me. Ha, ha, ha."

Caroline looked at her and Adam, studying them, then concluded, "Instant sexual attraction."

Not at the moment!

"Go . . . away!" she ordered Adam, at the same time smiling as she tried to hide her upset from the others.

"Not a chance!" Adam said, just before accepting the glass from Marcus and taking a huge slug.

To Marcus he said, "Do you mind if I stick around? I promise I won't interfere with any of your fun and games."

Marcus was not happy to have Adam there, but he also wouldn't mind his joining the club, Adam had told her that when he'd mentioned his wife and her involvement with this group.

Conflicted, Marcus glanced around the room. "Anyone uncomfortable with Adam staying?"

They all raised their hands.

"Wanna give him a trial? Half hour or so and he's out of here?"

Tentatively, the hands went up, one at a time, except for Sam who probably didn't want any competition.

Marcus nodded and said, "I'll be right back."

As he walked away, Marcus dropped his toweling robe.

At which view, Adam muttered, "You're not in Kansas anymore, Dorothy." Simone wasn't sure if he was talking to himself or to her.

Marcus went over to a panel on the wall that controlled some kind of sound system. Instantly, the room flooded with music . . . theme music to match the night's role playing. Loud and raucous beats caused everyone to relax and laugh. "Bum dee dee bum, bum dee dee bum, bum dee dee bum . . ." This time it was "Save a Horse, Ride a Cowboy!" that broke the silence.

"This ought to be fun," Adam remarked to her with a roll of the eyes. "By the way, what's your exit plan?"

She blushed.

"You and Dr. Cowboy have no exit plan!" he guessed.

"We do so, but you're screwing it up."

"*Screw* being the keyword in this motley crew of deviants."

"Go . . . away!" she repeated.

"I sense a little hostility here."

Just then, faintly and then getting louder, could be heard, even over the loud music, the sound of sirens in the distance. Marcus lowered the volume so they could be heard, coming closer and closer. Police, then ambulances.

"What's that?" she asked Adam.

"My exit plan," he said, then shouted to everyone in the room. "Hurry up and get out, folks. I think there might be an accident out on the lake. I thought I saw some activity down on the docks when I drove in. Hurry! You don't want any cops knocking on your door."

While the club members rushed for the door, Adam gave Simone a shove, hard, in the other direction and motioned with his head at Gabe for him to follow. When she didn't move fast enough, he pinched her butt, hard. "Hurry up. I'm parked out back."

"Our rental car's out front," Simone pointed out, rubbing her behind. "Pinch me again and I'll shoot you."

"With those toy guns?"

"With the pistol I left in the car, which we need to get—"

"Forget the damn car. If Pitot finds out what you're up to, you're dead meat." He was frog-marching her now, as Gabe rushed to catch up with them.

"Marcus wouldn't find out if you hadn't shown up like a lackwit knight in pinstripe armor."

"I don't wear pinstripes."

"Aaarrgh!"

"I'll get the rental car and our clothes," Gabe suggested. "Better that we don't leave anything traceable behind." As Adam was about to protest, he quickly added, "Don't worry, I can handle it." He removed the chain and medallion recording device from his neck and handed it to Simone. "We got some good stuff, boss."

"Yeah, thanks for your help, Gabe."

"Gabe? Not Dr. Larry Storm? Surprise, surprise! One of your Legal Belles looney birds, I suppose," Adam commented snidely as he shoved her into the passenger seat of his Lexus, causing her skirt to ride up and his eyes to about bulge out.

"Bite me!"

"Definitely," he said. "Later. After I've paddled your ass."

"Another pervert!"

"You have no idea."

Chapter Sixteen

T hanks for nothing . . .

Simone refused to speak to him during the one-hour drive back to Houma, which really pissed him off, more than he was already pissed off. He was the one who should be angry here, not her.

"Do you realize what a goat fuck that was about to become back there? If you and the nutcake doctor didn't participate in their games, Pitot would have retaliated, and it wouldn't just be kicking you out. Believe me, killing is the most merciful of things that psycho does to his enemies."

When that didn't prompt any reply, he told her, "I pulled in some favors to get a pal of mine and his friends to ride a couple vehicles into the area with their sirens going. Even so, Pitot might investigate and wonder if I had anything to do with the interruption."

Did she express concern on his behalf? Not even a little.

"Or you. He might wonder if you two were involved."

Still no concern, not even for herself or her employee.

He couldn't in all honesty let her think there was imminent danger, though. "I'm pretty sure we're safe in that regard."

Did she thank him then? Hah! Not even a blink of the eyelashes, which he was pretty sure were fake.

So, he tried a different tack. "You look hot in that outfit." And, man, did she ever! He could practically see her nipples through the straining fabric of her blouse, and the skirt had ridden up almost to the top of her thighs.

She shot him a glare that pretty much said he'd never see her in the outfit again. Too bad!

Which prompted his fool tongue to say, "I don't mind a bit of role playing myself. One-on-one, though. No sharing the goodies."

He thought her upper lip curled at that remark. And he noted that her lips were slightly swollen-looking. From his kisses last night, he hoped, not anything that might have happened back at Happy Horndog's.

Just to get back at her, he observed, "There will probably be butt cheek imprints on the leather seat you're sitting on."

That crudity caused her to shift uncomfortably. She was probably blushing. He couldn't tell in the dim lights of the highway.

Another ten minutes of silence, and he was back to being angry again. "I was worried about you. Do you ever consider other people when you take your risks?"

Silence.

"And how about your mother? Did it occur to you that Mike Pham won't like anyone who harbors his wife?"

That caused a jolt of surprise on her face, that he knew about Thanh and Adelaide Daigle. But then she immediately wiped all expression from her face again.

It was the indifference that was goading him. Mutual anger, he could handle. Indifference was somehow more insulting.

"To think I was almost falling in love with you!" he muttered.

Big mistake!

For the first time in more than a half hour she spoke, "Tell that to someone who cares!"

For the rest of the trip, they both remained silent, and when they got back to Legal Belles and he was about to get out and accompany her up the steps, she opened the passenger door and flew out, calling over her shoulder. "Stay where you are! I can take care of myself."

With those ominous words, he just sat for several minutes, watching as she looked under a potted plant on the landing, which must hide a second key, opened the door, and slammed it behind her. Even when the lights turned on inside, he still sat, fuming.

If that was the thanks he got for saving her, then so be it. He stepped on the gas and raised gravel as he shot away down the alley.

It was over.

How many times can a heart be broken? . . .

Simone was so angry, she could cry. And she did.

Then, she was so angry, she could throw things. And she did. Every item in her cowgirl porno outfit as she made a path toward her shower where she needed to scour away the sex club cooties.

Still angry after her shower, she stomped around her apartment in her fallback comfort clothes—oversize sweatshirt, running shorts, and thick cotton socks, no shoes.

"'To think I was almost falling in love with you!'" she mimicked Adam's words aloud in her empty rooms. It wasn't the reversal of his emotions that had her upset, *well, not quite*, but that clueless use of the word *almost*. Was there any woman in the world who wanted a man to be "almost" in love with her? Better he say nothing at all.

The jerk!

The problem was, there was no "almost" about her feelings for Adam. She was full-blown, heart wide open to be broken, Cajun Crazy in love with . . .

The jerk!

But, of course, the worst thing of all was his coming to rescue her. This was her job. If she couldn't take care of herself, she had no business doing it, whether it be law enforcement or Legal Belles. And, yeah, sometimes the job put you in touch with distasteful, even dangerous people, but those were the risks. Manageable risks.

Furthermore, he'd jeopardized the entire mission. It remained to be seen whether Marcus would connect the dots about newcomers, Dr. Larry and Diane Storm, Adam suddenly showing on the scene after all those years of disinterest, and sirens heading toward the lake lodge just as things were about to get interesting, *depending on your definition of* interesting. The repercussions could be disastrous.

Even though it was late, she called Helene, who would be worried about her. She expected to get her answering machine, but instead her partner picked up on the first ring.

"Are you okay?" she asked without preamble.

"I'm home, and I'm fine."

"You're home already? I thought you'd stay overnight in Nawleans."

"Things changed. I'll explain tomorrow."

"Did you get the goods on Pitot?"

"Oh, yeah."

"You sound funny."

"I'm just tired."

"Well, go to bed. I'll come in to the office early."

"It's Saturday. Don't you have plans?"

"I wish. I'm going over to my parents about nine. They want to take the boat out."

"Ooh, I remember the days on that pontoon."

"Wanna come along for the day? A little swimming, a little fishing, just relaxing."

"You have no idea how tempting that is, but I have too much to do." Plus, Adam had planted the idea in her head that her mother might be in danger. She would need to go over to The Gates to check on her.

"I'll see you on my way, then. If you're not up yet, don't crawl out of bed for me. I'll come up to the apartment."

She called Gabe, as well. "Just making sure you made it out safely."

"Piece of cake! They were in such a rush to change their costumes and lock things up that they never noticed me leaving. And turns out the sirens weren't headed to the lodge after all."

"I know."

"Adam's doing?"

"Uh-huh."

"Looks like he saved the day for us."

"We would have managed on our own."

"Probably. I'll bring your clothes and stuff when I come down to Houma this morning."

"You don't have to come all the way here on the weekend."

"No problem. Livia and I are going catfish noodling in the bayou with a group of friends."

Seems like everyone had water plans for the day. And wasn't it nice that Gabe could go from a perverted sex party to a fishing party with such ease? "How could you have made those plans when you didn't know we'd be done with the Pitot case last night?"

"If I'd been tied up, ha, ha, ha, Livia would have gone without me."

"Okay."

"Did you think I would leave you to your own devices, ha, ha, ha?"

"Very funny!"

"Anyhow, I'm anxious to see what kind of photos and audio we get from those computer chips," he said.

"Me, too."

"That party was a hoot, wasn't it?"

She pictured Marcus as a bull with a swinging penis, and Chantung as a horse, and had to laugh. "It was a hoot, all right." Then she added, "I hope we have a picture of you as the naked cowboy. Your girlfriend should get a kick out of that."

"Liv's already seen me as the naked cowboy. And the naked astronaut. And the naked biker."

He was probably kidding.

Then he added, "Too bad you wouldn't let me take a pic of you as *Deep Throat Cowgirl*. But then, I'm pretty sure your boyfriend, Adam, has that image imprinted on his brain forever. Did you see the look on his face when he first got an eyeful of you?"

She was about to correct Gabe's impression of Adam being her boyfriend. Not anymore. But she figured that would take too much explaining.

After she clicked off her cell phone, she made herself a cup of steaming chai ginger tea with a splash of honey and took it into the bedroom with her. It usually helped her sleep. It was three a.m. by the time she climbed under the covers. As she lay in the darkness, listening to the silence, she realized that she'd been expecting Adam to call and apologize.

But he didn't.

By five a.m. when the sun began to rise in a pink haze, she was still awake, and still waiting for a call that did not come. She realized then that he might not call tomorrow, either, rather today, or the next day, or at all. He might be as adamant about the rightness of his actions as she was about hers. That didn't make her any less certain of the stand she'd taken.

Her anger returned, and it was a cold, hard stone, which settled right in the vicinity of her broken heart. Her mother was right. She was Cajun Crazy. Again.

Shop till you drop . . .

Adam fully expected Simone to call him and apologize, then thank him profusely for saving the day—and her ass—in that centerfold cowgirl skirt . . . that made a man want to drop a coin for her to pick up . . . and the snap-button shirt that posed all kinds of unsnapping possibilities. He was still angry as hell. But he was mellowing as he pictured all the ways he would make her "pay" for his forgiveness.

But then he remembered the reason he'd been so angry, and still was. Simone was a stubborn risk taker who would be more likely to be engaged in a shoot-out at the local corral than baking brownies for the PTA. Not that she would have any reason to be involved with a PTA, or that he would want that kind of woman, unless he was thinking about marriage.

Which he was not.

But suppose he was.

He couldn't predict what Simone would do in any given situation. It would be crazy to bring a stick of dynamite into his home and hope it never went off. Bad comparison, but still.

When she didn't call before he fell asleep, he wasn't concerned. He intended to let her call go to voice mail, anyhow. He just wanted the satisfaction of knowing that she realized her mistake.

She'd said that she didn't care. Hah! He would call her bluff. She cared, all right.

But she didn't call that night, or the next morning, or while he tortured himself that afternoon strolling the aisles of Party Circus with Maisie, who thought everything was "So cool!"

He refused to buy Uncle Sam, Abe Lincoln, and Betsy Ross costumes for himself, his father, and Maisie on the premise that they would be ruined when going in the pool. But she did talk him into a dozen each of the Uncle Sam top hats and Lady Liberty tiaras.

Which made him think of the costumes he'd seen last night. In particular, the one worn by Simone, who, incidentally, had not yet called. But he soon cut off that line of thinking, or rather, his daughter did with her definitive ideas on what constituted a good party. Like they had to have twirly whirlys, cascade centerpieces that looked like rockets blasting out tinsel sparks, and window clings, whatever the hell they were.

His cart soon overflowed with flag décor table covers, banners, tiki lights, pool inflatable rafts, lawn pinwheels, and a huge flag and pole for the front yard, even a flag bathing suit for Maisie and, yes, for himself. In addition there were red, white, and blue paper plates, cups, napkins, straws, and balloons. And star-spangled nail polish, which he'd promised to help her put on.

"Oooh, look at that wavy flag cake mold. It serves twenty-four. PawPaw would like that," Maisie said, dropping it into their overflowing cart. "Make sure we get some food dye and red, white, and blue sprinkles."

"Of course."

Maisie missed the sarcasm.

"I thought Tante Lulu was making Peachy Praline Cobbler Cake."

"She is, but we have to have a flag one, too." She gave him that patronizing look that said he should know that.

"Okay, but no fireworks. We already agreed that we could see the fireworks being set off at the park from our backyard."

Reluctantly, she took several rockets out of the cart and put them back on the shelf. "How 'bout some sparklers?"

"Only if you promise not to light any unless me or PawPaw are with you."

She nodded.

As they were checking out, with not one but two carts, the bill came to almost four hundred dollars. Wincing, he asked, "What's our RSVP total so far?"

"Only sixty."

He shook his head and grumbled, "Where are we going to fit everyone?"

"Oh, Daddy! People circle-late at a party. Dontcha know that? They'll be in the pool, on the patio, dancing, in the house, everywhere."

She thought about all the possibilities, and beamed.

He thought about all the things he'd have to lock up.

Like Hannah's fragile pottery. And any legal documents he had lying around.

"Do I need to have the cleaning lady come in before the party?"

She thought for a moment. "No, but we'll prob'ly need her the next day." Then, with the astuteness of a five-year-old matchmaker, she said, "Why do ya keep checkin' yer cell phone, Daddy? Are ya waitin' fer See-mone ta call?"

Busted! By his five-year-old kid!

To atone for his lack of attention, he spent the rest of the afternoon by the pool with Maisie and his dad, who was barbecuing ribs for dinner. "So, do you have a final menu for the big party?" he asked.

"Aside from all the stuff that interfering old lady is bringing?"

Adam assumed that interfering old lady referred to Tante Lulu. "You mean that peach cake?"

"And much more. Okra poppers, bourbon beans, Creole mustard greens."

"Um, that's nice of her."

"Yeah, it is. But, holy smokes, she tends to take over."

"What are you making then?"

"Traditional stuff, like hotdogs, hamburgers, and salads, sliced tomatoes and cucumbers from my garden, skewers of andouille sausage with green peppers and mushrooms. Oh, and that blankety-blank flag cake, thank you very much." He could imagine the word his dad, a former cop, would like to use, but they both tried not to swear in Maisie's hearing.

"That was Maisie's idea."

"I've made it three times already, and the waves in the flag keep breaking."

"Aren't waves supposed to break?" he joked.

His father made a grunting noise of disparagement.

"Hey, I bet you don't know what a twirly whirly is," Adam said.

"Sure do. That's when a guy sticks his penis in a vagina and spins it around."

"DAD!"

"What? You asked what a whirly twirly was and I told you. Jeesh!"

"I said twirly whirly, and it refers to long strands of foil twists that are used for decorations. Like they sell at Party Circus."

"Oh. I like mine better." His dad grinned at him. "Ever tried it?"

He shook his head at his dad and stood, about to take a dip in the pool where Maisie was trying out one of the floats they'd bought earlier. The pool was fairly large for a residential pool—about thirty-six feet—but not that conducive to laps for a six-foot-one male. On a ninety-degree scorcher, like it was today, it would do fine.

Just then, he noticed someone coming around the side of the house and stopping by the gate into the backyard. Red hair. A blouse knotted at the waist. Short denim shorts. And sandals.

It was Sonia.

Talk about timing. He had been thinking about how things were probably over with Simone, seeing as how it had been fifteen hours since he'd dropped her off last night and still no call, and here stood a likely replacement.

Why then did he say with unintended rudeness, "Hey, Sonia. What are you doing here?" Immediately, he walked over and unlocked the gate. "Sorry. I was just surprised to see you."

"Didn't your dad and daughter tell you that I stopped by last week?"

"They did, but I was tied up with a trial."

"I read about it in the newspaper. Congrats," she said, waving at his dad and Maisie, both of whom were in the pool now.

"Thanks." He led her to a patio chair and asked, "Can I get you a drink? Iced tea? Lemonade? Beer?"

"Iced tea would be nice. No sugar."

"Sweet tea is all we have."

"Just ice water then."

When he came back with a frosty glass of ice water for her and a frosty longneck beer for himself, he sat down across from her. In his peripheral vision, he noticed his dad and daughter playing Capture the Goldfish with a lot of laughter and splashing. He wished he could join them.

Taking a long draw on his beer, he remarked, "So, you're not going to California, after all?"

"I am . . . but not for a while yet. The financing fell through, and my sister's working on a new proposal. It might be another six months before I leave. My boss at the yoga studio hadn't hired a replacement for me yet." She shrugged and gave him a flirtatious little smile that indicated they could resume where they'd left off.

He studied her for a long moment. She was a good-looking woman. Pretty. Flaming red hair that would catch anyone's eye, and a killer, toned body that would catch any man's eye. Why then was he feeling so . . . uncaught?

Truth to tell, this was the second time Sonia had come to his house, uninvited, and he didn't like it. Under his old policy, which might still be his current policy, he did not invite women into his home where they could meet his daughter. Simone had changed that, but that didn't mean he wanted women showing up here.

Would I feel the same if Simone popped in? he asked himself.

Before he could answer himself, she concluded, "You're upset that I've come here."

"Not exactly, but I do try to keep my personal and family life separate."

"I should have known when you didn't return my calls." She knocked the side of her head with the heel of one hand, as if to knock in some sense. "I'll leave," she said, face flushing, as she started to rise.

"No, don't." He reached across the table and put a hand on her arm, indicating she should sit. "I've been anal on that issue, and it doesn't work anymore, anyhow."

"It doesn't? Why is that?" She cocked her head to the side. "You've met someone?" she guessed.

"Well, sort of," he admitted, though not wanting to tell her that his new love was already an old love, or no love at all.

Sonia wasn't upset. Theirs had never been a serious relationship, just sex. Certainly no dating. So, they talked then about other things.

Finally, he said, "Why don't you come in the pool and stay for dinner?"

"I didn't bring a suit."

"You can wear what you have on, and I'll give you a sweatshirt for afterward. Besides, your clothes will dry off almost instantly in this heat."

She hesitated, then smiled. "You're on." Kicking off her sandals and taking off her watch, she ran to the pool and shouted to Maisie and his dad before diving in, "Marco Polo anyone?"

Thus it was seven o'clock before Sonia left, and he and his dad were sitting on the patio together once again. Maisie, after a day outdoors, had fallen asleep on a nearby chaise longue.

"That is one fine woman," his dad remarked after

Adam told him about Sonia's plans to go to California.
"Bet she'd stay if you asked her."

"Maybe."

"What's the problem, son?"

The problem was that it was now twenty hours, and
Simone had not called him to apologize, or at least try to
make up.

He told his dad about Simone and their "disagree-
ment." He ended by saying, "You were a cop, Dad. Am I
wrong to be concerned about the danger?"

"Danger goes with the territory. If you can't take the
fire, don't be toasting any marshmallows."

"Thanks a bunch."

"Seriously, we live in dangerous times." When Adam
was about to speak, his dad raised a halting hand and
continued, "But some jobs are definitely more dangerous
than others. It takes a certain kind of person to live with a
risk taker."

"It's one thing to live with a risk taker, and another to
expose your family—a little girl—to danger."

"Bull-pucky!"

He arched his brows at his father.

"You're just making excuses for being scared to death
of committing yourself to a woman again, and being
stabbed in the back."

"This isn't about Hannah."

"Isn't it?"

"Not totally. Honestly, Dad, was it so wrong for me to
be concerned about the danger Simone had placed herself in?"

"Your concern was commendable—your method of
showing your concern was insulting."

Whoa. That was blunt. "How so?"

"Simone is a trained professional, probably better suited

to protect herself than you are. You rushing in like that was like saying that you didn't respect her abilities." He shrugged. "Maybe you're just not suited to that kind of woman. No reflection on you."

Adam bristled at that assessment of himself.

"Don't you think that these are the kinds of things you should be discussing with her?"

"I suppose so."

"What? She's not taking your calls?"

Adam could feel his face heat. "I haven't called her."

His father blinked at him with disbelief. "And why is that?"

"I'm waiting for her to call me."

His father glanced at the cell phone sitting on the table in front of him, ominously silent. "How's that workin' for you?"

"Wiseass!"

They changed the subject then, and talked about the upcoming season for the Rangers, his dad's longtime favorite baseball team, and what would be expected of the Saints in football recruits come next fall. They also talked about the pool maintenance service, which was less than efficient, and a bonefishing trip to the Bahamas his dad was planning with some buddies for October. Plus, Maisie wanted to take karate lessons at a gym where his dad was thinking about offering classes in self-defense.

When his dad and Maisie were down for the night and Adam did a walk-through of the house to lock up, he had a chance to think about Simone once again. He was still angry, and he still thought he was right . . . or partly right. And, besides that, he had his pride.

Later, after an hour of being unable to fall asleep, he was reminded of the old proverb that said, "Pride goeth before. . . . something?" He couldn't remember exactly

what. He would think about it tomorrow. By then, hopefully, Simone would have called and he wouldn't still be
so angry/offended/hurt/confused.

Why did being right feel so wrong?

Using her noodle . . . or not . . .

Simone hadn't slept a wink. So, by seven a.m., she was
down in the office, catching up on paperwork.

She took the chips out of Gabe's medallion and her
earrings and inserted them, one at a time, into the special
device that fit into a computer like a flash drive. The photos they'd gotten, and the audio, were great, but they
would have to be edited and reduced down to something
manageable. She and Gabe would look them over when
he came in. A half dozen or so photos and an audio recording should be sufficient to satisfy Saffron Pitot's job.
The bill was going to be hefty.

Helene came in at eight, carrying two extra-large Styrofoam cups imprinted with Creole Grinds, that new
Starbucks copycat shop at the edge of town. "Double shot
skinny white mocha lattes with extra whipped cream,"
she announced, handing one to Simone and sipping from
hers as she sat down in the chair in front of Simone's
desk.

"Yum! But that's an oxymoron if I ever heard one.
Skinny and whipped cream?"

"Works for me. Anyhow, maybe I should have made it
a triple shot. You look as if you haven't slept at all."

"I haven't." When Helene was about to ask why, Simone said, "I don't want to talk about it."

"Okay, tell me everything about Pitot."

Simone proceeded to do just that, in detail, starting

with the skinny dipping in the lake. Many questions and much laughter later, they were both sitting before her computer staring at the photographs.

"Holy crap!" Helene said on seeing Heidi in the horse outfit. "Reminds me of those female erotica novels we read in college."

"The Anne Rice one!" Simone hooted with laughter. "The ones she wrote under a pen name. Oh, Lord, I forgot about those. Remember how we gathered in Patti Le-Braun's dorm room and read the passages aloud?"

"I never thought real people actually did that stuff."

When she flicked through the gallery of photos, James came up as a Mexican bandito.

"He looks almost normal," Helene remarked.

"Not when he turned around. His denims were ass-less."

Helene just shook her head.

But then Marcus the Bull showed up, which at first made Helene's jaw drop. "You've got to be kidding me!"

"That's the money shot," Simone told her.

Before Helene left, Simone asked, "Any chance Norah is going with you today?"

Helene just shook her head.

Helene and Norah had been partners for years, ever since law school. Simone had known they'd broken up before she returned to Louisiana, but Helene had never wanted to talk about it.

"I know how she used to enjoy a day out on the pontoon with you and your family," Simone remarked, hoping her friend would open up to her.

"We haven't talked for more than six months."

"Irreconcilable differences?" Simone asked.

"Oh, yeah."

When Helene didn't offer any more information, Simone dropped the subject. They discussed how and when they would give Saffron her photos and audio reports as well as a few upcoming cases before Helene left.

Gabe showed up then, dressed for his bayou excursion in Hawaiian floral board shorts, a sky-blue T-shirt, and flip-flops. He looked like a college surfer boy.

"Where's Livia?" she asked.

"She dropped me off while she went over to Starr Foods for some goodies. She'll be back in a half hour or so."

They discussed the material from the chips then what to delete and what to include in the final report.

"Do you have the technical ability to put this all together?" she wondered aloud.

"It's really not that complicated."

"Do you want to take the chips with you and work on them at home?"

"Not today. I'll be down the bayou, and I wouldn't feel comfortable with them sitting in my car. How about you put them in a secure place here, and I'll stop in for them on Monday? We'll have to make sure we have duplicates of everything, for your files as well as Mrs. Pitot's."

"Maybe I could have you deliver the reports to her and give you a chance to grill her about possible soap opera work."

"You would do that for me?" He tilted his head in surprise.

"Sure. Why not?"

"Thanks a lot. Are you sure you won't come with us today?"

"I have so much to do, and—"

"C'mon," he coaxed. "After last night, you need a little fresh air and sunshine to cleanse the pores."

She laughed. He had a point.

Thus it was that she found herself with a bunch of twentysomething guys and girls wading in muddy water, catching catfish with her bare hands, and hauling them onto the banks. There was much laughter, splashing, scratching of arms and legs, teasing, and total dunking. Although this crowd was only a few years younger than Simone, she felt somewhat like they were kids and she was the adult.

Fun was had by all, though, helped along by the vast amounts of beer and wine consumed. She was glad she'd come.

Even gladder—if there was such a word—was her mother when Simone pulled into the Pearly Gates, parked her car, and carried in a forty-pound dead catfish.

Scarlett greeted her with a long meow.

Which didn't fool Simone one bit. Her pet cat was more interested in the fish treat that would be in her bowl that night, rather than her missing owner, if it could be said that any person "owned" a cat.

"Ooooh, blackened catfish fer supper," her mother said.

Catfish were mean creatures when wrestling with humans, Simone had discovered today, and she didn't think she could eat any of the mud cats again in this lifetime, blackened or otherwise.

"Ooooh, *Canh Chua Dau Ca*," Thanh said, "Sour fish head soup."

That's all I need! Fish eyes staring at me while I eat.

After ascertaining that her mother and her guest were safe, and cautioning them to be extra careful, Simone went home. Only then did she allow herself to check her cell phone.

No messages!

On that happy, or unhappy note, she went to bed at seven p.m. On a Saturday night! And slept right through until Sunday afternoon.

And still no calls!

Chapter Seventeen

It's hard work being clueless . . .

Adam went to church with his father and Maisie on Sunday morning, figuring he might just "run into" Simone and have a chance to talk with her. No loss of pride in that. No need for apologies.

Can anyone say clueless?

Problem was Simone wasn't there, of course. Nor was her mother. He should have realized that her mother, who was harboring Mike Pham's wife, would want to stay out of the public eye. And he should have realized that Simone wouldn't be at church if her mother wasn't.

The person who was there was Tante Lulu, and she birddogged him out the aisle and into the vestibule after the services. "Well?" she wanted to know.

"Well what?"

"I ain't heard no wedding banns read yet? Whatcha been doin'?"

He inhaled and exhaled to show his impatience. "I have no plans to remarry, Ms. Rivard."

"Doan you give me none of that Ms. Rivard nonsense, boy. God laughs when he hears people talk about their plans. The only plans that matter are God's plans."

"And you think God has plans for me?"

"I know he does."

"You good friends with God then?"

She narrowed her eyes at him, wondering if he was being sacrilegious. "Some folks say I was waitressin' at the Last Supper."

He decided a change of subject was in order. "I understand you offered to bring a number of dishes to our Fourth of July party. Thank you for all your help."

"Huh? I'm jist bein' neighborly."

He was about to point out that she lived miles away from him, hardly a neighbor, but bit his tongue just in time. Besides, she was already off on another tangent. "What'd ya do with that St. Jude statue I gave ya?"

"Um. It's sitting on my desk." *Or in my drawer. I'm not sure.*

"Mebbe ya need a car weeble wobble one, and a big, life-size one fer the front yard, and—"

"You really think I'm that hopeless?"

"What do you think?" On those words, she wobbled off on blue orthopedic shoes that matched a blue dress that matched her blue hair, to harass one of her grandchildren—rather "grandnephews" since the old lady had never been married—who was walking out of church with Remy Le-Deux and his wife, Rachel, both of whom waved at him.

He escaped.

Only to find his father and Maisie standing outside his car talking to a group of young people from the Our Lady of the Bayou choir. He knew, he just knew, they were inviting even more people to the blasted party. Would they be having hymns in addition to the Swamp Rats wild Cajun music?

"See-mone was noodlin' yesterday," Maisie commented from the backseat as he drove home.

Whoa! Where did that come from? "How do you know that?" Adam asked.

"One of the choir members mentioned a party of folks, including her cousin, Randy, that caught eight giant catfish on the bayou yesterday, one of them fifty pounds," his father answered for her.

"See-mone was one of the people there. They caught the fish with their bare hands, Daddy. Thass called noodlin'," Maisie elaborated.

"I know what noodling is," he griped.

"Don't take your bad mood out on the girl," his father said.

"Sorry, sweetheart."

"Thass all right. PawPaw sez everyone gets their panties in a twist sometimes. But you don't wear panties, do you, Daddy? Tee-hee-hee! PawPaw sez that Uncle Dave should send you some man panties. Tee-hee-hee! When kin we go noodlin'?"

"Someday," he said, giving his father a glare. If Uncle Dave was there, he'd give him a glare, too. His dad and his jokes! Dave and his panty gifts!

But what really burned his butt was, *I was torturing myself all day yesterday waiting for her to call, and she was out partying on the bayou with some guy named Randy. I . . . am . . . a . . . fool!*

When he got home, he decided to go for a run, and gave up after a half mile. Even so, he congratulated himself for not taking his cell phone with him.

His father ruined his saintly effort by announcing on his return, "She didn't call."

To which, he said a foul word.

To which, his father said he would stick a bar of soap in his mouth when he was sleeping. But then his father softened his tone and said, "Just call her, son. You know you want to."

Yeah, he did. But, no, he didn't want to make that call. He wanted to talk to her when she called him. Which wasn't happening.

Finally, he did call, around nine p.m. on Sunday night, roughly forty-three hours since he'd seen her last. He got her answering machine, "Hi, this is Simone. I'm not available at the moment. Leave a message."

He left no message. What he had to say, and he had no idea what that would be, was best said to her, not on a voice mail.

He called again at ten p.m.

Another recording.

Again at eleven p.m.

Another recording.

He may not be leaving any messages, but her message was clear. She wasn't going to pick up for him. She didn't want to talk with him.

Maybe I waited too long.

He could swear he heard a voice in his head say, *Ya think?*

Maybe it was St. Jude, sitting up there on a cloud with God, making the latest entry in the big book he held in his hands: *The Clueless Men Hall of Fame.*

On the other hand, he could hold out as long as she could.

Now he heard laughter in his head.

It's not that she wanted him to grovel . . . much . . .

Simone knew that Adam had been trying to call her, but only because she'd checked her caller ID constantly. He'd left no messages.

What did he think? After almost two days of silence, he was suddenly going to make amends? *Big whoop!* Or maybe he was just calling to berate her some more. *Let him try!*

She still loved him. *Dammit!* But she would get over it, like a bad cold, like a rash that itched like crazy, like all the other love mistakes in her life.

The question was, had she ever really been in love before?

Not like this. *Dammit!*

After a joint meeting on Monday afternoon with Helene and Gabe, and viewing the material he'd put together in a visual and audio presentation, they called Saffron Pitot. She agreed to come into the office the next morning.

By Monday night, she'd had three more calls from Adam, one in the morning, one in the afternoon, and one in the evening. With the last one, he left a message, finally. "Call me." That was all.

Pfff! Not even a *please*! He could have at least said he was sorry, or better yet, "I love you."

She spent the night giving herself another hair-conditioning treatment. Much more of this and they'd be tossing her in salads.

The meeting with Saffron on Tuesday morning went well. Pitot's wife was pleased with their work and didn't balk at the bill they presented. When she saw the photo of her husband in the bull outfit, she merely laughed and said, "Old farts never die; they just keep making fools of themselves!"

After the meeting, Saffron agreed to go to lunch with Gabe to discuss soap operas. In fact, she was preening under the adulation of the much younger man who'd done his homework and researched all the old soaps she'd appeared in.

That afternoon Simone decided to make a quick visit to Chicago. She flew out Wednesday morning and when she got there tied up a few loose ends, like getting some of the furniture she'd put in storage delivered to Louisiana. But she didn't contact Jack Landry while she was there. That door closed weeks ago, for good. She did visit a specialty shop that that dealt in security devices mostly used by law enforcement. An FBI acquaintance of hers had recommended the out-of-the-way boutique.

When she returned on Thursday, BaRa informed her that a fuming Adam had come into the agency the day before. He'd been shocked to learn that Simone had gone out of town again. He probably thought she was doing another Pitot-type job. *Hah! Let him think that.* Or else he thought she was moving back to the Windy City. *Hah! Let him think that!*

Although . . .

While she'd been away, she'd gained a little perspective. Maybe if she and Adam sat down, they'd be able to resolve some of their issues. Her need for independence, his need to protect. Were they really so irreconcilable? She wasn't sure. He needed to respect her work.

So she was prepared, somewhat, when he stormed into her office late Thursday afternoon.

"Where the hell have you been?" he yelled.

Not a good start!

"I beg your pardon."

He combed his fingers through his hair with frustration and paced in front of her desk. "I've been imagining all kinds of scenarios. You dead in some alley. You hugging a concrete block at the bottom of Lake Pontchartrain. You being eaten by a giant catfish while noodling."

That last example drew her eyebrows into twin arches.

So, he knew about her catfishing. Did that mean he was jealous, or just mocking her?

"I was in Chicago," she informed him. "I left Wednesday morning and stayed overnight."

That stopped his pacing. "Why? Are you moving back there? Just because I might have yelled at you?"

"No, Adam, I am not moving back to Chicago. I went to arrange for some furniture in storage to be moved here."

"Oh." He had such a hangdog expression on his face that she almost felt sorry for him. Almost but not quite, because he still hadn't said the words she needed to hear.

"I called," he said.

Big fat hairy deal! "I know."

"A lot."

And I should care . . . why? "I know."

"Why didn't you call me back?"

"Because nothing has changed." *C'mon, Adam, say the words. Say the frickin' words!*

"When I left . . . that night . . . you said that you didn't care. Is that true?"

Oh, this is ridiculous! "You said nasty things, too, Adam. Did you mean them?"

He frowned with puzzlement. "What nasty things? What did I say?"

I give up! "If you can't recall, I'm not going to tell you."

"Why not?"

She rolled her eyes.

He had his hands in the pockets of his suit slacks, his hip cocked, just staring at her.

"What do you want, Adam?"

He didn't hesitate before saying, "You."

Her heart skipped a beat. She was touched, but it wasn't good enough. She needed two more words in front of the *you*. Even then, they still had problems, but it would be a start.

"How do you want me? As a dating partner again? As a hookup when it's convenient? Or more than that?"

"Isn't it enough that I want you?"

"No."

"Then, I don't know."

She tossed her hands in the air. "Well, you know what? Call me when you decide. In the meantime, I have work to do."

He left, his chin held up pridefully, his precious male ego still intact, but Simone heard him say to BaRa, who'd probably eavesdropped on everything they'd said through the half-open door, "I think I might have screwed up in there."

"Big-time," BaRa remarked, as only she could.

Suddenly, he turned around, came back into her office, moved behind her desk, and lifted her by the upper arms so that she was standing on tiptoe. Then he kissed her. He really, really, *really* kissed her. When he released her arms, she fell back into her chair.

And he stomped out.

She heard BaRa say, "Much better."

Knight in shining PJs? . . .

Simone awakened in the middle of the night to an annoying beep, beep, beep noise. That stupid smoke alarm! It was always going off, especially when something got burned accidentally in the bakery next door.

She tried hiding her head under a pillow, but the darn pinging just got more strident. In fact, it sounded as if another device had joined in.

What?

Just as she sat bolt upright, she heard the fire alarm go off down below. She jumped out of bed and realized immediately once she opened her bedroom door that the smell of smoke was everywhere, and it wasn't a burned cookie smell, either. More like . . . gas? Oh, my God! Was there a gas leak somewhere?

She rushed over to the door leading downstairs, opened it, then immediately slammed it shut. Flames were shooting up the steps. She could hear the sirens of fire trucks approaching already, alerted by the direct-to-station fire alarms in the office, no doubt. She grabbed her cell phone, handbag, and laptop and made her way down the back exterior stairs and around to the front.

Her building was a mass of flames, as were the two buildings attached on each side, the bakery and the dress shop.

She glanced at her watch. It was two a.m. How had this happened so fast?

Suddenly, there was a pop-pop-popping noise, followed by an explosion that caused the windows to blow out.

"Move back, move back," a fireman yelled to her and the small crowd that had already assembled.

One of the firefighters, Calvin Hebert, who'd graduated from high school with her, came up and put an arm around her shoulder. "This your buildin', *chère*?"

She nodded. "The one in the middle. How did it start?"

"We won't know till tomorrow, prob'ly. Or later. Why doan you sit yer sweet self down over there till we get the fire out? My boss will have questions, guaranteed."

She nodded and sat down on a bench across the street in front of Duff's Drugstore. Soon, someone came and put a blanket over her, even though she wasn't cold. The temperature was mild, even hot from the fire, and she was wearing a cropped-top pajama set, though she was bare-footed. *Oh*, she realized, *the blanket is probably for shock*.

She had just enough sense left to call Helene.

"What? What's wrong?" Helene asked after just one ring, before Simone even said anything. Wasn't it always bad news when the phone rang at this time of night?

"The building's on fire."

"Oh, my God! Are you all right?"

"Yes," she said, but her voice was shaky, even with that single word.

"And Scarlett?"

"She's still at my mother's, thank God!"

"Where are you?"

"Sitting on a bench in front of Duff's watching all our dreams go up in flames." That sounded overly dramatic even to her own ears.

"Oh, honey! I'll be right there."

Before Helene's arrival, someone else came. Her knight in shining armor. Again. Except this time he was her knight in white T-shirt, plaid pajama bottoms, and loafers without socks. His hair stood out in sleepy spikes. Not a white stallion or sword in hand, but there was a black Lexus parked down the street and he did hand her a clean white handkerchief, which came away sooty when she wiped her face.

"Adam!" she said. "How did you know?"

He sat down on the bench beside her and wrapped an arm around her shoulders, tugging her close. "John Le-Deux heard it on the police scanner. He called Luc, and Luc called me. Luc is over there, talking to the police chief." He was hugging her, and kissing the top of her hair, and tucking the blanket tighter around her. "I was so scared," he said in a choked voice. "Especially when they said there was an explosion."

He probably came here expecting to find a body, she realized.

"Do you think it was a gas leak?" she asked, just as she'd asked Cal.

He shrugged. "Maybe Luc will learn something."

"Look at the fire, Adam. The whole place will be gone." To her surprise, she wasn't crying. She must be in shock, after all. "All of Rachel's hard work gone—poof." Yep, definitely shock, or the onset of hysteria.

"Is there anything important that can't be replaced?"

"I don't think so, though I was partial to that fish rug."

He squeezed her in reprimand. "I'll buy you another fish rug. In fact, I'll buy you a shark rug, if there is such a thing. For legal sharks, get it?"

He was trying to be a comedian at a time like this? It was sweet of him, actually.

"Our business records are the most important thing, of course," she mused. "Critical files are digitized and stored in a secure web-based system at the end of every day, and we had some fireproof cabinets inside; so, that's one worry out of the way. But . . . oh, Adam! We're ruined before we even started."

"That's not true," Helene said. She'd just arrived and sat down on Simone's other side, giving her a warm hug, on top of Adam's arm that was still wrapped around her shoulders. Like Adam, Helene looked as if she'd just crawled out of bed, except she wore tights under a Yogi Bear sleep shirt with ballet slippers. Her hair was twisted into a loose knot atop her head. "We did it once, my friend. We can do it again."

"I wouldn't know where to start."

"We can find a temporary space and open for business again in a few days, you'll see."

"Hell, you can open up for business in my garage, if need be," Adam offered.

That got Simone's attention. She sat up straighter and stared at him. He'd released his hold on her by now. "You don't mean that." Not that she would take him up on the offer, but the fact that he made it, feeling as he did about the dangers of her business, said something. She wasn't sure what.

"Of course I mean it. You can even sleep in my bed." He waggled his eyebrows at her.

They all laughed.

"Seriously, I have plenty of room at my house. You can stay there until you get situated."

"No, she can stay with me," Helene said.

"I'm not staying with either one of you." With a shudder, Simone announced, "I'm going back to The Gates."

"Doesn't your mother have a guest?" Adam asked.

At any other time, Simone would have asked how he knew that, but then she recalled him mentioning the danger she'd placed her mother in during his tirade the other night. She'd failed to ask him then, in the midst of all her other problems. She couldn't think about that now. So she just shrugged in answer to his question. "I can sleep on my mother's couch."

"The same one where Cletus was sleeping?" Helene asked. "Eew! It probably still smells like beer farts."

Simone pretended surprise. "Helene! I can't believe you said that."

"I can't believe you two are sitting here discussing gas—and I don't mean the kind that probably started this fire—whereas I'm offering a perfectly good solution to a non-problem," Adam said.

"*Whereas* I can find my own solutions. He sounds like a lawyer," Simone said to Helene.

"Hey, I'm a lawyer, too."

"But you don't say *whereas* and *wherefore* in normal conversation."

"Aaarrgh!" Adam said.

Their discussion was cut short by the fire marshal who had a few questions for Simone. And then the EMTs examined her and wanted to take her to the hospital, just to make sure she was all right. She refused.

A large crowd had assembled by then, including the owners of the bakery and the dress boutique, both of whom were understandably distraught. The absentee owner of the buildings, a family trust in Texas, would be contacted by the police. There was some question about whether the gas ovens had developed problems, or whether a recent shipment of dresses from China had been flammable.

Luc came up then and told them that the fires would be put out within the hour, but it might be days before they had an answer as to the cause. They were advised to go home. There was nothing more to be done at the moment. Tomorrow they would see what could be salvaged.

Helene went home alone, reluctantly, and Adam insisted on driving Simone out to The Gates. "But what about my car? I'll need my car to come back in tomorrow . . . I mean, this morning."

"I'll arrange to get your car out there for you."

The deciding factor was when Luc came back from talking to some business people, no doubt rounding up business from the fire. Who to sue and all that. *That was mean*, she immediately chided herself. He was a caring individual. Although they hadn't had any contact until they were adults, he was her half brother, she had to remind herself. Family.

"Tante Lulu just called me. She heard about the fire," Luc announced.

Oh, boy!

"How did she hear about the fire from her house out

on the bayou?" Adam wanted to know. Little did Adam know how the bayou gossip line worked.

Simone, on the other hand, wasn't surprised. She did have a concern, though. "Please don't tell me that she's coming in. Not at this time of night! And, please God, not by driving herself."

"She wanted me to bring you out there to stay with her," Luc said. "I can't predict what she'll do if you don't show up."

"Tell her that Adam is taking me to my mother's."

Adam grinned at having won that argument, by default. He immediately wiped the grin from his face when he saw her glare.

But he grumbled the entire time they drove to the trailer park. "This is ridiculous. Waking your mother in the middle of the night. Staying in that little tin can like a bunch of sardines. My dad and Maisie would be perfectly good chaperones, if you're worried about your reputation, and I wouldn't make any passes unless you asked me to. C'mon, Simone."

She just let Adam ramble on.

"Everything's going to be all right, Simone," he told her. "I know you're overwhelmed right now, but things will look better in the morning."

It was already morning, she could have told him, and she wasn't feeling better. In fact, it was five a.m. and the sun was just coming up by the time they knocked on the trailer door. She'd told him that he could leave, but he persisted in being El Knighto and walked her up the path.

"Nice gnome!" Adam commented as they waited for her mother to answer the door.

At first, she thought he was making fun of her mother's home, but then she saw him glancing at the giant gnome sitting in a bed of pansies. "My mother has a thing about gnomes. There's a whole family of them in the back of the trailer."

"Maisie would love them. Who's the gnome's pal?" He pointed to the figure standing beside the garden dwarf.

"You don't recognize St. Jude? I thought Tante Lulu gave those statues to everyone."

"I didn't recognize him in a straw hat."

"The hat was my inspiration."

He smiled.

She might have melted a little bit at that smile—he did have a killer smile—but the door opened suddenly. "Oh, my God! Tante Lulu just called me. Come in, baby. Thanh is already putting on the tea. She makes the best green lotus tea."

Scarlett scooted out around her mother's bunny rabbit slippers and rushed over to pee on the gnome's foot. Cats had no respect. At least she hadn't watered St. Jude. Then, with the graciousness only cats can carry off, she meowed a welcome to Simone and hissed at Adam before scampering under the trailer to chase some wild animal, like a rabbit or its own feline shadow.

In fact, Simone felt a little bit like Alice in Wonderland who'd just fallen down the proverbial rabbit hole. Scarlett was the Cheshire Cat, of course, and her mother the Red Queen.

Simone turned to Adam . . . the Mad Hatter? "Thanks for everything tonight, Adam."

He took one of her hands in both of his and turned it over. Leaning down, he kissed the palm, then closed her fingers over it.

"I am so happy that you are alive and safe."

Had he put emphasis on *safe*? She should have been affronted at that reminder of the big stone wall between them, but she was feeling too tingly from his palm kiss.

Her mother put the final zinger on the night—morning—when she said, after eyeballing Adam as he walked to his car, "There's a voodoo priestess who lives two trailers down. I'm gonna have her put an anti–love potion curse on you, Simone, the kind that works against Cajun men with butts to die for."

And, Lordy, the Mad Hatter did, indeed, have a fine ass, she noted as Adam bent to slide into the driver's seat. First, he was her knight in shining whatever, then the Mad Hatter, what next? Devil in a Lexus?

Yep, her life was getting curiouser and curiouser.

Chapter Eighteen

Driving Miss Maisie . . .

Adam drove Simone's car out to the trailer park the following morning, with Maisie perched on the seat next to him, chattering away, as usual. The party, her friend's new bicycle, which was pink, how to make a Dutch braid, which was an inverted French braid for those not in-the-know, where to buy the prettiest hair ties. Anything and everything was a subject for her incessant talking, especially when she had a captive audience in a moving vehicle.

His dad was following in Adam's Lexus.

Actually, Adam didn't mind Maisie's chatter. He loved his daughter, energizer tongue and all.

He'd gotten a brief look at the fire site when he'd picked up Simone's vehicle, which had been parked on the street, and, in his not-so-professional opinion, the buildings were a total loss.

The area was cordoned off with yellow-and-black barricade tape, where several people stood just staring at the mess. He doubted Simone would be able to salvage much.

It would be a busy day for her today, and he hoped she would let him help. Knowing her, and the unresolved problems they had between them, he doubted she'd accept any of his offers. But he intended to try.

To his dismay, he saw a lavender convertible parked out front rather lopsidedly, half on the gravel driveway, half on the small lawn, almost knocking out St. Jude and the gnome. He knew what that meant. Tante Lulu was on the premises. Already!

Voices could be heard out back, so he and Maisie and his dad circled around the path leading to an awning-topped patio, surrounded by the promised gnome collection that Simone had alluded to. Maisie went about ballistic with delight, and Addie, who gave him a glower of unwelcome because he was a Cajun man *(Like I can help that!)*, soon went about introducing his daughter to the dwarf clan, each of whom had names. Cajun names. Alcide, Jolie, Sugah Bee, Hector, Tee-Bob, Claudine. His daughter was practically jumping up and down with excitement. He could almost guarantee that gnomes would be added to her birthday wish list.

Tante Lulu, sitting at a picnic table, gave him a little wave as she continued what appeared to be an explanation of St. Jude to the stunned-looking Thanh trapped on the opposite bench. Tante Lulu had that effect on people.

Today she had normal gray hair framing her wrinkled face like a helmet, but she wore the tiniest pair of blue jeans he'd ever seen on an adult with white sneakers and pompom anklet socks. (Fathers of little girls knew about pompom socks and skinny jeans and ballet slippers and the like.) On top, her shirt proclaimed, "Cajun Princess," and there was a picture of a girl riding a gator like a cowgirl. Maisie would probably be asking for one of those, too.

It appeared she was talking to Thanh about her miscreant husband when explaining the patron saint of hopeless cases because she made this remark: "Some men are as useless as pogo sticks in quicksand."

Typical Tante Lulu.

His father was checking out a few tomato and green pepper plants that Addie had planted at the back border of her small property. Mixed in between were onions.

While everyone was occupied, Adam slipped in the back door to the trailer. He needed to talk to Simone, alone.

He found her in the bathroom brushing her teeth. She must have just showered because her hair was wet and her face scrubbed clean. She wore a tight police academy T-shirt and a pair of jeans and sneakers that must have been left here at her mother's place when she'd been a high school or college student. The shoes had once been black and were now washed to a dull gray. The denim hugged her legs and cupped her bottom like . . . like he would like to.

The cat was sitting on the closed lid of the toilet, licking itself before spotting him. It gave him a "Not you again!" look, then jumped down and sauntered past him, probably putting a pound of cat hair on his black suit pants. He was dressed for the office.

That's when Simone noticed him leaning against the hallway wall, facing the open door of the bathroom, which had to be the size of a broom closet. She rinsed her mouth, spat in the sink, then dabbed at her mouth with a towel. "What?" she said as he continued to stare at her.

"Just admiring the view."

"Yeah, right. I look like someone who's been to hell and back."

"At least you're back."

"I assume you brought my car."

"I did. My dad followed me. He and Maisie are out back admiring the gnomes."

"Thanks for bringing the car. I didn't want to ask my mother for a lift," she said. Then, "You brought your daughter here?"

Why that should surprise her so much was a puzzle, until he recalled his old code of not mixing his women with his family, a code she'd been aware of. A code which was shot to hell since he'd met Simone.

"Yep. She'll probably think trailer parks are the epitome of cool after this."

"How bad is it?" Simone asked.

He knew she wasn't talking about trailer parks, but the fire remains, which he had to have seen when picking up her car. "Bad."

Her shoulders sagged, but then she straightened as if bracing herself. "I'm meeting Helene for breakfast. Then, we have an appointment with the fire marshal at eleven, and the insurance agent at noon."

"Already?"

"We have to start someplace."

"I could help with the insurance and stuff."

"I can do it. I know I had a meltdown last night, but I'm strong. I'll get through this."

"Atta girl!" he said, but what he thought was, *You have toothpaste at the corner of your mouth. Can I kiss it off?*

She set the towel aside. "Okay, spill. What has that worried look in your eyes? I can tell something's wrong."

I have telltale eyes? Man, that is not good for a lawyer. Maybe Simone can help me improve my body lan-

guage, or my body, or . . . uh-oh, she's glaring at me. "I want you to move into my house."

"Why?"

"Protection."

"You need me to protect you?"

"Very funny, smart-ass," he remarked and moved into the tiny confines of the bathroom, closing the door behind him, which forced Simone to be up close and personal.

"Now, Adam, my mother's outside. And Tante Lulu!" She tried to back away, but there was nowhere to go. "If you keep this up, my mother will be calling the police, and Tante Lulu will be calling the priest."

"I don't care," he said, and tugged her even closer. At first, he just hugged her, caressing her back. It was probably some adrenaline rush, posttraumatic reaction, but he felt the need to assure himself Simone was alive.

"This is insane," she said, even as she arched her body into his.

"How do you feel about PTSF?"

"Huh? Don't you mean PTSD?"

"Nope. Posttraumatic stress fucking."

"Where?" She laughed, craning her neck back to scan the room. "The shower?"

"Works for me."

"With our clothes on?"

"Works for me."

"Simone?" she heard her mother call from somewhere inside the trailer. "Are you still in the bathroom? You got any idea where that Cajun lawyer got tŏ? He's up ta no good, I know he is. He has that Cajun twinkle in his eyes, and I don't like the looks of his behind. I already told you that."

"My behind?" he whispered.

Simone put her fingertip to his lips so he wouldn't give them away.

He nipped at her fingertip.

When they heard Addie go back outside, Adam opened the door and led Simone into the living room. "There's something I need to tell you."

She narrowed her eyes at him. "About shower sex?"

He smiled. "No. About the cause of the fire."

She went suddenly alert and must have noticed the grim expression on his face.

"And why I want . . . need you to stay at my house . . . or in some safe house."

"Arson?" she guessed.

He nodded. "Originating in the Legal Belles offices."

She gasped. "Pitot?"

"I wouldn't think so. It's not his style."

"How about Mike Pham?"

He shrugged. "He's angry enough, but I'm not sure he's connected the dots yet between his wife, Helene as her divorce lawyer, and Legal Belles."

She thought over what he'd said, then asked, "How did you find out about the arson?"

"John LeDeux gave me the heads-up this morning as I was driving over."

"Why wouldn't John give me the heads-up? He's my half brother."

"I guess he knew how you'd react and wanted me to convince you that going into hiding might be the best route until the police investigate more."

"I am not going into hiding, and I am not moving into your house. Unless this is a proposal of marriage."

She was deliberately taunting him, he knew that, but still his face heated with embarrassment.

"I didn't think so," she said. "You should see the look

on your face, Adam. Relax, I'm not trying to rope you into some kind of commitment, and, with my record, certainly not marriage."

"Don't presume to know what I'm thinking. I'm here, aren't I? And I brought my daughter with me."

"Pfff! Your dad's probably got a rifle in the car, and you're probably packing heat under that suit jacket." When he didn't deny her accusation, she exclaimed, "Unbelievable! I do not need your protection."

"What *do* you need from me, Simone?"

"If you don't know, I'm not going to tell you."

He was heading back home a short time later with his father riding shotgun and his daughter in the backseat. He would drop them off and go into the office.

Suddenly, Maisie announced, "I have a secret."

"Oh?"

"Wanna know what it is?"

"It wouldn't be a secret if you told, would it?"

"It's not that kind of secret."

"What is it then?"

"I'm gonna get a mommy."

"Whaat?" He swerved and almost hit a guard rail.

His father chuckled and slapped his knee.

"Kind of hard for you to get a mother without me getting a wife, isn't it?"

"He's a rocket scientist," his father murmured sarcastically. He was in a grumbly mood because Adam hadn't stayed longer so that he could help Adelaide Daigle tie up her tomato plants. His old man had developed a thing for Simone's mother.

"Yer silly, Daddy. 'Course ya need a wife."

"From the mouths of babes," his father said. More sarcasm.

He decided to ignore the wife part and his father's

snarkiness. "Since when do we need a woman in the house? PawPaw is a great cook, we have a cleaning lady, and I go to work every day to pay for it."

"Thass not all girls do."

I know.

His father was shaking with silent laughter.

"What brought this on today, sweetie?"

She held out the little palm-size, plastic statue she'd been given. Everyone up and down the bayou had one of those by now. "Tante Lulu sez I should pray ta St. Jude if I want somethin' bad enough."

He should have known the bayou busybody had a hand in this.

"And why would you be telling Tante Lulu that you want a mother? You hardly know her."

"She guessed."

A likely story. "Do you have anyone in particular in mind?" he asked, knowing that his daughter might very well say Tante Lulu or the lady at the pet store or the girl who sometimes came to clean the pool.

Instead, she gave him a sly look and said, "Thass the secret."

Fireworks were the last thing she needed today . . .

By the Fourth of July, Legal Belles was open for business again. Sort of. A temporary office space had been rented in a strip mall near one of the Starr Foods supermarkets. A bit out of the way, but perhaps a downtown location wasn't necessary for the type of clientele they attracted.

Even though it was a legal holiday, Simone was going over to organize files and fill out more of the endless insurance papers. She was *not* going to the Lanier pool party. Not after the way Adam had been pestering her the past three days.

Her mother had been invited to the party by Adam's father, but she'd decided not to go, either, especially with Thanh Pham still being her guest. A cousin of Thanh's in Texas had invited her to come visit indefinitely, and Thanh's sister, Kimly, was going to drive her there this weekend. Mike Pham was still looking for his wife, but no overt threats had been made lately.

Simone's mother had become close with the Vietnamese woman and wanted to spend as much of the remaining time with her, which was no problem since she no longer had a receptionist job. No room in the temporary Legal Belles premises.

The arson case remained unsolved. Police were investigating Marcus Pitot and Mike Pham as persons of interest, but nothing more. Simone was doing her own investigation, as well, which was the spark that had set off the latest arguments with Adam. He still couldn't accept her dangerous occupation and cited the fire as further proof of his assertions.

Her last words to him, yesterday, were, "It's over. You and I are incompatible. Stop coming around."

His response had been the usual, "It's not over. We are not incompatible, just not on the same page, yet. And I can't stop. Dammit!"

"That *dammit* is so telling," Simone had said.

"What does that mean?"

"You do not want to care for me, dammit. I'm like a rash you hate but yearn to scratch, dammit."

He'd just grinned, as if *scratch* were another name for something else.

"At least come to the party, dammit," he'd coaxed. "Maisie will be so disappointed if you don't come."

"Aren't you worried about me exposing Maisie to my danger?"

"I'll be there to protect both of you. And my dad was a cop. And there will be plenty of other people there to make the party secure."

"Maisie won't notice my absence with the crowd. And I know what you're thinking. Me, a bikini, your smoldering eyes, the cool water of the pool, wet bikini, a little afternoon delight when no one's looking."

He'd blinked at her several times. "You took the words right out of my mouth," he'd lied.

Simone wasn't taking a chance.

When all else fails, bring in the big guns . . .

By two in the afternoon, half of the guests had arrived, the grill was sizzling, masses of food appeared, beer and pink punch flowed, water splashed, and the band was setting up. By then, Adam accepted that Simone was not coming.

No, *accepted* was the wrong word. He was royally pissed and not about to accept her stubbornness. He went into the house to get his Harley keys when the doorbell rang. Who would ring the bell when a party was going on? He stomped to the door, opened it, and just gawked, before bursting into a laugh. "Holy friggin' hell! Look what the wind blew in!"

"I heard you were having a party."

It was his brother, Dave, in full military gear, sporting enough stripes and medals and insignia to impress General Patton, if he were still around. He must have caught the attention of every female in every airport between Bagram and New Orleans.

Dave grinned as he dropped his duffel bag and yanked Adam into a huge bear hug. It was hard to tell who held on tighter. Although they didn't talk about it, Adam and his father worried all the time about Dave, knowing he could be smack dab in the middle of any danger spot in the world. Sometimes they didn't hear from him for months.

Can that be another reason why I'm such a stickler about danger?

Just then, there was a loud squeal followed by, "Uncle Dave, Uncle Dave!" Maisie flew across the room into Dave's arms, and he swung her around. "How's my Maisie Daisie doing? Didn't you know I would come for your birthday?"

"My birthday's not today."

"Oh, so it's a welcome home party for me."

His father stepped up then, and if Adam were a weeping man, now would be the time to do it. His father just stared at Dave, and Dave just stared back for a long telling moment before they hugged, too.

If that weren't enough drama, who should walk in then but Sonia, all hot red flaming hair, wearing a hot red bikini with a sheer cover-up and high-heeled wedge-type shoes that would do a hooker proud.

Dave's eyes about bugged out.

But then Sonia's did, too.

After the introductions, Dave prepared to follow Sonia and the others out to join the party. Before he stepped away, Dave asked, "Is she yours?"

Adam shook his head.

"Happy birthday to me," Dave said then with a wink.

Adam picked up his bike keys again and almost made it out the door before he was accosted by this apparition that had to be either Betsy Ross or Martha Washington or a little person in an old-fashioned flag gown with a bathing mobcap. It was Tante Lulu, of course.

"Boy, yer gettin' on mah last nerve," she said right off.

"Why? What did I do?"

She tossed her arms in the air with disgust. "Thass the problem. Ya haven't done nothin'." Under her breath, she added, "If brains were dynamite, he wouldn't have enough ta blow his nose. Lawyers!"

He didn't need to ask what she meant. "I'm going to get her now."

"And what're ya gonna do that's any different than the nothin' ya been doin' so far?"

Really, this busybody went too far some times. "This is between me and Simone."

"Oh? How's that workin' for ya?"

He clenched his fists. "What would you suggest, exactly?"

"It all depends on yer intentions."

"Oh, good Lord! This isn't the fifties. There are other things besides marriage."

"Not here in the bayou. Not if yer wantin' St. Jude's help."

He rolled his eyes.

"This ain't Cal-a-forny, and you ain't no hippie dippie free love kinda guy."

He sighed, wondering if he could leapfrog over her and escape. "Simone isn't any more interested in marriage than I am."

"Then, how come yer both so miserable?"

"She's miserable?" he asked and couldn't help but smile with a glimmer of hope.

"Let me ask ya one thing. Do ya love that gal?"

"Yes," he said, and was surprised that he hadn't even hesitated.

"And what did she say when ya tol' her that?"

"Um."

The old lady made a clucking sound of disgust and

shoved him aside as she went out the front door, which was still open.

"Where are you going?" She was so old she might have got her directions wrong, and thought the pool was that way.

"Outside ta pray ta yer St. Jude statue I brought for yer front yard. You need all the help you can get."

He used a little Cajun persuasion . . .

"Whoo-ee, baby! You could wave that flag over my bed anytime," BaRa said, staring out the plate glass window of the temporary Legal Belles agency.

"What?" Simone asked, glancing up from the file on her desk.

BaRa had come in to help her this morning but was about to go off to a July Fourth family barbecue with her twin sons.

Then Simone noticed the target of BaRa's appreciation.

It was Adam wearing a pair of flashy flag bathing trunks with a white tank top and flip flogs. He had driven in on his motorcycle and he gave the engine an extra rev, as if in anger, or to get her attention.

Honestly, the man never gave up.

And, honestly, a small part of her was thankful for that.

"Hi, Adam," BaRa said as she passed him by.

Adam nodded at her, but as BaRa went out and he walked in, he only had eyes for Simone.

"Lock up shop. You're coming to the party."

"No, I'm not. I already told you—"

"Here's the deal, darlin'. And, yes, I said *darlin'*. Live with it. Tante Lulu and her LeDeux gang have been making rumbling noises all day about some kind of half-assed Cajun Village People patriotic act where they do this sexy dance routine to woo a woman, or man. Sort of like Magic Mike on the bayou."

"I've seen their dance revue. It's outrageous, and totally embarrassing to the person they're targeting." She paused and felt her face heat up. "Me? They wouldn't!"

"They would. Imagine Abe Lincoln, George Washington, Lady Liberty, Betsy Ross, whom I'm pretty sure is Tante Lulu, Uncle Sam, Ben Franklin, a Star-Spangled Rockette, Yankee Doodle, Captain America, and a whole slew of military men and women strutting their stuff and taking it all off. All for the sake of true love."

Her jaw dropped. "You're making that up."

"I wish!"

"What would you be in this musical menagerie?"

"I have no idea, but my brother, Dave, just got home. I wouldn't be surprised if they commandeer his captain's uniform."

"Well, good luck with all that. I'm sorry you're having to deal with this, but . . ." She shrugged. It wasn't her problem.

"Have I mentioned that if I don't bring you back, they'll probably all come here to serenade you out in the parking lot? There'll be an even bigger audience. The news media will show up. Great publicity for Legal Belles, though, I suppose." He batted his eyelashes at her.

She wasn't sure if he was serious or not.

But she wasn't taking any chances.

"Do you promise that there won't be any serenading crap if I go back there?"

"I'll do my best."

"Just for an hour, and then I'm outta there."

"Sure."

Had she just been conned or what?

She knew that she'd been conned when he put her be-hind him on the Harley with her legs spread and her knees raised, hugging his hips. Then he proceeded to take every rough, vibrating road in Terrebonne Parish. She had to grab him around the waist to keep from falling off. By the time they got to his house, her lady parts had been jiggled to attention.

She hit him when she got off the bike, especially when he grinned at her, knowing what he'd done, and took her hand. That's when she heard, coming from the back of the house, reverberating around the neighborhood, the Swamp Rats belting out "Louisiana Man."

Yep, she thought. *My theme song.* Except that teenager-ish Britney Spears song "Oops! . . . I Did It Again" would be an even more appropriate signature line for her. And Simone was no teenager.

Still, it was a fact: Her Cajun Crazy was in full-tilt boogie mode.

Love is a Cajun kind of thing . . .

Adam was happy . . . happier than he'd been for a long, long time. It was the warm, heart-expanding kind of joy seeping out from within, radiating outward, that rarely comes in anyone's lifetime. A time to be cherished, and protected so that it would last, which it couldn't possibly do, being like a bubble or a wisp of dandelion fluff on the wind.

Corny, I know.

Now would be a good time for some reunion sex, if he could find a bedroom, or even a closet, where he could be alone with Simone. *Hmm. That sounds like a song title,*

"Alone with Simone." He grinned, not at all alarmed at his loopiness, not even when Simone elbowed him and hissed, "Stop smirking," while trying to tug her hand free.

"I'm not smirking," he said, refusing to release her hand. He wasn't letting her out of his sight today, not till they resolved their differences, or had reunion sex, or both. Meanwhile, he pretended to leer at her body in the spare bathing suit she'd borrowed from Charmaine. It was white, one-piece, and fit like a glove, low between the breasts, high on the sides. He couldn't wait to see it wet. "And stop trying to get away from me. The only way I'm releasing you today is if you let me watch your ass while you walk away. In fact, can I take a video with my cell phone? Up, down, up, down."

She stopped tugging.

He knew she was sensitive about her butt, with no cause. She was built like what his dad used to call "a brick shithouse." Not that he would mention that to her.

"Behave yourself. People are staring at us," she said.

He yanked her closer and kissed her shoulder, which was sun-baked and silky smooth and smelled like coconut oil. "They are not. They're having too much fun." And they were. "It's a great party, isn't it?"

"Yes," she admitted and relaxed beside him on the cushioned glider one of the neighbors had brought over to provide extra seating. He had plans for this glider, later.

There had to be at least seventy people of all ages, including a half dozen of Maisie's friends, standing about talking, dancing, sitting, and swimming as the Swamp Rats played one traditional Cajun song after another. "Jolie Blon." "Big Mamou." "Jambalaya." "Sugar Bee." "Diggy Diggy Lo." The band members all wore beachy kinds of shorts and T-shirts (including his favorite Bite

Me Bayou Bait Company ones) and flip-flops, more in the line of Jimmy Buffett than Doug Kershaw, even René with the washboard-type instrument hanging over his shoulders onto his chest.

"Wanna dance?" he asked Simone.

"Not a chance. Not in my bare feet."

"We could dance on the grass."

"You would use dancing as an excuse to make out."

He grinned.

"Stop grinning."

He grinned some more.

She just shook her head at him.

"How about some food?"

"If I eat another bite, I'll pop out of this suit."

"I can hope!"

"You're going to have enough leftovers to last a week."

She was right. Extra tables had to be brought in to accommodate all the food under a rented tent, not just that which his dad had made or ordered, or that which Tante Lulu had carted in, but many of the guests brought food or wine, as well, for their party contributions.

He loved the sense of community here in the bayou. And family. The LeDeuxs had taken him in like an adopted son, under the wide wings of the Big Mama herself, Tante Lulu. Every one of the nephews and nieces were here with their spouses: Luc and Sylvie, Remy and Rachel, René and Valerie, John and Celine, Daniel and Samantha, and a dozen or more of their children, including baseball great Andy LeDeux. The only one missing was Aaron LeDeux, Daniel's twin, who was out of town on some mysterious mission.

And family, of course, meant his brother, Dave, who was the primo guest of the day. With Sonia glued to his side, he regaled one and all with his war tales.

Maisie was in high heaven, flitting around like a butterfly in her star-spangled bathing suit. He'd never get her to sleep tonight.

John LeDeux walked over to them, a cell phone pressed to his ear, a longneck bottle of beer in the other hand. Clicking the phone off with his thumb, he put the device in the back pocket of his khaki cargo shorts, which rode low on his hips. He wore no shirt. "I've got news, folks," he said, hunkering down in front of them.

Adam was immediately alert.

And so was Simone who asked, "What? Not another fire?"

"The arson at Legal Belles. No, not a new one. You'll never guess who's responsible." He paused, setting his bottle aside, and told them, "Luther Ferguson."

"What? He's in jail," Simone said.

"He ordered the fire from the inside. Friend of one of his cellmates did the deed."

"We already knew that Ferguson had family money behind him," Adam told Simone.

She nodded. "What will this mean for Ferguson?"

"His jail sentence will be extended. I doubt if he'll get out before he's seventy, if then."

"Then the threat is over?" Simone asked.

"Sure is, sis," John said, squeezing Simone's knee.

John walked off to join his wife sitting on the edge of the pool, who could be heard warning her husband, "Don't you dare, don't you dare." He did dare, picking her up and jumping with both of them into the pool, causing a huge splash. Adam hoped his cell phone was waterproof.

Simone turned to Adam, "That is such a relief, that we know the truth, anyway."

He squeezed her shoulder and for just a moment she relaxed against him.

"You know I love you, don't you, Simone?" he asked, suddenly. To his surprise, the words came easily.

She straightened, and turned slowly toward him. "No, I don't know that, Adam."

"Why do you think I'm acting so crazy?"

"Maybe Cajun Crazy is catching."

"I love you," he said.

She just stared at him.

"I love you."

"Stop saying that."

"I love you."

She started to cry.

"Why are you crying?"

"Because I love you, too."

"Of course you do, darlin'."

And she melted, the way he'd hoped she would.

It was as simple, and complicated, as that. Men fought, women resisted. Or women fought, and men resisted. But love conquered all.

The only thing missing was . . . reunion sex.

Chapter Nineteen

A nd then there were fireworks . . .

It was a great party. Simone was glad that she'd come. Of course she was. The man she loved had told her that he loved her. That was a big, BIG deal.

Nothing had changed, though. They still had seemingly insurmountable barriers separating them, her job being the most glaring one, but they'd had no chance to be alone to discuss a resolution, if there could be one. She had to accept Adam's assurance that they would work things out.

In the meantime, the band played a wonderful mix of modern rock and traditional Cajun music, the food was spectacular, and the conversation was stimulating and fun. It touched her heart to watch Adam in an Uncle Sam top hat and flag bathing trunks dance a slow jitterbug with his little girl, who was adorable in a star-spangled bathing suit and a lopsided Lady Liberty tiara.

His brother came up to the patio table where she was sitting. A few years younger than Adam but with a much bulkier frame—all military muscle—Dave was a good-looking man. Especially when she'd first seen him in his uniform, but still double-take-worthy now in drab green shorts and a U.S. Army T-shirt. His hair was short, shaved on the sides and not much longer on top. A high and tight, she thought the haircut was called. Lots of male cops adopted the style, too.

Plopping into a chair next to her, he said, "So, you're the one?"

"Maybe."

"No maybe about it. My brother's batshit nuts about you."

"You just arrived in town. You know this . . . how?"

"By the way he looks at you."

She arched her brows.

"Like you're a hot fudge sundae, fifty-yard-line Super Bowl tickets, brand-new Porsche, and virgin nymphomaniac all wrapped in one pretty white package." He pretended to ogle her borrowed white bathing suit, which by now was covered by an open, white dress shirt of Adam's with the sleeves rolled up.

"All those things, huh?" She took a sip of her ice water, having given up on alcohol about two hours ago. "And how do I look at him?"

"Like he could butter your biscuit and lick it off any day, anytime."

"Daaaave!"

"Sorry. That was crude. I heard Tante Lulu say it." He held up his hands in mock surrender.

"Well, then, it must be all right." She smiled. "So, you're home on leave."

"Sort of."

That was . . . mysterious. "For *sort of* how long?"

"Not sure. I might take a temporary assignment at Fort Polk. Go inactive for a little while."

Definitely a story there, especially when her police skills detected a bit of sorrow in his pale brown eyes. She knew haunted when she saw it.

Adam came back then and squeezed a chair in between her and his brother. "Be prepared," he said. "The LeDeux looney birds are about to perform."

"Adam! You promised."

"Cross my heart. They gave me their word," he told her. "I wasn't too hot for the Richard Gere slash Debra Winger nonsense myself, wearing Dave's uniform."

"What about my uniform?"

"Ever seen *An Officer and a Gentleman*? The last scene?"

"Are you kidding? That's every grunt's go-to movie for getting laid . . . um, lucky. 'Scuse my language, ma'am," Dave said to Simone. Then, addressing Adam again, he added, "I could do that routine for you, bro, blindfolded." As proof, he began to sing "Wind Beneath My Wings."

"That would defeat the purpose, *bro*."

"Which is?"

"Which is *me* getting laid . . . um, lucky. Not you." Adam grinned at Simone. "Right, darlin'?"

"You're overdoing the *darlin'*s today, darlin'."

He grinned some more.

Maisie arrived and crawled up on her Uncle Dave's lap. The little girl had been clinging to her uncle, off and on, all day, afraid he would take off again for "Granny-stan."

"Let's go find PawPaw," Dave said, tossing a giggling Maisie up over his shoulder, then blowing a raspberry into her neck. "Betcha he's hiding in the garden shed, smoking one of those smelly cigars I brought him."

"Oh, Uncle Dave!" Maisie giggled some more.

Just then, René LeDeux, dressed like a hottie Ben Franklin with wire-frame glasses, shirtless except for a red, white, and blue vest, walked out onto the little stage to the sound of a loud drumroll. The band had already dismantled, but they'd brought their own taped music for the show that was about to begin. "Ladies and gentlemen, let me introduce you to . . . ta, da! . . . the Cajun Village People." With a loud version of "Macho, Macho Man . . ." adapted to "Cajun, Cajun Man . . ." the LeDeux men and women in full patriotic, cornball costumes strutted their stuff. Singing, dancing, gyrating, shimmying. They were really, really good, drawing numerous bouts of laughter and spontaneous clapping. The highlight of the entire performance had to be Betsy Ross, aka Tante Lulu, twerking. Or maybe it was George Washington (John Le-Deux) doing a very sexy striptease right down to white wig, buckled shoes, and very brief briefs that had battery-operated stars on them that flashed when he hip bumped his laughing wife, Martha (Celine).

After that, people started to straggle home, and by the time the fireworks were scheduled to start at nine in the skies over the park several blocks away, easily visible from Adam's backyard, there were only about fifteen people left. "Help me put Maisie to bed," Adam urged her.

"Won't she be upset that she didn't get to stay up?" Simone asked.

"Maybe, but look at her. She can't keep her eyes open." The little girl was planted, legs horizontal, feet not touching the ground, on the glider between Dave and the yoga beauty, whom Simone knew without being told was Adam's old girlfriend, Sonia. She wasn't sure how she felt about her being here, even if she wasn't involved with Adam anymore. "Besides, all her little friends left a long time ago."

He carried Maisie upstairs, with Simone following behind them carrying, at Maisie's insistence, a Lady Liberty tiara, a piece of Tante Lulu's Peachy Praline Cobbler Cake, which she intended to have for breakfast, and a garden gnome, which Simone's mother had apparently gifted the little girl, all of which she wanted nearby when she slept. Right beside the Chatty GI Jane doll that Adam had given her earlier that day. Apparently, the doll not only talked, saying such things as "Army gals rock, Army guys roll!" but also had a set of uniform changes, including day-of-the-week underpants.

Finally, the little imp was tucked in and had said her prayers, and God blessed everyone she could think of, including Simone, whom she hinted was part of some Tante Lulu/St. Jude secret. Leaving a night light on, Simone and Adam crept out into the hallway.

"I should go home now," Simone whispered.

"Not a chance!" He tried to back her up against the wall.

But she slipped under his arm. "The party's over, Adam."

"Hah! The party's just about to begin." He was feinting and parrying her every move.

She shook her head at his playfulness and dodged a pinch of her butt. The guy had a fascination with her behind. "You still have guests down there."

"Let my dad take care of them."

"Won't they wonder where you are?"

"Let them." He was eyeing her carefully, obviously planning his next move.

"We should at least go watch the fireworks."

"I intend to make my own fireworks," he said, making a successful grab for her, and opening the next door in the hallway. His bedroom.

And he was right. There were fireworks. And not just those that could be seen through the rear windows.

You could say it was his final argument . . .

Adam wasn't sure what to do first. Talk or make love. He decided to make love first to soften her up for the talk. He knew sure as stubborn Cajun women she was going to resist what he had to propose.

"Stand right there," he said, placing her in the center of the room, backlighted by the fireworks and the tiki flames outside. Someone had turned on the stereo and soft rock music played, a calming contrast to the raucousness of the day. Then he quickly shrugged out of his clothes and sat, bare-assed naked on the bottom corner of his bed.

She blinked with amusement at his nakedness, taking special note of one particular body part. "Nice rocket!"

The rocket lurched, but didn't take off, thank God! He wasn't going to be diverted into a quickie, if he could help it. Waving his hand at her, he ordered, "Take it off, darlin'. Slow and easy. I've been imagining this all day."

For once, she didn't argue. Instead, she eased out of his dress shirt and was shrugging her bathing suit down, inch by inch. She let it hang from her hips.

For a moment, he couldn't speak if he'd wanted to. His tongue had frozen in his mouth. He was probably having a tongue hard-on.

Her eyes fluttered shut, and she was swaying from side to side to the soft music. Her breasts were large, but not so large that they sagged. Just right to fit in his big hands.

Her dark hair, wavy from all their dips in the pool, lay about her bare shoulders. Her face was sun-kissed and slightly flushed, bare of make-up.

"More," he urged on a groan.

Without opening her eyes, she curved her lips in a little Mona Lisa smile, and proceeded to shrug out of the suit all together.

"Lord have mercy," he said. She was a goddess. Big, curvy, lush in all the right places.

"You're praying now?" Her eyes opened. She was teasing him, fully aware of her effect on him.

"Witch!" He spread his legs and beckoned with the fingertips of both hands for her to come closer.

When she stood close enough, between his knees, he kissed her belly. Her moan was all the encouragement he needed. He stood, took her in his arms, and let them both fall to the bed, which, unfortunately, caused the bed frame to crack and the mattress and box spring to fall through to the floor. Luckily, no one heard over the racket outside. Laughing, they couldn't care less whether the mattress was high or low.

"I can't wait," he growled, sliding on a condom and pushing himself into her body. "Sorry, but . . . holy hell!"

Her inner muscles were convulsing around him in a rapid-fire, rat-a-tat orgasm. Apparently, she couldn't wait, either.

He let his weight rest on her for a moment, forehead to forehead. "I guess some rockets just combust before launching," he told her.

"And some launch pads just self-combust," she said. "I didn't even kiss you silly like I planned."

He rolled on his side, removed the condom, and tossed it in a bedside wastebasket. Then, facing her, he brushed the hair off her face and said, "We have plenty of time."

"Do we?"

Okay, so now was the big moment. He was a lawyer. A trained talker. This had to be the best opening argument of his lifetime.

"We should get married. Soon," he told her. Best to present your case right up front.

"Whoa!" she said and tried to pull away.

He wouldn't let her. With his hands on her buttocks, he forced her to stay in place.

"I love you, Simone. And you love me. You told me so, and I'm holding you to it."

"That doesn't mean—"

"I want to be with you. All the time," he interrupted and gave her a small kiss. "I want to live with you. I want to sleep with you. I want to share my life with you."

"That doesn't mean we have to marry."

"It does when there's a child in the picture."

"Lots of people live together, without marriage, even with children."

He shook his head. "Not me. And not you, if you're honest about it."

"Adam, you don't want to marry again any more than I want to marry again."

"Actually, I do. Want to marry you."

"Why?"

"Because I love you." He shrugged. It was as simple as that. "Tell me the truth. Do you want to marry me, or are you just afraid?"

"My history," she reminded him. "Three failed marriages."

"Mine, too, but that doesn't mean I can't do better."

She sighed. His arguments were working. Maybe. "What about my job?"

He sighed then, too. "I can't promise not to worry, but I can promise not to interfere again. Or try not to."

"I don't know, Adam. I just don't know."

He rolled over, tucking her up against his side. "I had a short talk with my brother today. Apparently, he lost a couple buddies recently, and someone important to him. He didn't elaborate. What he did say, more than once, was, 'Carpe diem!' Seize the day! Treasure the present because you never know what tomorrow may bring."

"That's all well and good, but in reality you and I are like oil and water."

"In reality, sweetheart, how would you feel if we broke it off today, never to see each other again? In fact, let's take it a step further. Suppose I was the one to die tomorrow. How would you feel?"

"Devastated."

He shrugged, as if he'd won the case. "Marry me, Simone." He cupped her face with one hand and kissed a line down her jaw.

"My mother would have a bird." She arched to give him access to her neck.

"Maisie would be in high heaven. Marry me." He pressed her onto her back and moved his kisses in a line down her chest, between her breasts.

"What if we tried a trial living together? Private, discreet, my apartment, wherever that will end up being." She gasped as he licked one nipple, then nipped at it.

"No trials. No sneaking around, discreet or otherwise. Marry me."

When he began to move his mouth even lower, she grabbed his face with both hands and pulled him up and over her. "All right."

"What?"

"I'll marry you."

"You will?" He smiled. "This isn't just your Cajun Crazy speaking, is it?"

"You, my love, are going to be my last Cajun Crazy. My forever kind of Cajun Crazy."

He could live with that. He sealed the deal with slow lovemaking (his specialty) that caused more than a few fireworks . . . inside, not in the Louisiana skies outside.

When she lay splatted out with depletion an hour later, he reminded her, "We're going to be married."

"Uh-huh."

"I know what I want for a wedding gift, from you."

She cocked open one eyelid.

"Handcuffs."

But she got back at him for the fixation he had with the handcuffs she'd mentioned weeks ago. "I don't think we'll need a wedding planner."

Huh? He was thinking hot kinky sex, and she was thinking embossed invitations and reception halls. "Why is that?"

"Now that Maisie has proven how good a party she can throw, a wedding should be a piece of cake for her."

He chuckled.

"Provided she gets a little help from . . ."

He stopped chuckling. When she didn't finish her sentence, he thought she'd fallen asleep.

But then she added, ". . . from Tante Lulu."

Thunder crashed in the distance, or maybe it was just the fireworks.

Epilogue

And the craziness continued . . .

After three marriages, Simone did not want a big wedding. It would be embarrassing.

Adam had already done that, not interested in a repeat. No way did he want the whole tux/gown/frenzied wedding hoopla.

But Maisie wanted not just a big wedding, but an extravaganza of a reception. Guess who won?

"You'd think you were the one getting married," Adam had grumbled at his daughter.

To which, Maisie had replied, "I am, Daddy. This is *our* wedding."

He couldn't argue with that.

Thus it was that one month later, Adam Lanier married Simone LeDeux in Our Lady of the Bayou Church. Turned out that the Catholic Church had never recognized her three civil marriages as valid, so she was free to have a priest officiate over the rituals, which pacified Adelaide Daigle, somewhat. And gave Tante Lulu free rein to take over the event.

Lucien LeDeux gave his half sister away. Helene was the maid of honor, and Adam's brother, David, was the best man. Also, in the wedding party on the bride's side were BaRa, Sabine, Charmaine, and Tante Lulu. The ushers were John, Remy, and René LeDeux, and Adam's cousin Rusty Lanier. Maisie was the cutest flower girl in history with a white gown matching Simone's white gown, a mother-daughter kind of testament, they claimed.

At the reception, which was held at a local veteran's hall, Tante Lulu, in her pink bridesmaid gown (Maisie's choice of color for the wedding theme), wobbled around on her matching high heels. She finally accosted Aaron LeDeux, a pilot, who had been avoiding her for weeks. "Where ya been hidin', boy?" she asked.

"Don't you be throwing any thunderbolts my way, old lady," Aaron replied with a laugh. "I'm not interested."

"Lak that matters when St. Jude is in the buildin'!"

But then her eyes were caught by a handsome man in uniform standing near the bar. It was Adam's brother, Dave, in full dress uniform.

"Hmmm," she said and wandered off. Lots of couples had been avoiding her that night, having heard about the strange phenomena of all the LeDeuxs being suddenly pregnant. "As if I had anythin' ta do with that!" she murmured to herself, then grinned.

Later that night, after making desperate love for the first time since the Fourth of July party, thanks to Tante Lulu's interference and insistence on celibacy before marriage, Simone gave her husband the promised wedding gift. A pair of handcuffs.

They immediately tried them out.

They worked.

In all the right ways.

Then Adam said, "I have a present for you, too, darlin', but it's nothing you can unwrap."

She glanced down at the finally flaccid organ between his legs.

"Not that," he said and pinched her butt, one of his favorite parts on his new wife. "I'm thinking about leaving my law practice with Luc."

She raised her head to stare at him. "Why?"

"Well, how would you feel about a new name for your agency? Legal Belles and Beaux?"

"Oh, Adam! You would do that for me?" Tears welled in her eyes. "It sounds perfect."

Reader Letter

Dear Reader:

Did you have as much fun reading *Cajun Crazy* as I had writing it? Guess we all need to get our crazy on now and again, whether it be for Cajuns or Vikings or Navy SEALs or whatever.

Cajun Crazy is the eleventh of my bayou adventures featuring the outrageous Tante Lulu. If you haven't tried them, start with *The Love Potion*, which is Luc and Sylvie's story, and don't forget the most recent, *The Cajun Doctor*, featuring pediatric oncologist Dr. Daniel Le-Deux. Next up will be the pilot Aaron LeDeux, Daniel's twin brother, in *Cajun Persuasion*.

Although I've never lived in Louisiana, I have a love for that state—every bit of it, from the swamps to the cities. Perhaps there's a genetic memory, though I can't find any Southerners in my family tree. However, my grandmother, who was a Butler, always claimed she was descended from Rhett Butler. Yes, I know that Rhett was a fictional character. Still . . .

One time when I accompanied my husband on a business trip to New Orleans, I went off sightseeing on my own in the French Quarter. I came across this historic house that had a plaque out front saying that it was open to visitors. Turns out it was the former residence of author Frances Parkinson Keyes and was once home to General Beauregard. When I knocked on the door, a lady in an antebellum gown welcomed me and showed me around. Then we had tea, as if I were an expected visitor. Truly, I felt as if I'd stepped back in time.

And did I mention that my oldest son is named Beau?

Please let me know what you think of this and all my other books. I love to hear from readers at shill733@aol.com, or visit my website at www.sandrahill.net, or my Facebook page at Sandra Hill Author, or sign up for my mailing list to get the occasional newsletter at www.sandrahill.net/mailinglist.html.

Wishing you smiles in your reading,
Sandra Hill

Chapter One

The Big C strikes again . . .

The first time Dr. Daniel LeDeux met ten-year-old Deke Watson, Deke asked him what it felt like to have sex. The second time they met, Deke asked what it felt like to die.

Lying back in one of a dozen leather reclining chairs at the Juneau, Alaska Pediatric Medical Center, with a first dose of chemo blasting into his IV, Deke looked like any other pre-adolescent kid, iPod blaring in his ear, baseball cap turned backward on his head, freckles dotting his pug nose, a wide mischievous grin on his face. He was a little on the thin side, having been feeling lousy for a long time and only recently diagnosed with Chronic Myelogenous Leukemia. CML.

"Seriously, if I'm gonna die from this crud, I'd like ta know what it's like ta boink a girl." He batted his stubby eyelashes at Daniel with fake innocence.

Boink?

Deke was joking, of course. At this stage, he was full of hope for a complete remission, as he should be. No time, or need, for fearing death. As a pediatric oncologist, Daniel had seen hundreds of cases, many of which defied the odds for survival. No need for a miracle here. Unless Deke's CML morphed into AML, Acute Myelogenous Leukemia, his chances were good. Deke's question was a blatant guilt trip ploy to get some info Daniel might not otherwise be inclined to share.

While Daniel checked his patient's pulse and heart rate, he said, "I think those kinds of questions should be put to your dad, don't you?"

"Sure. If I had one!"

Daniel arched his brows.

"He skipped out when I was five. Cokehead."

Daniel nodded. Not an unusual story. He recalled now that Deke's mother, Bethany Watson, a special ed teacher, had been raising him single-handedly for a long time. Dealing with childhood cancer was a kick in the gut for a couple; it was a body blow for one parent to handle alone. He had to admire her bravery.

"If you don't wanna give me the goodies . . ."

"Goodies?"

"The details about sex," Deke explained. "You could always just give me a *Playboy* magazine . . . you know, if you're too shy to talk about sex. One of the old magazines, not one of the new PG versions." More batting of eyelashes.

Daniel laughed. "Nice try, kiddo."

"My buddy Chuck says it feels like every hair on your body is doin' the hula, and your cock is like a train racing to the finish line."

Cock? A ten-year-old using that word? Daniel shouldn't

be surprised. Kids today knew things that would have
been shocking twenty years ago. Still, he stopped checking the latest white cell count on Deke's chart to stare at
him. "Chuck has had a lot of sex, huh?" Now, that *would*
shock him.

Deke ducked his head sheepishly. "Nah! He's only ten,
too, but he *has* seen a *Playboy* magazine. *Three* of them.
The good ones, too. He has older brothers."

"Wow! A man of experience!" Daniel could remember
the time his identical twin, Aaron, now a pilot, had shown
him a stash of *Playboy* magazines he'd hidden under his
mattress . . . a cool trade scored with AJ Coddington for
five Snicker bars and a Big Blaster water pistol. Come to
think of it, they'd been about ten, too . . . more than
twenty years ago.

That evening he went to his mother Dr. Claire Doucet's
house for dinner. Already he could hear Barry Manilow
crooning through the sound system he and Aaron had
given her for a Christmas gift last year. Big mistake, that.
Now they got to hear Barry in every room of the house
and outdoors on the patio. Their mother and Melanie
Yutu, her longtime significant other, best known to them
as Aunt Mel, had attended dozens of the crooner's concerts . . . thought nothing of flying cross-country, one end
of the United States to the other, to hear him in person.

Sad to say, he and Aaron knew the words to every Barry
Manilow song ever written, and there were lots of them.

But tonight he had something else on his mind. After he
sat down at the dining room table, he asked Aaron, who'd
also been invited for dinner, "Do you remember those ratty
old *Playboy* magazines you used to hide under your mattress?"

Aaron grinned at him. "No, I don't think I do. Unless
you mean . . . oh, let me see . . . um, Karin Mantrose, May

1992. Turn-ons: Being naked on a fur in front of the fire-
place. 36–20–34. Which had nothing whatsoever to do
with that Sherpa bath mat I bought from Walmart with
my paperboy money. Uh-uh."

Daniel grinned. "Or DeLane Velasquez, June 1991,"
Daniel reminded him.

"Turn-ons: Bubble baths for two," they both said at the
same time, then gave each other high fives.

"How about Patti Ann Jones? Remember that one,"
Daniel said.

"How could I forget? Her ideal date was with a brown-
eyed, curly-haired male."

"And our hair was curly in those days. We were sure
she was just waiting for us to grow up." It was amazing
what stuck in a young boy's head, Daniel thought. Hell, a
man's head, too.

"You two are idiots," his mother said as she placed the
big tureen of jambalaya on the table. "Thirty-something
adolescents!"

Coming up beside her, Aunt Mel scoffed, "Any gal
with a twenty-inch waist beyond the age of twelve is an-
orexic or wearing a corset."

"Could someone please turn down the volume on that
music? I can barely hear myself think," Daniel said.

"Barry is best at full volume," his mother asserted, although she did go over and turn a knob so that "At the
Copa" was only a distant backdrop.

"What brought up the skin mags? You're not usually a
memory lane kinda guy." Aaron leaned back in his chair
and studied him in a way he knew would annoy Daniel.
"Oh, don't tell me. You met a centerfold today at the medical center. You have all the luck!"

"I wish! No, it was a young kid, a new cancer patient,
who wanted me to buy him a *Playboy*."

"Don't you dare," his mother said. "With all the mal-practice suits today, you could be sued. Somehow they'd find a way to prove that pornography causes cancer." His mother was a GP in a small medical group that struggled under the burden of monumental malpractice insurance premiums.

He noticed his mother's hand shaking as she sat down next to him and placed a napkin on her lap. Reaching over, he took her hand in his. "Mom? What's up?"

She and Aunt Mel exchanged odd glances.

Oh, this is not good.

"Tell them," Aunt Mel prodded, her eyes welling un-expectedly with tears.

Definitely not good. Aunt Mel was not a crier.

Squeezing Daniel's hand, which she still held, his mother took a deep breath and said, "I have cancer."

He and Aaron said the same foul word under their breaths. To show how serious the situation was, neither woman reamed them out, as they would normally.

For a moment, Daniel felt faint with shock, but then he choked out, "What kind of cancer?" Being an oncologist, that was the most important question he had to ask.

"Uterine."

The most deadly. "What stage?"

"Two. It's already spread to my lymph nodes."

Oh, shit!

"And that's all I'm going to say on the subject tonight," she declared. "I'll show you all the records tomorrow, and you can start interfering in my medical care then. For to-night, I just want to have a nice family dinner."

He and Aaron, who was equally stunned, looked at each other. They didn't have to be twins to read each oth-er's minds this time. Their mother was in big, big trouble.

"I knew it!" Aaron stood angrily. "Mom, I even asked

you last month if you were sick when I noticed how much weight you'd lost, and then I caught you at home in the middle of the day, puking your guts out. You said it was the flu."

His mother shrugged. "I didn't want anyone to know yet. I was waiting for the right time."

"There's a right time to discuss cancer? Coulda fooled me, and I've been dealing with it for ten years. How long have you known?" Daniel narrowed his eyes when his mother squirmed in her seat.

"Three months, and don't take that tone with me, Daniel. I have a right to handle this any way I want."

Daniel stood now and shoved Aaron in the chest. He had to have some way to vent his fury, and, yes, fear. "You knew something was wrong and didn't tell me? I'm a doctor, lamebrain!"

"Mom's a doctor, too, in case you hadn't noticed." Aaron shoved him back.

"Yeah, but she's a GP, not a specialist."

"Whatever!"

"Both of you, sit the hell down and listen," Aunt Mel yelled.

Duly chastened, they sank back into their chairs and watched with disbelief as their mother calmly served up the jambalaya and salad, then passed slices of warm bread to each of them. Aunt Mel poured iced tea into four glasses.

They expect us to eat? Now?

"And don't be such sad sacks," Aunt Mel added. "Things aren't hopeless. Your mother and I are still going to Hawaii this summer." They had been planning that two-week vacation for years. Icing on the cake was the fact that good ol' Barry would be performing there at the same time for a few days.

Four months away, Daniel thought. *Please, God, let her get a chance to wear that lei. Help her and I'll lobby for Barry Manilow songs, rather than Muzak, in the hospital elevators . . . a penance for all my past sins . . . and any forthcoming ones, too.*

Nine months later . . . prayers are answered, but not always the way we expect . . .

Daniel's eyes burned, and he blinked back tears as he approached the little house on Arctic Lane.

His mother had died two days ago at the far-too-young age of fifty-three, after what had turned into a painful battle with cancer, despite several trips to the Mayo Clinic, and some experimental treatments outside the U.S. Cliché though it was, death had been a blessing. Didn't make the loss any easier, though.

And now here he was, asking for another dose of heartache. He should have developed thicker skin by now, considering his specialty, but instead he felt like he was at the end of his rope. He had no business coming to this particular house over which the heavy cloud of hospice care hovered. His work as a pediatric oncologist had ended when Deke left the medical center last week, for good. In-home nurses had taken over.

The hospital lawyers would deem it unwise, from a legal standpoint, for a physician to involve himself personally with a patient. Especially off-premises.

Lawyers! They couldn't know, or care, how close Daniel had gotten to the kid over these past nine months, even with all the time he'd taken off for his mother. There was just something about Deke that touched him, deeply.

He was dragging with him the most pitiful example of

mankind. Jamie Lee Watson, once a promising Marine lifer, now a thirty-five-year-old thin-as-a-skeleton, nose-bleeding cocaine addict. Apparently, the man had seen things in Iraq that only drugs helped him forget. Daniel had found the whereabouts of Deke's father last week, but it had taken him all that time, when he wasn't at his mother's bedside, trying to get the man halfway lucid, showered, and dressed in clean clothes. The new, barely improved Jamie Lee was not a happy camper.

"This is a train wreck about to happen," Jamie Lee complained.

"Not if I can help it."

"My kid . . ." His words trailed off as he choked up, fully aware of Deke's rapidly deteriorating condition. "My kid doesn't need a loser like me."

"He needs you, all right."

"Why?"

"Because you're his father. Simple as that. He doesn't care if you're the President of the United States or a circus clown."

"Bethany is gonna have a fit."

"She's the one who asked me to find you."

Jamie Lee stared at him with the most incredible hope in his bleary eyes before he masked the emotion by rubbing his hands over his face, a face which Daniel had personally shaved for him, removing a year-old beard. Jamie Lee would have probably slit his own throat.

Before Daniel had a chance to knock, the door flew open and Bethany smiled . . . a smile that did not reach her bloodshot eyes. "You came."

It wasn't clear if she was referring to Daniel or her long-absent husband.

Daniel stepped aside and shoved Jamie Lee forward. "Go for it, buddy."

"I am so sorry, Bethany," Jamie Lee said. That apology covered a whole lot of ground, Daniel suspected.

She nodded, seemed to hesitate, then opened her arms to give Jamie Lee a comforting hug. Almost immediately, she stepped back, putting space between them.

"Deke's been in and out of a coma for days, but he asks for his daddy when he wakes up." She laughed, but there was no mirth, just an odd tone of near-hysteria.

With a squeeze to her shoulder, Jamie Lee walked into the dining room which had been converted into a sickroom with a hospital bed and medical equipment. The oxygen machine whooshed away while an obscene number of tubes ran from the child's frail body, no attempt to hide his bald head under its usual baseball cap. A nurse moved away from the bed to give the stranger room. Daniel and Bethany stood in the open doorway, watching.

It was odd the things you noticed in times of crisis. Birds chirping outside the open window. A Disneyland souvenir glass on the sideboard. A framed photo showing a much younger Deke with his mother and a guy in a buzz cut and military uniform, all of them smiling.

"Hey, slugger," Jamie Lee said, clearly uncertain what to do, where to put his hands. But then he leaned over and kissed his boy's cheek. "That's what I always called him. Slugger," Jamie Lee nervously told Daniel.

Miraculously, considering his sedation, Deke's eyes fluttered open. "Dad?"

"Yeah, it's me," Jamie Lee choked out.

"I prayed . . . that . . . that you . . . would come," Deke finally got out. Talking was difficult at this stage.

"That's me . . . the answer to a little boy's prayer," Jamie Lee muttered.

"Am I dead yet?" His little hand clung to his father's. "Are you an angel?"

Jamie Lee started to weep then. Hell, they all had tears in their eyes.

"No, I'm hardly an angel, son. Just your daddy."

"I'm afraid. Will you stay with me?"

"As long as you want, slugger."

And he did stay with him for the next five hours, never moving from the seat the nurse had pushed behind him, never releasing his son's grip on his hand, until Deke slipped away. The death was almost an anticlimax.

Daniel had gone back to his office for several hours and returned just in time. As he left for the last time, he wondered how many more of these cancer deaths he could handle without going insane.

A dog is a dog, no matter the breed . . .

Samantha Starr walked down the corridor of the French Quarter courthouse with her new lawyer, Lucien LeDeux, at her side. They were headed toward a conference room where they would meet with her horndog ex-husband Dr. Nicholas Coltrane (aka Nick the Prick), his shark lawyer Jessie John Daltry, and an associate judge for the Fourth Circuit Court of Appeals, District of New Orleans.

"Don't say anything," Luc warned her. "You know the good doc will try ta rile you into a hissy fit, which won't sit well with the judge. Just let me do all the talking."

"I'll try."

"Not good enough. I've studied the records, *chère*. You're paying Coltrane as much alimony as you do because of your outburst last time."

She stiffened and raised her chin haughtily. "Or because the judge was a female influenced by my ex's dubious charms. Nick commented on my lack of sex appeal as an excuse for his adultery, and the judge didn't even reprimand him."

"Huh? No way! You are as hot as a goat's behind in a pepper patch."

"Charming."

"Oops. That's my Tante Lulu's favorite Cajun saying. Hang around her long enough and she wears off on you."

Samantha knew and even worked on occasion with Louise Rivard, better known as Tante Lulu to everyone, and she was outrageous in appearance, actions, and general reputation. Not the role model Samantha would set for herself.

Luc grinned. "Anyhow, don't let the asshole put you down."

"Oh, please! I am what I am." Samantha was five-footten in her bare feet. When she wore heels, she was taller than Nick's five-eleven frame, which had annoyed him to no end. If that wasn't bad enough, her body was covered with freckles from forehead to toes, and not the attractive kind. Once, in a drunken rage, Nick had likened her freckles to tobacco juice spit on her by a redneck farmer. Orange spittle. As for her bright red hair . . . no more! She paid a fortune to her hairstylist to keep it a more subdued auburn.

Samantha hated that she'd taken so much care with her appearance today . . . white, long-sleeved, Chanel pantsuit with a fitted peplum jacket, matching stiletto pumps, and tailored, jade-green, collarless, silk blouse . . . to match her green eyes, her only feature that she really liked. Her auburn hair was swept off her face in a neat chignon. Emerald drop earrings in a platinum setting and her great-grandmother's emerald-and-diamond filigree ring were her only jewelry. Unfortunately, there was no way to cover the freckles on her hands, face and neck.

She hadn't dressed to impress Nick, but for her own self-esteem which always tanked in his presence. "I don't need phony compliments."

"The dickhead has done a job on you, darlin'. Talk about!" Luc just shook his head. "We can discuss that later. Maybe you should have stayed home and let me handle this."

"No. I am not going to let him continue to bleed me. Did I tell you that a friend of mine saw him in the South of France? He was on the freakin' French Riviera for a month. A month!"

Luc sighed. "Yes, you told me. His lawyer says it was a medical conference."

"For a month? What kind of medical conference lasts a month? SDU? Slimy Doctors United?"

Samantha had been married to Nick for five years and divorced for another five, but she was still paying for that mistake. And not just with the continuing humiliation of his serial adultery, or the very public, acrimonious divorce. Nope, the jerk had demanded alimony, that on top of her having paid his way through medical school. And he kept wanting more and more.

It wasn't just that Nick knew the salary and benefits she drew from her family business, not to mention stock she owned in the company and a sizeable savings account. But he was aware of the gold coins and bullion, worth anywhere from a million and a half to two million dollars, depending on the market, stored in her bank safety deposit box. It started out as a million dollars in gold, a gift her grandfather gave on the birth of each of his grandchildren. In her case, it had almost doubled in value. Being of conservative Scottish stock, her grandfather preferred hard, cold metal, over stocks and bonds. Portable wealth. Since that gold wasn't "earned" during their marriage, the courts had denied Nick access to it, over and over. But he kept trying.

During the course of her relationship with Nick, she'd met many of his physician friends, and they all seemed to be focused on their net worth and what expensive toy they could buy next. Very few were in the profession for the good they could do. And most had been divorced at least once, or were blatant adulterers. And talk about the conversations when Nick and his gynecologist buddies got together! If she heard the joke "I've seen more pussy than Hugh Hefner," one time, she'd heard it a hundred.

Thus, her bias against doctors. It was an unreasonable bias, to lump all male doctors into one assumption. She realized that, but perhaps it was understandable.

"SDU? Sounds like a sexual disease. But see, that's the kind of remark that will get you in trouble." Even as he chastised her, Luc had to smile. "All we need is time. Wish you had contacted me earlier, but not to worry. I've got investigators checking into his activities. We're gonna nail his sorry ass to the wall, one way or the other."

"I wish I'd hired you sooner, too. My old lawyer, Charles Broussard, was a lovely man . . . a friend of my grandfather . . . but not the sharpest knife in the drawer, not a barracuda like Daltry."

"I eat big fish for breakfast," Luc bragged.

He probably did. That, or fried gator kidneys if his crazy aunt had any say.

Samantha put one of her recently manicured fingernails to her mouth and began to gnaw nervously.

Luc slapped her hand away. "Enough of that! You have to walk in there as if you own the world. Fearless!"

"Pfff! How do I do that with a man who looks like some kind of Norse God in Armani? And a lawyer who sharpens his teeth on people like me?"

"No, no, no! Daltry is a shark, guar-an-teed, but, dar-lin', you hired yourself an even badder shark. A Cajun shark. The best kind." He waggled his eyebrows at her. "Here's a clue on how not ta be intimidated. When I'm in court, if it's a man tryin' ta disconcert me, I just picture him naked, walkin' down Bourbon Street with a string of Carnival beads looped around his . . . um, family jewels. If it's a woman, I picture her, naked, too, but with a be-hind the size of a bayou barge, doin' a Cajun shimmy snake dance. In both cases, people are laughin' their asses off at them."

Samantha's jaw dropped open before she burst out with a giggle.

And that was how her ex-husband and his lawyer saw her as she and Luc entered the auxiliary courtroom. And, to her surprise, Nick was the one who looked discon-certed.

"Game on, Samantha?" Luc whispered in her ear.

"Game on," she agreed, leaning in to his ear.

*At Avon Books, we know your passion
for romance—once you finish one of our
novels, you find yourself wanting more.*

May we tempt you with . . .

- **Excerpts** from our upcoming releases.

- Entertaining **extras,** including authors'
  personal photo albums and book lists.

- Behind-the-scenes **scoop** on your favorite
  characters and series.

- **Sweepstakes** for the chance to win free books,
  romantic getaways, and other fun prizes.

- Writing **tips** from our authors and editors.

- **Blog** with our authors and find out why they
  love to write romance.

- **Exclusive content** that's not contained
  within the pages of our novels.

Join us at
www.avonbooks.com

An Imprint of HarperCollins*Publishers*
www.avonromance.com

Available wherever books are sold or please call 1-800-331-3761 to order.

FTH 1013

*G*ive in to your Impulses!

These unforgettable stories only take a second to buy and give you hours of reading pleasure!

Go to *www.AvonImpulse.com* and see what we have to offer.

Available wherever e-books are sold.

AVONIMPULSE